Where have you been all my life?"

"Oh, Gina." Brady ran a hand across his somber face and took a deep breath. "Where have you been all my life?"

"California."

"No. Now that I think about it, you've been here all the time. Since I was 19, anyway."

"Nineteen? What are you talking about?"

"I remember you visiting the summer I was 19. You must have been 15."

"Did we meet?"

"Not exactly, but I knew who you were."

"That Lindstrom girl."

"Mm-hmm. I watched you hanging out with Lauren and Liz. You looked like such a snob."

"What'd I do?"

"Nothing in particular. You were just too cute to be for real. Between that and your heritage, I concluded you were a snob."

"You thought I was cute?"

He chuckled. "Cute as a bug's ear with a Miss America smile."

Her skin tingled. "Hmm, I see. And being cute made me a snob?"

"Well, all three of you were snobs. After all, you were Lindstroms."

"I never stood a chance."

"Not really…"

Sally John is the author of three books and a former teacher. Much like Brady in *A Journey by Chance,* she and her husband, Tim, live in the country surrounded by woods and cornfields. The Johns have two grown children.

A Journey by Chance

SALLY JOHN

HARVEST HOUSE PUBLISHERS
Eugene, Oregon 97402

Scripture verses are taken from the New American Standard Bible®, © 1960, 1962, 1963, 1968, 1971, 1972, 1973, 1975, 1977 by The Lockman Foundation. Used by permission.

Scripture verses are also taken from The New English Bible, © The Delegates of the Oxford University Press and the Syndics of the Cambridge University Press 1961, 1970. Reprinted with permission.

Cover by Garborg Design Works, Minneapolis, Minnesota

Published in association with the literary agency of Alive Communications, Inc., 7680 Goddard Street, Suite 200, Colorado Springs, CO 80920.

A JOURNEY BY CHANCE
Copyright © 2002 by Sally John
Published by Harvest House Publishers
Eugene, Oregon 97402

Library of Congress Cataloging-in-Publication Data
John, Sally D.,
    A journey by chance / Sally John
        p. cm.—(The other way home ; 1)
    ISBN 0-7369-0880-3
    1. Women—Middle West—Fiction. 2. Middle West—Fiction. I. Title. II. Series.

PS3560.O323 C47 2002
813'.54—dc21   2001043632

Printed in the United States of America

02 03 04 05 06 07 08 09 10 / BC-MS / 10 9 8 7 6 5 4 3 2 1

This book is dedicated to those women who have been the touchstones of my writing journey.

❧

Thank you:
Irene Frank, for teaching me how to write fiction
Pat Teal, for nudging me into that first contest
Jere Johnson, for suggesting that my characters portray faith
Doris Fell, for your wisdom and trailblazing
Jill Carter, for smiling at that first manuscript
Elizabeth White, for prying loose my wings
Margo Balsis, for the critiques and prayers that carry me

❧

A special note of thanks goes to Kelly Parrish
for enthusiastically sharing her expertise of horses.

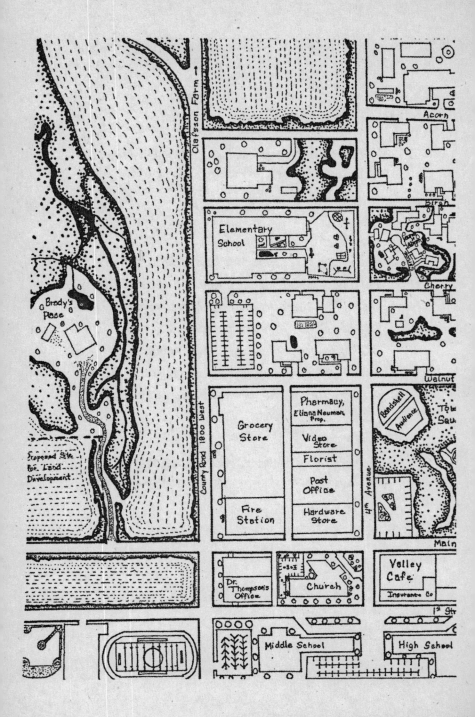

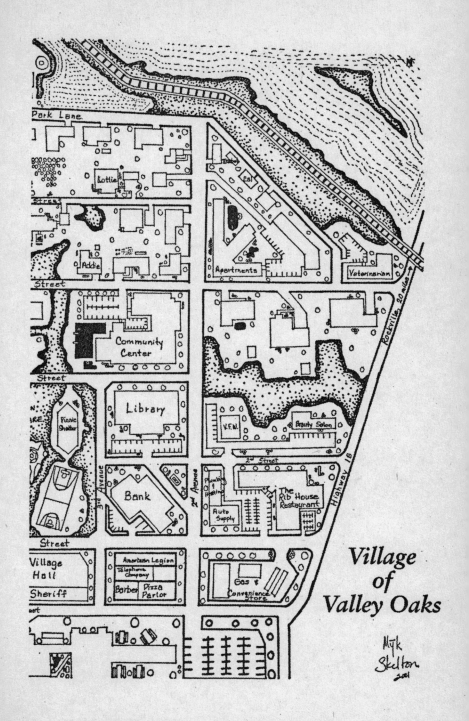

Village
of
Valley Oaks

Prologue

*Thou hast traced my journey and my resting places,
and art familiar with all my paths.*
—Psalm 139:3

"It's all settled then." The young woman's determined tone lingered in the soft spring air. Cross-legged on the ground, she plucked at the short grass that clothed the grave.

"Yep." The man unfolded lanky arms and legs and stood. The pronounced angles of teenage years contrasted with the mature weariness etched in his jaw.

She turned her petite face toward the barren cornfields. A light breeze played with her long blonde hair. "It's not what we planned."

"But it's for the best."

"I'm so sick of that platitude."

He stuffed his hands in the back pockets of his jeans and twisted his mouth. "You're happy with the tombstone?"

"It's perfect," she whispered, now studying the upright slab of white marble. "And you're okay with the name?"

"Mm-hmm. It's appropriate, the two last names."

"Remember 'Ode on a Grecian Urn'?" She looked up at him, a sparkle erasing the flatness of her eyes.

A corner of his mouth lifted in a half smile. "Senior English. I remember you liked it, and I got a D on the test."

"It reminds me of that. The stone links us together forever, engraved with our names, but," her eyes went dead again, "we're suspended there. Not together in reality."

Neither spoke for a few moments.

"Maggie," he said, "think of it as a road marker, pointing us in different directions. We traveled this far together, but now there's a fork in the road."

"I like my ode better."

"Bullheaded." His tone teased. "I'll take you home."

She stood and glanced at the nearby pickup. "Thanks, but I need to walk." She patted the front of her loose overblouse.

"All right."

There was an awkwardness in their stance as they looked at each other.

She swallowed, then shrugged. "Well, have a nice life, Neil."

He held out his arms, and she stepped into his embrace. "You, too, Mags. You, too."

One

Thirty-five years later

Gina Philips stood at the library's checkout counter and directed her words in a hushed tone toward the back of a small, gray-haired woman. "Excuse me?"

Bent over a desk just beyond the counter, the librarian did not respond.

Gina drummed her fingers on the wood surface. How badly did she want this novel? No, the question was—how long could she survive in Podunk without at least a mental escape? Four weeks of family gatherings stretched before her like a desert highway. At high noon. She swallowed the hushed tone. "Excuse me?"

Still the woman didn't budge.

There was always the hooch Great-Uncle Peter had supposedly hidden in the cellar. She wrinkled her nose at that preposterous thought and realized just how crucial it was that she have this book. She raised her voice to soccer fan level. "Excuse me!"

The woman twirled around and patted her chest. "Oh, my! You startled me." She shuffled over to the counter, a distinct frown pinching her aged face, and pulled off her glasses. They dangled from a pearl chain. "We don't allow loud talking in the library. May I get you something *else?*" Her tone was polite enough, but her emphasis on "else" expressed an obvious displeasure.

11

Gina wasn't too pleased herself. This was her fourth request for help. Plunk her down in the middle of the University of Southern California's stacks—no problem. This one-room library, however, baffled her. She slid the novel toward the woman. "I'd like to check this out."

"Do you have a borrower's card?"

"Not for this library. I—"

"What township do you live in?"

"Township? I don't know. I'm just visiting here in...uh... Valley Oaks." She bit her lip. She absolutely had to stop thinking of it so rudely as Podunk. "But I have a driver's license and credit—"

"No, no, no." The woman shook her head, enunciating each no with a twist. "It's against our policy to check out books to nonresidents." She slipped on her glasses and inspected the book.

"But my aunt—"

"Where did you find this book?" she asked tersely.

"On the shelf. The new release section—"

"Tsk, tsk." The woman's lips were decidedly pursed now. "Impossible. You could not have found it there. We have a very long waiting list for this book. It's a bestseller. It wouldn't be on any shelf."

Gina clenched her jaw. "I didn't pull it out of midair! I found it—"

"Hattie," a male voice interrupted from behind her. "I'll check it out for the lady." A man stepped forward and flipped a blue card onto the counter.

Gina glanced to her side and saw a long, tanned arm beneath the rolled-up short sleeve of a white T-shirt. She craned her neck to peer at the rest of him.

Hattie tsk-ed again. "But I have to find the Reserved list first." She rummaged through a drawer.

"Of course, Hattie. You certainly know how to keep this library humming smoothly."

The woman beamed.

He tilted his head toward Gina and, beneath the peak of a dingy green cap, winked.

Unbelievable! Was he attempting to pick her up? "Uh, that's all right—"

"Ah, here it is!" Hattie studied a piece of notebook paper.

"So," the guy was addressing her again, "do you like his other novels?"

"Um, yeah."

"He's quite a storyteller. This new one's received great reviews."

"Oh!" Hattie looked up at the man with a confused expression. "Well, *your* name's next on the list."

He winked now at the older woman. "I thought so. Just check it out on my card, and we'll let the visitor here read it first."

"That's not standard procedure. Do you realize you're responsible for what happens to this book? Do you even know her?"

"Well," he leaned forward, his elbow on the counter, and lowered his voice, "I know she's a Lindstrom."

"As in Darryl?" Hattie stuck her head toward him and matched his conspiratorial tone.

"No. Martin."

"Oh. That one that took off to California?"

He gave a slight nod. "Lottie's niece."

"Probably here for the wedding," she surmised.

Gina's eyes widened.

"Mmm." It was a noncommittal grunt. He straightened and pointed to a cart behind Hattie. "You're holding another book for me. That red history one there. I ordered it from Rockville."

The woman busied herself with the computer.

"Look," Gina said as she inched backward, "it's your turn for the book. You should have it." She slung her backpack over her shoulder and stepped behind him.

"Nonsense." He swiveled around and thrust the book out, cutting off her escape. "I insist. Just make sure you get it back by the due date." He grinned.

"Right." She took it from him and bolted for the exit. "Uh, thanks."

"Hey, are you—"

Gina let the glass door swish shut on his words, less concerned about making polite conversation than fleeing the eerie discomfort of listening to these people discuss her. She hurried across the library's front yard, shoving the book into her backpack. Her mother had warned her. Everybody knew everything in Valley Oaks, population 1,947. She had been in town less than 24 hours and already two total strangers knew exactly who she was and why she was here. Not only that, they discussed this information in front of her as if she didn't exist!

She hoisted the bag across her shoulders and pulled on the ancient bicycle's upright handlebars, loosening the wide tire from its anchor. The small effort sent rivulets of perspiration down the back of her neck. She hoped she had tucked a banana clip in her luggage. Her mother had warned her, too, of the Midwest heat and humidity. Gina assumed it was an exaggeration, but this late morning air was like a layer of invisible, sticky flannel, impossible to shake off.

"Thought the bike might be yours." The guy was beside her again. "I'll give you a lift."

"No, thanks. I'm not going far." She straddled the bike. "But you probably knew that." The words spewed out in a sarcastic tone, as if her manners were still tucked away in a suitcase, too.

"Yeah, I knew that, but it's going to storm." He grasped a handlebar and held out his book. "See those clouds? I can toss the bike into the back of my pickup."

She glanced at the sky. Sickly green clouds hovered. "I won't melt." She held fast to the bike.

"We're not talking raindrops here. There's a severe weather warning, which means wind and lightning. And it comes up fast."

As if validating his prediction, thunder rumbled and a raindrop pelted her head. She took the book from his hand and stepped away from the bike.

He slung it atop his shoulder, carried it to a cream-colored truck parked at the curb, and dumped it in the bed. "Get in!"

Gina stood on the sidewalk. A gust of wind whipped her hair across her face, adding to her discomfort with this whole situation. She didn't even know the guy's name. Why would she get in a vehicle with him? She'd never do this sort of thing in California. Crimes happened here, too, didn't they?

"Need some help?" He nodded down toward her leg.

He had noticed then. Noticed? Shoot, he probably knew the whole story about why her left leg couldn't quite keep pace with the right. "No."

"Let's go then." He climbed in and started the engine.

Gina marched her slightly uneven march to the passenger door. The injury really didn't slow her down all that much, but it was noticeable to others. The guy couldn't know the whole story, though. Her mother had promised not to tell the whole story to anyone in Valley Oaks.

She yanked open the door and came face-to-face with a large golden retriever. The dog tilted his head in a friendly expression. Ignoring him, she said in a bristly tone, "Look, mister."

He peered around the dog.

"I don't even know your name. Why would I get in a truck with you?"

A horrendous clap of thunder exploded directly behind her and reverberated in her chest. She stuck her right foot on the running board, propelled herself onto the seat, and slammed the door shut, squishing herself against the dog.

The stranger burst into laughter and pushed the gear stick. "Lay down, Homer." The dog obeyed, and he slung his arm across the back of the bench seat, looking over his shoulder. Still laughing, he maneuvered the truck out of its parking spot.

In spite of the cool air flowing through the vents, Gina felt unbearably hot.

His laughter subsided as he moved his arm to shift. The grin settled into a smile above a square jaw. His tanned face was narrow and angular, like the rest of him, and somewhat creased, as if he spent a lot of time facing wind and sun. A tuft of dark blond hair stuck out below the cap that proclaimed "Nothing runs like a Deere." He glanced toward her and held out his hand. "Brady Olafsson."

She snubbed the handshake, totally giving in to her edginess and not worrying about where her manners were hidden. "Where are you taking me?"

"Nice to meet you, too. I'm taking you to your Great-Aunt Lottie's."

"Why?" She scratched the dog's ears and settled as best she could with the backpack mashed into her shoulder blades.

"Simple deduction. If you were staying at your Aunt Marsha's, you'd be out at the farm and not biking to the library. Your grandparents have passed away. Your cousin Lauren's apartment is small. Your uncles and numerous cousins are possibilities, but they all have families or live outside of town, whereas Lottie lives alone, three blocks from here, in a two-story. Hence the bicycle."

She glowered at him.

He threw her a smile. "Common knowledge in a small town. I also know you're from Los Angeles."

"Close. By the way, I am *not* a Lindstrom."

"It's your mother's maiden name." He lifted a shoulder. "That makes you one here in Valley Oaks."

If she had to endure others like this guy spouting off her family history, the town would positively undo her fairly quickly. She gazed out the side window and berated herself once again for agreeing to this extended visit in Valley Oaks.

Valley Oaks. Now that was a misnomer. Those trees bending in the fierce wind were maples. Not one oak tree sprouted from land flatter than the Pacific on an ugly surfing day.

"Here you go." He pulled into the driveway, scrunched the parking brake and hopped out.

The endless ride had probably taken all of two minutes. Gina shoved open her door into a privet hedge, patted the dog goodbye, and squeezed out.

With the bicycle balanced upside down on a shoulder, Brady loped through the drenching rain to the garage at the end of the driveway. He was rangy looking. Extremely long arms and legs.

The wind was howling now, flapping her hair in every direction. Fat raindrops ricocheted off the sidewalk and soaked her. She ran to the covered front porch as the guy raced past her and shouted, "See you around, Gina Philips!"

Her thanks caught in her throat as he slammed his door shut. He knew her name. What didn't he know?

Four weeks in this place was definitely, absolutely, without a doubt going to be way too long.

〜

He wasn't surprised.

Brady drove down the two-lane county highway, the wipers furiously beating buckets of rain off the windshield.

He had been curious, but he hadn't really expected anything different. The snobby California 15-year-old he remembered had grown into a snobby California young woman. Still cute as a bug's ear, with thick, just-above-the-shoulder, milk chocolate brown hair and eyes the shock of brilliant, late spring green.

Absent, though, was the 1,000-watt Miss America smile that had caught his attention when he was 19. After all these years he could distinctly recall how it was nothing less than dazzling. Today he hadn't glimpsed even a semblance of a smile. And how in the world could she give poor old Hattie such a hard time?

"Well, Homer," he addressed the dog snuggled against him, "for Aaron's sake we'll be nice to her. At least for wedding stuff, huh? It won't hurt me to walk Dr. Angelina Philips up and down the aisle."

Now that he thought about it, didn't the groomsmen usually just wait down front? Lauren, his cousin's fiancée, had mentioned they would escort the bridesmaids up *and* down the aisle. He wondered if that had anything to do with the woman's limp? It was her limp—wasn't it?—that had tugged at him, prompting him to offer the book. And drive her the few blocks home.

He gave his head a slight shake and turned onto the gravel lane that led through cornfields. In the distance a leafy canopy of oak trees welcomed him home.

Wedding-related activities were obligatory, but they wouldn't consume the next four weeks. If he had to spend time with a Lindstrom, he'd just as soon keep it to a minimum.

Two

Gina's mother and Aunt Lottie greeted her as she carefully laid her wet backpack on the rug just inside the front door at the foot of the staircase.

"Oh, sweetie," her mother said, "I was worried."

"Mother! I'm 28 years old."

"So?" She patted her cheek.

Gina noticed that her mother's naturally curly and almost naturally blonde hair was frizzy. Uh-oh. Even cool, calm, collected Margaret Philips appeared uptight after spending less than a day in her hometown. She wasn't even called by her name here. Sophisticated Margaret, manager of women's clothing for Southern California's largest department store, was reduced to *Maggie*.

"Did you ride that bike in this rain?" Margaret's tone was reminiscent of the days when Gina would miss curfew.

Aunt Lottie answered for her. "No." She moved away from the lace-curtained window. "Looks like Brady's truck."

"Yeah, Brady Oleo something," Gina replied. "He was at the library."

"Oleo?" Margaret asked.

Aunt Lottie laughed, her plump hands folded at the waist of her flowered apron. "Olafsson, Gina. Say Olafsson. It's a good Swedish name. Maggie, you remember the Olafssons, don't you? Oh, goodness!" She clapped a hand over her mouth. "Of course you do. Well." She lowered her hand and smiled brightly. "How about some nice cold iced tea with our sandwiches? We'll take lunch to the cellar."

19

"Sounds great." Gina watched her great-aunt waddle off toward the kitchen. She was short, on the rotund side, still sharp and active at the age of 89, still living alone in this big old house. Snow white hair, fluffed weekly at the hairdresser's, framed her round cheeks. Gina smiled. "Aunt Lottie," she called after her, "no sugar, please!"

"Oh, a little sugar won't hurt you!" she called back.

Gina pulled the book out of her bag. "Mother, why are we going to the cellar?"

"Tornado watch."

"What's that?"

"If I remember correctly, it's when the entire town goes outside to watch for a tornado. Except for cautious, elderly women. They head to the basement because it's the safest place if a tornado hits, which it never has in Valley Oaks." Shoulder braced against the front door, she shoved the humidity-swollen wood into its jamb.

"Do we have to shut the door? It's stifling in here."

"It's raining in. Ah, summer in the Midwest. I had hoped Aunt Lottie would have had air conditioning installed by now. You can live with the heat and humidity for a few weeks, can't you? It means so much to her to have us here."

Gina looked into her mother's emerald green eyes, so like her own. They were tired. "No problem. Aunt Lottie's a hoot. Worth the trip. Are you okay?"

Margaret gave a slight shrug. "It's always a little rough at first. So many old emotions hit all at once."

"Oh, Mom! Don't let it get you down. It's just Podunk, Illinois—"

"Angelina Philips! This is my hometown. My heritage is rooted here, and so is half of yours. Please don't use that derogatory term in my presence."

"I'm sorry. I just hate seeing you upset. If you're upset, who's going to pamper me? I'll be forced to act my age, and then I'll have to give up whining. You have spoiled me rotten these past eight months."

"Only eight months?" She smiled. "Gina, it's just emotions and not only the negative kind. Now, promise me something?"

Gina hid her exasperation by turning to drop the backpack in the coat closet. Her mother had been riding this strange emotional roller coaster for some time now, supposedly a normal event for women her age, but Podunk had definitely intensified the situation. Nothing would be gained by pointing that out, so she swallowed her frustration and turned around. "Promise you what?"

"Well, I know your future is up in the air right now, and you're anxious to attend to that matter, which means you are not thrilled about spending an entire month here—"

"I chose to come, Mother. I want to be here for Lauren's sake."

"I know, but I also know it will be difficult for you."

That was an understatement. One short visit to the village library and her teeth were on edge.

"Will you just try to keep an open mind? Look for the positives in Valley Oaks. It's not California, but it's not a bad place."

Gina made a conscious effort not to roll her eyes. As they wound their way between overstuffed chairs and doily-covered end tables, she heard the solemn ticktock of the grandfather clock, erasing the seconds one by one. This interminable time would pass. Sweating the small stuff with her mother would only heighten the discomfort. She agreed to keep an open mind toward Po...make that Valley Oaks.

Margaret stood at Aunt Lottie's kitchen sink, her hands submerged in hot, sudsy water, and stared out the window. Storm clouds were dispersing and the sun had broken through, its heat coaxing steam from the wet grass. Sweet fragrances drifted through the screen, mingling with the scent of lemony detergent.

Odd how such a simple act as washing dishes soothed, how it centered her. She should do it more often. But then, maybe back home it wouldn't have the same effect.

Back home. She thought of her shiny white ceramic tile countertop and, just outside the window, the brilliant red bougainvillea covering the patio wall. San Clemente, where she was Margaret Philips, career woman with a very full social calendar, a talented daughter, and a handsome husband...

She sighed. Margaret Philips didn't even exist here in Valley Oaks. She was Maggie Lindstrom, always had been, always would be. Maggie or Magpie or Mags, depending on who was speaking. She imagined a collective Valley Oaks voice. *You remember Maggie. Daughter of Martin and Mary...good, hard-working folks...tragic how they were killed in a car accident, only around 60 years old when it happened out on Highway 72; you know that curve. Marsha Anderson is her sister. That's right, they've got three older brothers. Everybody loved Maggie. She was a good student, cheerleader and homecoming queen, worked at the Tastee Freez. Ended up marrying a guy from Chicago, but all through high school she went with Neil—*

"Maggie, I'll help with those dishes."

She looked over her shoulder at Aunt Lottie shuffling into the kitchen. "No, I'm going to wait on you. Just sit and visit with me."

"Talked me into it." She angled a chair toward Maggie and sank into it with a slight groan. "Rainstorms remind my knees they've been at work for almost 90 years."

Maggie smiled. It was the closest her aunt would come to a complaint. "I've been admiring your perennials. They're so beautiful, as always. Shall I put in some tomato plants for you? I hope you still have the garden patch behind the garage."

"It's there. Can't say much has changed outside that window in 50 years, except the elms are gone and that maple is taller."

"Everything is so lush, not dry like my yard."

"Do you miss Valley Oaks?"

"I don't know." She began washing the dishes, remembering how 35 years ago she had turned her back on all this. Her dream had been to spend her life here, out on the farm. The memories swirled, uprooting adolescent joys, guilt, anger, crushed hopes. "Out of the blue I get these incredibly intense emotions from the past. Like now." It came then, a familiar burst of internal fireworks. Maggie grabbed a dishtowel and wiped perspiration from her face.

Aunt Lottie chuckled. "That happens, honey, especially around your age. You feel like you're losing your mind?"

Maggie blinked back tears and took a deep breath. "It's crazy. I feel like buying a wild purple dress or eating an entire bag of chocolate chip cookies."

"Or taking four weeks off from work?"

She nodded. That had been such an off-the-wall decision, like many others of late. "My boss agreed I needed an extended vacation. I just feel so *ungrounded*."

Aunt Lottie nodded. "So you came home."

"So I came home." She resumed washing the dishes. "I thought it might help to reflect on the past. Figure out where I'm going."

"That's a wise decision, honey. What does Reece think?"

"Reece? Oh," she shrugged, "that I'm crazy. He can't fathom why I simply don't fix the problem."

"Husbands can't always understand. But God does, and that's all that matters."

"I'm counting on Him. There doesn't seem to be anyone else at the moment." Except for...she stopped the thought from forming.

"God's love is always unconditional. Will you take Gina to the cemetery?"

She nodded. "It's time."

"I agree." Aunt Lottie went to a cupboard and pulled out two tin canisters.

"What are you doing with the flour and sugar?"

Aunt Lottie rummaged on a shelf. "Ah! I knew I had some." She held up a bag of chocolate chips and smiled. "Homemade is so much better than store-bought."

In the warm twilight that evening, Maggie watched her sister Marsha back out of the driveway. Gina had left earlier to shop with Marsha's daughter Lauren.

"Maggie." Aunt Lottie stood beside her on the covered front porch, waving. "Now I don't want you worrying about making long-distance phone calls."

"I won't." She followed her inside through the screen door.

"You've got to keep those communication lines open with hubby, you know." She turned at the foot of the staircase and smiled. Her words grated, but that round face and sparkling eyes were the epitome of sweetness. "I haven't heard you call him yet, and I thought maybe you're concerned about the money. I'm not rich, but I've got more tucked away than I've time to spend."

Maggie's heart melted. Aunt Lottie, her mother's older sister, had two grown children of her own, four grandchildren, and three great-grandchildren. Still, since the death of Maggie's mother 25 years ago, Aunt Lottie had embraced her sister's family as if it were her own, liberally giving her time and energy and money. "Aunt Lottie, you have been so generous with us." She chuckled. "Do you know what a dual income means? With an independent daughter whose school bills are paid and not one grandchild to spoil?"

Aunt Lottie grabbed her hand and squeezed it. "Of course I do, dear. That wasn't the point. Good night." She climbed the stairs, pulling heavily on the banister, setting one foot at a time on each step, her knees creaking audibly.

"Good night. I'll close up."

So what was the point? Communication lines. "And I'll call Reece," she muttered to herself as she walked to the kitchen.

Communication lines hadn't been open for some time, not for real communication anyway. She knew the difference. Oh, they talked. They lived together, went out for dinner with friends together, shared work stories, fussed about Gina's dilemma. Yes, they talked...but they didn't communicate.

She picked up the receiver from the wall phone and sat at the formica-topped table. The old-fashioned kitchen was bright and cheery, even at nighttime. White cabinets reached all the way to the high ceiling. Intermittently slicing through the daffodil yellow walls were white doors with clear glass knobs, leading to the pantry, back staircase, back porch, and basement. The swinging dining room door was usually propped open.

She listened to her own voice on their home answering machine. No surprise there. "Hi, Reece. Well, we're here, trying to keep cool. Gina's fine. I thought the humidity might bother her hip more, but she seems to be handling it well. Tomorrow we have the two celebrations for Aunt Lottie's birthday, so we won't be around the house much. Talk to you later."

Maggie bit her lip and hung the phone up on the wall behind her shoulder. He was traveling, of course. Somewhere. She hadn't paid attention to his schedule. She had simply stuck his itinerary in the suitcase and left it there when she unpacked. It didn't really matter, did it? If she wanted, she could try his cell phone. No matter where he was, the cell phone was in his pocket.

If she wanted.

What she wanted was to talk to John. Other women had close female friends. How was it her closest friend was a man?

They had met at a party last September. What was the connection again? Lillian's friend Deirdre was a friend of the Millikens who knew him. She stood across the buffet table from him, pondering an unidentifiable concoction. They laughed about it.

"John Beaumont." He introduced himself.

"Margaret Philips." She shook his hand.

Chatting, they wedged themselves into the crowd, away from the table. He said he was a professor at Long Beach.

She smiled. "English lit."

"It's that obvious?"

"It's that obvious."

He wore a tweed jacket, gray corduroys, and oval, wire-rimmed glasses. His wavy black hair was sprinkled with silver, his dark eyes intense. His movements were slow, deliberate, and yet there was a distracted air about him. His accent was East Coast.

"Tell me," she teased, "there must be a pipe in your pocket?"

He pulled it out just far enough for her to see it.

Their talk covered current bestsellers and the Japanese display at the art museum. He wore a wedding band, but didn't mention his wife. She told him that her husband had bowed out of the party. Reece was with a land acquisition company. She bragged about Gina, their veterinarian daughter who talked to elephants.

Innocuous beginning. It could have been anyone.

Reece should have been beside her.

Three days later Gina misjudged her elephant. Maggie waited through interminable hours, gagging on the scent of antiseptic, head pounding at the stark, fluorescent whiteness. Waited while they put her child's body back together again.

Reece should have been beside her then, too.

Three

"Lauren," Gina eyed her cousin in the driver's seat, "when do I get to meet Mr. Right? Or should I say Dr. Right?"

She sighed. "God has given me such a perfect partner. Aaron is so wonderful."

"So you've told me." Gina smiled. "Once or twice."

Her cousin was on cloud nine, which made her whirlwind personality even flightier than usual. Lauren resembled their mothers, who were sisters, in personality as well as looks. Vivacious, petite, naturally curly, gold-blonde hair. Only the eyes were different. Gina's cousin's and aunt's were a ginger brown, her mother's emerald green.

Except for sharing her mother's eye color, Gina always felt the odd woman out in this group. She was taller, more solidly built with medium brown hair and a medium personality to match. Her demeanor was decidedly more calm, which was a plus for being a veterinarian.

Although the cousins lived thousands of miles apart, their growing-up years had often intersected. Lauren visited California, sometimes for entire summers. Every spring they and their mothers met in Phoenix. Gina's mom had an annual business meeting there, but her rooms at the resort were always large enough to accommodate the four of them. The tradition continued during and after their college years, and they seldom missed.

Lauren threw her a smile as she turned a corner. "Aaron's tied up tonight, but he'll be at Aunt Lottie's birthday party tomorrow."

A year ago Lauren had re-met Aaron Thompson when he returned to Valley Oaks to take over the practice of the local doctor. He had been a few years ahead of Lauren in school. As teens their paths hadn't romantically crossed, but when the physician met the high school's band teacher, it was love at first sight for both of them.

Gina reached over and squeezed her arm. "I am so happy for you."

"I feel like I'm going to burst! I don't see how I can keep this up for four more weeks."

"You could elope." Gina gazed out the window and noticed they were already beyond the town limits. They sped along the highway, past rolling fields of corn planted in rows so neatly they looked like colorful pages of typed words. The sun was low on the horizon, and the short green stalks glistened in the streams of light against the black earth. "That's a beautiful sight. How do they make the rows so straight?"

"Well, I don't know," her cousin grinned at her, "but Brady could tell you. I heard you met him this morning."

"Unbelievable! How did you hear that already?"

Lauren giggled. "News gets around fast in this town. You'll get used to it. So what'd you think?"

"What do you mean, what'd I think? Was I supposed to think something?"

"Oh, I thought you might be impressed with his looks. Or how friendly he is, or just how homespun he is in spite of the fact that he is our most—"

"Wealthy, eligible bachelor. I know. Aunt Lottie told me."

"Not bachelor. Well, he is that, too, but I was going to say our most famous author. Actually, he's our only author."

"Author? Aunt Lottie said he farms with his dad."

"She doesn't catch everything these days."

Remembering the lunch-in-the-cellar conversation with their great-aunt, Gina laughed. "You won't believe what she does catch. She mentioned he looks good in a white T-shirt."

Lauren joined in the laughter. "Isn't she a stitch? Anyway, he does farm, but he also writes these awesome Christian books. So what did *you* think of him in a white T-shirt?"

She moaned. "Tell me you are *not* playing Cupid."

"He is going to look terrific in a white tuxedo with his dark blond hair." Her cousin glanced at her. "You told me Steve is old news, right?"

"Mm-hmm. You are playing Cupid. I suppose you've paired me with this Brady for the bridesmaid-groomsman thing."

"It was a perfect match, Gina! Aaron and I put our best friends together and my sister and his brother. You and Brady were the only two favorite cousins. He and Aaron are the same age, 32, and were good friends growing up." Lauren threw her a smile. "And you will look so good together. You're both tall—"

"I'm not that tall."

"Yeah, but you're the tallest in the bunch, perfect for his 6'4". And his tanned face with the white tux and your eyes with the chartreuse dress..." Lauren sighed.

Gina rolled her eyes. The details of a wedding. "We didn't hit it off too well, but I suppose I could be nice to him for your sake."

"You're not pining over Steve, are you?"

"No, not in the least. That relationship never could have gone anywhere. It just fizzled out. Having the boss as my significant other was not a smart move on my part."

"But you had so much in common, since you're both veterinarians."

"I'm sure that was part of the initial attraction. But when things got complicated at work—" She bit her lip to stop herself from saying too much. "Well, it just got complicated." If she mentioned that Steve faced difficult choices and ultimately chose the ones that were not in her best interest, it would sound gossipy and demeaning. In spite of everything, she wouldn't stoop to that. He was just doing his job. His version of it, anyway.

"Is your leg all right?" Lauren's voice was concerned. "I've been praying about that."

"Thanks." Her cousin prayed about everything, just like the aunts did. It must be a small-town thing. "It healed fine and usually doesn't hurt. I bicycle and wear a brace for long hikes. My jog's just a little lopsided."

"Well, what happened? All you've told me was that you got hurt at work and had to take a disability leave of absence." Lauren glanced at her. "Or maybe you don't want to talk about it?"

Gina shrugged a shoulder. "Not really. It was...complicated. I don't think I've sorted it all out yet. Let's talk about more cheerful things, like your wedding. Or the family!" She'd heard enough about the wedding. "Tell me all about the cousins."

She listened with only half attention. The other half occupied itself with pushing aside memories. They were a year's worth in the making, still too vivid to easily ignore. She was a vet employed at the Wild Creatures Country in Orange County, California. She had chosen the elephants over the Park. Steve, her boss and romantic interest, had chosen the Park over her. Worse than ending their relationship, his choice had ended her career. It was simple. Heartbreakingly so.

But her heart had healed. If God created hearts, He made them with incredible resiliency. As with her leg, though, her heart moved in its own uneven beat. There were some emotional dances she'd have to sit out. Emotional dances like following your dreams and doing what you love to do. Or trusting people.

"Disability leave of absence" stretched the truth, but it was the most she could handle for now. To admit out loud that she had been fired was still beyond her ability.

Four

Gina sat at a round table, plunked down in the precise center of the Valley Oaks Community Church reception hall. She felt like a buoy anchored to a floating chair, afloat in a sea of humidity peopled with unfamiliar faces. The entire church membership, perhaps even the entire town, had turned out for Aunt Lottie's birthday celebration. Wall-to-wall tables filled the sunny room that easily accomodated the hundreds now noisily milling about, hemming her in.

She pulled at the scooped neck of her chamois-colored knit cotton top. The label read 100 percent cotton...but it wasn't breathing this afternoon. She discreetly picked at the matching wrinkled linen skirt, easing it off of her lap, and wondered where to dump her cup of too-sweet punch and find a glass of ice water.

The outside temperature was 90, the humidity 95 percent. Inside it must be—

She stopped the petulant line of thinking. It wouldn't change anything. And she had certainly spent long enough wallowing in self-pity these past months. *Look for something positive*, she reminded herself.

Across the room her mother was overseeing the placement of the candy dishes and plates of white sheet cake. She gravitated toward such tasks at hand, which was why she was so successful as a manager. Between this open house and the coming wedding and reception, she would easily find outlets for her skills.

Aunt Lottie was beaming, her white hair freshly fluffed this morning, her new dress a pretty pastel floral print. She was 90 today...just like the temperature.

"Hello."

The masculine voice came from behind her. It was soft, well-modulated, with a whispery hint to it. And it was definitely familiar.

Brady Olafsson came into view and pulled a folding chair out from the table. "May I?"

"Why not?"

He sat beside her and stretched out his long jeans-covered legs, blocking any escape. "How's it going?"

"Fine." She noted that his blue jeans were almost brown with dirt. Mud clung to the thick soles of his—she blinked—work boots. Unbelievable.

He removed a grimy white cap with "Seed" something or other imprinted on it and finger-combed his short hair off of his high tanned forehead. "Just fine? That's somewhat of a generic reply."

"Kind of like the question." She met his gaze and found the robin's-egg blue eyes Aunt Lottie had described along with her white T-shirt comment. With a hint of green shading, they weren't quite a true blue.

The corner of his mouth lifted slightly, and he crossed his arms over his chest. Today's T-shirt was a faded red. There was a tear in the neck seam. "May I get you some more punch?" He eyed her three-fourths-full cup.

"No, thank you."

"How's the book?"

"I, uh, um..." Now that sounded inane. She swallowed the embarrassment she felt about not yet opening the library book he had so freely offered. "Actually, I haven't had a chance to start it. I'd be happy to give it to you."

"No, I'm sure you'll get to it soon enough. Last night you had your bridesmaid gown fitting, wedding errands, and dinner with Lauren."

Her eyes widened.

"Then today there's Lottie's birthday celebrations—"

"How do you know this stuff?" Her tone was incredulous.

"Word travels fast in Valley Oaks." Brady winked. "You know how you can tell if you live in the Midwest?"

She stared at him, sensing it was a rhetorical question.

"When your car breaks down outside of town and news of it reaches town before you do." He grinned.

Gina blinked in reply.

"Yep, that's how you can tell." He stood. "Well, I just thought I'd spend a few minutes getting to know you, since I've been appointed your escort for the wedding."

Escort? Something about this homespun guy really annoyed her. "All that entails is walking together up the aisle."

"Up *and* down."

"Up *and* down?"

"Rehearsal and wedding, up and down. Then there's the rehearsal dinner seating. The reception line. Sunday brunch—"

"Brady!" Lauren pushed her way through the crowd toward them, carrying a fork and plate of cake above her head.

He leaned over and gave her a brotherly peck on the cheek. "Hello, Princess Bride."

She smiled. "I'm glad to see you two are getting acquainted."

"I've been entertaining your cousin with some Midwest humor."

"The Midwest jokes? Did you tell her the one about the elevator?"

He shook his head, then turned to Gina. "You know you live in the Midwest if using the elevator involves a corn truck."

Lauren burst out laughing. "That's my favorite."

Gina remembered her promise to be nice. She stretched her lips sideways in a sort of smile. She didn't have a clue as to what a corn truck was, let alone what it had to do with an elevator.

"Tell her the neighbor one."

Brady glanced down at her. "You know you live in the Midwest if your nearest neighbor lives in the next area code." He laughed with Lauren.

"I love these! Do the corn one."

"You know you live in the Midwest if you can eat an ear of corn with no utensils in under twenty seconds."

They roared while Gina allowed herself a tiny smile. That one was almost funny. The image of someone scarfing down an ear of corn that fast—

"Gotta run, ladies. See you tonight." He sauntered off.

"Isn't he cute, Gina?" Lauren sat down and took a bite of cake.

"Uh." She didn't want to offend her cousin. The guy was obviously a good friend. "Well, he's sort of attractive, if you like tall, thin guys."

"Didn't you date a couple of basketball players in high school? Tall and thin type?"

And in college... One or two... She didn't offer the information that would only add fuel to Lauren's Cupid bent. Besides, she had outgrown that infatuation years ago.

Lauren held a forkful of cake in midair. "As a matter of fact, I distinctly remember a conversation we had our junior year. You planned to marry a basketball player and live out in the country and raise horses."

"Long time ago." Gina changed the subject. "What did he mean, he'd see you tonight?"

"Actually, us. At Annie and Alec's." Alec was Lottie's grandson.

"I thought that was a family dinner for Aunt Lottie." She thought of the myriad of cousins and second cousins and their children that she had met so far today. Being related to anyone in this town loomed a very real possibility. "This guy's not related to us, is he?"

"Nope, not yet. Do you want some cake?"

"No, thanks." Inwardly she cringed at the thought of the thick frosting, chock full of shortening, slithering down her cousin's petite throat, making its slow journey toward arteries. "What do you mean, not yet?"

"Well," she swallowed, "I am marrying his cousin, so that makes him a cousin-in-law. A distant relative to all of us, I guess. Anyway, Aunt Lottie likes him a lot. He and Vic have been good friends since grade school."

"Vic is Alec's brother. Which makes them some sort of cousin, right?"

She nodded, her mouth full of cake.

"Lauren, how can you eat that stuff and stay so slender?"

"It's this month! It must be the stress. I'm eating everything in sight. I hope my gown still fits. Oh, you haven't seen it yet. It's so absolutely gorgeous. Let's run over to my apartment now." She popped the last bite of cake into her mouth. "Then we'll stop by Aunt Lottie's so you can change. Most of the wedding party is going bowling tonight, after the birthday dinner. You'll want to be casual."

Lauren had always been on the bubbly side, but at this special time in her life she gurgled like a regular fountain of effervescence. Gina doubted the schedule would ever slow down enough to make time for reading, let alone figuring out her own future. Maybe, though, it was just what she needed.

Now if only "most of the wedding party" meant everyone except Brady "Mr. Homespun" Olafsson, she just might be able to relax.

Dear God, Brady paused, then ploughed ahead, *she's like a porcupine.*

He sat at his desk, head in his hands, elbows propped either side of the laptop computer, praying.

He imagined God's view on the subject of one porcupine named Gina Philips. If God's voice were audible to Brady, His reply would probably be along the lines of, "Yes, well, I created porcupines for a purpose, you know."

Brady groaned.

"You're holding some things against her, and it shows."

This was true. *I'm sorry.*

That part was easy, but he knew that writing this afternoon was out of the question unless he came clean before his heavenly Father, the source of his creativity.

Okay. The past is not her fault. Help me to give it up.

He heard the silence.

She is a snob, though. All right, help me to ignore the stiff, sharp spines of her porcupine personality.

"They will hurt. But they're not poisonous."

Brady breathed a hasty "amen." It would be tough to face Gina Philips again tonight, but he felt relieved that he had addressed his crummy attitude toward her. He didn't know how to let it go, didn't even know if he *wanted* to let it go. At least he had asked for help. Not a total cop-out.

He opened a file on the computer. He was working on his fourth novel in a series called *The Nazarene.* The last few lines he had written were part of an imaginary scene with Jesus joking with a tax collector, a man who cheated others in order to increase his own wealth. A man who did not deserve the kind attention of God's Son.

Brady stared at the screen.

Of course he had to let his crummy attitude go. What right did he have to keep it?

He thought again of Gina's stiffness, of her nonresponse to his jokes. What *would* make her laugh?

Five

Maggie sat at the big round oak table in her sister's farmhouse kitchen. The room was typical country, full of gingham checks and spicy aromas and windows framed in white lace that looked out every direction onto fields. The double sink, butcher block countertops, and wooden floor were of recent history, but the old cupboards were original, now painted white with forest green doors and adorned with new white ceramic knobs.

It was comfortable and homey, just like Marsha, whose husband, Dan, had grown up in this house. Their daughters were on their own. Liz was married and had a baby. Lauren had an apartment in town and in just a matter of weeks would be married. Only young Danny, a college student, remained at home. The in-laws lived down the lane in the "grandparent house."

She watched her sister fixing potato salad at the island counter. A chocolate cake cooled on a rack, waiting for frosting. "Are you sure I can't do anything?" Maggie asked.

"I'm sure. This part's under control. It's the wedding that unnerves me. You can help with that."

"Well, the house looks great, and so do you."

"I've gained. I look like a plump version of you, Magpie."

"Not plump, just less bony." She sighed. "I've lost interest in eating regular meals. One night I ate a can of black olives for dinner."

"Oh, boy. Maybe you should try the hormones."

"Reece keeps saying," she lowered her voice and cocked her head, "'can't the doctor give you a shot or vitamins or *something?*'"

Marsha chuckled. "Men, always full of quick solutions. Is that why you're not doing it?"

Maggie smiled. "Maybe. I've discovered a heretofore unknown ornery streak."

"I noticed that when you were 12."

"You did not."

"Did to."

"Anyway, except for unpredictable tears and hysteria, I'm fine."

"Oh, is that all?" Marsha replied in a sarcastic tone. "Just a little hysteria?"

"It keeps life interesting. It's definitely weird, this feeling of being out of sync with myself."

"I can hardly wait."

"Maybe it won't affect you the same way. I wonder why Mom never told us about this season of life?"

Marsha shrugged. "Different era. Have you told Gina?"

"Poor baby. Living back at home, she's gotten the full brunt of my craziness. I'd snap at her, then bake her cookies, which she definitely didn't want while lying around in a body cast. So I'd eat them."

"Body cast." Marsha shuddered. "Do I get to hear the full story now?"

Maggie shook her head. "There may be a lawsuit, and Gina is just coming to terms with a job change. It's not a topic for discussion yet. What concerns me is that she really hasn't cried about it. That's not normal. I mean, her whole life has been turned upside down."

"She'll reach the end of her rope, and the tears will come." Marsha dried her hands on her apron and sat down at the table. "I can't believe you're going to be here an entire month. You know I really appreciate it. You're always such a help to me."

Maggie smiled. "And you're always such a help to me. Isn't it strange how life has kept you and me apart?"

"What's really strange is how we're living out each other's dreams. I'm on a farm where you wanted to be, and you're far away from Valley Oaks with a sophisticated career."

"Like you wanted to be." Tears sprang to her eyes. "Why didn't we get our dreams, Marsh?"

Her sister went to the counter and brought back a box of tissues. "I call it chance journeys, Maggie. God takes us on these different routes, not the ones we think we want, but the ones that are best for us. I am so content and at peace with this life, I could pop."

"Well, I'm not like that with mine."

"You, dear sister, don't count right now. As you said, you're out of sync with yourself." She paused. "Maggie, you know God loves you."

"I should know. You've told me often enough." She smiled through her tears and blew her nose. "But what does that mean exactly?"

"It means you're important to Him. Between Gina's accident, your instability, and Reece being Reece, you're going through an extremely difficult time. God listens and He comforts."

"What do you mean, 'Reece being Reece'?"

Her sister sighed. "If he can't fix something, he avoids it. It's what makes him so successful business-wise. Fair enough?"

Maggie shrugged.

"This is a long healing period for both you and Gina. Has he been traveling more than usual?"

Well, that would be hard to determine. "When he's around, he tries."

"I know he does. He's a good man, but at a time like this, his personality may leave something to be desired."

A chill flowed through her. Marsha had struck a chord, one Maggie didn't want to linger on. She changed the subject. "I went to the cemetery. Your roses are beautiful."

"My roses?" Marsha looked puzzled.

"On the grave."

"I didn't put any roses there."

They stared at each other for a moment. "Who, then?"

Marsha shrugged. "Beats me." The clock ticked away the seconds. "Did you tell Gina?"

Maggie shook her head.

"She's met Brady, you know. Things will come out."

She sighed. "I know. Better from me than someone else. I will. Soon." It was one of the ghosts from the past, one she was determined to eliminate. "I'll make time tomorrow." She sighed again. Maybe she should write a to-do list. A to-do list of ghosts.

"Come on, Magpie." Marsha stood. "It's time for Aunt Lottie's party."

Six

Lottie's grandson Alec Sutton and his family lived in a big old farmhouse, although they were not farmers. Some years ago the town had expanded out to the place, eating up farmland along the way. Still, their home provided the old-fashioned amenities of a large kitchen and a private, rambling backyard that ended in someone else's cornfields. It was the perfect place for a large family birthday dinner.

Brady climbed from his truck and pulled out his bachelor contribution to the potluck: a bag of chips and two six-packs of cold pop. He headed down the gravel drive full of parked vehicles toward the backyard, then rounded the corner of the house. Groups of noisy people were scattered about, sitting at picnic tables or in lawn chairs. Babies rolled on blankets, toddlers crawled through the grass, older children played badminton. Under an old, solitary tree stood Gina Philips, staring up at the oak's canopy of green leaves.

He meandered through the groups, greeting several acquaintances. Someone relieved him of his food. He kept one eye on Gina, preparing to greet her. Might as well get it over with.

Her hair was twisted up off of her neck with some sort of tortoise-shell-type clip. She wore a pale yellow T-shirt and blue jeans. He wondered why she didn't wear shorts like most of the women did on such a warm afternoon. She couldn't be self-conscious about her slender shape. Maybe it had something to do with the limp, something she didn't want to call attention to? It wasn't exactly an obvious gait, rather subtle, more of a favoring one leg over the other. Now, as in the library, she stood leaning on the right foot.

He stepped beside her. "How's it going?"

She didn't turn, just continued staring upward. "Well, I finally found an oak tree. One solitary oak in the entire town. It does not explain why this place is called Valley Oaks."

"Hmm. Maybe you're looking in the wrong place."

"I've seen every square block. It takes about two minutes."

He bristled at her cutting remark about the town, then reminded himself it was true. "Is there something up there?" He studied the leaves above them.

"A bird. Hear that song?"

He listened a moment. "Like a squeaky swing?"

She looked at him then, her eyebrows raised as if in surprise. "Yes. I can't find it. What is it?"

He shrugged. "I don't know. Just part of the summer song. Like the frogs and cicadas and crickets."

She turned again to the tree. "It's an exquisite tree, all by itself here," she murmured.

He stared at her upturned face and wondered where the porcupine had gone.

"Brady!" His good friend Vic approached. They slapped each other's shoulders and shook hands. "Glad you could make it. Gram will appreciate it. Well, I hear you and Gina are paired up for the big wingding."

"Yep," he agreed, smiling inwardly at the panicked expression that crossed her face. "We're just getting acquainted here."

"I'll let you get back at it. Just wanted to ask if you'd help me out at the grill in awhile?"

"Sure, be glad to."

"Thanks. Well, Gina, you're in good hands. He and I go way back." Vic sauntered off.

Brady turned toward her. "Way back, as in tricycle days."

"Not as in cousins? Everyone else here is some sort of *relative*." She cocked an eyebrow.

He had never seen anyone raise just one brow. She was clearly challenging his right to be here. He decided to ignore her snooty remark and not defend himself. "Speaking of being related, can you figure out how you can tell if you're in the Midwest?" Brady studied her, wondering what the porcupine would do. Would she have the audacity to just walk away?

She broke the eye contact and tucked a stray piece of hair behind an ear.

He noticed her tiny gold hoop earrings. He hadn't realized before how tall she was or how fit she looked in a T-shirt and jeans. Her eye makeup was subtle, her face fresh in its natural state. A trace of rosy gloss outlined the somber pose of her lips.

She met his gaze. "You know you're in the Midwest if every other person you meet is your cousin."

He nodded. "Not bad. I think you're getting the hang of it."

She rolled her eyes.

Heads up! Porcupine is back.

"But you," she said, "and my second or third or whatever cousin Vic is, are just friends?" Her cool tone indicated that friendship wasn't quite enough to warrant including him in today's family gathering.

But she had asked a question! How long could he keep her talking? He'd give her the long version. "He and Aaron and I—"

"Aaron is your cousin, right?"

"Right. We all graduated from high school together. Aaron and I adopted Vic's Grandma Lottie and late Grandpa Peter. The three of us lived out in the country.

Around here every country boy needs a town home to hang out in, and their door was always open for us. If we were hungry, or didn't have time to go home between school activities, or if the snow got too deep during basketball practice, our moms knew where we'd be. Lots of good memories. One time—"

Her eyes glazed over.

"I suppose it's hard for a big-city girl to relate."

She lifted a shoulder and looked toward the house. "Orange County is a sprawling place. I didn't live close to the schools, but there were always late buses and car pools."

"And probably not much snow."

"Uh, no. Not much snow."

Brady glanced discreetly at his watch and crossed his arms. Could he break the earlier church basement encounter of four minutes? "Does it get this hot where you live?" He leaned against the tree.

"Hotter in the summer. The humidity seldom makes a difference, though. A hundred degrees at the Park just slows us down a bit."

"The Park?"

She gazed out at the cornfield now, but her eyes seemed focused elsewhere. "The Wild Creatures Country. Where I work. It's semidesert, but full of eucalyptus trees and plants. Nowhere near this green, though. This...this *verdant*."

Hmm, nice vocabulary. "I think I heard that you're a veterinarian?"

She looked at him. "You know you live in the Midwest when your car breaks down outside of town..." She didn't finish the joke of how fast news traveled. "I really should get reacquainted with my cousins."

"Sure." He winked. "I'll catch up with you later at the bowling alley." Brady grinned at the expression on her face.

It was nothing short of disbelief. He just might beat his time yet.

Gina opened her mouth as if to speak, then closed it. She turned, took a few steps, hesitated, then came back. "Look, don't take this the wrong way, but I really don't need to be part of a *pair* except for the wedding ceremony itself. All right?"

There was only one way to take her huffy comment. But Brady, always slow to give in to his temper, chose the teasing route...again. "I get it. You must be engaged to some possessive-type guy?"

"No!" Her face flushed. "It's just... just..." she sputtered, then pressed her lips together.

He straightened his posture and uncrossed his arms. Maybe they'd better get it over with, dredge up the past that wasn't really their personal past, but one that still affected them both. "Hey, I don't know what your mother told you, but—"

"My mother?" Her voice rose.

He took a deep breath. On second thought, this really wasn't the place. "Gina, I'm just trying to be friendly. I promised Aaron."

"Yeah, well, I promised Lauren." Her face was flushed, but she lowered her voice. "That makes us even. Let's just do it from a distance, okay?"

"Okay. Fine with me."

"Great!" She walked away.

Good golly, she is the prickliest woman I have ever met! And the most unnerving! If he had been alone, he would have kicked the tree. He gritted his teeth.

Sorry, Lord. I take back the porcupine remark. She's an out-and-out thorn. From You, I suppose?

My mother?

Fighting down the urge to stomp, Gina tried to walk casually across the yard, away from the insufferable Brady Olafsson.

What did he mean about what my mother said? What does my mother have to do with any of this? Oh!

The guy was either just down-home hokey or extremely desperate for a date. Whichever, he was annoying, and she wanted no part of him. *Catch me at the bowling alley? Unbelievable!*

All she wanted during the next few weeks was some special time with Lauren, her Aunt Marsha, and Great-Aunt Lottie. She wanted to enjoy her cousin's wedding and become acquainted with all the rest of her cousins. She wanted time to stand undisturbed under an oak tree and listen to a bird's odd song. And she wanted time to contemplate her future.

Is that asking too much?

She climbed the back steps and entered the air-conditioned kitchen where a group of women stood talking as they prepared food. Her mother's voice rose above the others.

"Marsha, you're just not mean enough. You never have been. I'll go with you to the florist's. I'll be the mean aunt and get this straightened out."

The others laughed, but Gina knew her mother was capable of zeroing in on a problem and fixing it, no matter how uncomfortable she might make others feel. It sounded as if they were in the middle of wedding details. Her question about what Brady had meant would have to wait.

"Gina!" Lauren's sister Liz noticed her by the door. "Saw you out there with Brady."

Anne turned to her with a grin. "Isn't he funny? He'll keep you entertained during all the wedding brouhaha, that's for sure."

Anne was married to Aunt Lottie's grandson Alec. Gina liked this distant cousin-by-marriage. Anne and Alec Sutton's wedding was one of those rare Valley Oaks memories she treasured. Anne was a down-to-earth, fun-loving, stay-at-home mom of three. Her dark hair and eyes hinted at her Native American heritage.

Liz said, "If you want to give up your bridesmaid spot, I'll walk with Brady. Even though he was years ahead of me in school, I always had the biggest crush on him."

"Probably still do," Lauren teased.

"Well, I realize I'm happily married and have a darling baby girl, but Brady Olafsson is still the best-looking guy in town."

"We all know he's the richest anyway."

There was laughter and Gina joined in. She doubted the statements were true, but it just felt good to be welcomed into the family. Even as the relative who had traveled the farthest and not visited in 13 years, she wasn't treated as a stranger. For an only child with no family on her father's side, it was a pleasant sensation. In spite of small-town nuisances like Brady Olafsson and everyone knowing everything, there was a distinct comfort in belonging.

Now if she could only figure out how to get out of the bowling excursion.

Seven

Gina hadn't been inside a bowling alley since...probably not since she was 15 years old and visiting Valley Oaks.

It hadn't changed. Loud laughter, a continuous thumping of balls hitting the wooden lanes, and the crashing of pins echoed off the low ceiling. The scent of French fries mingled with stale air and damp shoe leather. Someone else's shoes.

Oooh. She wrinkled her nose, scooted around in the molded plastic chair, and stared at her bare feet in sandals. A clammy rented bowling shoe dangled from her hand.

"Here, Gina." Lauren sat down beside her and handed her a pair of white athletic socks. "I brought these for us."

"Whew, thanks! You're a lifesaver."

"Are you any good?"

"I doubt it. It's been a long time."

"Did you meet everyone? Most of them are in the wedding. A few couldn't make it, and a few brought spouses. We thought it'd be fun to divide the group in half for two teams. Since there are eight guys and eight gals, we can keep the couples together."

Gina leaned over to tie her shoe and mumbled, "Wouldn't want to split up the couples."

She mingled with others, trying to learn the names. Brady seemed to keep his distance, making it easy for her to avoid the richest, most handsome guy in town. She smiled to herself.

Lauren's fiancé, Aaron, sought her out. They had met briefly at Aunt Lottie's dinner, but because he arrived late, his time had been occupied with meeting all the relatives.

She liked him. He obviously adored Lauren. Like his cousin Brady, he was tall with blue eyes and blond hair. The resemblance ended there. His mannerisms were gentle, an attentive doctor's personality. He asked her intelligent questions without prying and was grateful that she had agreed to be in the wedding and able to spend a few weeks beforehand in town. He didn't tell her any jokes.

She soon began to relax. She reminded herself that this was part of the special time she wanted to spend with Lauren. Maybe she could just let go for a bit.

It wasn't until she stood at the end of the lane with a heavy ball in her hand that she realized bowling was a new activity since her injury. She'd have to gauge her steps carefully in order to keep her balance.

It didn't quite work. As the ball dropped from her fingers, her left leg gave way and she rolled ungracefully onto her side. Her legs flew up as first her elbow, shoulder, and then head hit the floor.

"Ow!"

Her feet plopped down and she lay still, taking inventory. There was no hole to crawl into.

She was lying in a *bowling* alley, literally in the alley itself, set somewhere in the middle of *cornfields*.

Her friends were *thousands* of miles away.

Her leg wasn't right.

Her job wasn't right.

The plastic hair clip was cutting into her head.

The weather was unbelievably *putrid*.

Could life get anymore dreadful than this?

It could. She sensed Mr. Homespun himself would be the first to her rescue.

"Are you all right?" Brady asked as he knelt beside her.

She burst out laughing.

It had been a long time since Gina had laughed so freely. What an absolutely ridiculous situation!

Brady helped her to a sitting position. She pulled the clip from her hair and continued laughing while she rubbed the back of her head.

Aaron and then Lauren peered over Brady's shoulder. "Are you all right?" they asked.

She nodded and giggled.

"Can you stand up?" Brady held out his hand.

She wiped tears from her eyes.

He grasped her hands and pulled her to her feet. "Is that a smile on your face?" He leaned toward her and scrunched up his eyes.

"Probably," she giggled. "So what if it is?"

"Well, it's about time. Welcome to Valley Oaks, Gina Philips." He tilted his head toward the alley. "Care to pick up your spare?"

One lone pin stood in the right corner. How in the world had she done that? She shook her head. "I don't think so. Bowling just got crossed off my list of fun things to do."

"Oh, come on. I'll catch you this time."

She laughed again, along with him. Eventually the others talked her into rolling the ball down any which way she could. She walked to the end of the lane, holding the ball in both hands, then dropped it with a little "oomph" to send it on its way.

She missed that spare, but never her turn. The evening turned out to be rather enjoyable.

Even Brady Olafsson seemed less annoying.

After church the next morning, Aunt Lottie napped. Gina and her mother settled on the front porch swing with unsweetened iced tea and gently pushed, creating a slight breeze in the hot afternoon.

"Well, that was different," Gina commented.

"What was?"

"Church. Kind of informal."

"Not like home, that's for sure. The pastor makes Jesus sound, oh, I don't know. Maybe approachable is the word."

Gina nodded. "Everyday and real. Like the people. Although Brady Oleo wasn't everyday. He wore a nice pair of jeans and no cap."

Maggie's forehead creased.

"You missed him at the open house. He wore mud-caked boots and jeans! Unbelievable."

"That's the Olafssons." Maggie stared out at the street.

"Did you know—" The phone shrilled through the screen door. "I'll get that."

Gina hurried to the kitchen. "Hello."

"Hi, Gina. How are things in Podunk?"

"Dad! Hey, I promised not to call it that. How's work?" She always asked him about work. It was synonymous with "How are you?" As a top executive in a national land development company, he traveled more than 50 percent of the time. Work was his life.

"I'll be in Chicago in a couple of weeks, and I may run down to *Valley Oaks*."

"Very good, Dad! Mother would appreciate that emphasis."

"Well, I'm not coming to the garden spot to sightsee. Our Midwest division ran into a snag on some nearby property. I said I'd look into it. On another subject, nothing new here yet on the Park situation. How are you dealing with that issue?"

Gina answered her dad's straightforward question in a like manner. "I'm not. I don't want to even *think* about it. I'd rather plan the future."

"All right. It will work out, honey. Don't worry."

He chatted with her about other things, keeping her on the phone, she knew, until she calmed down. He was a good dad.

While her mother talked with him, Gina sat outside. Her thoughts drifted over the full schedule that prevented her from focusing on the future. She remembered Brady's comment under the oak tree as her mother rejoined her.

"Mom, you know that Brady character kind of rubs me the wrong way. He's just so friendly, but at the same time I sense a chip on his shoulder or something. Kind of like he's not being *genuinely* friendly toward me. Anyway, we were getting into it about being paired up. I said the ceremony was the only necessary time for that, and then he definitely lost his down-home attitude. He said, 'I don't know what your mother told you,' but he never finished the sentence. Do you know what he's talking about?"

Her mother stopped pushing the porch swing and looked out at the street. "Your dad and I were just talking about some memories. He said you should know." Her voice trailed off. "Gina." Maggie looked at her then, and there was sadness in her eyes. "I need to show you something. It may answer your question. I'll get the car keys."

Gina sat frozen on the swing. Why would there be an answer to that question?

Open, rolling fields surrounded the town of Valley Oaks. Maggie drove Aunt Lottie's old car to one of the edges of town. A few minutes later Gina's stomach tightened as they turned into an old cemetery enclosed on three sides by soybean fields. Cows grazed on a distant rolling hill. They parked along one of the narrow gravel lanes and climbed out.

"Is this where Grandma and Grandpa are buried?"

"Yes. Do you remember coming here?"

"Not really," Gina replied, "just that we brought flowers to a cemetery."

She walked behind her mother between tombstones, many more than a hundred years old with worn lettering. It was a well-maintained place with neatly trimmed grass. They stopped before a small, pink-flecked marble stone. Fresh white roses filled an attached metal vase.

Gina read the engraved name. Rose Lindstrom Olafsson.

Lindstrom? Her mother's maiden name.

Olafsson?!

She read the dates. The girl was born 35 years ago. And she lived only three days. Gina felt as if a hand clutched her throat. "Mom?"

Unshed tears swam in her mother's eyes. "It was before hyphenated names were fashionable." She gave her a tiny smile. "I did have another middle name in mind. Engraving four names cost…" Her voice trailed off. "I made a mistake, but I didn't want her to leave without her mother's family name."

Gina sat on the soft grass and let the news sink in. She had a sister.

"Sweetie, I was married to Brady's father." Maggie sat down beside her.

Another shock wave rolled through her. A baby *and* a husband? Hearing out of the blue that her mother had such secrets was disconcerting. She listened without comment to the story that began at Valley Oaks High School almost 40 years ago. Her mother and Neil Olafsson dated and fell in adolescent love. By the end of their senior year, she was pregnant.

Their families had never cared for each other. The Olafssons were wealthy farmers. The grandparents had been able to purchase land during the Depression rather than lose it like so many others. On the other hand, the Lindstroms, a family of seven, lived in town, not far from the railroad tracks. Grandpa Martin worked in the factory that built the tractors and combines that the Olafssons purchased.

"I stayed home from college and worked, determined that I was on my own and that I would make it work. By October, Neil was fed up with his family. We were legally adults and so much in love." She shrugged. "We eloped. His parents almost disowned him. Mine let me live at home while he went back to school. Rosie was born December 27."

Maggie wiped a tear. "Her skin felt like velvet, like a rose petal. There were complications. Anyway, we were too young. When she died, we didn't have to be married. Neil went back to school. I went to a different one." She sighed. "I never would have lasted as a farm wife. We got divorced. I met your father. End of story."

Gina didn't think so. "Why didn't you ever tell me?"

"And tarnish my image?" She gave her a sad smile. "I felt so guilty. I wanted to be the perfect mother to you. There was never a right time. I'm sorry."

"I remember calling you old-fashioned and uptight and mean and stricter than any mother on earth had a right to be."

"I didn't want you to live with the baggage I had. I should have told you why. Your dad always told me to. It was the only major thing we disagreed on. I'm so grateful I found him. Without him, I wouldn't have you."

Now Gina cried. They sniffled for a few moments. "Did you bring these roses?"

She nodded. "But some were already here. I thought Aunt Marsha probably brought them..." Her voice trailed off again.

Was this the chip on Brady Olafsson's shoulder? "Do you think Brady holds this against me? But why would he?"

Her mother dabbed at her eyes. "Oh, I imagine he's heard poisonous remarks at impressionable times growing up here. Neil's mother—that would be Brady's grandmother—always blamed me for getting pregnant. Then for Rosie's death. Then for the divorce. I couldn't win. I'm sure I was known as 'that hussy.' You're probably referred to as 'that hussy's daughter.' In a small town like this, the past never goes completely away."

"Is that why you left?"

"Partly. Partly because Valley Oaks was not your Chicago-native father's kind of town."

They sat quietly. A light breeze played with Gina's hair. Knowing that she had a sister felt...well, she wasn't sure how to feel, not that there was much to be done about it. Still...maybe her sharp sense of aloneness could soften just a bit by the simple fact that nestled in her family tree was a half sibling.

"Mom? Do you think she's in heaven?"

"If Jesus is real, I know she is."

Eight

The house was quiet. Gina was out somewhere with Lauren. Aunt Lottie had fallen asleep on the couch while crocheting. Maggie set down the book she couldn't concentrate on.

She should call Reece, tell him that Gina now knew the deep, dark secret.

With a shake of her head, she reworded the thought, erasing the angry tone. *I told Gina about Rosie and we're fine.* Yes, they were fine. Her daughter's mature compassion amazed her. The upheaval of the past few months had drawn them closer together, more as equals, as friends even. While Maggie's unpredictable emotions tore down stoic walls of perfectionism, Gina had been able to tease her and, in more serious moments, confess that her mother was much easier to relate to these days.

As this new relationship blossomed, hers with Reece deteriorated. Marsha had asked if he traveled more. He could scarcely be gone more than he had been in recent years unless he simply moved out of the house. On the surface their marriage appeared the same, but she knew they weren't connecting on a deeper level. Yet at times she wondered if it were all in her imagination, simply a result of this unstable time.

He needed to hear what happened yesterday, and she needed to apologize for mentally stomping her foot and snapping at his suggestion. She thought again of what she would tell him. This was positive news. Why the angry tone?

Maggie went to the kitchen, lifted the phone receiver from the wall and carried it through the back door, stretching the cord to its limit. It was a pleasant evening without last week's stifling humidity. The sun was almost hidden behind the garage. She sat on the top step and dialed Reece's cell phone number.

It rang and rang and rang. She disconnected and tried again. After ten rings she cut it off. If he didn't answer, the stupid thing was supposed to automatically roll into voice mail. She glanced at her watch and subtracted two hours. Evelyn, his secretary, might still be at the office.

Someone else answered. Before she could ask for her husband's voice mail, she was on hold, a Vivaldi concerto assaulting her eardrum.

Her internal thermostat did its spontaneous overheating number. Perspiration seeped through every pore. Her heart pounded, resonating in her head and chest. She rested her elbows on her knees, blinked back tears, and bit her lip. This had nothing whatsoever to do with summer, absolutely nothing whatsoever to do with anything except pure frustration and anger at not being able to reach her husband when she needed him. She wondered if years and years worth of bottled-up frustration now flowed.

Evelyn got on the line. Maggie had always liked the woman and tried now to keep up her end of the polite chitchat. Reece was in New York, probably at a restaurant at this hour. Unavailable. At last she was connected with the voice mail.

"Reece, it's me. Margaret." She coughed a self-deprecating laugh. "Guess you could figure that out. Your cell number didn't work. I don't know why." She wiped her brow, steeling herself to drop the complaining tone. "I took Gina to Rosie's grave yesterday. She's fine with it, of course. Just as you knew she would be. She is a darling, isn't she?

Call me so I can apologize for snapping at you." She paused. "I miss you."

She did miss him, had been missing him for a long time, but suspected the feeling wasn't mutual.

She ran her fingers through her hair, then dialed another number, fully aware that she had promised not to, fully aware that sometime between the unanswered ringing of the cell phone and the Vivaldi concerto she had decided to break that promise.

The answering machine clicked on. The soothing, professorial voice stated simply, "Please leave a message."

She waited through the beeps. "Don't pick up. I just need to talk one-sided." *To someone who will listen,* she added silently. "I told Gina yesterday. She was so precious about it all. Are all my fears this unnecessary? I don't think she'll hold it against me. She seems to appreciate seeing all sides of me—"

"Hi."

She closed her eyes. "You weren't supposed to answer."

"You weren't supposed to call."

"I'm sorry."

"Don't apologize." There was a smile in his voice. "I wanted you to call, remember? But we did agree it would be best for your sake to go it alone." He paused. "How are you?"

"Not very well at the moment. Actually, I'm doing a thoroughly good job of botching my going it alone."

"Sounds as if things went well with Gina."

He was coaxing her thoughts to focus on the positive. She knew his deep brown eyes would be twinkling pools about now, subdued by thick black lashes and wire-rimmed glasses. "They call me Maggie here."

"Maggie?"

She let him ponder that for a moment.

"Maggie," he repeated. "Hmm. It suits you, I think. The 'you' that you let me in on sometimes. Do you like it?"

"Confession time." She smiled softly. "I do, I really do."

"Ah, the beginnings of an authentic identity?"

"Just a baby step."

"Two baby steps. Authenticity with Gina as well as yourself."

"I miss you, John."

"Margaret," he breathed.

"I'm sorry."

He didn't reply for a moment. "You need a friend there. Tell your sister."

She bit her lip.

"It's the next baby step. Pretty soon you'll have taken one giant step in authentic relationships and, I suspect, found a large piece to the identity-slash-future puzzle. Nothing to lose, right?"

She exhaled sharply. "No. Nothing to lose."

He waited, patiently, politely. She knew he would let her end the conversation.

"Okay."

"Okay."

"Thank you, John."

"You're welcome...Maggie."

She heard the grin, imagined the crinkled crow's feet behind the glasses. "Bye."

"Goodbye."

Maggie held the phone against her forehead and blinked back tears. If only—

"Who's John?"

She looked up, over her shoulder. On the other side of the screen door stood Marsha.

Nine

Brady grabbed a sport coat and tie from the closet, just in case his editor chose an upscale Chicago restaurant. An upscale one that allowed jeans. On that point he wasn't conceding.

He laughed as he strode out the door and to his truck. Contract for book Number Five was signed. Today's discussion over lunch would be the gist of Number Six. The critics loved his work.

He didn't *have* to wear a suit!

He flung his arms wide and whirled around, whooping loudly. *Thank You for that, Father.*

Brady gazed at his log cabin house. At his 122.7 wooded acres that glowed now in slanted shafts of early morning sunlight through the oak trees.

And for this.

And for not having to major on planting corn the rest of my life!

Well, he could go on with the list, but it was time to leave. The "girls" would be waiting. When Lauren had heard he was headed to Chicago on Thursday, she begged for a lift and offered her mother's van so that she and her wedding entourage could sit comfortably for the 90-minute ride. They had shopping to do, and Gina hadn't seen the city in 20 years. Could he just stay an extra hour or maybe two?

He wasn't adept at saying no to a sweet, pretty woman asking a favor. And Lauren was genuinely both.

With a wry smile, he climbed into his truck. It was a wonder he could still recognize such feminine traits. When his fiancée, Nicole, left him for another man and another lifestyle in California, he had buried himself in work. The escape route had surely been a gift from God. When he emerged from it, his second book had just been released to rave reviews. Now, at last count, the combined sales of the first two novels had reached 200,000.

Much to his surprise, he had noticed a tender streak emerge. His fictional characters took on depth. He had a soft spot for readers who bothered to write and tell him how they liked his books. He became more involved with community affairs and enjoyed the people of his hometown, unlike his former tendency toward aloofness.

Still, he fiercely guarded his privacy. He turned down most speaking invitations and had done only one major book tour. He liked living and working alone; he could not imagine doing anything else. It was easy to keep his distance from sweet, pretty, unattached females not only because he knew better, but because he had found contentment apart from them.

And so while his tender side could not say no to Lauren, his practical side knew it wasn't a serious disruption to his life to say yes. Their company would make the drive go quickly. Perhaps he could spend the extra time at the Art Institute.

Or he could take notes on Gina Philips. Given the reputation of her parents, she probably never stood a chance. She had a mother who had left her first husband, and a father who traveled on business most of the time. Except for a brief period at the bowling alley Saturday night, Gina was the epitome of a thorny character, a perfect blueprint for one of his Number Six characters.

Well, as long as she didn't smile. That Miss America smile of hers could still make a guy weak in the knees.

Gina felt embarrassment.

She climbed into the minivan, mumbled a hello to Brady, and headed to the far backseat. How should she greet the guy, a practical stranger, who had the same half sister as she did? *Oh, by the way, I just heard our parents were married...something you've probably known your entire life?*

Good grief! Did this mean they were related?

No, of course not.

They weren't even anywhere near being *step*-related. Absolutely none of the business of her mother being married to Brady's father 35 years ago had anything whatsoever to do with her or him. There really was nothing whatsoever to feel embarrassed about.

Gina determined to put the entire story out of her mind and enjoy the day. She had visited Chicago only a few times as a child, when her dad's parents lived there. He didn't have the extended family the way her mother did.

She wished there would be time to visit one of the zoos, but this was obviously a shopping crowd. Well, except for Brady. He had a business meeting and would meet them later. Lauren sat up front with him now, glad to give him the driver's seat. Her sister Liz sat in the back with Gina; her two friends Isabel and Abbey were in the middle. The four of them were bridesmaids and on a mission to help the bride purchase her honeymoon trousseau.

They were a fun group of women, eager to laugh. And sing. Lauren was the school district's band teacher, Abbey its music teacher, Liz the church choir director, and Isabel an announcer for the local Christian radio station. Gina soon relaxed.

As the freeway lanes multiplied and traffic thickened, skyscrapers came into view. The city looked enormous. She listened with half attention as the others discussed where to meet. With a start, Gina realized that she didn't have to make a decision about the schedule or anything. That felt good for a change. She could postpone her personal, heavy-duty decision-making thought processes for today at least, couldn't she?

She needed a job. There was no denying that, but things were out of her hands for now. Four applications had been mailed seven weeks ago. One more went out last week. Those were out of her hands.

Still, it seemed inadequate. She'd have to continue her research tomorrow. Her experience with zoological parks was extensive in a way and yet specialized. From the time she was 16, she had worked in some capacity at the Wild Creatures Country. Finally, three years ago she had received her degree as doctor of veterinary medicine and completed all the licensing requirements. When the Park needed an assistant vet to care almost exclusively for the large animals, her dream had come true.

Her parents tried to encourage her, promising that when the time was right, she would find a job. Dad would laugh and say some elephant somewhere would need her services sometime.

It was the "somewhere, sometime" part that unnerved her. She was a planner and had never been so long without step-by-step details solidly organized in her Day-Timer. She even had a page for listing future projects, some scheduled for ten years down the road. Even those were up for grabs now.

And then there was that nagging impression that she kept shoving aside, a fear she never intentionally put into words, although it popped into her mind at times. Like now. *Could I really do it again? Could I really stand face-to-face with an elephant—*

She clenched her jaw, cutting off the thought, forcing her attention back to the present. She was taking this day off!

Glancing forward, her eyes locked with Brady's in the rearview mirror for a long moment. Had she spoken aloud?

She looked out the window. The fear was so audible in her head, she sometimes thought others must hear it. No doubt, though, it was probably written all over her face.

Oh! Why doesn't that man mind his own business?

∼⌒∽

The brakes screeched as Brady jerked the van to a stop alongside the curb. "Water Tower Place, girls!" he shouted. "Have fun! Get moving! Here comes a bus! Meet me at 2:30! Don't be—"

Gina climbed last from the van, then with a wave slammed the door shut on his instructions. As the vehicle peeled away from the curb, a bus whooshed into its place.

She stepped onto the sidewalk and immediately felt the urge to crane her neck. The soaring height of the buildings was unbelievable! She moved in a slow circle, chin up. Someone jostled past her. There was a tangible sense of excitement in the big-city air. While she gawked, the others discussed their agenda.

"I vote for lunch."

"It's only ten o'clock!"

"Well, we want to stop later at Field's in the Loop for ice cream. Maybe we could hold lunch off until then."

"Gina's got goosebumps."

"It's freezing today!" Gina rubbed her arms. In spite of sunshine, the air was cool. "What happened to hot and sticky?"

"Didn't you listen to the weather forecast? Cold front. This is 20 degrees below normal."

"Yeah, and hot and sticky was above normal for early June," Lauren explained. "Let's go sweater shopping for you first. It's not going to warm up much today."

They ducked into the nearest department store and as a group chose a thick cotton, short, navy blue cardigan that matched her ivory slacks and top. The price stunned her.

"Is this a group payment, too?" she asked only half-teasingly.

"Welcome to Michigan Avenue," Isabel offered.

Lauren gave her shoulders a squeeze. "Single doctors can afford something a little special now and then, right?"

Employed single doctors, Gina silently amended. The fact that she probably needn't spend any more money along their shopping route was a comfort.

The women made quick work of the tall, impressive indoor mall called Water Tower Place, then headed back outside toward a bookstore. It seemed an odd choice for trousseau hunting, but Lauren and Abbey explained there were teaching materials there that they couldn't find anywhere near home.

The group fanned out, and Gina wandered toward the new releases. Maybe she could spend some money to buy that novel she was reading and give the library book back to Brady. It would take care of the debt that gnawed at her every time she opened the thing.

She studied the new release selections. The name "Brady" jumped out at her.

Brady.

Brady Olafsson?!

Gina stared. There was the man's name...on a book...on a hardback, new release novel...in Chicago. He was an *author?*

Well, she knew that. Lauren had told her that.

But...

She picked it up and turned it over. There was his photograph. It really was him.

Oh, my goodness.

She flipped it back over. *Rivers in the Desert. Number Three in the series, The Nazarene. Over 200,000 of Numbers One and Two Sold.* The cover's artwork was attractive. A beautiful woman in long white robes sat on a stone step alongside what looked like a well. Her face glowed, and she appeared to be looking expectantly at something not in the picture.

Gina flopped it to her other hand and studied the color photo. It covered three-fourths of the jacket. The background was a mass of unfocused spring green leaves. Brady leaned nonchalantly, raised elbow resting against a tree trunk. The other hand balanced on his jeans-covered hip. He wore a pale yellow polo shirt that enhanced his tanned face and short blond hair. And he was smiling. A very nice smile that softened the square jaw and sharp angles of his face. It wasn't the grin that irked her so.

"That guy's books are awesome."

Gina glanced at a young woman beside her, an employee straightening books on the shelf. "Oh?"

"And he is sooo cool. He came here once for a signing. He's even better-looking in person, and really, *really* tall with shoulders...well, just look at his shoulders." She pointed to the picture. "Perfect for crying on, know what I mean? And he was the friendliest author we've ever had. It was like his personality just filled up the whole place."

"Hmm. I haven't read his books."

"Really? Well the first two are in paperback now, but we just sold our last ones this morning. They're on back order!"

"It says they're a series. Should you read them consecutively?"

"No, they're great stand-alones. Oh, excuse me." The clerk left.

The embarrassment Gina had felt early in the morning returned with intensity. Why wasn't she aware that this Valley Oaks resident, her cousin's friend, was a well-known author? Probably because she didn't know the name before last week...she never picked up historical fiction. And she had been a bit preoccupied with her work...for the last 12 years or so, thousands of miles away.

Hadn't Lauren said the books were Christian? This was a huge bookstore that carried all kinds of books. This was a *major* bookstore in Chicago that carried on its new release shelf a hardcover book written by Brady Olafsson of Valley Oaks, Illinois.

Gina was stunned. There was no other word for it. Mr. Homespun was a bestselling novelist, and no one had even mentioned it! Aunt Lottie apparently wasn't aware of the magnitude of that "something he had published a while back," as she described it. Lauren had said the books were... what? Awesome. The same word the clerk had used and with the same emphasis. Lauren had not indicated he was nationally known. Well, in truth, Gina hadn't paid attention to what she said.

Would it have made a difference if she had? Probably not. He still would have been an annoying nuisance with a chip on his shoulder. After the visit to the cemetery, though, she had a pretty good idea of the source of his attitude.

If she was going to keep running into the man for the next few weeks, she needed to get over her embarrassment. Perhaps the best defense would be to arm herself with information, to protect herself from being caught again by surprise.

She knew about Rosie. She'd better learn what she could about this farmer who wrote awesome novels in his spare time.

Gina carried the new release by Brady Olafsson to the checkout counter. It seemed that a good place to begin learning about the man would be to read about the Nazarene.

Ten

It was 3:30.

Brady stomped into a Marshall Field's elevator, jabbed his thumb against the top floor button, then bit back the first word that sprang to mind. He wiggled his thumb. It didn't appear to be fractured. He exhaled sharply.

Women!

Of course they would be late. He knew it. He just knew it. From the moment he told Lauren sure, come along, he knew she and her friends would miss the 2:30 meeting time. He knew he'd be hanging out in the city long after his lunch was over.

He had stood on the corner of State and Monroe for 30 minutes before spotting them rushing toward him, shopping bags bumping along among them. That was at 2:58. There was still a sliver of a chance they could race two blocks to where the van was parked and hit the freeway by 3:15.

That was before their breathless apologies and excuses and stories, before he noticed Gina Philips wasn't with them. With a sinking feeling he realized rush hour would be in full swing before he could sort through their babble. He suggested they continue shopping and meet again at 6:00. They had a better idea! They were taking him to dinner at 5:30, at an Italian restaurant just a few blocks away. And meanwhile could he take a few of their bags to the van and then fetch Gina?

The elevator doors swished open now. Brady stepped out, loped past the elegant Walnut Dining Room and into a large, bright space of food merchandise displays and open eating areas. She was supposed to be at a table near the first window he would see on his left.

He saw her, elbows propped with head in hands, bent over a newspaper. Her left leg was stretched out and resting on another chair. Lauren told him that Gina had tired from so much walking. After stopping here for ice cream, she convinced the others to finish their shopping without her. She would stay put and read until someone came for her at 2:20.

Obviously she was a patient woman. He, on the other hand, had run out of patience some time ago on the first floor of this huge store that covered an entire city square block, trying to figure out where they hid the elevators. He wouldn't have minded so much meandering around downtown Chicago by himself, but now he faced two hours alone with a lame porcupine. What was he supposed to do with her?

He approached the table. "Hello."

She glanced up at him, then quickly looked back down.

Brady's stomach twisted. Her face was tear-streaked. "Gina?" His anger instantly dissipated. He pulled out a chair across the table from her and sat down. "Are you all right? Does your leg hurt?"

She buried her face in a paper napkin and shook her head.

He would have chosen a porcupine over a crying woman any day. She looked as if she needed a hug. "Can I do something?" *Besides give you a hug,* he added silently.

She took a deep, tremulous breath. "No." Her eyes were liquid emeralds. "It's—" Her lower lip quivered and she bit it.

"What?"

She pointed at the newspaper and winced. "My elephant died."

"Your elephant?"

"Delilah." She caught the puzzled look on his face. "Oh, she wasn't *mine* mine. I mean, I took care of her at the Park. She was special. She—" Her face crumpled again.

He had forgotten she was a vet. "I'm sorry. Was she sick or just old?" Totally of its own accord, his hand covered hers on the table.

Gina's eyes widened and her breath caught. "Uh, no." She shook her head slightly. "She wasn't sick or, uh, old. Um, it's kind of a long story."

"It must be a shock." His touch seemed to have staunched the flow of tears. "And you just found out, sitting here in downtown Chicago?"

She glanced toward the window, nodding. "I thought I'd buy a big-city newspaper and read some real news."

"Stuff you can't get in the *Valley Oaks Weekly Times*?"

"No offense."

"None taken. My copy of the *Tribune* is in the van." He smiled.

"Van. Oh my goodness!" She slid her hand from under his and looked at her watch. "What time is it? We're late, aren't we? I'm sorry."

"No, it's not your fault. The others were late, so we've changed plans." He stopped, thinking of how her hand had felt beneath his. It was broad with long, slender fingers. Strong. A doctor's hand.

She hurriedly folded the newspaper and stuffed it into a shopping bag, gathered it along with her purse, and lowered her leg. "The rush hour traffic must be impossible here."

"Mmm, yes, it is. It's best to wait it out. We're, uh, going to meet for dinner at 5:30." Again he stopped. Her eyes were still red. There was a speck of dried tear salt on a cheek. He resisted the urge to rub his thumb over it. Her chocolate hair was smoothed back into a ponytail low on her neck. She wore the tiny gold hoop earrings.

"Oh." She glanced at her watch again. "Well, I can stay put. I'm sure you have things you could do."

He gave himself a mental shove. A good-looking chick sat across the table from him. One of the world's most fascinating cities lay just beyond the window. Now what exactly was his problem? "Let's go exploring. I had the Art Institute in mind."

A blush tinged her cheeks. "Well, I, uh, I think I've walked my limit today. I should have worn my brace, but I wasn't expecting a major hike across concrete—"

"I'm sorry." Where was his mind? "Of course. That's the whole reason you're sitting here. Well, let's see...we could, um, ride. How about a bus tour? They leave every 15 minutes or so."

She shrugged, sniffled, looked out the window, bit her lip. And then finally smiled. "Okay."

Something inside of him melted. The porcupine would definitely have been easier to deal with than Gina's Miss America smile.

$\sim$

Delilah was dead.

Gina wiped at the corner of her eye and gazed up at the passing skyscrapers. *Let it go. You're in Chicago, riding on top of a crowded double-decker bus, sitting next to an annoying nuisance who is being incredibly kind and hasn't told a joke for at least an hour.*

"Are you cold?" Brady asked her.

"A little." She crossed her arms and willed herself to stop shivering. The sun still shone from a brilliant blue sky, but despite her new sweater the breeze still felt cool from many open windows on the upper deck.

"Put this on." He had shrugged out of his sport coat and was holding it open for her.

"Thanks." She leaned forward to let him drape it over her shoulders. "You don't need it?"

"Nah, I was getting too warm."

The bus slowed to a stop and the tour guide's voice, amplified through a loudspeaker, began describing a huge Picasso sculpture that covered a large area of a plaza on their right.

"Well, I'll be switched," Brady drawled in an exaggerated manner. "I can't tell if that's a horse or a cow." He craned his neck to look around her through the window.

"What?"

He glanced sideways at her, his eyelids half closed. Most of those blue-green eyes hid behind thick blond lashes. "Well, the thing is," he continued the drawl, "you know you're from the Midwest if you can tell a horse from a cow at a distance. And gosh durn it, in this case I can't tell."

He sounded absolutely pathetic. She burst out laughing.

"And I'm about as Midwestern as they come. Born and raised on a farm."

She wiped her eyes again. At least the tears were caused by laughter this time. He was helping, bizarre as that thought would have sounded this morning.

When he found her in Marshall Field's, she had just read the news about Delilah. Of course the elephant's death hadn't been a surprise, but all the same, knowing that it had happened grieved her. If Brady hadn't walked up at that moment, she didn't know what she would have done. Probably bawled until an employee intervened and called security.

He had saved her from that embarrassment, but she couldn't think straight. Brady offered a plan, and it was as if he threw her a lifeline. Instinctively, she grabbed hold.

He waited while she stopped in the ladies' room to splash water on her face and assess the damage. Her face was a wreck. She popped open the barrette at the back of her neck and brushed back the loose strands of hair. Good thing she hadn't applied mascara this morning. She blew her nose one more time, found eyeshadow and a compact in her purse, and fixed what she could, all the while imagining what this news meant.

Delilah's death would have an impact on the lawsuit, but there was nothing to be done about it except fret. Better to go with the flow and take a bus ride. Her attorney and other vets were in control now. She had to put it out of her mind.

Brady offered his arm when she stumbled getting into the elevator. Ibuprofen had helped the throb in her leg, and the swelling about the knee had lessened, but things were still a bit stiff. She grasped his elbow for a moment, and he took the shopping bag from her hand. Inside the bag was mint chocolate candy she had found for Aunt Lottie, a towel set Lauren had admired, and Brady Olafsson's newest release. Before picking up the newspaper, she had read the first chapter of his book. The story and writing style quickly caught her attention.

Once they reached outside, Brady easily hailed a cab that whisked them a few blocks to a busy intersection where a tour bus sat waiting just for them, it seemed. He quickly purchased two tickets and ushered her to the upper level where they found the last available seat. Nonstop from the elevator to the bus he talked of his impressions of the city. He even struck up a conversation with the taxi driver and learned he was from Morocco and had a wife and two kids.

Her stomach ached. The grief simmered just below the surface. If she had been there, could she have prevented the elephant's death?

"Wanna hear another one?" Brady peered at her closely.

She blinked. "What?"

"Do you want to hear another joke? You look lost in space again."

She turned her head toward the window and swallowed. The bus was moving.

"Would it help to talk about it? I've been told that sometimes I can listen instead of talk."

She shook her head. It was too soon to put the feelings into words. They would be incoherent. Another lump formed in her throat. She didn't want to cry in front of him again! The bookstore clerk's remarks about Brady's shoulders sprang to mind. She had been right—they appeared the perfect height and breadth for crying on—but Gina wasn't about to test out the theory. She kept her face toward the window.

"Of course, we are strangers. I certainly wouldn't be inclined to tell you what's bugging me either."

She looked at him now.

He stared beyond her, out the window. His hair was just long enough for the breeze to catch it, lift it up.

They had progressed beyond total strangers. She nestled in his jacket, warmed in its roominess. The laid-back farmer was an author and a perfect gentleman and completely at home in the big city. These things she knew about him. And she knew he liked to tell jokes. And she knew she simply had to end this verge-of-tears nonsense. "It's your jokes, Brady."

He raised his brows.

"Your jokes are bugging me. As a matter of fact, they drive me bonkers."

He snorted. "You obviously don't understand them. Anybody who says 'bonkers' would not appreciate my sophisticated jokes."

"Bingo." She smiled. "How did your meeting go?"

He missed a beat and stared at her for a full minute. "That sounds like an invitation to get acquainted."

She shrugged.

He shrugged back. "It went well. My editor is in from New York for a couple of days. We had lunch and discussed my next book. Ironed out a few wrinkles."

"I'm sorry I didn't even know about your books until today."

"Don't apologize. There was no reason you would know, was there?"

"I guess not. I've never paid much attention to historical fiction."

"It's funny. Even in Valley Oaks, not everyone knows about them."

"Shouldn't you be on a book tour or something for the new release?"

"Just got back. I have a couple of things coming up in August, but then I'll stay put through harvest season. I can pretty much make my own schedule."

"How did you come up with the idea? I mean, a fiction-alized account of Jesus' life? For adults?"

Brady settled back into his seat. "I just always wondered what went on between the lines in the Bible. Really, what was it like to walk for miles on end wearing sandals? And the people who came to Him, what were their personalities, their backgrounds? I guess I've been imagining for a long time. Church was pretty boring when I was a teenager."

"Did you major in creative writing?"

"Nah. Agriculture with a minor in English." He grinned. "For real. You can't make a living at writing. I taught English for five years at a high school over in the next county. Writing and farming kept getting in the way. Now I write full time, but still help out on the farm with my dad and brother."

"Do you have any sis—" Gina stopped herself.

"Two living sisters. And then, of course, there's Rosie. You're missing the sights." He nodded toward the window. The bus had stopped again.

"Brady, I didn't know about Rosie until three days ago."

He stared at her, disbelief wrinkling his brow. His jaw muscles tensed. "How could you not know?"

"My parents never told me."

"That's outrageous! The entire town has known for 35 years."

"Well, I'm not part of the entire town. My mother had her reasons. It's not like it would have made a difference to anybody in San Clemente, California, that my mother made a mistake at the age of 18."

He shook his head. "It's our personal history, which makes it public record in Valley Oaks, which means it was often referred to in my presence." There was an edge to his voice. "It had a hand in shaping who I am."

Obviously she had hit a nerve with this subject, but that didn't give him the right to fuss at her. "It's not my fault, is it?"

He exhaled. "No, it's not your fault that your mother left Valley Oaks."

Gina was stunned. *That* was the problem? Not that a child was conceived out of wedlock and the teenagers married too soon, but that her mother had *moved*? She sensed it best to probe no further. She and Brady were, after all, just strangers, thrown together for a brief moment in time for the sole purpose of participating in a wedding.

Eleven

"I said I'll take Gina home." Brady's tone was adamant, almost belligerent.

Liz laughed. "Okay, okay. She's all yours."

Having just returned from Chicago, the group of six stood on the quiet street outside Lauren's apartment building. It was after ten o'clock. In the dim light of a street lamp they unpacked the van and discussed the most logical way for the other five to go home in two vehicles. It was becoming obvious that Brady's tolerance threshold for illogical women had been crossed.

"I don't know," Isabel mused. "You sound a little cranky. Maybe we shouldn't let her go with you."

Brady grabbed Gina's one shopping bag from the pile and headed across the street to his truck. "Good night, ladies," he called over his shoulder.

"Isabel!" Lauren hissed. "Stop giving him such a hard time! We want them to be alone together." She gave Gina a quick hug and sang out, "Thanks, Brady!"

The others chorused their thanks while Gina followed the guy who was becoming her all-too familiar escort. At this point she was too tired to care who drove her home. Once again she climbed into Brady Olafsson's truck.

They rode in silence. It had been a long day. She enjoyed the delicious Italian dinner, but the slow, busy restaurant delayed their exit from the city. Although rush hour was over, they encountered an accident on the freeway, and traffic was held up for a while. She had fallen asleep in the back.

Brady remained cheerful through it all. After their curt discussion on the bus about their parents, they had changed the subject. He was friendly enough toward her, but seemed aloof as before, as if that chip had perched itself back up on his shoulder. She didn't exactly mind; she had enough problems to occupy her energies without delving into his.

It was odd that he pressed to take her home.

With a start she realized she really hadn't thanked him for the bus tour. On top of everything else, she seemed to be developing a knack for rudeness. She knew better. "Brady. Thank you for the bus tour."

"You're welcome."

"And for, um, well, coming to find me when you did." Her stomach ached again as she remembered reading about the elephant. How could life get so messy in just 28 short years?

"Guess it was God's timing." His voice was soft. "Couldn't have our guest crying all by herself in the middle of downtown Chicago."

"God's timing? I doubt He'd care about something like that. There are too many important things going on in the world."

"But this was important to you, and you're important to God. That's the whole point of Jesus walking on earth in the form of a man, to tell us that He does care about all the nitty-gritty details of life."

"Is that what you write about?"

"Yeah, I guess basically it is."

"From what I read on the book jacket, the characters are everyday people."

He pulled into Aunt Lottie's driveway. "You read the book jacket?"

"Actually I bought the whole book."

"Thank you." The porch light illumined his face. He was grinning like a little kid.

"You're welcome. You're the first nationally known author I've ever met. Thought it would be appropriate to get a copy. Well, thanks for the ride." She reached for the shopping bag between them on the bench seat.

Brady placed his hand over hers. "Do you mind sitting here for a minute? I need to say something."

"Um, okay." She felt it again. It was like in the department store. His hand on hers gave her an instant sense of well-being, as if some invisible protective covering gently enfolded her.

He removed his hand and cut the engine. "I was out of line on the bus." He stopped. As he turned toward her, the front porch light threw a shadow across his face.

She surmised that he referred to his snappish response to her not knowing about Rosie. "Well, I can't imagine what life is like in Valley Oaks. I can't understand what growing up here with this knowledge meant."

"Likewise, I just can't imagine you not knowing. I apologize. Look, I know this is uncomfortable, but can we talk through it so that we can stop trying to avoid it?"

"I take it this is what's been bugging you?"

"Mm-hmm."

"Brady, I don't know if I have it in me tonight. I am exhausted."

He looked toward the windshield and drummed his fingers on the dashboard a moment, then turned back. "To tell you the truth, I won't sleep tonight until I air this thing. Five minutes?"

She slid down until her head rested back against the seat. "I guess I've only been avoiding it since this morning. I imagine every time the Lindstrom-Philips family came to town, you've been avoiding it."

"I'm pretty much faced with it all the time, what with all your cousins around. And now my cousin is marrying a Lindstrom. Kind of impossible to avoid it."

"Why is it so difficult for you? Every family tree has a skeleton in its closet. It's not like you're responsible for putting it there. Not to mention it's almost ancient history."

He was silent.

"Can I just tell you what I know?" Gina didn't wait for a reply. "After the baby, after Rosie died, our parents felt they didn't need to stay married. Obviously they concluded they were too young, weren't ready."

"Your mother ran off with another guy."

"That's not true! Your dad went back to school and my mom went to a different one, determined to stay single. She eventually met my father, and they eventually married and moved from Chicago to California."

"My father never finished college, he was so hurt and humiliated."

"And my mother wasn't? What makes her responsible for his college decision?" Gina took a breath, willing herself to calm her voice. "How old are you anyway? 32, 33?"

"Almost 33."

"Well, I'm 28. My parents were married two years before I was born. That means they *met* after you were born. I'd say your dad wasn't all that hurt to get into another marriage so soon."

Only the sound of their breathing broke the silence. The windows were closed against the night chill.

"Whenever Dad and Mom argued," Brady's tone was flat, "or if he got mad about anything like low corn prices, I'd panic. I was convinced he would run off and find Maggie Lindstrom and leave us all behind."

"Why in the world would you think something like that?"

He ran his fingers through his hair. "I was taught from day one, by my Grandma Olafsson, to despise the entire Lindstrom clan because they bewitched my dad."

Gina was stunned.

"I spent a lot of time with Grandma when I was little. She and Grandpa lived with us when he became ill. She took care of us while Mom worked in the fields with Dad. She was proud. Back then the gossip was fresh enough to still hurt her. She told me all about it. Said the Lindstroms were to be despised, but we often went to Rosie's grave."

He exhaled loudly. "I imagine the whole thing diminished her in the town's eyes. Looking back, I can see that would have been tough on a woman like Grandma. But she was always kind and giving to us kids. I guess I never thought of questioning her word."

"Perhaps it would have been the same if I'd grown up around my grandmother. How did you and my cousin Vic and Aunt Lottie manage to be such good friends?"

"Well, technically they're only Lindstroms by marriage." She rolled her eyes.

"And Lottie had this way about her, one of the truest Christian ways I've ever seen. She didn't take sides in the issue. Grandma knew she still respected her and wasn't talking behind her back. So, the Samuelson branch was accepted."

Gina shook her head in disbelief. It was so archaic. She wondered, though, if there was any merit to Brady's childhood fear. "Is your parents' marriage all right?"

"Oh, yeah, it's solid, with just the usual ebb and flow. How about yours?"

She smiled. "It's fine."

"Gina."

"What?"

"I'm sorry."

"For what?"

"For holding this against you. Just because you're a Lindstrom, I treated you as being partly responsible for this black mark in my family history. And that sounds totally ridiculous."

"It's like some family feud that no one can remember the cause of."

"Yeah. Kind of scary how you trust adults and don't even question some of the stuff they tell you."

"What's scary is finding out at my age that my mother was married and had a baby who died. Makes me wonder if I've missed anything else."

"Do you know about Santa Claus?"

The giggle started somewhere deep inside of her, like a volcano rumbling. When her laughter erupted, Brady joined in, filling the truck cab with loud guffaws.

Gina's giggles slipped away into a yawn, and she reached for the shopping bag again. "Are we finished?"

"No." His laughter subsided, and he cleared his throat. "Do you forgive me?"

Unbelievable! "I don't even know you, Brady Olafsson, and you want my forgiveness for that chip on your shoulder?"

"Ouch. Maybe I don't want to get acquainted with you."

"Suit yourself." She yawned again. "I'm going to bed." With that she shoved open her door. It scrunched against the neighbor's hedge. "I can't get out."

"Here, come this way." Brady took the bag from her and got out, then moved aside as she slid out. They walked toward the front porch. "This feels familiar here, walking in the dark across Lottie's yard. With a girl. Oh, I remember. I dated Sherri once."

"Vic and Alec's sister?"

"Mm-hmm. For some reason she was spending the night at her grandparents. Gina, that's what Valley Oaks is like. Pockets of memories everywhere. Literally everywhere because it's such a small place."

"Hmm. I'd probably have to drive at least 20 minutes between my Orange County pockets of memories."

He stopped at the bottom porch step and handed her the shopping bag. "Such different backgrounds. Well, good night."

"Good night." She climbed the three steps and crossed the porch. All in all it had been a good day. In spite of the tragic news, she felt comforted, as if she'd been carried through the worst part, and she had even laughed. All because of this guy. Hand on the screen door, she turned.

He still stood on the sidewalk.

"Brady. I can't see the chip anymore."

"Really?"

"Really. I forgive you."

He smiled. "Sleep tight, Angelina."

She went inside and shut the door. Angelina? Now how did he know her real name?

Her mother's words replayed, *Everybody knows everything in Valley Oaks.*

Gina groaned. Who would ever choose to live in a place like her mother's hometown?

Brady pulled on a sweatshirt, then carried ham sandwiches and a glass of milk to the screened-in porch located off of the kitchen. Homer, his golden retriever, padded at his heels.

The night was cool and clear, perfect for sitting out on the porch. It was a square room, decorated with a mishmash of hand-me-down patio furniture: couch, armchairs, and chaise lounge all made of wood and covered with nondescript cushions. Small end tables held reading lamps, one of which he had already turned on.

Another door led outside to a deck that surrounded three-fourths of the log cabin-style house. Just beyond the deck was a pond. Stars twinkled in the still water. Now and then a few tree frogs hummed. The bullfrogs' song was absent tonight. Too cold for them.

"Here you go, Home." Brady settled into a chair, then handed his dog a sandwich.

His mind was full of Gina Philips. While munching his snack, he pushed aside her smile, which had a tendency to scramble his thought processes, as did her tears. If he hadn't glimpsed both, though, he never would have been motivated to admit what he had just admitted to her tonight in the truck.

He was glad now that he had broached the subject of their shared heritage, glad that she had spoken boldly without mincing words. Her perspective shook him up. It was idiotic of him to hold against her something that hurt his grandmother's pride so many years ago. How had he not realized that before? Were the words and fears of his childhood that insidious?

Did he harbor other prejudices that were holdovers of older generations?

Dear God, help me to see myself clearly and change what doesn't honor You. Thank You for using Gina to open my eyes. Let me see her now. She seems fearful, distrustful.

He opened up the *Chicago Tribune* and quickly scanned the articles until he found a zoo-related headline, most likely the one she had been reading on the top floor of Marshall Field's.

It was a short piece. An elephant had died at a California wildlife preserve. This Delilah had made news eight months ago when she attacked a Park employee. There had been rumors of abuse at that time. Officials stated the incidents were unrelated. The employee could not be reached for comment.

What did this have to do with Gina? The woman was obviously hurting. It was written on her face, in her cross response to old Hattie at the library, even in her shortness with him whenever they met.

Brady turned off the reading lamp and stared out at the pond and dark outlines of oak trees. It came to him then...the touch of her hand beneath his. On the heels of that impression came a distinct, irresistible urge to hold it. His emotions flew through the dark, catapulted over the tree-tops, bounced against the stars, then tumbled back to race around the pond.

What was this?

He only knew that the woman intrigued him. And that he hadn't been intrigued in a very, very long time.

He wondered if it was too late to call her and invite her to see the oak trees.

Maybe tomorrow.

Twelve

When Gina and Lauren left for Chicago, their mothers headed out on their own shopping trip. Alone now in the car with Marsha, Maggie wondered how best to broach the subject of John. She had put her sister off long enough.

"Well," Marsha interrupted her thoughts, "I'm not sure we'll be able to find you a wild purple dress with red flowers at the mall. Do you want to head up the interstate? The boutique shops in Thompkins should have more to offer. And then there's the new outlet mall about 20 miles beyond that."

"I've got the whole day if you do."

"Let's do it then." She turned her attention from the highway long enough to throw her a smile. "I know the girls won't be back until late."

"I agree." Maggie chuckled. "They said Brady wanted to leave before three o'clock and miss rush hour. The guy has obviously never taken a group of females shopping in downtown Chicago. Tell me, what's he like?"

"As Lauren says, he is the gen-u-ine article. He truly is a nice guy. They're in good hands. He won't leave them stranded when they don't show up on time."

"It is rather odd that my daughter and Neil's son would end up spending time together."

"Only in Valley Oaks, huh?"

"Right." She took a deep breath. "Thank you for being patient. Do you want to hear it now?"

Her sister glanced at her. "Only if you want to tell me, hon."

"I need a friend, sis. Promise you'll still love me, no matter what?"

"Of course."

"Think about it. I'm going to tell you something that you will disapprove of."

Marsha was silent for a moment. "Magpie, Jesus disapproves of a lot of things I do and say and think. But He is compassionate and still loves me anyway. When I know He disapproves, I ask His forgiveness and I know He gives it."

"Well, I ask your forgiveness."

"You don't need mine. You need His. I know you've told Him you believe He is God's Son and that He died for you. You asked Him to forgive all your past sin. But do you spend much time getting to know Him?"

A couple of years ago her sister had explained this plan of God's. Maggie understood it was the way to get in a right relationship with Him and had accepted that fact, but beyond that, Jesus didn't affect her day-to-day living. "I usually go to church on Sunday."

"It takes time." Marsha smiled at her. "A little bit every day. Tell me why you think you need forgiveness."

"I haven't committed any major wrong, but I feel guilty."

"What's up?"

"You asked who John is. He's just a friend." She gazed out the side window at the passing cornfields. "I better start at the beginning. Reece has been traveling more and more. You know, I used to think that when Gina was out of the house, he and I would have more time together. I've seen less of him in the past two years than ever." She took a shaky breath. "It's wearing me down."

"That's understandable."

"It is?"

"Of course. You're being neglected."

"But he's always been such a good provider. I shouldn't feel neglected just because he's doing his job."

"Maggie, I'm not judging or condemning Reece, but he isn't providing something you need on a deeper level. Have you talked to him about this?"

"I've tried. He loves what he does and, you know, he's so good at it. He says he loves me and our marriage and the way things are, that we'll have plenty of time together when he retires, which could happen within five years. Though I doubt he'll ever completely retire." She sighed. "Whenever we discuss this, he'll make sure we go out for dinner, always with friends."

"You've always trusted him, haven't you?"

"He's never given me a reason not to, although lately I've wondered. Why does he choose travel over me?"

They rode in silence for a few moments.

Maggie hesitated continuing the discussion that would lead to territory that for them personally was uncharted. Once she spoke aloud words to describe a close relationship with a dear man who was not her husband, other words would follow. Ultimately, words like adultery and divorce would become a part of their vocabulary, making that territory no longer uncharted and therefore making it...familiar. Comfortable. Acceptable.

She wasn't sure she wanted that. "Have you ever felt neglected?"

Marsha nodded. "Sure. You know what farming is like, especially during planting and harvest seasons. I could gain 50 pounds and shave my head and Dan would never notice. Add three children and the fact that my in-laws live a stone's throw away. Stir in years of unpredictable weather wreaking havoc on crops and emotional stability. Voilà." She threw her a sad smile. "You've got the makings for wishing my best friend's mailman husband was available."

"But you said you're so happy you could pop!"

"Deep down I am. But there have been moments, some that lasted for months at a time. Dan and I both recognized that we weren't on the top of each other's priority list. We had to make conscious efforts to work on our marriage."

"Unlike Reece."

Her sister shrugged. "He takes you to dinner."

"Mm-hmm." Maggie stared ahead at the long, flat stretch of interstate. "I'm not having an affair. At least not in the physical sense. I am just so lonely, Marsh."

"Maybe angry, too?"

"No," she replied quickly. Not angry. Lonely made sense. Angry was too...out of control. She leaned forward, flipped the fan to high, the temperature to cold, and turned her face toward the vent's blast of freezing air. She heard her sister's stifled sigh. "I am not angry."

"Where did you meet him?"

"At a party, last September. One of those work-related events I was compelled to attend. He was the friend of a friend of a friend. We just sort of enjoyed talking. He's an English professor at Long Beach." She turned the fan back down and straightened. "A month later we ran into each other in the cafeteria of the hospital where Gina was. Reece was out of town. Again. My child was suffering. I was distraught."

She drummed her fingers on the door's armrest. She'd skip what he looked like in his tweeds...disheveled wavy hair, black sprinkled with silver...brown-black eyes...calm voice...gentle mannerisms. The fact that he was a widower with no children. The way he simply listened!

"How old is he?" Marsha interrupted her reverie.

"Reece's age. Fifty-six. The third time we bumped into each other was at a local family-type restaurant. I eat there often because lone diners don't stick out like a sore thumb, and everyone is friendly." She blew out a noisy breath. "I guess the third time was the proverbial charm. We met there again, sort of by accident, and then we planned on it once a week or so. We've browsed through bookstores and art galleries and that's all. Neither of us wants more."

"Yet. There's a yet in your tone."

"Yet," she conceded, then laughed disparagingly. "I'm supposed to use this time back here to figure out who I am. I don't even know if I'm Maggie or Margaret. I need to be quiet for a while, come to grips with some old ghosts. Then maybe I can get a handle on what comes next."

"What do you want to come next?"

"I don't really know." She saw pain etched in her sister's profile. "There's absolutely no physical contact."

"But your hearts have connected." A tear trickled from the corner of Marsha's eye.

"Our hearts have connected," Maggie whispered. "He is my best friend."

Marsha wiped at her eyes, blinking to keep them focused on the highway before her. "This is dangerous territory, hon."

She nodded. "And I am petrified."

The next morning Maggie tapped softly on Gina's door, then peeked inside.

"I'm awake," Gina mumbled from under the covers. "Mmm, do I smell coffee?" She yawned and stretched.

"You do." Maggie slipped open the shades while Gina plumped pillows and sat up. Morning sunlight streamed through the two open windows. Warm air chased away last night's coolness, promising rising temperatures today. She handed her daughter a mug of coffee, kissed her forehead, then sat beside her on the bed. "You must have had a late night."

"Thanks. No, just a long day. A really long day. What is this?" She inhaled the steaming liquid and took a sip. Her eyes widened. "Mom! This is real coffee!"

Maggie smiled. She still loved surprising her daughter, still loved watching her wake up in the morning on rare occasions such as this. Her tousled hair framed her face, a lovely feminine version of her father's with strong chin, olive skin, and striking dark brows that accented her green eyes. "Aunt Marsha and I went up the interstate to shop at some boutique-type places. Lo and behold, I found a Starbucks."

"Mmm. It's great. Did you find a purple dress with red flowers?"

"I did. It's absolutely wild. My sister may disown me if I wear it to the wedding, but it's perfect for the reunion. What did you think of Chicago?"

"I loved Chicago! So exciting. It was the perfect antidote to Podu—excuse me. Valley Oaks. Look in that shopping bag. I bought Lauren some towels she liked. We didn't have a shower gift, did we?"

"Good idea." She admired the towel set, then pulled out a book. "What? Oh my goodness. Brady Olafsson?" She turned it over and gasped at the resemblance to his father, Neil.

"Do you believe it? Do you believe we didn't even know?"

"Marsha never mentioned that he's an author. This looks like a major publication."

"It is."

"Interesting. How did you get along with him?"

"Well." Gina looked out the window.

Maggie sat back down. "What's wrong, sweetie? Is the chip still there on his shoulder?"

"Delilah died." She quickly brushed tears from her eyes.

"Oh, no." They looked at each other for a speechless moment. Maggie knew it wasn't a total shock to her daughter, but the circumstances coupled with Gina's tendency to grieve over the death of any animal meant this hurt deeply. "I'm so sorry, hon. How did you find out?"

Gina sipped her coffee. "Well, I bought a newspaper. Then we walked for miles and my leg—don't say anything."

Maggie pressed her lips together and made an imaginary zipping motion.

"I should have worn my brace."

"Can we look at it?" When Gina hesitated, Maggie knew it must ache. "If your knee's swollen, I'll get you some ibuprofen."

She pulled aside the sheet.

Maggie fought the onslaught of queasiness that still came whenever she looked at her daughter's scars. Angry fuchsia colored ridges crisscrossed her knee, one rope-like vine continuing along the thigh, marring the youthful skin. Evidence remained of holes where the pin had been inserted. *It could have been worse. It could have been worse.* She swallowed. "Doesn't look too bad. Does your hip hurt?"

"Not much. Anyway, we stopped for ice cream on the top floor of this wonderful, huge, old, old store—"

"Marshall Field's on State Street." She pulled the sheet back across Gina's leg in spite of the heat wafting through the window. "Grandma Philips took you there once when you were very young."

"Really? Lauren said Aunt Lottie took them a few times through the years. Anyway, I stayed put while the rest of them kept shopping. I read about Delilah in the paper. Then Brady came to pick me up. By then it was too late to avoid rush hour traffic, so the others had decided to meet us later." Her eyes widened. "There I was, stuck with Mr. Homespun for two solid hours."

Maggie giggled.

"It wasn't funny!"

"The look on your face is. Whatever did you do?"

"Told him to leave, but he invited me to go sightseeing on a tour bus. Mother, he really was a perfect gentleman, and I had a good time. He did get obnoxious, though, when we talked about your divorce."

"How's that?"

"This is unbelievable. He blamed you for ruining his dad's college career by running off with another man."

"Oh?"

"All you have to say is 'oh'?"

Maggie shrugged. "It's Valley Oaks, Gina. There's so much talk about everything, some of it's bound to get twisted. You just can't take it all to heart."

"Well, when he brought me home, he apologized for his attitude. He explained how it was ingrained in him by his grandmother."

"Just as I thought."

"Right. And, get this, he asked me to forgive him for the chip on his shoulder."

"He sounds rather…authentic."

"Yeah, I have to admit, he's beginning to seem that way. Mom?"

Maggie smiled to herself. "Mom" in that tone meant Gina was going to say something heartfelt. "What?"

"How's your and Dad's marriage?"

She blinked, waited for her heart to beat again, waited for the sensation of her body melting into liquid to pass.

"I mean," Gina turned for a moment to set her empty mug on the nightstand, "it seems fine. Brady said his great childhood fear was that his dad would split. I realized I never had that fear. Thank you for that, by the way."

She reached out and patted her daughter's hand.

"Now he knows his parents' marriage is solid. But it prompted the thought..." She paused, then finally locked eyes with Maggie. "Dad's not around much, is he?"

"That doesn't mean he doesn't love me. That we don't love each other."

"I know."

She took a deep breath. Gina was no longer a child. She was in fact her equal, as any friend. But was it right to burden her, inflict doubts that might be groundless? No...but she had to be honest. "Of course it's difficult, all his traveling. I hate it, actually. I miss him, but it won't be this way forever. He can retire soon, you know."

"Is he coming for your reunion?"

Maggie thought how he had made it only once out of the three times she had attended. Why would he come for this one? "We should hear from him today. It depends on some meeting schedule. Now I'm changing the subject. Aunt Marsha thinks that Lauren doesn't know you've lost your job. Haven't you told her?"

Gina frowned. "Not exactly."

"Why not?"

"I just don't want to talk about it with anyone yet! I'd only cry."

"Honey, maybe it's time you do cry over it."

Gina looked out the window.

Maggie pressed her lips together to stop exasperation from coating her next words. "Even when you were a little girl, you always bottled things inside until eventually you'd just burst over some insignificant frustration. Wouldn't you rather burst with your cousin than with," she waved her arm, "oh, I don't know. Rather than with the librarian when you're upset about not being able to get online?"

Gina raised an eyebrow. "Don't worry about it, Mother."

"Well, I will." *Just leave it alone.* They'd had similar conversations. She took a breath. "You could save it until you're my age. Then you can just burst all over the place. Laugh and cry and buy wild purple dresses with great splashes of red flowers and not give a hoot about what anyone else thinks. Want to see it?"

Her daughter smiled. "See what? You burst all over the place?"

"You've seen that. No, I mean my dress."

"I'd love to see your dress."

Thirteen

Gina stood in Aunt Lottie's kitchen, coiled phone cord stretched across it to reach the sink where she stared unseeing out the window. She listened patiently to her father's voice on the other end of the line. He spoke in his curt business tone, which comforted her because she knew it meant her problems were on his agenda. He would take care of things.

"If word hadn't leaked that Delilah was dead, we may not have known in time. But Ben was ready for a confrontation." Ben was her attorney. "He showed up on their doorstep with the vet and a court order. There was obvious evidence of neglect, perhaps of abuse."

"One and the same," she muttered.

"At any rate, based on that combined with your testimony, Ben thinks you have a case now. He can prove the Park's negligence was a direct cause of your injury. He's filed already. You're suing for 25 million."

"Twenty-five million?!" she exclaimed.

"We know you're not interested in the money, but it'll get their attention, encourage them to move on it. He needs to schedule your deposition. Once your story's recorded, they'll want to settle out of court as quickly as possible. When can you come?"

"Dad, can't it wait until after the wedding?"

"It's best to move on it. They won't want any more bad publicity than they're getting now. We need to seize this opportunity."

She closed her eyes. "Tonight's the shower. Tomorrow—"

"Gina, don't give me your schedule. How about a week from next Monday or Tuesday?"

She squeezed the phone between her chin and shoulder, then crossed her arms tightly over her midsection. Lunch rumbled in her stomach. "For how long?"

"Just a few days." His voice softened. "We won't let you miss the wedding, honey."

"Okay."

"Okay. Let me talk to your mother."

"Hey, are you coming for the reunion tomorrow? Mother's got this wild purple dress. It's got a high neck, but the back—well, let's just say, there isn't much of one! I don't think she should go alone, Dad."

"I'm not worried about a bunch of fat old farmers."

Gina winced at her dad's harsh tone. He never could mix lighthearted topics into his business mode. "I'll get Mother. Bye."

"Gina," he added.

"What?"

"Put this out of your mind. Go do something fun, like watch the corn grow."

"Right. Goodbye." She rolled her eyes and called her mother to the phone.

Maggie entered from the dining room and raised her brows at Gina. It was a look that indicated her side of the conversation had been easily overheard by Aunt Lottie, Aunt Marsha, and Lauren, who all sat in the adjacent room.

Gina thought as much. Aunt Lottie didn't believe in cordless phones, which meant that when the kitchen phone rang while she was standing next to it, Gina could either answer it or rush through the house, up the stairs, and down the hall to the bedroom phone.

She sighed. While talking to her father, she had been aware of her mother's voice trying to keep a conversation going around the oddly quiet lunch table. Oh, well. She needed to tell them sometime. Might as well be now. Evidently Aunt Marsha already knew she didn't have a job. She'd just give them the straight facts, leave no space for emotional interpretations.

As she entered the dining room, Aunt Lottie asked sweetly, "Troubles, dear?"

She nodded and slid into her chair. "One of my favorite elephants died at the Park. Her name was Delilah."

"Delilah?" Aunt Lottie laughed. "Oh, my!"

"She was such a flirt. I swear, she'd wink and," Gina stood and swayed her hips, "sashay around like this whenever she saw a bull."

They laughed. Lauren asked if she died of old age.

Gina shook her head. "She was only 25. Sixty-five would have been an old age. Actually there have been some problems at the Park. I'm not supposed to talk about it yet because of the lawsuit. That's what Dad called about."

"Lawsuit?" Aunt Marsha exclaimed.

"Um." She studied her fingers splayed on the white linen tablecloth, willing herself not to cry.

"Gina," Lauren urged, "we're thousands of miles away. Who are we going to tell?"

"I know there's no one here who would care. Well, my accident was in part due to the administrator's negligence. And, um, because of those extenuating circumstances, they let me go."

"They fired you?" The hurt in her ginger eyes softened the bluntness of her words.

"Yes. So Dad got a lawyer for me. They seem to think I have a case."

"Oh, Gina!" Lauren jumped up and hurried around the table to hug her. "I'm so sorry. Why didn't you tell me?"

She returned her hug. "Like I said. It's complicated. And I didn't want to think about it while I was here. This is a month devoted to you and your wedding, not to worrying about my problems."

Aunt Marsha murmured her concern, and Aunt Lottie announced, "You can trust that when God closes a door, He'll open a window. There'll be another place for you."

Gina smiled. "I hope so."

"That was like your dream job," Lauren remarked. "What do you want to do now?"

"I'm looking for a similar vet position."

Just as her mother hung up the phone, it rang again. She called Gina to the kitchen, then handed the phone to her with a shrug.

"Hello?"

"Hi, Gina."

"Brady. Hi."

"Ah, you recognized my voice."

"I should hope so. I listened to it for hours on end yesterday." His soft voice, with that whispery hint to it, was pleasant over the telephone. With a start she realized its effect was one of immediate comfort. Like yesterday.

"Uh-oh. Sounds like maybe you won't be interested in my invitation." He paused.

"Well," she teased, "are you going to run it by me or not?"

"Promise not to bite my head off?"

"What makes you think I'd do a thing like that?"

"Experience." He chuckled.

"Ha, ha."

"Okay, here goes. I thought you might need a lift to the couples' shower tonight. I'd be glad to swing by and get you. It's outside of town; could be difficult for you to find."

Gina listened to the quiet emanating from the dining room.

"And there's something I'd like to show you, if you could be ready early, say about 4:00?"

She weighed the thought of the planned shopping expedition with high-strung women against this voice that was having a decidedly calming effect on her. She thought of her father's advice to have fun—

"But if you have other—"

"Well," she interrupted, "can we watch the corn grow?"

"Sure." The grin in his voice was obvious.

"I'd love to. Four o'clock or 3:30 would be fine." No way the women would be back by 3:30. It gave her an easy out.

"Three—? Sure. See you then. Bye."

Gina met the four expectant faces with a shrug. "Brady," she stated, knowing the name would explain everything to them. "You don't mind if I skip the outing this afternoon, do you?"

Lauren laughed and clapped her hands. "Not in the least."

She pointed a finger at her cousin. "Keep that up and I'll change my mind."

Fourteen

"Unfortunately, I've had a change of plans." Brady glanced at her, then focused again on his driving. They sped in his truck along a two-lane highway north of town, a new route for Gina. "I hope you don't mind."

"Since I didn't know what the original plans were, I guess I don't mind." She watched him drive, his right wrist slung over the steering wheel, his left elbow propped on the open window. He wore a yellow cap today, with some other sort of "Seed" proclaimed on it. White T-shirt, blue jeans, and work boots completed the ensemble.

"We might get to the original plans yet today. My brother just called on the cell phone while I was driving over. He needs some help. It shouldn't take long. Maybe you'd like to see the family farm? You did ask if we could watch the corn grow."

"My dad's idea of a joke. Sure. Whatever it takes to keep me out of the mall."

"More shopping?" His tone was incredulous.

"It's what you do three weeks before a wedding. Today is Aunt Marsha's turn. She had bought a blue dress, but my mother said that just won't work. Rule number one for the mother-in-law is to wear neutral tones and keep her mouth shut."

He laughed. "Good advice for a lot of people."

"You know, you wouldn't last three minutes on a Los Angeles freeway driving like that."

"Like what?"

Gina scrunched down in the seat and mimicked the positioning of his arms.

He winked. "Wouldn't catch me driving on a Los Angeles freeway in a million years."

"You sound rather closed-minded on that subject."

"Just not interested in the place."

"Have you ever been to California?"

"I was in Los Angeles once."

"Once isn't even a blip on the screen. L.A. alone is so multifaceted, you couldn't begin to form an intelligent opinion based on one visit."

"Would you want to live in Valley Oaks?"

"Not in a mil—" She stopped. "It's just not my kind of place."

"Hmm. And how often have you visited?"

"I don't know. When I was growing up, every other year or so."

"For three days at a time."

"Well…"

"Hardly counts. Guess we're evenly closed-minded." He lifted his forefinger off of the steering wheel as a car sped by in the opposite direction.

"Guess so. What did you just do with your finger? Looks like some sort of secret code."

He grinned and turned onto a blacktop drive. "Just a wave."

"A wave." Gina eyed the long drive bordered on the left by a cornfield. To the right was a big field of thick green grass enclosed on four sides by a white split-rail fence. In the distance stood a large, white house. The whole scene belonged on a postcard. "This is beautiful. Did you grow up here?"

"Yes. My great-grandparents built the original house around 1910. Rooms have been added through the years."

The two-story white house with black shutters resembled a square colonial. Attached to both sides of the square were wings, one of which appeared to be a screened porch. Evergreens, smaller trees, and bushes dotted the long front yard. White barns and other smaller buildings to the right of it were separated by a large blacktop area. It was nothing like the few farmhouses she knew. It was almost elegant. Maybe all that talk of the Olafssons being wealthy hadn't been an exaggeration. Recalling the humble home her mother grew up in with four siblings, she thought it no wonder the family looked down their noses at the Lindstroms.

"Do you have neighbors?"

"Sure. Down the road a piece." He glanced at her out of the corner of his eye. "In the next area code."

She narrowed her eyes at him. No neighboring homes were in sight, but she had heard this one. It was a Brady joke. "I don't believe it."

"Suit yourself." Just beyond the house he parked outside a barn. "I can show you the house later, if you'd like." They climbed out of the truck. "Do you mind helping if we need it? Ryan is the only one around at the moment, and he gets pretty queasy with this sort of thing."

"What sort of thing?"

The sharp neighs of a horse drowned his answer. She followed him into the barn and immediately saw what sort of thing this was. A wild-eyed chestnut reared in its stall. A chain was draped over her nose, cutting into the skin.

"Ryan! Let up!" Brady shouted above the animal's cries as he went toward her, pulling on gloves. "You're making it worse."

Gina barely took note of the smaller version of Brady standing nearby, lead rope in hand. While the brothers argued, she stared at the horse, fighting down the nausea that quickly spread from the pit of her stomach. What ripped through her was the unbearable pain and terror so evident in the animal's eyes and unnaturally pitched cries. Like a blow to the head, they wrenched aside all sense of equilibrium.

It was Delilah all over again.

"Gina!" Brady yelled. "Grab a coat from the hook over there and cover up your clothes. The Banamine's up in that cupboard. I'll hold her steady while you—"

She ran blindly out of the barn, away from the pain and terror.

It was Delilah all over again.

A corner of her mind knew she was hysterical, knew she raced without direction, but that corner was a powerless observer. Sobbing, she stumbled past buildings and fences, across blacktop, gravel, dirt, then onto grassy, uneven ground.

Her throat ached and her lungs burned. She sank onto long, soft grass, her chest heaving as she gulped for each breath.

She had no sense of time, but only of a consuming grief. She crossed her arms over her head and buried her face against her bent knees.

The crying wouldn't stop. The grief intensified.

"Oh, God! I can't bear this."

She hadn't cried like this...ever. Not when her pets died. Not when her best friend moved. Not when Steve told her he couldn't respect, let alone love, a nonteam player. Not when Steve publicly questioned her veterinary expertise. Not when the body cast sapped her strength like a desert noonday sun. Not when she lost her job. Not when friends stopped returning her calls. Not yesterday when she learned Delilah had died.

Was she making up for all those times? Why now? Why here with a bunch of strangers?

The answer came. It was because a horse begged for help, and in that instant she knew she'd never again help another animal.

"Oh, dear God, help me!"

"Gina." Brady's voice seemed to come from a great distance.

A moment later his strong arms enveloped her.

She jerked away, elbowing him in the ribs. "I'm fine." Her tears had slowed, but she still sat in the grass, knees curled up, head buried in arms, lost in anguished thoughts.

"I beg to disagree, Dr. Philips."

"I am fine." She enunciated each word, her voice low, and peered up at him through swollen eyes. He was sitting beside her. "I will be fine."

He pulled a handkerchief from his back pocket and dabbed at her cheek. "Gina," he whispered, "just let it go."

The will to not let it go was gone. She began to cry softly. This time when his arms came around her, she didn't struggle.

He stroked her hair, nudging her to lean against his chest.

In the stillness she became aware of his heart's rhythmic beating against her ear. Its measured cadence seeped a calm into her chaotic mind. There was the clean scent of laundry detergent on his T-shirt soft beneath her cheek. The hand near her face that smoothed her hair smelled of just-scrubbed, soapy freshness. Nestled in his arms, she relaxed against him and wiped tears from her face. He handed her the hankie.

Her shaky breaths subsided. She felt like a silly child—

"Gina?"

No, not a child. She felt like a grown woman being comforted by a very physical male with a gentle, whispery voice that sent a tickle along her spine whenever she heard it. He was a mere stranger whose heart had the audacity to care that she was hurting.

"Know how you can tell if you're in the Midwest?"

A Brady joke. She shook her head.

"When you find a weeping woman in a waterway."

She smiled. "Nice alliteration." Her voice was thick and scratchy from crying. "What's a waterway?"

"What we're sitting in. It's a path through the cornfield, a channel for water to flow into. The seat of your khakis are probably grass stained. Though I imagine that's the least of your worries at the moment. You know, it might help to talk."

There was an almost imperceptible tightening of his arms, just enough to crack open the door to her reluctance to talk about it. "How's your horse? Is it colic?"

"Good diagnosis, Doctor. Ruby will be fine." He chuckled. "And so will Ryan. I made him plunge the Banamine down her throat. It was good practice for him. He always avoids these situations."

"I'm so sorry." She sniffled.

"It's okay." He rested his chin on her head. "Tell me what happened."

Glad that she couldn't see his face, Gina began. "She terrified me. Some vet, huh? I'll never ever be able to—" She choked.

"Shh. Never ever say 'never ever.' Nothing is a forever 'never' in this life. Why don't you start at the beginning? You are a vet, right?"

"Was."

"Hey, you don't stop being one because something scared you. Was it Delilah?"

"Mm-hmm." She listened to his heartbeat for a few moments, letting it flow through her like a healing balm on bruised emotions, sensing that it would somehow give her the ability to tell the story without falling apart again.

She took a deep breath. "She was one of the animals I cared for. I was an assistant and helped with the elephants and some of the other large animals. Rhinos and giraffes. Anyway," she swallowed, "Delilah was being abused. In my opinion anyway. Her keeper was young and inexperienced. He used the ankus all the time."

"What's that?"

"A long stick with a hook on the end. And he chained her. I treated her for the wounds he inflicted on her, and they said it was just a necessary part of the training! Like I didn't know the difference!"

"I take it you reported it?"

"Yes. To my boss. When that went nowhere, I talked to administrators and board members."

"What was their response?"

"Two asked me to keep them informed. One day an animal rights group picketed outside the Park. I was blamed, but I hadn't told anyone on the outside. I didn't want bad publicity. Other employees began avoiding me like the plague. Steve, my...uh, boss, said I wasn't acting like a team player and I'd better get my act together.

"Oh, Brady, I couldn't stand by and not say anything! Delilah got worse. She was so sad. Her keeper didn't even take care of her feet properly. Do you know about elephants' feet?"

A chuckle rumbled through his chest against her ear. "No."

"Well, they need regular pedicures because they're confined in a zoo setting. Out in the wild they walk miles every day. Their pads and toenails just naturally wear away. Without that or the pedicures, they get infections. Life-threatening infections. And this idiot, Jared—" She took a breath. "At least he was alert enough to suspect she had one. I went in to take care of her..." Gina's mind went blank.

"And?" he prompted softly.

The nightmare rushed back. The two-and-a-half-ton elephant swayed...not in her usual manner...it was a nervous movement. She seemed to avoid eye contact with her, tilted her head oddly. Of course the infection would bother her.

Gina patted her thick hide, talked to her. Jared slipped through the tall, open doors. "Hey!" she had called. He was supposed to stay. He was the animal's handler, the one who trained her how to lift her foot so they could inspect it.

The tall doors mechanically swished shut.

Delilah bowed her head and Gina knew...not soon enough to move. "She attacked me."

Brady tightened his hold. "Dear God!" he whispered.

"Full body slam against a concrete wall." Gina's tone was flat. "She had been secured and couldn't reach me, but I could hear her. I'd swear she was crying."

"Where was the keeper?"

"Gone. It was almost as if..." She bit her lip. "As if it were planned."

He caught his breath.

"Brady, I've never said that out loud. It was just a split-second feeling."

"How long before someone found you?"

She lifted a shoulder. "I passed out."

"How badly were you hurt?"

"Um, three months in a body cast. Most of the damage was to my hip and knee. That's why I walk funny." She felt wrapped in a cocoon, a small world where she could speak freely and feel safe. She closed her eyes. "The press got wind of it, and I talked. I knew it would cost me my job, but that seemed beside the point compared to lying around in a piece of itchy plaster not knowing if I'd ever walk again." She sighed. "And wondering if Delilah was suffering."

"Do you have a job?"

"No. I went back and lasted a week. They gave me assignments I couldn't possibly keep up with even in good health. It was their way of creating a reason to fire me. My father hired an attorney. They want to file a lawsuit because it would help the animals get the attention they need, but then again it'd probably jeopardize my potential future with any zoo. Was this more than you asked for?"

He leaned back then so he could look her in the face. "Maybe a little." He smiled. "But at least now I know why you didn't want to help with my horse."

She returned his smile. Her eyes felt almost swollen shut. Her throat ached from her earlier sobbing.

"Thank you for telling me." He brushed a finger gently across her cheek. "Tear tracks. When did it happen?"

"About eight months ago. It has been the worst eight months of my life. I'm even living back home with my parents. I feel like such a loser."

"Of course you do." He grinned. "It'll get better. Now for the important question. What do you want to do with the rest of your life's journey?"

Fresh tears sprang to her eyes. "I thought I wanted to be a vet...until I saw your horse."

His laughter sang out over the cornfields.

Gina didn't mind because while he laughed, he drew her back into the circle of his arms.

Fifteen

Maggie squirted a dab of cream into her palm, then worked it into her hands as she climbed onto the bed, all the while smiling to herself.

She couldn't remember the last time she'd had as much fun as this evening. Goodness, it was after 1:00 A.M. and she was still wide awake. Of course the pot of coffee she drank at the restaurant might have something to do with that.

But no, this was more than caffeine. She felt energized, as if an old pilot light was relit somewhere deep in her being, igniting youthful emotions. Not only emotions, but whole thought processes as well. If the room were larger, she would attempt a back flip.

Well, a cartwheel anyway. She giggled, envisioning how less than an hour ago she and her friends had performed a cheer in the restaurant parking lot.

She turned off the lamp now and slid to the foot of the old twin bed so she could look out the window. Stars flickered through the tree tops. A gentle breeze out of the west promised relief from the heat sometime before dawn.

They had all been there tonight—Susie, Jane, Rita, Judy, Lynn, and Donna. Her closest and dearest friends through school, all members of the cheerleading squad that graduated 35 years ago, gathered together the night before the official class reunion.

They had met for dinner at a landmark restaurant in the city. "City" was a bit of a euphemism for Rockville, the large town 20 miles down the highway situated along the river

112

bank. It boasted factories, an airport, movie theaters, restaurants, a junior college, and a shopping mall. Compared to Valley Oaks it was a city. Compared to Los Angeles it was simply a midsize town and Valley Oaks was a village. At any rate, it had been and still was the "happening" place.

The old friends' rapport was instant, sweeping away the years in the time it took to exchange hugs. Laughter erupted and didn't subside until someone noticed dimming lights and the waitress's yawns.

It was their common background. A startling realization occurred to her now. She had more in common with them than with anyone she knew in California. Granted, any group of women her age would find the same similarities these friends had found: at least half would be divorced, some remarried, some would be grandmothers, most would have in-depth knowledge of various weight-reducing diets, most would have colored the gray, and 99 percent would know that adolescent unsettledness didn't hold a candle to this stage of life.

Beyond that, though, only these friends knew as she did what it meant to grow up in Valley Oaks. Each other's mothers had a hand in molding them. They shared the same influential characters, from school staff to family doctor to pharmacist to librarian to pastor to county sheriff. Between them they had cried a river of tears and filled every nook and cranny of Valley Oaks with their giggles.

Soaking up the past nourished her. She felt a twinge of the overall contentment and joy that had accompanied her through childhood. Had she known them since? The contempt of Neil's mother had whittled away at them. When Rosie died, they fled completely.

Then she met Reece, and he had helped her pick up the pieces. Although they were happy together, it was never quite the same. There was always guilt and fear hanging about the fringes. She assumed it was part of growing up. Baggage.

Come to me as a little child.

What were those words? They sounded like something from...church. Did Jesus say them? Children didn't have baggage. Is that what He meant? To be like that with Him?

But what do I do with all this grown-up stuff? I can rationalize all I want, but I should feel guilty according to God's law. I conceived a child out of wedlock. I'm thinking of leaving my husband. My second husband. I'm afraid of making a mistake. I'm afraid of death.

Maggie inhaled deeply. She had never admitted so much to herself in one sitting. What was it her sister kept telling her about guilt and fear? If we tell Jesus about what we do wrong, He forgives us, which means we don't have to feel guilty. The future is in His hands, so we don't have to fear it.

The stars blurred. *Dear God, I'm sorry for the wrong things I've done. I'm sorry for Rosie. I'm sorry for considering divorce. But you know how lonely I am! Help me to figure out my future. Take away my fears.* She paused. *Help me to figure out my past and be like a little child again.*

Odd. Reece wasn't part of her childhood. He didn't fit in here. If she became Maggie again, albeit a responsible version, would he like her?

Sixteen

"Oh," Gina groaned and leaned closer toward the mirror. "You look great this morning." Yesterday's crying jag in the cornfield plus a late-night reading session were well documented in her puffy eyelids. Who would have thought the bursting point her mother warned her about would come in the presence of Brady Olafsson?

She sat down at the old dark wood vanity table in what used to be the bedroom of Aunt Lottie's daughter and brushed her hair. Although she looked a sight, at least she felt rested and of a mindset to sort through a myriad of thoughts that seemed to be fighting for attention.

For one, last night's couples' wedding shower had been a disaster. Absolute disaster. Lauren had gotten upset with Aaron and left early, pulling Gina in tow.

Just when Gina was getting used to being with Brady.

Being with Brady?

That phrase wasn't right! Totally inaccurate. Back up, girl.

Brady had been...a gem, really. He brought her back to Aunt Lottie's after the cornfield incident, whatever *that* was. Catharsis maybe? Emotional tensions had obviously erupted and flowed away in a flood of tears. It had drained her, but left her feeling stronger than she had in a year. She probably should have seen a counselor sometime in recent months. Instead she saw a terrified horse and a friendly farmer-turned-author.

But it seemed to be just the right therapy.

After that there wasn't enough time to do the other thing Brady had planned, and so they stopped at Aunt Lottie's house. Thank goodness no one was there to ask why her slacks were grass stained. He waited while she changed and washed her face. They arrived at the shower a few minutes late. Gina thought she detected a raised brow or two in the crowd. Maybe it was her imagination. Or the fact that nothing escaped the collective small town's notice.

Or was it the fact that her own mental brow was raised at herself when she realized she liked walking in with Brady Olafsson? And then there was the moment when she caught his attention across the crowded room just to smile at him. Later he walked up behind her and whispered in her ear, asking if she were all right. That tickle went down her spine again now, just remembering. And then there was her profound disappointment when Lauren begged her to leave with her, which meant she couldn't ride home with Brady.

Good grief!

Gina vigorously brushed her hair, yanked it back, twisted it up in a clip, and ignored her hunger pangs.

Anyway, she was thoroughly intrigued with his book. The story was the most thought-provoking thing she had ever read. Jesus jumped off of the pages. Had He really been like that in life?

She had always imagined Him somewhat of a pious, know-it-all who told people to believe in God or else they'd be sorry. Actually, God's Son would have a right to that attitude. But if that were the case, why would thousands flock around Him? Why would they invite Him to parties?

Why would He cry over someone who couldn't walk?

Because He was God's Son, then in some supernatural, spiritual way after He died, He came alive again. She had always heard that, even believed it could be true, but it didn't make a difference to her everyday life.

Until now. Would He cry over someone who couldn't walk quite evenly?

"Okay," Gina spoke aloud to the hairbrush in her hand. "Jesus, if You're there, I mean here, I want to get to know You better." She closed her eyes. "May I? And will You help Lauren and Aaron deal with their problem? Amen."

Her stomach rumbled. She hurried out to the hallway, hoping Aunt Lottie had prepared a megabreakfast, like blueberry pancakes and bacon and eggs. Halfway down the stairway she stopped.

Uh-oh. The last time she was this hungry for a meal it was the beginning of an extra ten pounds...and of a relationship with Steve.

~

One large breakfast and a medium-size lunch later, Gina peddled the old bicycle across town toward Aaron's office.

Her mother had tried to persuade her to stay out of what didn't concern her. Gina disagreed. After Lauren's second tearful phone call, not to mention last night's dragging her away from the party, she was convinced it did concern her.

Problem was, she sided with Aaron. In her opinion Lauren was being downright silly. And she was on her way to tell her cousin's fiancé to stick to his guns.

Gina turned a corner, fairly certain she couldn't get lost in the small, flat town. She'd never be able to bicycle this far at home. The hills were too steep and the traffic too thick.

Valley Oaks was an old town with a town square in the center. She rode through the business district, much of which was turn-of-the-century brick buildings. All the basics were housed within a couple of blocks of each other: post office, pharmacy, bank, hardware store, florist, café, barber shop, sheriff's office. The library was in a newer brick building. The grocery store was close by, housed in something called a Morton building. From the outside it looked to her like a huge blue tin box. There were homes of all shapes and sizes and ages, filling every street that branched out from the town square.

To Gina the town had the feel of a movie set. Everything was so compact, and everyone spoke or waved to everyone they passed, including her. People could probably walk to take care of any kind of everyday business. Unreal.

She turned another corner and followed Aunt Lottie's directions to the doctor's office. The sight of Brady's pickup parked in a small lot caught her attention first, then she noticed behind it was a low building with a sign in front that read Valley Oaks Clinic, Aaron G. Thompson, MD.

She wondered what Brady was doing here and tried to ignore the sensation that she was glad at the thought of seeing him again so soon. As she braked near the sidewalk, he walked out through the door.

"Gina!" He smiled. "Hi."

"Hi. How did Aaron survive last night?"

He shook his head and flipped on a white cap. "Let's just say the man has lost his bedside manner. I'd hate to be in need of medical attention right now. I hope that's not why you're here."

"No, I just wanted to talk to him."

Brady raised his brows. "Help smooth things over?"

"Not exactly. Lauren's a basket case, but what can I say? She's brought it on herself."

"You mean all that business last night was *her* fault?"

"Yes, I do. She wants me to tell him that he can come apologize anytime he's ready and remind him that yellow roses are her favorite. I told her I would, but I also said she owes him an apology, not vice versa."

"Don't women stick together in cases like this?"

"Gender has nothing to do with it. Lauren reacted illogically and irrationally. Pure and simple. Is it all right if I park my bike in the grass here?" She pushed it off of the sidewalk.

"Illogical and irrational?" He sounded perplexed.

"Yeah." She propped the bike against the kickstand and looked back at him.

There was amazement in Brady's raised brows and slack jaw. His hands were on his hips. "A woman is not supposed to accuse another woman of being illogical and irrational."

She crossed her arms. "She's not? Oh. And exactly where do you get your information, Mr. Olafsson?"

He pursed his lips. "That's not the point. Let's take a ride." He strode past her. "I'll get your bike."

"Whoa, wait a minute. I'm here to talk to Aaron— Brady!"

He perched the bicycle on his shoulder and headed toward his truck.

"You can't do that."

He tossed the bike into the truck bed where it clattered. "I just did."

"I'll walk home." She stomped down the sidewalk toward the medical office.

"Gina, I already reminded him that yellow roses are her favorite."

"Fine," she tossed over her shoulder. "I'll leave out that part."

"I also told him," he raised his voice, "to go apologize."

She whirled around. "You what? He didn't do anything wrong!"

Brady took a step toward her, his eyes narrowed. "This is none of your business or mine." His voice was low and threatening. "If you go in there, then I'll go tell Lauren she has every right to be angry, even call off the wedding, until my cousin stops behaving like a—" He clamped his jaw shut.

She stared back at him. "Is that blackmail?"

"No. It's what I told Aaron I was going to do. But I won't if you're with me." He held his hand out toward her, imploring. "Please. Come and take a breather with me."

Well, she definitely didn't want Lauren hearing Brady's opinion. It would only encourage her to continue in her silliness. On the other hand, here was Brady Olafsson, persuading her once again to follow him into his truck. "Don't you have writing or farming to do?"

"I'm ahead of schedule in the writing department and waiting for the corn to grow in the other." He winked. "And Ruby's fine."

She rolled her eyes. "Do all women just hop in your truck when you wink at them?"

"Usually."

She shook her head and walked ahead of him toward the parking lot. She could always call Aaron later. And besides, being nice to Brady was becoming less of a chore. Actually it was becoming downright enjoyable.

He'd show her the oaks.

Brady glanced at Gina. She stared through the windshield, a slight frown wrinkling her forehead. He wondered if it mirrored his own.

He wasn't that far ahead of schedule in writing, but that wasn't what was bothering him. He had to get his mind off of fixing Aaron and Lauren's dilemma.

No, that wasn't quite it either.

He had to get his mind off Nicole's leaving him four years ago. He had to stop asking himself if he had listened better, if he had not done what Aaron was doing, would they be married today?

He had said as much to his cousin. It was all the advice he could offer. He certainly had no business going off to comfort Lauren. His spontaneous coercing of Gina to divert his attention from all this had been a bit extreme. The phrase "any port in a storm" came to mind.

But on the other hand, why not? The porcupine quills had softened into silky feathers. He enjoyed talking with her. She was great to look at, even when tears streaked her face and hid the Miss America smile. The damsel in distress scenario in the cornfield had surprised him, as did his response. It must have been God's response. With almost any other woman it would have been a natural to hold her, but not Gina. Maybe he could become friends with a Lindstrom after all.

"Brady," she interrupted his thoughts, "where are we going?"

"It's a surprise. It's what I wanted to show you yesterday. Do you have something planned for this afternoon?"

"No. Actually, I think I've given up on my agenda for this month. Sitting still and reading want-ads is simply not on the calendar. Maybe it's Lauren's influence. She's like a whirlwind flying from one activity to another. And now this fiasco from last night. You really think Aaron should apologize?"

"Well, they probably both should. But he did arrive late, after promising not to."

"He's a doctor! He can't predict how many really sick people need to be squeezed into the day's schedule. The guy didn't even eat or change his clothes, and he would have gotten a speeding ticket if he didn't know the sheriff."

"He has office hours. His receptionist should be able to juggle things a little more efficiently."

"Brady, that's unrealistic. I worked with animals, from 7:00 to 4:00, and I can't tell you how often at 3:45 one of them got sick or hurt. Waiting until the next morning allows a more serious condition to develop."

"Stop me if I'm getting too personal, but this begs the question: Did you have a significant other waiting patiently for you?"

"No." She bit her lip. "Not waiting. He was the head vet, usually working with me."

"Ahh." This answered one question he didn't realize he had until just this moment. "Your boss?"

"Mm-hmm. Former, on both counts. Anyway, Lauren should recognize by now that she's Aaron's first priority, but it won't always look that way if someone's health hangs in the balance."

"How does she know it if it doesn't look that way?"

"Because he called to tell her what was going on, and he eventually showed up with red roses and an apology. Ooh," Gina shuddered, "I cannot believe she threw the flowers on the floor. Anyway, she can also tell because he would have made it up to her in some way. *That* she knows from experience already."

"Sounds as if you've figured this all out. Your head vet must have been like that?"

She groaned in reply. "Steve was nothing like that. That's how I figured it out. Can we change the subject?"

"Why didn't you speak up more on the Chicago trip?"

"What do you mean?"

"You're so logical. Now *that* group needed some logical direction."

She laughed. "They had a cast-in-concrete agenda, and I had no idea where we were. I was strictly along for the ride that day. Though I admit it was tough to keep my mouth shut at times."

"Do you have an illogical, irrational bone in your body?"

"Nope. They're a total waste of time and energy."

"Well, Dr. Philips, how then does a man romance you?"

Gina didn't answer.

"Whoops, that was off limits." He turned from the highway onto a gravel lane.

She looked out her side window. "It's just been so long, I can't remember offhand. Where in the world are we?"

"My place."

"All this is your place?"

"Just the road. That cornfield belongs to a neighbor who leases the land to my father to farm. The land to the left has been sold to a development company, which means I have a problem right through here." He slowed for the curve. "See the ravine there? That's my land, but the road flows into this company's land because it was easier to build it here. The man who owned the land gave me an easement. He died and his heirs weren't required to abide by the contract."

"So you don't have permission to use this?"

"Right. We're negotiating new terms, as they say."

"Technically you're not landlocked. You could build another road through the ravine."

"For a small fortune. Then on top of that, I'm not looking forward to having neighbors fill up the place."

"Oak trees!" Gina exclaimed. "Oak trees?"

He smiled as they entered the woodsy area with its canopy of leaves above the lane. "Told you you were looking in the wrong place all this time."

"These are yours? Oh, Brady, this is absolutely beautiful!"

"Welcome to the original homestead of Valley Oaks. It's where the name comes from." They wound through trees for another quarter of a mile.

"How much land is yours?"

"A little over a hundred acres. Mostly wooded."

She caught her breath. "A log cabin! You *live* here? In the midst of all these oaks?"

Brady parked the truck and they climbed out. "And walnut, cherry, elder, and hickory."

"Was the house here? It looks like the Ponderosa place on those old *Bonanza* shows."

"No, I built it. The remains of the original aren't far." His golden retriever raced out from behind the house, barking excitedly and wagging his tail.

Gina knelt to pet him. "Hey, boy. What's your name again? Some old author."

"Try ancient Greece," Brady hinted.

"Mmm, Aristotle?"

"Homer."

"Hey, Homer!"

He watched his dog fall in love with the childlike woman vigorously rubbing him down. He swallowed. "Do you want to stay for a bit?"

"Oh, yes!" She looked up at him, emerald eyes sparkling, and smiled. "Can I see all 100 acres?"

"Sure." He smiled back at her, aware that he had been holding his breath, waiting for her response. It seemed that he had just stumbled onto how to romance Angelina Philips.

That is, if he were so inclined.

Seventeen

"Magpie, you look sensational." Marsha smiled at her sister. "Only you could pull off wearing a purple dress splattered with giant red flowers."

Maggie twirled. "It is fun, isn't it? Well, I think I'm ready." She stepped to the small mirror hanging next to Aunt Lottie's front door and inspected her hair.

"Where's Gina?"

"She called from *Brady's* house. He's cooking dinner for the two of them."

"You're kidding. How'd that come about?"

"I don't have a clue." She rearranged a stray blonde curl. "Evidently they ran into each other on the street somewhere and started talking. He invited her to his place. Where does he live anyway?"

"He bought the old Crowley homestead and built a house on it."

"Really?" She pulled a lipstick from her purse and applied it. "Gina will love that. All those woods and animals. I suppose he has a dog." Her eyes met her sister's in the mirror. "Now this is odd."

"Very odd. Gina and Brady, getting along, eating dinner alone. Maybe they're hatching a plan to get Lauren and Aaron back together."

"Haven't they talked yet?"

"Not as of 30 minutes ago." Marsha shook her head. "That girl is as stubborn as her aunt."

Maggie snapped shut her purse. "Ha, ha. Okay, I'm leaving." She turned toward the stairs and called, "Bye, Aunt Lottie."

"Goodbye, dear. Have a nice time. I'll be right down, Marsha."

"Maggie." Her sister's face showed concern.

"It's all right, Marsh. Reece believed I would have more fun without him, and that's probably true. He wouldn't know anyone."

"But still—"

"He's not like Dan. I mean, he couldn't be. He's been on the road most of our married life."

"Well, sometimes Dan resembles glue."

"Except during planting and harvest."

"True."

Maggie smiled. "Appreciate the glue, sis. Besides, you're just saying that to make me feel better. We're different. We married different men; we have different lifestyles. For the reunion tonight, I'm fine. Okay?" She hugged her sister.

"Have a great time. Remember how to get to the club?"

"I remember. Bye."

Maggie walked out the front door and down the porch steps to Aunt Lottie's car parked in the driveway. She was used to engaging in activities by herself, driving herself, being responsible for herself. It really wasn't the traumatic event it would be for Marsha. She was complete without a man at her elbow.

Then why John?

She dismissed the thought and backed into the street. Pregnant with Rosie, she had vowed to always remain independent. Soon after marrying Reece, they didn't need her paycheck. He never would have minded if she spent her days volunteering wherever, but she chose to work. She craved the independence it offered. With that independence came the ability to take care of herself.

That way it hurt less when Reece flew off to Timbuktu twice a month.

By rote now she turned corners, eventually picking up the county highway east of town. She nudged the old car up to a conservative 58 miles per hour, the fastest it could handle without shimmying. At least the air conditioning worked. She turned the fan on full blast, swiveled the vents toward her face.

It was what she had wanted. Wasn't it?

Tonight she would inevitably watch certain couples. Were Neil and Barb happy? Would his wife still have that contented glow on her face that Maggie had spotted ten years ago? What if Maggie had stuck it out? Now that would have been true stubbornness. Would she glow after a lifetime of running a household and being her farmer husband's right hand?

She shook her head. This wasn't about "what ifs." It was about getting a handle on the old Maggie and equipping herself to deal with the consequences of today with a new, confident outlook.

She glanced in the rearview mirror. Well, she definitely had a glow about her, too, but it didn't have a thing to do with contentment.

⌒

"Aww, come on, Mags. It's tradition." Neil Olafsson held his arms out to her. "Homecoming king and queen dance one together."

Maggie looked up at the man who owned a large chunk of her youthful past. There was something familiar about him, but it had grown vague after all these years, almost as if their story happened to someone she had only read about.

"It's not exactly tradition for our class. I have successfully avoided this dance at every reunion, whether I attended or not."

His arms dropped to his sides. "You always were stubborn about the dumbest things." He winked, taking the edge off his words.

"Was I really?" She remembered her sister saying that.

Couples shuffled near them as slow strands of an old beach tune filled the dimly lit, crowded room. The music wasn't the din of ten years ago when no one could speak in less than a shout. Tables surrounded the parquet dance floor. A disc jockey, flanked by enormous speakers, stood at one end, buffet tables at another.

"Mags, Barb doesn't mind. Does Reece?"

She gave her head a slight shake.

"Heck, after 35 years, nobody does. Why should you?"

Indeed, why should she? Valley Oaks was filled with a new generation, one that didn't condemn her. If tonight was part of her journey through the past, then spending a few minutes with her first husband seemed...acceptable. "No reason." She placed her left hand on his shoulder.

Neil led her into the midst of the other dancers. "You look prettier than ever."

She smiled. "You're looking good yourself."

His blue-green eyes were still bright and friendly, although the crow's-feet were deep. The ruddy complexion told of a lifetime spent outdoors in all kinds of weather. Gray had overtaken most of the blond hair that was noticeably thin and revealed more of his forehead than she remembered. His height hadn't diminished. Nowhere near overweight, he had filled out some, softening the sharp angles of his youth.

"Reece around?"

She shook her head. "Business. How's the farm?"

"Can't complain. I picked up a son-in-law, but unfortunately lost one full-time son in the process."

"The writer? I saw one of his books. You have to admit, that's exciting."

"Well, it's his dream, so I don't give him too hard of a time. Not many get their dreams in this world."

"You and Barb look contented, as if your dreams came true."

Surprise crossed his face, then he smiled. "I suppose they have. She just gets better and better with age. We celebrated our thirty-third last winter. Went to Hawaii. She still works in the fields with me sometimes. We've got four great kids. And a granddaughter."

"You're a grandpa? Congratulations! And you're doing what you always dreamed of doing."

He nodded. "God has given us much. How about you?"

An involuntary shrug lifted her shoulder. She stopped herself from replying "fine." If she insisted on exploring other people's states of mind, she'd better have some description of her own figured out. And she'd better be able to ignore the twinge of envy when she heard a husband sing praises about his wife. While she hesitated, compassion clouded his eyes.

"Do you believe in God, Mags?"

"More than ever."

"Faith makes all the difference."

"I understand who Jesus is now. Your mother used to tell me often, but I..."

"I know. She was pushy."

Maggie didn't add that the woman also succeeded in single-handedly pushing her away from God. "And we were know-it-all kids, determined to do what we thought was best."

"We all have to make our own way. What about your dreams?"

She glanced away. "After...after, well, us, I didn't dare dream anymore. But it has been good." She smiled at him. "I just ploughed ahead without too much thought. I love California. I have a daughter who is absolutely beautiful inside and out. Reece thrives on his work and takes good care of me. I enjoy my job and have time to do volunteer things."

"Sounds good."

Maggie nodded.

A quick drumbeat followed on the heels of the fading slow song. They stepped apart.

"Tell Barb hello if I don't see her tonight," she said.

"You want to come tell her now?" He pointed over his shoulder.

"I'm going this way. Haven't talked with Shelley Michaels yet."

"Thanks for the dance." He leaned over and gave her a quick kiss on the cheek. "That wasn't too difficult was it, Queen Margaret?"

"No. It was nice catching up with you." She turned to go, not wanting to watch him with his wife. What was hard was not that it was Neil with Barb, but that she had never known that kind of adoration from Reece.

"Hey, Mags." He grasped her elbow.

She looked back at him.

"You know, it's never too late to dream." He smiled and moved away through the dancers.

It was one of those moments that stretched, shoving aside the present. Dream? When had she last considered a dream? Weren't dreams only for the young? What in the world would she dream for at this point in life?

Perhaps...a husband who cherished her so much he would clear his calendar in order to attend her reunion, just to be near her, just so she could share it with someone she loved?

It was a little late for that.

Eighteen

Brady and Gina huddled together in his basement, shoulder to shoulder, arms brushing, and peered into the freezer chest.

Brady glanced down at her. "I hope you're not a vegetarian. After all, you are in the middle of cattle and hog country, you know."

"No way. All I've seen is corn and soybeans. Don't you have any tofu?"

"Bleagh! Nope, just T-bones and pork chops."

"I'll have a T-bone. A big one." She grinned at him. "I am famished!"

"Sounds good to me." He grabbed two packages from the freezer and shut the lid.

"Have I got time to catch a bullfrog?" Her eyes sparkled up at him. They'd been sparkling all afternoon.

"You'll never catch a bullfrog."

She laughed. "Yes, I will. Let's bet that if I get one, you do the dishes. If I don't get one in 20 minutes, I'll do them."

"You're on." He looked at his watch. "On your mark, get set—"

She bounded up the stairs, Homer at her heels.

While the meat defrosted in the microwave, Brady watched from the porch. About ten yards away, Gina crouched at the pond's edge, almost hidden in the tall grasses. He smiled. From the moment she heard the bullfrogs' foghorn chorus, she had been determined to catch one.

She had fallen in love with his place. They spent the afternoon tromping through the woods. Her excitement grew by the minute. They spotted a myriad of birds, followed deer tracks, surprised pheasants from their hiding place, picked wildflowers, threw in a fishing line, and shimmied along the tree trunk that lay across the creek. In the upper meadow, she gasped at the sight of a soaring hawk. At the sound of the tree frogs' song, she stood still. When the bullfrogs' deep hum resonated through the woods, she giggled.

It was another dimension of her personality. Another one he would not have imagined she possessed. That she was smart and serious was a given because of all her work entailed. Her uneven gait had tugged at his heart, arousing protective instincts...until her opinionated attitude indicated how independent she was. Her tears in the cornfield revealed a fragility that meant she was, after all, human. Not a porcupine, not a despicable nonentity named Lindstrom, not really a thorn in his side.

But it was these few hours of witnessing her expression of pure joy in nature that connected with his heart. It seemed to be...unraveling it.

A loud splash from the pond caught his attention. Gina was lying prone, elbow-deep in the water.

"Whoa!" she yelped and jumped up, her hands cupped together above her head. "I got one! I got one!" She screamed with laughter. Her jeans and T-shirt were covered with mud.

"Well, now what?" he shouted. "Frog legs for dinner?"

"No! I just want to kiss it. See if a prince pops out."

To his amazement, she lowered her hands to her face and peered into them for a moment, then held them to her mouth. He heard an exaggerated smacking noise. With a squeal, she flung the frog back into the water.

"That one's a dud, Brady! Got any more?"

He found dry clothes for her, sweatpants and a T-shirt left by a young cousin. While he grilled the steaks outside, she rummaged around in the kitchen and completed the salad and baked potatoes. They met on the screened-in porch where she had put place settings on the small wooden table. She had even lit two candles, a soft light in the dusky woods.

"I moved your laptop to the kitchen table," she said. "I hope you don't mind? It's so nice out here."

"Good idea. I practically live out here when the weather's like this, not too hot or cold." The woman was invading his space, had the audacity to touch his computer—and he was grinning?

She hiked up the too-large sweats and sat down across from him. The baggy shirt sleeves hung below her elbows. "I hope you invite me back so I can go prince-hunting again."

"Of course." After saying grace, he asked, "So a prince is included in your life's plan?"

"Seriously, no. I mean, you can't exactly write in on your calendar the day you're going to meet Mr. Right. I hope to have a family some day, but who knows? How about you? Is there a Miss Right on your horizon?"

"Well, I thought so once, but..." He shrugged. "It didn't work out."

"Mmm, this steak is perfect."

"Thanks."

She eyed him over a forkful. "So why do you think Aaron is in the wrong?"

"Thought we dropped that subject."

"Not forever. Now we've calmed down. We can discuss it. Don't you think?" She smiled sweetly. "It doesn't mean we're going to impose our views on them."

He frowned for a moment. This would hit a little too close to home, but those beautiful spring green eyes across the table encouraged him. "Okay. Despite the fact that I appreciate Aaron's position as a doctor, he needs to be more obvious about letting Lauren know she's first in his life."

"What else can he do?" Her voice rose.

He held up a hand. "You said we had calmed down."

She closed her eyes. "All right. Go ahead. I'm calm."

"A couple of those patients yesterday could have been referred to a doctor in Rockville. It's only 20 miles away. They weren't emergencies."

Gina pressed her lips together.

Brady continued. "Lauren wouldn't have gotten so bent out of shape if she felt secure in his love. He's not doing or being all he can. This has happened before. Yes, she's going to have to accept that it will happen again. But his one phone call should have been five or six. 'I'm thinking of you. I'm running late. Hang in there, sweetheart.'"

Gina opened her mouth to say something.

"Wait," he held up a finger, "I'm not finished. The roses should have been delivered at the time he was to arrive, and they should have been yellow."

"The local florist didn't—"

"Somebody within a 30-mile radius had yellow. There should have been a handwritten note with them that said, 'I love you.' When he arrived, he should not have stopped to talk with others and filled a plate with food. Instead, he should have gone directly to her, ignoring everyone until he greeted her and kissed her as if no one else were around." He took a breath. "He should have held her longer the night before."

She stared at him, hands in her lap, dinner forgotten. "That is the most illogical, irrational thing I have ever heard."

"But it would work."

She raised a brow. "How do you know?"

"Because my ex-fiancée told me it would have worked for her."

She swallowed. "Oh."

He waved a fork toward her plate. "Your steak is getting cold."

"Oh. Right." She fiddled with her napkin. "Were you writing at the time?"

"I was teaching and farming full-time, trying to write in my spare time. All those things were more important than she was. At least it looked that way, and maybe they were, or else you'd think I would have done things differently. Anyway, I don't want to see Aaron make the same mistake, especially with Lauren."

"Does she live in town?"

"Who?"

"Your ex. I'm sorry. I'm being nosy."

He shrugged. "No problem. She lives in Los Angeles."

"Oh." She thought a moment, tucking her hair behind an ear, and whistled softly. "Strike two against women from California?"

That hit home. "You know," he bristled, "maybe if you minced your words a little, you'd be a lot more fun to talk to." He felt like a heel as soon as the words were out of his mouth. "Gina, I'm sorry."

She bit her lip and concentrated on her plate.

He reached across the table and grasped her wrist. "I am sorry. I told you no problem, but I guess it still is at times."

She met his eyes. "Whew! For a minute there I thought I had just swung the third strike without even trying."

"Well, you know, since you're a California native, that puts you in a different game. The other game involves only Illinois women who move to California."

She reached across the table and brushed at his shoulder. "There, it's almost gone."

The chip on his shoulder. He grinned. "And I do enjoy talking with you, probably because you don't mince your words." He peered down at his shoulder. "Is it gone now?"

Gina laughed.

~

While Brady prepared dessert for them, Gina sat curled up with a sleeping Homer on the couch. A small lamp provided soft light in one corner of the porch. She sipped coffee, staring through the screens at the darkened outlines of trees. The bullfrogs croaked one at a time, their throaty voices answering each other from different points around the pond.

It seemed odd, but she felt so safe with Brady. Brady Olafsson...of all people! She really hadn't felt safe with anyone in a long time. Her parents were great, but there was always that natural barrier between the generations. Her world was so different from theirs. And she often hesitated opening up completely, sensing that she did not quite live up to their expectations. After all, she was jobless and had had to move back home. There were no grandchildren on the horizon. In recent years there hadn't been enough time for cultivating close friendships, the kind that allowed you to pour out your soul.

Then why did she do just that with Brady yesterday in the cornfield? Probably because she needed to so desperately, and it really didn't matter with him because he was a stranger. What he thought of her or whom he would tell were meaningless.

His comforting response was sweet, though. It paved the way for these hours today of just hanging out with him, away from the stresses of the wedding and her future plans. She never would have imagined from their first meetings that he was so easy to be with. It was also hard to imagine he was a famous author. He shouldn't be such an ordinary guy.

Brady stepped onto the porch and handed her one of two white bowls he was carrying. "Warm black raspberry crisp with vanilla ice cream."

"Mmm." And he baked as well as cooked, a definite plus for her ravenous appetite today. "Thanks. I saw tons of wild berry bushes in the woods. Did you pick them?"

"Just this morning."

"You are full of surprises, Mr. Olafsson." She took a bite. "Mmm. This is wonderful."

"Thank you. May I ask you something personal?"

"It seems we've been doing a lot of that today without asking permission."

"Yeah, I guess so." His eyes held hers for a moment. "It's kind of like we're in that territory where just about anything is fair game because after a couple weeks we'll never see each other again."

"Exactly. It's an interesting place, isn't it? I totally unload on you yesterday, unlike I've done in years with anyone. I feel like this great weight has been removed, and we don't even know each other. Are you a counselor, too?"

He shook his head. "No, just a shoulder available at the right time."

Gina thought of the bookstore clerk's comment about Brady's shoulders. Words caught in her throat. It wasn't just his shoulders. It was his long fingers smoothing her hair, his low voice whispering comfort, his heart beating against her ear, his cheek resting atop her head...a shiver went through her.

"Cold? I'll get a sweatshirt."

"No. It's just the ice cream."

"You do have that blanket practically in your lap," he referred to Homer, whose golden fur spread around him on the couch beside her.

"One that snores. So what was your question?"

"Oh yeah. Well, after watching you with my dog and the princely frogs," he grinned, "I was wondering if you'd consider working with small animals. How about a pet vet?"

She set aside her empty bowl and wrapped her arms around Homer, avoiding the piercing blue-green gaze. "Since the summer I was 16 I've worked at the Park in some capacity, from selling popcorn to giving tours to mucking out stables. My dream was to become a vet for the elephants, giraffes, rhinos, and tapirs. Then I accomplished that dream. I had my life planned, the whole thing. But now..." She shrugged, trying to shake off the turmoil of yesterday that was beginning to rattle again.

"I don't mean to pry."

Was her face so easily read? "I just haven't come up with an alternative plan yet. I don't know what I'm doing with the rest of my life."

"Most people face that dilemma at least once before reaching your age. And how many do you know who have careers related to their college degree?"

She shrugged again and turned toward the screens. "I guess I may have to come up with Dream Plan B."

She had never met a man like Brady. From his writing she sensed that he knew of things she had intentionally ignored most of her life. God had His place, she had hers. They intersected on occasional Sunday mornings. Some people, like Lauren and Aunt Lottie, thought it could be otherwise. She looked back at him. "Aunt Lottie said that when God closes a door, He opens a window. What is that supposed to mean?"

"That He's got something better planned for you."

"Why would He bother with me?"

"Because He loves you."

"But I'm just a regular person."

"Gina, we all are. We can't earn His love; that's why He sent Jesus."

"Your book is wonderful. I never thought of Jesus being a real person before."

A tiny smile lit up his entire face, softening the masculine angles.

She grinned. "You look like a happy little boy right now."

"What you just said. It's exactly what I hope readers will get, you know?"

"The point being that He showed us what God is like?"

Brady leaned forward in the chair, propping his elbows on his knees, and nodded. "That, and to tell us that the only way to be in a right relationship with God the Father is to believe that Jesus is who He said He is, the Son."

"And what does that mean?"

"Well, there's a logical explanation for it all."

Gina smiled. "Logical is good."

"Thought you'd like that. God created us, and so of course He loves us, but He gave us a free will. We get to choose whether or not we want to let Him be Lord in our lives. Okay so far?"

"Okay."

"Being imperfect humans, we're always going to do things our own way. Trouble is, God demands perfection, and He demands payment for doing things our own way."

"So what chance do we have?"

"Jesus. He paid the penalty. All we have to do is accept that fact."

"And then we'll live happily ever after?"

"Eventually, but not during this lifetime. We still are imperfect humans. The difference is we know we're forgiven. There's great comfort and freedom in that."

She frowned.

"Illogical?"

"Too simple."

He smiled. "I know."

"So what does He want from me?"

"Just tell Him you believe in Jesus and that you want Him to be Lord of your life. He'll do the rest."

She remembered her morning thoughts and her jaw dropped. "This is weird, Brady. I was wondering about Jesus earlier today, and I told Him I wanted to get to know Him better. And here we are having this conversation."

"That's not weird. It's logical. You asked Him for something and He answered."

She stared at him. "I suppose I should tell Him I believe in Him now. Should I close my eyes or kneel?"

"You don't have to."

"How about outside?"

Brady stood and reached for her hand. "Under the stars is my favorite place to talk to Him."

She placed her hand in his, and they walked out the screen door, across the deck and down a short distance to the pond's edge. The smooth water mirrored the navy blue sky. Both sparkled with the silver glitter of a zillion stars.

Brady dropped her hand and backed away. "She's all yours, Father."

Gina smiled and turned back toward the pond. In a shy whisper she began to address the unseen that she had always sensed was expressed in nature and the animal world. "Okay, God. Father. I believe what Brady said, that Jesus is Your Son. Please forgive me for not doing things right. Please live in me now. Be Lord of my life." She paused. "Do I say amen now? Okay, amen. Oh. And thank You."

She gazed at the sky. There was no thunderous answer, no zapping in her heart...just a single, unbidden tear that slipped from her eye.

"Brady," she called out. "I don't feel any different."

He strode to her side. "He didn't promise feelings."

She grinned up at him. "Of course not. They're illogical and irrational."

With a loud laugh, he wrapped his arms around her.

Nineteen

Gina looked through Aunt Lottie's screen door. "Uh-oh, Mother, here comes Lauren, and she's not dressed for church."

Maggie peered over her daughter's shoulder. "Her face looks ready for an argument. I think she's still mad at you, honey."

"Can you and Aunt Lottie go without me? I'd better get this straightened out." Her tone was resigned. For the first time ever she had anticipated going to church without thinking of it as a duty and now this.

Lauren stomped up the front porch steps. "Gina Philips! Where have you been?"

"Oh, Lauren, Aunt Lottie told you I was at Brady's last night." She held open the screen door. "Come on in."

"I know. She told me the seven times I called. Didn't you come home?"

"It was after eleven o'clock. I thought it was too late to call. Why didn't you just come out to Brady's? I know you're good enough friends."

"Because then it would be three against one. The two guys and you, my traitor female cousin." Lauren's petite face scrunched in a pout.

Gina rolled her eyes. "Aaron wasn't there and besides— Oh, let's go upstairs and we'll talk, okay? I want to get out of this dress. It's hotter again today, isn't it?" She led the way up the staircase.

In the bedroom, Lauren plopped on the bed. "Didn't you see Aaron?"

"You two haven't talked yet?"

"No!"

Gina hid her look of disbelief by turning toward the closet and kicking off her flats. "I was on my way to deliver your message—and mine—when I ran into Brady. He was just coming out of Aaron's office."

"Oh, swell," she whined. "I can just see it. The three of you plotting—"

"Lauren! Brady agrees with you! He thinks Aaron hasn't made you feel secure enough." She slipped out of the summer dress. "Trust me, your message was delivered to him, but not by me."

"Really?"

"Really. The whole thing and then some." She found a hanger for the dress. "Evidently Aaron's as stubborn as you are since he hasn't called by now. I didn't even get to tell him *not* to call you. Why don't you call him?"

"Gina, do those hurt?"

"What?"

Her cousin nodded toward her leg.

"Looks awful, doesn't it?" She glanced down at the raised, reddish-purple, rope-like scars that ran down her thigh and over the knee. "No, they don't hurt. I can have plastic surgery done, but at the moment I have no desire to go back into a hospital for the sole purpose of enduring pain and agony just to look presentable in a pair of shorts."

"Gina." Lauren's voice was quiet. "I don't know if I want to marry him."

She sank onto a stuffed armchair. "Oh, Lauren."

"He's not going to change."

"No, he's not. It's good for you to accept that fact. He is a doctor. His patients will often come before you *in his schedule.*" She sighed. "But not in his heart, Laur. That's another fact you can just accept."

Her cousin's lower lip protruded. "I don't want facts. I want unbridled passion."

Gina burst into laughter. "Then go after Brady. He seems to have it wired. He told Aaron he should have kissed you in front of everyone the other night as if no one else were there."

"He should have."

"That is totally irrational. Aaron doesn't think that way. But if that's all you need, he'll just learn a few things that he can do to help you feel better. He's a good, solid man who has probably bought you a pair of diamond earrings or something to make up for missing half the shower. Isn't that irrational enough?"

"He missed three-fourths. The gifts were already opened."

Gina groaned. "You know you both need to apologize. Who broke the ice the last time this happened?"

"He did."

"Well?" She sprang up and went to the closet. "I'd bring you a phone, girl, but it's down the hall attached to a wall jack. What are we doing today? I have jeans or jeans to wear. Are jeans all right? Oh, I have these." She pulled out a pair of khaki capri pants. "If they still fit. I've been eating like a horse."

"Gina, how can you be so chipper? I'm calling off my wedding, and you're yapping on and on." She bolted upright. "Oh my goodness! What happened between you and Brady last night anyway? You two were together for an awfully long time."

Gina found a khaki-and-white striped shirt. "We really had an enjoyable time. Do you believe it? The guy can be all-right company." She pulled the shirt on over her head and tucked it into the pants. "He took me all over his property.

Amazing place. He cooked dinner for us, great steaks and this luscious black raspberry crisp. And we had the most interesting conversation. He told me about Jesus and how if we accept Him, we're right with God. So I asked Jesus to be my Lord because I never have. Then we found constellations, and then he brought me home." She held out her hands, palms up. "There you have it. I think we're friends. Maybe. For the duration anyway. So you've got to go through with the wedding. That's why we're being nice to each other, you know."

"Gina! You're a Christian? I mean, like what I've been preaching at you for years?"

"I guess so. It just didn't make sense when you told me."

Lauren rushed to her side and gave her a hug. "This is great! I've been praying for you."

"I know. Thanks."

"You're not as uptight as when you first got here."

"It's my understanding that God has things under control. Do you want some lunch?"

"I think I just had breakfast."

They headed down to the kitchen where Gina rummaged in the refrigerator. "So, what are we doing today?"

"Well, I had planned on going to Brady's brother's college graduation party at the farm. With Aaron. Now, I don't know."

"Lauren, just call him. It's not that big a deal." She set out fixings for a ham sandwich on the counter. "You know you want to marry him."

"Maybe I'll just go and run into him there. See how it goes."

Gina sighed. "How old are you?"

"You can come with me."

"I wasn't invited. And I'm not dropping in on my mother's first husband's private wingding. Which reminds me. Did the whole family swear to secrecy about that or what? Why didn't you ever tell me my mother was married before and had a baby?"

Lauren studied her nails. "We did swear to secrecy. My mother said it was up to your mother to tell you. Anyway, give me a piece of that ham. This is not a private wingding. All friends and relatives are invited. You just said you were friends."

"Not *friends* friends." The phone rang and she went to it. "More like acquaintances who are spending an inordinate amount of time together. Hello?"

"Hi." It was Brady's soft voice.

"Hi." Her intimate tone betrayed herself. He was rapidly turning into someone beyond acquaintance.

"Why aren't you here at church? Need a ride?"

"No." She turned her back to her cousin's curious face. "I'm too busy trying to talk Lauren into meeting Aaron. Halfway, at least."

"Ah, good girl. He's not here, so I can't work on him. I'm calling to invite you out to the farm this afternoon. My parents are having an open house for Ryan, my brother you almost met the other day. He just graduated from college."

She tried to imagine it...Maggie Lindstrom's daughter surrounded by disapproving Olafssons. "Uh, sounds like a family thing. It's natural that your parents would mind. But thank—"

"Gina." He paused. She heard him inhale a deep breath. "My grandmother is dead. I'm the only other one who minded."

She smiled. Absolutely no trace of a chip. "You more than made up for things last night, Brady. Why are you being so friendly?"

"Because of your Miss America smile. I'd rather see it than your scowl."

"Now you're skating on thin ice, mister."

"If you need a ride, I'll come by for you about two o'clock."

Lauren was actually jumping and twirling in front of her. Gina turned her back to the spectacle, wrapping herself in the long cord. "How about if I come with Lauren?"

"That'll work. I'll make sure the groom is there. It'd be a shame for them to cancel. I was just beginning to look forward to being your escort."

"Uh-huh. Well, I still don't need one," she teased, smiling to herself. "See you, Brady."

"Bye."

Ignoring her cousin's pointed stare, she unwrapped herself from the cord and hung up the phone, then resumed fixing her sandwich.

"Well?" Lauren squealed.

"Well what?" She pulled two more slices of bread from the bag. Two sandwiches sounded appealing, especially with the whole wheat bread she had managed to find at the local grocery store.

"Gina!"

"What? Oh, I'm invited to the graduation party, and Brady's going to make sure Aaron is there so that you two can make up."

"I gathered all that. I mean, you were flirting with him and smiling—"

"Flirting? I was not flirting."

"Call it what you want, but you don't sound like *just* acquaintances. What was he saying?"

Gina shrugged. "Some nonsense about a Miss America smile and being my escort. Do you want a sandwich?"

"I think he likes you."

"And I like him. When you and Aaron celebrate your twenty-fifth, I'll come back for the open house and be nice to him because I'll want to. Now back off, Cupid, and let's eat."

Twenty

In spite of Brady's reassurance on the phone, Gina was apprehensive as she and Lauren drove to his parents' farm. Besides helping her cousin deal with her dilemma, she'd have to deal with being scrutinized by the entire Olafsson clan.

She had asked her mother about it.

"Gina, it's history. Whenever I return to Valley Oaks, the memories overwhelm me at first because they hit all at once, lots of happiness and lots of pain and not all related to the Olafssons. I've met Neil's wife Barb a few times over the years. She's a very nice woman who doesn't seem threatened by the past. Stop worrying. Just go and enjoy yourself." She winked. "And tell me all about their house and furnishings when you get back."

Gina glanced at Lauren now. She drove with one hand, while chewing the nails of her other. "Did you pray about this?"

"What?" Lauren stared at her.

"Pray. Watch the road. Brady told me God is concerned about every little thing, so you should probably pray about this."

"I have."

"Then it will work out for the best. Relax." Silently she told herself the same.

The beauty of the Olafsson farm struck her again as they turned onto their lane. It was picture-perfect on a slightly warm, sunny afternoon. An iridescent blue sky shone above the pure greens of the fields and whites of the fences, barns, and house.

Lauren parked her car behind a long line of others. A woman waited for them to get out, then hurried over to Gina. She was short and more plump than slender. Her light brown wavy hair was brushed off of her face, and she wore a denim jumper.

"You must be Gina Philips." She smiled and shook her hand warmly. "I'm Barb, Brady's mother. Welcome to our home."

Relief flooded Gina. "Thank you." She smiled.

"And Lauren," Barb said, "I have a very unhappy nephew moping around in the upper meadow."

Lauren's face looked stricken. "What do I do?" she asked Gina.

"Oh, go to him, Laur. Try to apologize before he can." Barb patted her shoulder. "You'll sort it out."

As she walked away toward the barns, they went to the house. "Your farm is so beautiful," Gina said.

"Thank you. The house is becoming too large with the children grown and more or less gone. The boys work with their dad, but only Ryan lives here. And I'm sure that won't be for long. We have one grandchild, though, and another on the way, so we're working on filling it again. How's your mother?"

Gina was only slightly taken aback at the direct question, probably because of Barb's genuine friendliness. "She's well, thank you. She's busy helping Aunt Marsha with the last-minute wedding details, playing the mean aunt role when necessary with caterers and florists."

Barb smiled. "I'm sure that's a big help. Marsha always was on the quiet side."

"You know Aunt Marsha?" *Of course she would! This is Valley Oaks.*

"We were classmates, a few years behind your mother. I was sorry I didn't get a chance to chat with Maggie last night at the reunion."

What?

"You know," Barb continued, "she and my husband graduated together. Now I want to say something that I hope will put you at ease. I don't know what Brady has said to you, but I want you to know that my mother-in-law was an intimidating woman. However, I never allowed her to speak ill of your mother in my presence. And Neil never spoke ill of her. Of course, he is a man of few words anyway."

Gina felt herself relax. "Not like his son?"

Barb laughed. "Not at all like Brady."

A large crowd was gathered in the backyard. As Brady approached, his mother excused herself.

"Hi, Gina." His blond hair shone in the sunlight. A short-sleeved plaid shirt, tucked into blue jeans, covered the ever-present white T-shirt.

"Hi." Suddenly self-conscious, she fought the smile that insisted on controlling her facial muscles. She wanted to scowl at his penetrating turquoise gaze rather than smile and be reminded of a— What had he called it? *Miss America smile.* "Uh, we've sent Lauren to apologize to Aaron."

A grin softened his angular features. "Glad to hear that. Come meet my dad."

She hesitated. She had just hurdled one obstacle, his mother, and was midair over a second, which was the star-tling affect Brady Olafsson was having on her heartbeat. The physical presence of this tall, good-looking man was scram-bling her thoughts, and it seemed it just shouldn't be so.

"My mother's the one who can bite when she wants to. Dad's a lamb compared to her." He crooked his elbow out toward her.

She looked at the blond hairs glistening on his tanned forearm and thought that he was too real to touch. He was practically a stranger, but touching his skin would be too intimate considering these odd emotions racing through her.

"Practice." He pointed at his arm. "For up and down the aisle, you know."

Gina gave herself a mental shake and hooked her wrist through the crook of his elbow. It was just Brady, friendly wedding ceremony partner, annoying teller of jokes. "Right."

Neil Olafsson was a slightly shorter, less angular version of Brady with gray streaks throughout his thinning blond hair. *Nowhere near as handsome as Dad,* she thought.

He shook her hand. "Nice to meet you, Gina."

"Thank you."

He smiled. "I talked with your mother last night. She seems to be doing very well."

It was a casual comment. The son's early furor was obviously not the father's. Gina smiled back at the man. "She's my favorite mom."

"Be sure to make yourself at home. There's plenty of food."

As he walked away, Brady leaned over her shoulder and whispered in her ear, "That wasn't too bad, was it?"

She exhaled. "No." It really hadn't been at all. More difficult to deal with was the tickle his breath sent around her neck.

Gina met countless others, including the mayor, barber, postmaster, and a good-looking deputy sheriff named Cal Huntington.

He shook her hand. "I'm surprised we haven't met yet."

"How's that?" She flexed her fingers, glad that his grip hadn't permanently mangled them. Her neck was going to get a crick in it. They sure grew them tall around here.

"Well, what with you being a California *freeway* driver and me patrolling our little old two-lane county roads, it seemed inevitable." He emphasized a drawl. "Figured you don't drive under 70."

"I don't, but have you seen Aunt Lottie's car?"

His grin softened the iron jaw and square cheekbones. Clear green eyes bore into her. His build resembled a stone fireplace. Although he seemed friendly enough, she was glad not to be breaking any laws.

Anne approached, accompanied by a female version of Brady, tall and blonde, though more athletically built than slender.

Gina returned Anne's hug. It was good to see a familiar face at last. "Gina, this is Brady's sister, Britte Olafsson. She's my boss."

"Hi, Gina." A smile lit up her face. "Welcome to the farm. It's about time we met. My brother keeps talking about you."

Gina glanced at Brady deep in discussion with Cal. The tips of his ears turned pink. "I'm nothing like whatever he said."

Britte laughed. "He does write fiction."

"Exactly. How are you Anne's boss?"

"Only on paper. She's my assistant girls' basketball coach at the high school, but she leads me more than I lead her."

Isabel greeted them, then turned to Britte. "Can we meet at your house on Thursday? My bathroom is still under construction."

"No problem."

Anne said, "Gina, has Lauren invited you to our book club? She's been too busy to come lately, but you're welcome to join us any time. You don't need to read the book. We're rather informal."

Isabel laughed. "Informal is right. We could call it 'ladies night out slash counseling session slash what can I pray about for you slash let's all paint your living room slash book discussion if there's time' club."

Britte nudged Isabel. "Scare her away, why don't you? I don't think *I'm* coming next week."

"You just said we could meet at your house."

"Oh, yeah."

Gina joined in their laughter.

Brady touched her elbow. "Hungry?"

When wasn't she hungry these days? Definitely not a good sign.

After eating a plateful of fried chicken and the best homemade potato salad she had ever tasted, she and Brady strolled out to a pasture to see Ruby.

"Brady, I just can't imagine living with all this wide open space. Tell me you never get tired of waking up to this glut of nature."

"I never tire of waking up to this glut of nature. Unless it's the fifteenth straight day of subzero temperatures with a 35 mile-per-hour wind out of the north."

"Oh." She giggled. "Now that's impossible to imagine living with."

"Well, it doesn't happen too often." They walked behind a barn through scrubby grass. To their left an endless cornfield disappeared on the horizon. "Speaking of your imagination," he said, "I think that's what must make it easy for you to see God. Your imagination and your keen awareness of nature."

"Could be. I never *didn't* believe in God's existence. Nature and life are just too complex to not be designed by a higher being. I remember feeling close to Him the day we watched the condor hatch. Here we all were, looking through the glass, holding our collective breath. I mean this magnificent bird is almost extinct, and we witnessed the first birth of one in captivity. It was incredible. Absolutely incredible. What?"

He was looking at her, an indecipherable expression on his face. He shook his head and turned away. "Nothing. That does sound incredible."

"It's true!"

"Gina, I didn't mean not credible. You must think of Valley Oaks as quite the backward place."

She bit her lip at the truth of his statement.

"It's an everyday occurrence for you. Maybe not the birth of a condor, but births of all kinds of exotic animals we've never even heard of here. Not to mention caring for wild animals like elephants, making it possible for thousands of visitors to enjoy such grand creatures. Sounds pretty special to me."

"Yeah, but I got fired."

He squeezed her shoulder. "You'll find another place. There's Ruby."

They stopped at a fence and watched the chestnut horse grazing nearby. Brady whistled and she cantered over to them.

"Feeling all right now?" Gina cooed. She stood on the fence and leaned over to pet her. "Oh, I like you much better this way."

There was a peace about the farm that Gina embraced, letting it soak through to the very marrow of her bones. She spent much of the afternoon with Brady as tour guide. They roamed around the silo and through barns, one of which contained a full-size basketball court. She climbed on tractors and a combine. He took her through the house, indicated family photos mounted on the walls, and talked of his great-grandparents, who had built the original portion.

She protested that he spent too much time with her, ignoring the other guests. He shrugged and murmured something about all of them knowing what a combine was. They lingered in the backyard at the picnic table full of desserts and munched on gooey chocolate brownies.

Lauren, all smiles after her reunion with Aaron, found them. "Gina, ready to leave?"

Before she could reply, her cousin's words tumbled over Brady's, both offering her options so that she could stay longer.

"Take my car," Lauren said. "The keys are in it. I'll go with Aaron."

"I'll take you home." Brady's words piggybacked hers.

"If you want." Lauren raised her brows.

"If you want." Brady smiled.

She didn't know if it was his smile or the soft earth-scented breeze that lifted his blond hair or the peaceful rhythms of the family gathering, but she chose to stay.

Brady took her to see the cattle. Straddling the three-wheeler behind him, she placed her hands on his shoulders. After ten minutes of racing down a grassy lane, he veered onto a field of scrubby weeds. Gina squealed as they thumped across the uneven landscape, never slowing. Her arms intuitively encircled his waist, the only solid hold available. When they flew up a slight rise and soared, she pressed her face between his shoulder blades and screamed.

The wild ride ended near a patch of willows. She climbed off and, in spite of her laughter, fussed at him for his maniacal driving habits, vowing to never again get in or on a vehicle with him. He laughed at her.

Their laughter grew louder as they mimicked the lugubrious expressions of nearby cows and tried to out-stare them. After a time they gave up and sat on the ground, each chewing a long blade of grass, and discussed the raising of cattle.

Gina sensed lengthening shadows and glanced at her watch. She jumped up. "Oh, no! I'm going to be late. Aunt Lottie is having everyone over tonight, and I promised to help."

Brady winked as he stood. "Guess we better hurry back as quick as we can on the three-wheeler."

She frowned at him, but he knew she was only teasing. The thought of ending the afternoon with her arms wrapped around Brady Olafsson felt...well, reassuring. As if everything was right with the world.

Brady parked near the car and cut the engine.

"Thank you, Brady." Gina braced her hands against his shoulders and swung her leg over the three-wheeler. "It was such a relaxing afternoon."

"I'm glad you came." He tried not to notice how pretty she looked with flushed cheeks and wind-blown hair. He tried to act reasonably average rather than expressive and risk revealing his infatuation with her.

She smiled and opened the car door. "We are making progress, Mr. Olafsson."

"Progress?"

"In our relationship. I mean, could you have imagined two weeks ago inviting me to your parents' farm and, on top of that, me accepting?"

He shook his head. "Was I really that obnoxious?"

"We both were."

"You weren't."

She raised an eyebrow.

"You were just preoccupied with your job."

"Lack of one," she corrected. "Still, that was no excuse to be rude and refer to Valley Oaks as Podunk."

He cringed. "I take it back. You were obnoxious."

"I've got to go." She slid into the car. "Please tell your parents thank you?"

"Sure. Are you comfortable with driving? It's not a freeway out there."

"I'll go slow, if that's what you mean." With a little wave, she closed the door.

He watched her drive off. He didn't know if that's what he meant or not. He didn't know exactly what he meant. He only knew that they were indeed making progress in their relationship.

For the duration, anyway.

There was no relationship outside of the duration. There was only a Lindstrom named Angelina Philips who lived in California.

Two strikes, he reminded himself.

He wanted to send her flowers...

Not to mention you've sworn off women...

No, not flowers. An exotic plant, maybe...

You know how your focus on work flies out the window...

Or an oak tree seedling...

Friends for the moment...You don't need another companion...

A frog. Maybe a special one...made of rubies and diamonds...

Least of all you don't need to lose control...

God has control. Not me! God...

He threw the vehicle into gear and roared off toward the barns.

Twenty-One

Maggie stepped through the back door into the kitchen just as the phone rang. She, Marsha, and Aunt Lottie were planting marigolds around the vegetables in hopes that the strong-scented flowers would discourage a seemingly bountiful supply of rabbits. It felt soothing to comb her fingers through rich, Midwestern soil again. Sweet memories of gardening with her grandmother hovered.

Wiping dirt from her hands with a paper towel, she went to the phone. "Hello?"

"Hi."

It was Reece. Her skin tingled. She hadn't worked through last night yet, the fact of him not being at the reunion. "Hi." She balled up the paper towel.

"I'm home for a couple of days. Got in late last night. I'm looking at all your potted plants on the patio. Is there anything you want me to do with them?"

She wiped her brow with the back of her hand. Ramon, the gardener who cared for their small plot of grass and did the heavy trimming, promised to water her flowers while she was gone. "Is the soil dry?" She heard the sliding door of her kitchen swoosh open.

"I'll check. We had Santa Anas recently."

She pictured Reece in chinos, polo shirt, loafers, striding across the flagstones, holding the cordless phone to his ear. The breeze would catch his silver hair at the crown, lightly fluffing it.

"Some of the leaves are a little droopy. Yep, the soil feels hard as bricks."

157

"Then water them."

"I didn't want to interfere with Ramon's job."

Maggie's neck and face were burning now. "He'll know if they've been watered or not. If they're dry, water them. It's not that complicated." She grabbed a dish towel and fanned herself. *Ask me about the reunion, Reece.*

"Ran into Bill and Jane at the store this morning. I told them there wasn't any cream for my coffee and only one egg was left, so they invited me over for dinner tonight."

She pulled at the collar and short sleeves of her sticking shirt. "Guess I haven't figured out yet how to keep the refrigerator stocked with perishables long distance." *The reunion, Reece.*

He laughed. "That's not like you. Well, we've decided the week's schedule. I'll be in Chicago Thursday and Friday. I thought you might rent a car and come up for dinner, but every waking hour is booked with partners and clients. I'll drive down Saturday and stay for a couple of days. I booked a seat for Gina to come back with me to L.A. on Mon—"

"*Now* you're coming?" Her voice rose. *A week after the reunion?*

"There's that easement problem just outside of Valley Oaks, of all places. I offered to look into it. I figured it was a good excuse to see you and Gina."

"You need an excuse?!"

"Are you feeling all right? You sound a little tired. Podunk getting you down?"

Maggie buried her face in the dish towel, soaking up hot tears. Reece had always avoided her discomfort, had always held Valley Oaks in disdain, had always seemed to take her for granted. Why was that? Because she allowed him?

"Margaret? Are you there?"

Well, it was getting tiresome. "No, I'm not all right, Reece. I wanted you here last night, for the reunion. Oh, the reunion? Thank you for asking. I had a wonderful time. I laughed and danced until 1:00 A.M." She paused for a breath and yanked her shirt out of the waistband of her shorts.

"The reunion! I forgot! I'm sorry."

"Sorry that I had a good time?"

"Of course not. I knew you'd enjoy yourself without me."

"That's not the point!"

"Margaret, are you sure you want to stay there the entire month? You're supposed to be relaxing, but you sound awfully upset."

"Reece, sometimes life is just plain upsetting. We'll see you on Saturday."

"O-okay," he said in a tone of "whatever you say." "Give my love to Gina."

She waited a moment, then said a perfunctory "Bye" and hung up.

And how about me? Who will give your love to me if you don't?

She stomped up the back stairway, peeling off her shirt. Her skin was boiling and damp to the touch.

She knew now that her sister was right. She admitted it. Right or wrong, she was angry. As a matter of fact, she was exceedingly angry with her husband.

With her daughter as companion, Maggie drove down back county roads chock full of memories.

"Why the sudden interest in genealogy, Mother?" Gina asked.

"I don't quite understand it myself. At your age, I wasn't the least bit interested. Thanks for agreeing to come, by the way."

"Sure. I figured we both needed a breather from the wedding planners. Whew! People are busier here than in Los Angeles."

Maggie smiled. "I know it seems that way, especially around Lauren and Marsha."

"I thought it was time we caught up with each other."

"I did too. Anyway, to get back to your question. It seems the older I grow and the further away I get from my roots, the more I feel a need to get back to them. Maybe because before I know it, I'll just be one of those roots, rotting under the ground."

"Mom!"

"I mean, I think I'll be with God, but what's the whole purpose of my life here and now? I wonder if there isn't some sort of direct, meaningful link between the past and the present. Between who my ancestors were and who I am today. If I get a handle on the past, maybe I'll better understand myself and where I'm going." She chuckled. "Goodness, that sounds like an elderly version of an adolescent's 'Who am I?', doesn't it?"

Gina laughed. "Yeah. But when you think about it, it makes a case for God. The fact that there's this pattern of families throughout the ages. In one sense it seems random, that because these parents happen to live here, these children were in a certain situation that caused them to meet and marry and have children. But in another sense, I think that all points to a Designer."

"I agree. That's the other thing. The older I get, the more I believe God is real and He's involved in the here and now. Otherwise, this world is just too crazy."

"Well, I've decided I believe in Jesus now, too."

"Really?" Maggie smiled at her daughter and reached over to squeeze her hand. "I think that's a significant development, sweetheart. I believe He's who He said He was."

"The way Brady explained it all, it makes sense."

"It does. When did this happen?"

"Saturday night at his place. I haven't had a chance to tell you much."

"He cooked dinner for just the two of you?"

"He's really a nice guy. I liked his parents, too. But Neil is nowhere near as good-looking as Dad is."

Maggie laughed. "You're right. But he was some basket-ball player. Tell me about Brady's place. You said it's beautiful."

"A hundred plus acres of beautiful. Except for an ease-ment problem, the place is absolutely perfect for a wildlife preserve. We roamed around it all afternoon."

Something tugged at Maggie's memory. "Aunt Marsha said it's the old Crowley place."

"Is that the original Valley Oaks homestead?"

"Yes. Years ago, when your grandmother was young, folks wanted to rebuild the house, make it a museum. I guess there wasn't enough interest."

"Brady said the town built up east of there, nearer the railroad tracks."

"Charles Crowley was an early leader, started a lot of things, but he farmed all of his land that wasn't wooded. He named the place Valley Oaks, but wasn't about to share his trees or his land. Where's Brady's house?"

"Do you know where the road starts, off of the highway? Then there's a ravine?"

Maggie nodded.

"After the road curves right around that, it curves a little to the left, then straightens for about a quarter of a mile. His Ponderosa house is at the end of that lane. Smack-dab in the middle of trees. It's about three-fourths of a mile east of the original house site."

"You're talking like a true country girl, Gina. What I remember of the Crowley place is it wasn't in the middle of the woods. It was— Oh my goodness. Did you say easement problem?"

"A bunch of land was just sold for development, and a small section of his road runs through it. The farmer he got permission from died last year, and his children sold the land. Sounds like a legal mess."

Maggie's stomach tightened. "Your father's coming to town because of an easement problem."

"His company bought that land?"

"I imagine so. There probably aren't too many other areas just outside of Valley Oaks that are headed toward development and have an easement problem."

They were silent for a moment. Then Gina said, "Kind of weird that Dad will be tangling with the Olafssons, huh?"

"He's been tangling with them for years. Now he gets to do it in person."

"What do you mean for years?"

Maggie slowed the car as they entered the county seat town, 20 miles from Valley Oaks. "Well, I was an emotional basket case when I met your father." She smiled softly. "He tended to blame the Olafssons. That's why he usually didn't come with us when you and I visited here. Whenever I was too strict with you as a teenager, guess who he blamed? When I avoided church involvement, he knew it was because Neil's mother pushed religion on me."

"Whew. I thought Brady's chip was bad."

"Mm-hmm."

"Maybe Dad has mellowed by now." Gina's tone was hopeful.

"Maybe," she replied, though seriously doubting it was possible. Perhaps she should suggest he put aside personal— With a start she realized it wasn't her problem.

"Wow," Gina interrupted her thoughts. "Is that the courthouse? It's beautiful."

She drove toward the three-story stone building that filled almost an entire square block. "They knew how to build courthouses." She parked alongside the curb. "Let's go meet our ancestors."

⌒

Maggie was pleasantly surprised that Gina's enthusiasm matched her own. After spending hours pouring over faded handwritten ledgers of county marriages, births, and deaths, they returned home with a stack of copies of licenses and certificates.

They sat at the dining room table, munching tuna sandwiches and fruit salad, sharing their finds with Aunt Lottie. Maggie smiled to herself when she noticed her daughter bite into the white bread without even a hint of a grimace.

"Aunt Lottie, look at this one," Gina exclaimed.

Tears filled the older woman's eyes. "My parents' marriage certificate."

"My great-grandparents! Johanna and Andrew Anderson. And look at the back here. It says this is where they were born. In Sweden! I've got to look at an atlas. And those are their parents' names and even their mothers' maiden names. Just imagine, they had to come all this way on a boat and maybe wagons. What if they hadn't come? You wouldn't be here and I wouldn't be here. Everything is a result of someone else's decisions before us. Isn't that awesome?"

Aunt Lottie giggled like a little girl. "Awesome. Just like God."

"Yeah! It's like He had His finger on all of us, down through the generations."

"Psalm 139. He knew us in our mother's womb."

Gina's nonstop chatter stopped. "He would, wouldn't He? That's in the Bible?"

Aunt Lottie nodded and closed her eyes. "Thou didst weave me in my mother's womb." She paused. "Thine eyes have seen my unformed substance; and in Thy book they were all written, the days that were ordained for me, when as yet there was not one of them."

A sense of stillness enveloped Maggie, as if a large, invisible cocoon wrapped itself round her, blocking out the world with all of its noise, its pulsating energies. The room faded from view and for one brief moment she knew she was not—would not ever be—alone.

"Wow," Gina breathed softly. "That is so beautiful."

Aunt Lottie nodded. "God's Word is beautiful and powerful."

"I don't remember hearing about my great-grandparents. Tell me what they were like?"

Aunt Lottie told them stories about their hard-working ancestors who farmed in the area at the turn of the century. She was up to the time of the Depression and how they lost their land when Gina had to leave.

"I want to hear more later, Aunt Lottie," she said. "I promised Lauren I'd help her clean their new house. Do you believe they just got possession today and want to paint and recarpet the whole place in two weeks?" She stepped around the table and kissed both of them goodbye. "Thanks, Mom. I love all this newfound family."

"You're welcome. We'll come by in a bit with Aunt Marsha. Now don't overdo it."

Gina fluttered her eyelids. "Oh, Mother."

She grinned. "Hazards of the trade. Goodbye," she called to her daughter's retreating back.

"Maggie," Aunt Lottie said, "Reece called this morning. He wanted you to call him. Something about changing his schedule in Chicago so you could come."

The cocoon slithered down, wrinkling in a pile at her feet. "Oh." She started to gather the dishes.

"It must be hard having him work out of town so much of the time."

"It is."

"It's not like the old days."

Maggie carried a load to the kitchen, then returned to finish clearing the table.

"Seems like today," Aunt Lottie continued, "everyone just has too many choices. When Peter made me mad, I knew come nighttime, I'd have to climb into bed next to him. And vice versa. We didn't have anywhere else to go."

"Uncle Peter made you mad? He was the kindest man I ever knew."

"He was very kind." Aunt Lottie chuckled. "Oh, honey, he was a man. Never hung up a towel in his life. Forgot my birthday now and then. Only remembered one anniversary, our fiftieth, and that was because everyone kept talking about it. Smoked too many cigars." She sighed. "We had our ups and downs, some more serious than others. But every morning and night he hugged me."

Maggie's throat tightened.

"Now I don't want you to feel funny about pushing those two twin beds together when Reece comes. A married couple needs to be close when they get the chance."

"Aunt Lottie!"

"I'll just call Alec and have him come over—"

"I will not have my cousin rearranging my bedroom."

"Well, call him anyway." She stood slowly, her gnarled hands pushing against the tabletop. "I mean Reece. He said he would be in the office all day."

"I really don't have time to drive to Chicago. Lauren's band concert is Thursday night. I promised I'd go. Friday we simply must finalize things with the caterers." Her stomach muscles tightened. "Besides, he'd be preoccupied with business. He'll be here on Saturday." Soon enough.

Aunt Lottie shuffled toward the doorway.

Maggie thought she looked pale. "Do you feel okay?"

"Just tired, honey. I'll lie down until Marsha comes. Say a little prayer for you and Reece."

Maggie bit her lip. She doubted that a little prayer would make up for all those years' worth of missed hugs. It wouldn't even change her mind about not calling him.

Twenty-Two

When the call came from the zoo, Gina struggled to slip into her professional demeanor. So much had happened in recent months to obliterate it.

She at least managed to relay that she was available to come to Seattle for an interview late next week. Almost numb from an onslaught of conflicting emotions, she didn't know how she felt. After hanging up, she went out to the backyard and sat in the old Adirondack chair. The shady spot kept the hot 86 degrees from being unbearable.

First of all, she needed a job as soon as possible. But did she want to be a veterinarian in a zoo setting again? *That's what I'm trained for, what I'm experienced in, it's my lifelong dream...but can I do it?*

Despite the summer heat, a chill went through her.

She could work with other animals. Smaller, domestic types. She could go back home, scour the huge Los Angeles area for a vet office that needed an assistant, learn as she went.

She could go back to school, become a teacher of veterinary medicine. Somehow. Somewhere.

This was avoiding the subject.

What did she think about the job interview? What would they think of her? On the application she had explained the trainer's lack of control, the accident, and subsequent dismissal. She had been honest.

Well, for the most part anyway. She hadn't gone into detail about her complaints. Her ineptness when she returned to work. Her lawsuit.

But surely her complaints were valid. Surely she had the animals' best interests at heart. Surely she would have regained skill and confidence given time. And the lawsuit? Simply a formality. A necessary complication. A legal way to shake up the administration and protect the animals.

Oh, she was still thinking in circles. She needed to talk out loud and get another opinion. Mother was gone, but she was too close to the situation anyway. Lauren was just too plain giddy. Friends back home had drifted away, especially those from work.

She leaned back in the chair and closed her eyes, telling herself to calm down. The heat enveloped her, and she thought of how different the air was here. Unpolluted, and yet so thick it seemed tangible, as if you could grab a fistful of it.

In the stillness she heard that one bird's odd song...like a squeaky swing, back and forth, back and forth.

Brady.

She opened her eyes.

Brady?

It made perfect sense to talk to Brady.

And that was exactly why she wasn't going to call him. It shouldn't make perfect sense that a new acquaintance was the person closest to her heart.

She shouldn't be noticing how good-looking he was, how soothing his voice was, how comfortable it was to bury her face in his shoulder. She shouldn't be wanting to roam through his beautiful acreage or putter around his rustic kitchen.

Oh, for goodness sake, she shouldn't be missing the man after three days.

Maybe it was his books. She had finished the first one and started another that he had given her. His portrayal of Jesus taught her why He was God, and it warmed her heart. There were practical lessons in seeing life from God's point of view, but this warming trend that flowed toward Brady made no sense whatsoever. But he had been the one to help her understand what a relationship with God meant. Of course she would be grateful to him for that.

It just didn't help that he was so...her type.

She sighed.

What would he say? He would say pray about it.

"Dear Father, please help me sort this out. About the job, I mean." She paused in her murmured prayer. "Okay, about Brady, too. Friendship is one thing, but I suppose You know what I'm feeling." She winced. "Attracted. And I'm sure You know perfectly well I am not interested in that sort of relationship right now, especially not in Valley Oaks! Amen."

Aunt Lottie poked her head out the back door. "Are you all right, honey?"

Gina nodded. She loved how she called her honey. You just knew the woman would do anything for you. Like listen.

In the dining room, Gina rejoined Aunt Lottie at the round oak table where they had been crocheting when the telephone had rung. That is, Aunt Lottie had been crocheting, often stopping to guide Gina's fingers in the intricate pattern of the piece that covered the table.

The women had spent many hours in recent days doing this. It was a pleasant diversion that made Gina feel as if a corner of the early 1900s still existed. In that corner loud music had been replaced with the rhythmic ticking of a cuckoo clock. Instead of frantically searching for a job, she was getting to know her great-aunt. Rather than mall shopping for a wedding gift, she was creating a unique one.

She flexed her fingers. Well, if not wedding gift, perhaps first anniversary. "I wish I would have known how to do this a few months ago while I was in the hospital."

"I'm just so sorry about that, honey, and about your job."

"I know. That phone call was for an interview. In Seattle. And I'm not sure what I think about it. Since I've been talking to God more—"

"And knowing He's listening."

"Yes. I'm wondering how I'm supposed to pray about this?"

"I don't think there's a right and wrong way to pray. Prayer is just talking to God. Tell Him what you need. He knows it anyway, but He wants you to ask. Otherwise, when the need is filled, you might forget He did it."

"But how do I know whether or not this is the right job?"

"Did they offer it to you?" Her blue eyes sparkled in her round face.

"Well, no. I have to go for the interview next week in Seattle."

"Then there's nothing to worry about."

"But I don't know if I want this job."

Aunt Lottie smiled. "Of course not. You haven't been there yet. This reminds me of the car story. You can sit in a car and turn the steering wheel all you want, but it's not going to go anywhere until you turn on the engine and step on the gas pedal. Life is like the car and you're the driver, but God does the steering. And He can't steer unless you get moving."

"So I should just go for the interview and see what happens?"

She nodded, her fluffy white curls catching the sunlight shining through the window. "Step on that gas pedal and don't worry about any of it. Just do whatever He puts before you. Right now you're healing, I think."

Tears sprang to Gina's eyes. "Mm-hmm."

"And all you really had to do was get ready for a wedding and spend some time with an old lady. Now you have the possibility of getting a job. So it would seem this is something good from God to investigate."

"I guess it's one of those windows you mentioned before?"

"See? He opened it right up. But you have to promise me something."

"What?"

"Don't be gone too long. I'm getting used to having you here."

Gina hugged her great-aunt, thinking how she was getting used to being here.

Twenty-Three

Thursday night most of Valley Oaks turned out for the weekly summer band concert and monthly ice cream social in the town square. The three women took Aunt Lottie's car because the three blocks was farther than the 90-year-old cared to walk.

Gina scanned the area that was quickly becoming packed with people. She wondered if Lauren was there yet, but in reality she knew she wasn't looking for her cousin. She wanted to see a blond man, taller than the rest of the crowd and wearing a white T-shirt and jeans.

Her heart sank. Maybe he didn't come to these things.

In the shelter, a group of men churned ice cream makers. Women arranged cakes and pies on the tables. Children played on nearby playground equipment. Park benches were arranged in rows in front of the band shell. As the local band teacher, Lauren would conduct the group of musicians, a mixture of teenagers and adults.

While Aunt Lottie and Mother settled in at a picnic table, Gina stood in line to buy desserts. She peered over her shoulder, hoping and yet willing herself to stop such nonsense. A casual friendship did not warrant this eagerness, this grin that threatened to erupt if she caught sight of Brady.

Balancing three plastic bowls of soft vanilla ice cream and chocolate cake, spoons, and napkins in her hands, Gina spotted him near the end of a line and veered that direction. His back was to her, and he was talking with some people who didn't look familiar.

"Brady!" she interrupted, the unbidden grin spreading across her face.

He turned only half way around from his group to greet her. "Oh, hi." He eyed the bowls. "Hope you left some ice cream for the rest of us."

"There's plenty. Would you believe I've never eaten homemade ice cream in my life?"

"That's what growing up in California can do for you." He glanced at his group that scooted forward in the line a few inches.

"Brady, guess what!"

"Mm." He shrugged and shook his head. "What?"

"The zoo in Seattle called me yesterday! And now I'm trying to figure out how to fit God into this decision-making equation. I need to talk to you."

"Uh, yeah, sure. Your ice cream's melting. Maybe sometime later?"

She heard the hesitation in his voice, noted the sporadic eye contact. Enthusiasm fizzling, she consciously kept her smile in place and backed away. "Yeah, okay. Later."

Gina hurried through the crowd toward Mother and Aunt Lottie, pondering the obvious change in Brady's demeanor. He wasn't the least bit friendly. She decided he must be preoccupied with something.

As the evening progressed, she found herself preoccupied...with Brady. While eating and visiting with Aunt Lottie's friends and moving to the benches in front of the band shell, she kept one eye on him. From a distance with other people he appeared his usual self, smiling and laughing with others, tilting his head in that way of his to catch some shorter person's words.

She tried to shake it, but couldn't. Was he ignoring her? Maybe her mother intimidated him. Maybe he didn't want to meet her. Gina had certainly had difficulty meeting his parents. It seemed even more likely that he would avoid hers. And yet...that didn't sound like the Brady she knew.

Knew? She didn't know him. This emotional tie between them was her imagination, sprung from a couple of special moments. A couple of special moments did not make a friendship you could count on. Was she still that naïve to trust, of all men, a virtual stranger?

And besides, he had a life and friends before she came to town. Of course he would be active with them in this type of setting. He wasn't required to introduce her.

Why didn't he at least stop by to say hello to Aunt Lottie?

Gina pushed aside thoughts of Brady and gave her attention to Lauren up front welcoming everyone. How her flighty cousin could focus on conducting musicians would have been a puzzle if she didn't know the perfectionist side of her. Now she turned her back on the audience, and Gina noticed her rigid spine and the blonde curls brushed just so. She held the small baton aloft, and the crowd and band alike stilled for one long moment. As the first notes of a Sousa march blared forth, Gina felt a sense of pride flow through her. This was her cousin at work, and it was a beautiful sight.

At intermission, Maggie said Aunt Lottie was ready to go home and she would take her. Wanting to hear the entire concert, Gina said it would be an easy walk for her and told them goodbye. As she watched them stroll slowly along the tree-lined sidewalk in the twilight, it crossed her mind that Brady could come over now if he had a mind to.

She noticed him on the other side of the benches, standing and talking. *Oh, well.*

Waiting for the concert to resume, she looked for the first twinkling of evening stars and listened to the strangers all around her chatting. The band shell glowed under its arch of bright lights, creating an unrealistic aura and adding to Gina's feeling of not belonging.

Which was fine with her, of course. Actually she didn't belong anywhere these days, and so it should come as no surprise that of the two people she knew in this place, one was in the program and the other was...preoccupied. Or choosing to ignore her. Where were all her other cousins and the wedding party members she had met?

Oh, it didn't matter. It was just Valley Oaks, a temporary stop on the way to a new life. Her future plans had begun to take shape yesterday with the scheduling of an interview. Aunt Lottie's advice made sense. She would just get the car going, so to speak, and let God do the steering. She didn't need Brady Olafsson's opinion. Nor his company, for goodness sake.

Gina's temper seldom flared. It usually did a slow burn, giving her time to notice the danger signals and figure out what was going on and plan logically what course of action to take. Now she couldn't hear the music. The luscious ice cream and cake had rolled into an uncomfortable lump. Her neck felt hot. Typical signals.

What was it? Brady did not owe her friendliness. Good grief, a couple of weeks ago his sappy friendliness offended her.

No, it wasn't Brady. It was Gina herself. It was her reaction to this man. What was she doing, feeling hope and expectation in regards to him? And of all things, *trusting* him?

She was just vulnerable, which was perfectly understandable considering the eight months she'd just been through. She'd get a new life, far from Podunk—

"They're playing your song." Brady's mouth was at her ear.

Gina jumped in her seat.

"Let's dance." He pulled her to her feet and off to a nearby grassy area where a few couples swayed to the slow music. Before she could protest, his right arm was around her waist, his left hand holding her right. His face was in shadow. "Recognize it?" he asked softly.

Gina stumbled and gritted her teeth, stopping the curse before it crossed her tongue. Stupid leg.

He deftly maneuvered them into another position, tightening his grasp of her waist, enabling her to regain her balance. "Sorry. Too fast." He was charming her again, taking the attention from her injury. He began singing. "Where does your journey lead from here? Down roads unseen, midst stars flung wide?" He hummed a few bars. "I forget the rest. Do you know it?"

She shook her head, so close to his shoulder. He surrounded her, holding at bay the confusion that threatened to overwhelm her.

"Hmm, nice rendition with the trumpets. It's your song." He hummed again. "You know, because you're trying to figure out what to do next." He began to sing, "Where does your journey lead from here? Da-dum-dee-dum-dee-dum-dum..."

Why couldn't she respond lightheartedly? Dance with him, joke with him, chat with him? Why this tightness in her chest, this dizziness at his peppermint-scented breath on her cheek?

"So you got a phone call?" he prompted.

It was a little late to pick up that conversation. She didn't have time for this crazy mixture of comfort and anger. He didn't owe her anything, and she certainly didn't owe him anything. She stopped in her tracks and pulled his hand from her waist. "It's past my bedtime." With that she turned and strode down the darkened sidewalk in the direction of Aunt Lottie's street.

Exits were simple in Podunk. No crowds to push through, no handbag to go fetch, no traffic to struggle against heading toward the freeway. It was going to be easy to leave the place.

"Where does your journey lead from here? I have but one request of you dear: that, your hand in mine, I'll walk alongside 'til life's journey is complete."

Brady hadn't forgotten the words. He just refused to say them out loud. Even now as he watched her go, he struggled against them as they reverberated in his mind.

More devastating was that uneven gait of hers that tugged at his heart.

Lord, this can't be from You. I don't want this! I am doing just fine. We are doing just fine, You and me. Working, minding my own business, helping out in the community, singing at church.

What is this?! It was a cry that pounded in his throat.

She was at the corner of the park now, under the street lamp, stepping down from the curb.

He had avoided her, hung close to others, but still she came to him, that smile lighting up her face, excited about news, wanting to tell him, eager to know where God fit in.

And he had snubbed her.

I have neither the time nor the energy for this! He continued the argument with himself and with his God.

He had watched her before the concert. He should have gone over to meet her mother. A rational, polite human being would have done that. He even chose to ignore Lottie, a dear old friend.

When they left, Gina sat alone, her face a mask. And then that song had started. The old tune caught his attention. *Where does your journey lead from here, Angelina Philips?*

He owed her that much, to ask her what her news was, to listen to her plans, to pray for her. Guilt flooded him for snubbing her tonight, for not calling her all week. Before he could talk himself out of it, he slipped to her side, pulled her from the bench.

"Down roads unseen, midst stars flung wide?"

The damage had been done. She was stiff in his arms, her voice cold.

Now, down the street, she disappeared from view, swallowed in the darkness.

"I have but one request of you, dear."

No, I have several. He hurled his staccato thoughts against the music. *That you go back to California immediately. That you never again turn your beautiful smile in my direction. That you ask someone else about your newfound faith. That you take your endearing mixture of vulnerability and independence and just let me be!*

Would he always regret not going after her?

"Counting each moment with you as eternity held fast."

God, I don't want this!

It was as if God pummeled a chisel into that one corner of his heart, that part that had turned to stone over the years. In one final blow He snapped it off now, leaving a gaping wound.

A searing pain ripped through Brady's chest. Love shouldn't hurt like this, but he knew that's what it was. His heart relentlessly pumped it through the wound, and he knew there was only one relief. He had to give it away.

He ran.

She could not have walked the entire distance yet. Could she have? He had to reach her before she went into the house.

He flew along the park's sidewalk, over the curb and across the quiet street, between parked cars and down another sidewalk. *End of the block, end of the block, end of the block.* His feet pounded out his only thought.

He swerved at the block's last front yard, ran through the grass and jumped a hedge, narrowly missing a tricycle. He was on Lottie's street.

Where was she? *Where was she?!*

There! Just beyond the street light.

"Gina!" he shouted as he raced toward her. "Gina!" Three more houses.

She turned and spotted him, but didn't stop until at last he reached her side, breathless. They were almost to Lottie's front yard.

"Gina." He stared at her face, unreadable in the shadows. She gave her head a slight shake.

What could he say? He gulped a deep breath, then crooked his elbow toward her.

"I've told you," she clipped her words, "that I don't need an escort."

"But I do," he whispered the plea. "I do, Angelina."

She just stood there.

He waited, his arm still bent in hope. He had no choice. There was nothing else to say, nothing else to do. Would she let him love her? The moments ticked by. Only his labored breathing broke the silence. His arm tired.

Slowly she took half a step toward him, then seemed to hesitate, her head bowed.

Brady closed his eyes, blocking her hair from view, lest he reach out to touch it. At last he felt her hand, strong, soft against his elbow...cool fingers slipping along the inside of his forearm.

Gratitude flooded through him. He covered her hand with his, bent forward and rested his cheek atop her head. "I'm sorry," he murmured into her soft hair.

She gave an imperceptible nod, not enough to break their contact, but enough to say she understood.

It was a long, perfect moment, eyes closed against the precipice that he knew lay before them. Whatever happened, his life would never be the same again.

"Your hand in mine, I'll walk alongside 'til life's journey is complete..."

He inhaled deeply the scent of her hair. When he held her in the cornfield, he had fought to ignore it. Now he drank it in, a garden of sweet summer flowers flooding his senses. His throat ached at the nearness of her, and his heart hammered. He swallowed and heard her shallow breaths.

He let go of her hand and traced his finger along her chin. As he cupped her cheek and tilted her face, his only regret was that he could not clearly see the spring green eyes...nor those exquisite lips. But he knew she was looking at him and that the Miss America smile was hiding, waiting...

He lowered his mouth to hers and thought for certain he felt the earth move.

They sat on the old wooden swing that hung on Aunt Lottie's front porch. The only lights came from the row of citronella candles placed on the railings alongside and behind them, a few stars twinkling between treetops, and the street lamp half a block away. Like most of the other houses, the windows were dark. It was well past midnight.

Gina sat in one corner with her bare feet curled beneath her, facing Brady, who sat in the other corner. He sprawled with an arm flung across the back of the swing and his long legs stretched to the wooden slats of the floor, gently pushing the swing back and forth.

Earlier, out on the sidewalk when their kiss ended, she had at last found her voice and wondered aloud if maybe they should talk. Arm in arm, they walked to the porch. She had stuck her head inside to dim the lights and call out to her mother that she was going to sit outside for a while. Her hands trembled when she lit the candles, but that was no surprise. Her entire body still trembled from Brady's touch.

They had sat in silence for a while, unsure where to begin. Finally she asked, "Now what?"

Brady's low voice was huskier than usual. "I don't have a clue."

Gina didn't have a clue as to how they had come to this, let alone what it meant. She had just reached the point of admitting to herself that her feelings for this man were developing beyond the point of reasonableness. He was unlike any she had ever met. Physically, of course, he was the type that attracted her: tall and slim. Beyond that, though, he was so totally different in his demeanor with his goofy jokes and his kindness. And then there was his log cabin of a house and his woods and his writing profession and his spiritual depth.

She never gave it a thought that he felt anything toward her. His odd behavior at the band concert indicated he did, after all, consider her immaterial to his life and she better just nip in the bud any sort of trust or warm feelings she felt.

And then out of the blue he chased after her, said he needed her, and then kissed her. Her response almost scared her to death, but there was no getting around it. No one had ever kissed her like that before.

"You don't have a clue?" she had repeated his words.

He shook his head.

It was all so illogical. She had no response except a tickle in her throat that soon turned into uncontrollable giggles. Brady's deep laughter joined in. Soon the swing was wobbling as their bodies shook with laughter. The matter was settled. They had nothing to talk about along those lines, but spent the next few hours learning a myriad of details about each other.

At the moment they were discussing favorite childhood books. Brady wasn't hungry, but Gina was just finishing off a can of honey-roasted peanuts, a follow-up to a bag of pop-corn.

"You certainly eat a lot, Dr. Philips."

"Only at certain seasons."

"Like fall or winter?"

"Um, not exactly." She grinned, unable to contain how delicious it felt to be so comfortable with someone. "More like, um, when someone has captured my attention in," she shrugged, "a special way."

"Oh, Gina." He ran a hand across his somber face and took a deep breath. "Where have you been all my life?"

"California."

"No. Now that I think about it, you've been here all the time. Since I was 19, anyway."

"Nineteen? What are you talking about?"

"I remember you visiting the summer I was 19. You must have been almost 15."

"Did we meet?"

"Not exactly, but I knew who you were."

"That Lindstrom girl."

"Mm-hmm. I watched you hanging out with Lauren and Liz. You looked like such a snob."

"What'd I do?"

"Nothing in particular. You were just too cute to be for real. Between that and your heritage, I concluded you were a snob."

"You thought I was cute?"

He chuckled. "Cute as a bug's ear with a Miss America smile."

Her skin tingled. "Hmm, I see. And being cute made me a snob?"

"Well, all three of you were snobs. After all, you were Lindstroms."

"I never stood a chance."

"Not really. Anyway, that was probably the beginning of this love-hate feeling for you."

"What does that mean?"

He reached over and tucked a strand of hair behind her ear. His eyelids were half closed. "I heard your real name was Angelina. It didn't fit the family reputation. How could a Lindstrom be an angel? But...you looked like an angel. Bright and flawless. Thus, the love-hate feeling." He paused. "And now since the hate is gone—" He stopped.

Only love remains, she silently completed the thought and swallowed the lump in her throat. "Those are strong terms, love and hate."

"Perhaps."

"We hardly know each other."

"Mmm. How about intense dislike and intense infatuation?"

"I don't know if I can put it into words."

"We don't have to."

"It's been a rough year. My life is a tangle of loose ends."

"I know."

"Good grief," her voice rose, "I'm leaving in two and a half weeks!"

He took her hand and squeezed gently. "Shh. I know."

"Oh," she groaned, "this was definitely not in my Day-Timer."

"I find life is much more interesting without those things. God fills in more of the blanks that way."

"Brady, that is such a foreign thought to me, it's incomprehensible."

"You'll learn." He stroked her hand with his thumb.

She rested her head against the back of the swing, watching his face in the flickering candlelight. They sat that way for a long while, holding hands, at times conversing quietly, at times dozing. Reluctant to let the moment of this awakening end.

Twenty-Four

It had been such an ugly time. There was no reason on earth to ponder it 35 years later, but Maggie couldn't shake the memories. They had slithered in before dawn and now clung to her, as thick and heavy as the muggy air that filled the upstairs bedroom. Weighted down by them, she lay in bed long past her usual rising time, literally unable to begin a new day.

The face and voice of Neil's mother remained startlingly clear after the dream. Maggie recalled her uncharitable, teenage comparison. Dottie Olafsson always reminded her of a bulldog with her square face, jutting jaw, forehead etched into a permanent frown. The harsh, unyielding personality didn't stray far from the image.

Maggie flushed now as she replayed sniggering conversations with the other cheerleaders as they spied her boyfriend's mother sitting primly in the bleachers. They had been shameless. On the other hand, the woman seldom smiled and never cheered for her son. To Maggie's motherly heart that seemed the greater sin.

Neil, the youngest child and only son, obviously took after his father in every way. Their life was farming and basketball, their needs few, their personalities undemanding, their faith practical. When Maggie met Neil Sr., he welcomed her as easily as turning a page in a book, as if she were quite simply what came next in his son's life.

Dottie felt threatened, forcing Neil to choose. His fierce, adolescent loyalty to Maggie pitted him at odds against his mother, even more so than did his sports, which she viewed as straight from the devil. Years later Maggie realized that it was another hint suggesting she and Neil would never make it. Were his actions more in defiance of his mother than those of true love?

The two of them had been too young to know true love. They had tried, at least, to take responsibility for their actions and married, determined to make a go of it. Maggie had attempted building a relationship with her mother-in-law. She called her, kept her updated on the doctor's reports. When Neil came home for Christmas break early in December, she joined the Olafsson household until Rosie was born on the twenty-seventh.

Her own parents had been greatly disappointed in her foolish choices. They didn't hide that, but neither did they hide their love and support. Aunt Lottie had been a tremendous comfort in those days as well. Still, it was Dottie's negativism that coated the memory. Every chance she had, in subtle and not-so-subtle ways, she condemned Maggie. During the short while they lived under the same roof, the tension became unbearable. Maggie was not faultless in the situation. At 18, she didn't possess an ounce of graciousness, nor did she know the power of holding her tongue. Sometimes Neil sided with his mother. In the end, the woman wore her down.

An ache now clutched in her midsection, twisting quickly upward, squeezing her chest, clamoring into her throat. Maggie buried her face in a pillow, catching the sob just as it burst forth.

Rosie was born too soon.

Grief pummeled Maggie like ocean waves. It felt as raw as if it had all happened last week. Tears soaked her pillow. The grief only intensified.

"It's your fault! She died because you're guilty. It's all your fault..." Dottie's accusations filled her head.

"Dear God."

Slowly the prayer formed. Little by little it absorbed the other voice.

"Dear God, I'm sorry. I'm sorry. I'm sorry. If Dottie—"

Don't blame her.

The tears stopped.

I don't blame you. Don't blame her.

It wasn't an audible voice, just new thoughts. Incredibly new. "What can I do to make up for it all? So that You'll forgive me?"

Jesus already did it. All you have to do is ask.

Yes, it was what Marsha kept telling her. So simple... "Please forgive me."

You're forgiven. Now forgive her.

Maggie wiped tears from her face. "What?"

Forgive her.

She froze. The impression of those two words gripped her. Her sister's gentle voice came to mind. What had she said? Forgiving simply meant letting it go. Don't demand payment from the one who wronged you.

"I can't."

I'll help.

It will free you.

Dottie was wrong, but then so were you.

Maggie sat up and shook her head. This was too, too extreme.

Too extreme.

But...this was, after all, a season of extremes. *And I am so very, very tired of clinging to this. It's so foolish. She's dead.*

"I forgive her. Oh, Lord, help me."

She took a deep breath. Then another. The morning air promised rain. Good. It would wash away the heat, clean the dry, dusty landscape, add a fresh sparkle to the air.

Maggie smiled to herself. That was kind of the way she felt.

"Gina, what's with you?" Lauren eyed her cousin over a forkful of garlic chicken and rice.

"What?" Gina raised her brows and bit into a steaming slice of garden pizza.

They sat in the food court at the mall, taking a lunch break from shopping. Their mothers stood in line at one of the other restaurant counters, waiting for their orders.

"What do you mean, what? You haven't stopped grinning all morning, and your eyes look like a raccoon's, like you didn't sleep last night. Something's up."

What could she say? That she and Brady were now on kissing terms? They hadn't seemed to define any terms other than that. "Well, Brady and I talked a long time last night after the concert, on the front porch." She grinned. She couldn't help it.

"How long?"

She shrugged. "Two."

"Two hours?"

"Uh, 2:00 A.M. Actually, 2:45 A.M."

Lauren's eyebrows shot up. "A quarter to three?"

She nodded.

"And?"

She tilted her head. "And...and we're having dinner tonight."

"Okay. That's nice."

"Mm-hmm. Dinner." In an effort to contain another grin, she shoved more pizza into her mouth.

Lauren's brown eyes narrowed as she studied her. "Did you sit together on the swing or did one of you sit in the chair?"

"Swing. Together." She took another bite.

"Ha! You are avoiding this subject. Obvious giveaway, cousin." She leaned across the table and enunciated each word. "Do you like him?"

"Sure. He's a nice guy."

Lauren burst out laughing. "It's written all over your face!"

The other women set their trays on the table and slid onto the two empty chairs. Maggie asked, "What's written all over her face?"

"She has a crush on Brady."

Crush? Gina took another bite of pizza and thought about it. That was probably an appropriate enough description.

"Brady Olafsson?" Maggie's face looked stricken.

Aunt Marsha laughed. "Yes, ma'am. There is no other Brady in Valley Oaks. Gina, all I can say is, welcome to the club."

"Olafsson?" her mother repeated. She still hadn't picked up her fork.

"What do you mean, Aunt Marsha? What club?" Gina asked.

"The Brady crush club. One out of every two females in Jacob County feels that way. He is the best-looking, friendliest, most eligible bachelor around."

"Does he know this?"

Aunt Marsha laughed again. "He always has some female hanging on his arm. I would suspect he is aware of it."

This was a new twist. An unreasonable stab of jealousy poked her. "Does he date any of them?"

Lauren giggled. "Not the married ones, but he often has a companion with him at different functions. I thought he was with somebody last night, but evidently not, since he spent half the night with you."

Maggie's styrofoam cup slipped from her hand and coffee sloshed over its sides. "Half the night?"

Gina sopped the liquid with her napkin. "We talked on the porch, Mother. So," she turned back to Lauren, "he's not serious about anyone?"

She shook her head. "Not since Nicole left him. That woman really did a number on him. She had a gorgeous diamond, and they looked so happy together. Then she started traveling with her job, and one day she called him from California and said she wasn't coming back. Aaron said he was pretty shook up over the whole thing. He swore off serious relationships with women. That was four years ago."

"Gina."

She looked at her mother.

"How serious are you?"

"Mom, I just met the guy two weeks ago, and I didn't like the first thing about him then. And now…" She raised a shoulder. "He's just a friend."

"And you're eating like a horse." Maggie raised an eyebrow. "I think I'd better meet him."

Twenty-Five

Gina felt like a teenager. Evening plans, which included Brady picking her up and meeting her mother, reeked of official first date material. She rolled her head, relaxed her shoulders, and took a deep breath.

She had spent a long time at the mirror and in the closet. She wasn't ready when she heard his knock downstairs. Maybe she was avoiding her initial reaction to him? Evidently from Lauren and Aunt Marsha's discussion, she was the latest in a long line of females who eagerly held his proffered arm. Of course he would attract many. No reason for her to get too starry-eyed. And besides, she was leaving in two weeks.

Careful not to muss her French twist, she slipped on a short-sleeved black knit dress. It was midcalf length and dressy without being too fancy. She added pearls and heels and took a deep breath, fighting down the anticipation.

Dear God, thank You for Brady's friendship. Please don't let me...don't let us make a mistake.

"Amen," she said to the mirror. "Just stay cool and aloof." She smiled. "A little."

At the top of the staircase she heard her mother say, "You look exactly like your father."

"That's what I said, didn't I?" Aunt Lottie added.

"I hear that often." There was a grin in his voice.

As she descended, all three looked up. Her eyes locked with Brady's, and she knew cool and aloof were out of the

190

question. They didn't stand a chance under his intensely approving gaze.

"I-I'm sorry I wasn't ready on time."

"No problem."

"Tell us where you're taking her." Aunt Lottie prompted with a smile.

"The Landing."

Gina noticed his black slacks and the soft, short-sleeved pale blue shirt that set off his tanned arms and face. His blond hair glistened. He towered over Mother and Aunt Lottie.

"Where is that?" Maggie asked.

"Up the river, about ten miles north of Rockville."

All four moved toward the door, Brady and Maggie murmuring polite phrases about meeting each other. Gina sensed their initial face-to-face had gone smoothly. Both were smiling.

"Don't be late." Maggie bit her lip. "I didn't mean that."

"She forgets I'm not 16," Gina explained.

"Brady." Maggie sighed and glanced at her. "Sorry, honey. I do know your age. Brady," she paused, "take good care of my daughter. Please."

He hesitated a beat, keeping eye contact with her mother. "You can trust me, Mrs. Philips."

"Call me Maggie." She hugged Gina, squeezing her extra tightly. Her voice caught as she whispered, "You look so beautiful."

Had she missed something?

She left the question behind the closed screen door and slipped her arm through Brady's. "Hi," she whispered.

He patted her hand, almost absentmindedly. From his profile, he appeared somber. Maybe she couldn't leave the question behind. They walked down the porch steps.

"Everything okay?" she asked.

"No."

Her heart sank. It was that old family feud business. She should have—

"The thing is," he said softly, "I'm having an extremely difficult time preventing myself from kissing you."

She stared up at him as they walked along the front walk.

He took a deep breath, still not looking at her. "And your mother knows it. I find both of these things rather, uh, disconcerting."

Apparently she had missed something, but it seemed to have been an undercurrent rippling right before her very eyes. Talk about disconcerting!

He held open the passenger door of the car while she slipped inside. As he walked around it, he waved toward the house. Maggie and Aunt Lottie still stood behind the screen door. She lifted the corners of her mouth and waved to them as the car pulled away from the curb.

Car? "Where's your truck?" She ran her hand across soft red leather. It was a small, two-seater, old model sports car.

Brady drove hurriedly through town. "Traded vehicles with my brother for the night. Look." The car squealed to a stop on a side street. He cut the engine and unfastened his safety belt. "Can we start over?"

Just as she was rebuilding her cool and aloof armor, he turned toward her. Again the defenses melted away. "Hello."

Slowly, he smiled, his eyes crinkling. "Hi. How are you?"

"I don't really know. My head is swimming." Inwardly she cringed. She shouldn't have admitted that. "How are you?"

"I feel like I've been hit by a semi."

Her eyebrows shot up. "Oh." *Oh my.*

"Mm-hmm." He leaned over and softly kissed the corner of her mouth, then straightened. "You look beautiful tonight. Shall we go?"

Words caught in her throat. In less than a minute they had settled into the comfort of last night. There was no denying a connection with him.

He winked, depressed the clutch, and turned the ignition key. They headed out of town and were soon on the two-lane highway. "I like your mother."

"Really?" she scoffed in a teasing manner. "She is a Lindstrom, you know."

"Ooh, that was low."

"But deserved." She smiled at him.

"Touché." He shifted into fifth, then reached for her hand. "Seriously, no hard feelings along those lines?"

"Seriously, no." She squeezed his hand.

"I liked her mother-grizzly spirit."

Gina rolled her eyes. "I can't remember the last time she met my date at the door."

"Well, these are unusual circumstances. I mean, I am an Olafsson."

"That's true."

"And it's probably been kind of tough on her watching you go through this time, being hurt and losing your job and all."

She thought of her mother's special attention in recent months, of the hours she spent at the hospital, of worry etched on her face whenever Gina cried because of the pain. The way she blanched when she looked at her leg. "Very tough. She's always fixed things, you know? This she couldn't fix. But she was...there for me."

"You said you moved back home months ago?"

"Mm-hmm."

"And she hasn't met a date at the door for some time. Let's see...exactly how long has it been since you've had a date?"

"I don't think that's any of your business."

He shrugged. "I was just curious if we're talking lo-ong time."

"Brady, we're talking desperate time."

"Desperate? You mean it's been so long that you're desperate?"

"Tell me now, why else would I say yes to an Olafsson in Podunk?"

"You really know how to build up a guy's confidence. Want to know how long it's been for me?"

She grinned. "No."

"It's been—"

"I said no!"

"Not very long. But I have to say, as far as a kiss goes, we're talking desperate time."

"Brady!" She punched his shoulder.

"Hey, with the remarks you dish out, you're fair game, sweetheart."

He teased, but the term of endearment warmed her.

"And," he continued, "I sincerely hope you're not expecting a romantic evening."

"Well, of course I am. I told you I was desperate."

"You're out of luck. We have reservations at The Landing. I asked for a window table that overlooks the river. Sunset view. The décor is burgundy and black. Elegant. Linen tablecloths. Two forks. Three if we get the cheesecake or chocolate torte. Lemon wedge in the water goblets. Soft, chamber-type music. They have raspberry-flavored butter. Fresh fish entrees. Soft candlelight."

"That's not romantic?"

He shook his head. "Nah. In the Midwest romantic is picking up dinner at the fast-food drive-through and renting a hunting instructional video."

Gina laughed until her side hurt. Desperate or not, she knew Brady Olafsson was having a considerable impact on her life.

Twenty-Six

With synchronized footwork, Maggie and Marsha kept the porch swing going at breakneck speed. They giggled like little girls.

"Aunt Lottie might yell at us," Marsha warned.

"Remember that one time she did?"

They squealed in unison, and Maggie relished the silliness. She and her sister both needed a respite from real life. Wedding details had been discussed. They had examined the emotionally draining details of forgiving Dottie Olafsson. She had unloaded her apprehensions regarding Brady. The handsome young man couldn't hide his adulation of Gina. The thought of her fragile daughter being in close proximity to that kind of attention unsettled her. Would he capture Gina's heart and thoroughly confuse her?

Marsha had declared a recess from heavy-duty subjects. They scanned the movie listings for a comedy, chose one, then started their silly swinging, waiting until it was time to leave.

"Reece comes tomorrow."

"Maggie, we called recess."

"I don't want to deal with him right now."

"Don't. Wait until tomorrow."

"You know what I mean. I'm starting to get a handle on myself, but he'll bring in the here and now and all that entails."

Marsha sighed. "I don't have an answer, sis. Just be honest, be yourself, and let God take care of things. Pray about it. I'll pray about it. Why don't we go to the movie now?"

Maggie watched as an unfamiliar white car pulled into the driveway. Her feet fell behind the synchronized pushing and the swing wobbled crookedly. "Better pray quick, Marsh."

"Why?" She followed her sister's gaze toward the drive. "Who's that?"

"Reece."

"Kind of early, isn't he?"

"Only by about 15 hours."

The first time Maggie laid eyes on Reece Philips, nothing much happened. She was in her junior year at Northern Illinois University. He was older, working on his MBA. He was an assistant to one of her business professors and in her classroom Mondays, Wednesdays, and Fridays.

It was ten weeks before she noticed his friendly, energetic personality, his clear gray eyes, and his wide, masculine mouth. That came about only because they happened to be standing near the same exit door during a torrential downpour.

It was another month before she confessed to her roommate that thick black hair and a height under six feet were indeed attractive. She even went so far as to muse that racquetball could probably be as exciting a sport as basketball.

Reece, on the other hand, admitted to noticing her the previous year. According to him, she was the cause of a few relational dismantlings. He knew that he hadn't met the "right one" as long as he remained intrigued with a green-eyed stranger whose enticing blonde hair swished almost to her waist as she strode across campus or cleared tables in the student union.

An air she carried about herself fascinated him. It was a hint of delicacy, of sadness. Hesitant to enter her world, he watched from a distance until, quite simply, he could no longer. The rainstorm had been a godsend.

When she told him about Rosie, he didn't flinch. He sent white roses that first December twenty-seventh while they were apart during Christmas break. He introduced her to his friends. By spring, she was laughing again and falling in love with him.

His mind was made up; hers wavered. He gave her space and was incredibly patient. It wasn't until a month before they received their degrees that she consented to marry him, consented to follow him anywhere.

She had followed him first to the altar at a chapel near the school, not her home church in Valley Oaks. Next, they moved to Chicago, then to California. Their life had been rewarding together. They liked each other, shared similar interests and the same friends. He spent almost as much time with Gina as she did during her growing-up years.

Ten years ago Gina graduated from high school. Nine years ago Reece got the big promotion. As Vice President of Acquisitions, he oversaw everything west of the Mississippi River. He began traveling even more frequently and for longer periods of time. Maggie's world changed. While he still included her as much as possible, his driven personality remained in high gear and directed him toward places she couldn't follow either physically or emotionally.

Something inside of her disintegrated.

Whenever she tried to explain it, he brushed away her concerns like flies from a picnic basket. She meant the world to him, he'd say. He'd do anything for her, he'd say, then change the subject.

She knew he was hiding again, hiding from that hint of sadness that had been too long buried and now, like a submerged buoy, flung itself to the surface. Something had to be done about it.

Well, she was doing something about it, but now, here he came. Interrupting the process. He would push it back down, pretend it wasn't there. She would follow his lead, save it for another day, accommodate him.

Or not.

She watched him climb from the car. Eighty degrees and he wore his usual: suit pants—light gray today—and a white long-sleeved shirt. The cuffs were rolled halfway up his forearms and the powder blue tie was loosened. His hair, still thick but conservatively cut, was more salt than pepper, with a silvery sheen that almost glittered in the sun's late evening rays. He opened the back door and pulled out his briefcase.

Numbness crept over her, as if switches were being clicked off, shutting down whatever it was that energized the ethereal sense of emotions. This dulling was familiar; she didn't know why the sight of her husband triggered it.

He spotted her and Marsha and grinned. She went down the porch steps to greet him.

"Reece, what are you doing here?"

He embraced her and murmured, "Oh, you know me and Podunk-I-mean-Valley Oaks."

"I know. That's just it. You hate it."

He kissed her quickly, then dropped his arms. "Not exactly hugging weather, is it? You look hot in those blue jeans. Lottie has air, doesn't she? Hey, Marsha!" He climbed to the porch and gave his sister-in-law a brief hug.

They exchanged pleasantries, and then Marsha announced she was leaving. Reece protested. "Let's all go to dinner. We'll pick up Dan—"

"No, no, no." Marsha was adamant. "You two need some time alone—"

"I want to go to a movie," Maggie interrupted.

They both turned puzzled expressions toward her.

"Marsh and I were going to a movie."

"I thought we'd go to dinner." Reece smiled. "Is that one place still there in Rockville? They had decent prime rib—"

"We just ate chicken salad." She knew she sounded like an obstinate child, but so did Reece, barging in on the middle of something and demanding his own way, however politely. "I'm not hungry for anything except for popcorn with extra butter and a large diet soda with lots of ice. I want to eat it at the freezing theater, and then I'd like ice cream at O'Malley's."

Marsha had a distressed look on her face. "Maggie," she admonished. "Reece probably hasn't eaten."

She turned to her husband. "Want some chicken salad? It's made with mayonnaise, though, not your favorite, and there are eggs in it."

Reece had always been undemanding on the surface. Intense and driven, but always undemanding. She had seen him harried, in stressful situations, frustrated with her or Gina, and yet his pleasant mannerisms never diminished. She had heard stories about him in business situations, going for the jugular with positive words and a smile on his face, resulting in the other guys thanking him. But Maggie had never intentionally pushed him to the wall like this. Best friends didn't take perverse delight in such things, and he had been her best friend. Had been. When did it become past tense?

"Margaret, if you want to go to a movie, we'll go to a movie. I'll eat popcorn, too." He smiled his genuine smile, deepening the creases in his cheeks. "Ladies, please tell me this season of life will pass and my Margaret will return."

Marsha sighed. "It will pass."

"But," Maggie warned, "it sometimes takes ten years."

His jaw dropped. "Ten years?! What's a husband to do?"

The sisters looked at each other. *Tell him, Marsha,* she pleaded silently. *Tell him what I don't understand! Tell him what you said about him not giving me something I need.*

Marsha squeezed her brother-in-law's arm. "Hang on. I hear it's a bumpy ride."

Maggie blinked at them. Yes, it was a bumpy ride. An incredibly bumpy ride. And she felt as if her last link to shore had just been cut.

Twenty-Seven

Aunt Lottie cooked up a storm Saturday morning. Aunt Marsha and Uncle Dan brought homemade caramel rolls. Lauren brought doughnuts. Favorite cousins Alec and Anne brought fresh strawberries from their patch.

Gina thought it was great. Dad had arrived ahead of schedule and everyone stopped by to say hello. With food. She smiled now, watching her 90-year-old great-aunt flirt and her father tease as they stood beside each other at the stove, one cooking bacon, the other veggies and scrambled eggs. He wore shorts and a polo shirt. He didn't have his contacts in yet, and his wire-rimmed glasses added to his sporty appearance.

Odd that Dad didn't visit more often. Everyone loved him. Of course there was that issue with the Olafssons. Nice guy though he was, Dad didn't hide well his disdain for Valley Oaks in general. It was where she'd learned it. A bad habit that Brady kissed away once and for all last night...

"Gina." Dad's voice broke into her reverie. "You going to tell me about your new friend?"

She glanced at her mother, who smiled as she walked past carrying a stack of plates toward the dining room. "I told him he's a very nice Olafsson. Must take after his *mother*." It seemed she had been impressed with Brady. This was her first smile of the day. She appeared fresh enough with her curly hair still damp from a shower and a trim white T-shirt tucked into navy walking shorts. Her eyes, though, looked as if it had been a toss-and-turn night, and she definitely seemed out of it.

"Uncle Reece," Lauren interjected as she walked into the kitchen, "he's going to be my cousin-in-law. He's a good guy."

"You're marrying an Olafsson?"

She wrinkled her brow for a moment, thinking. "No, he's Aaron's cousin on his mother's side."

Dad shook his head. "It's amazing nobody marries their own cousin in this town."

"Reece," Aunt Lottie said, "did I ever tell you about my cousin who married Clint Eastwood's aunt?"

Her father laughed heartily. "Do you think we're in the will?"

Aunt Lottie punched his arm. "Well, you never know. That marriage means we are related. Gina, honey, hand me that bowl, please. I think we're ready."

They all sat around the dining room table. Several conversations continued simultaneously. Aunt Marsha announced that the menu for the reception had to be decided today, and once again the choices were discussed. Gina heard Aunt Lottie tell her mother that someone had called while she was in the shower but he didn't leave a message. Dad asked Alec about the school superintendent, whom he was to meet later in the morning to talk about the new housing development. Lauren asked what time she and Aaron could pick her up. Brady had invited the three of them over for dinner that evening.

As she scooped the last of the nutty caramel topping from her plate onto her fork, she got her father's attention. "Dad, is your company's concern really Brady's neighboring property?" She put the fork in her mouth and sighed, savoring the sensation of dissolving sugar.

He nodded. "Afraid so. Neil Braden Olafsson Jr. is the name on my contact sheet. What did you tell him about me?"

"That you're hard-nosed," she smiled, "but that he'd like you anyway."

"Fair enough." He reached over and ruffled her hair. "Okay, what's he like?"

"You're getting that steely business edge to your voice."

He eyed her over the rim of his coffee cup. "It's a father's edge, brought on by the fact that I waited up for you, but evidently not late enough."

"Mother," she called down the table, "remind him how old I am."

Her mother was head-to-head with Aunt Marsha and didn't respond. Gina noted she was also having one of her conspicuous hot flashes. Her neck and face were beet red; perspiration stood out on her forehead and upper lip.

She turned back to her dad. "I think he's hard-nosed, too, but I like him."

Dad smiled. "How come?"

She shrugged. *He dries my tears and hugs me in cornfields?* "He's compassionate. He listens to me. He makes me laugh. He gives me a new perspective on God and how Jesus is real."

"Hmm. Sounds like a rather significant influence. Your mother told me he writes Christian novels."

"I want to show them—"

Her mother touched her shoulder as she walked behind her. "I'll bring them down."

"Thanks. Dad, they really are unlike anything I have ever read or heard before. They're a step beyond church. Did you ever think that God wants to be involved in our everyday lives?"

"I know He does, when we need Him. And I know He has given me one special daughter."

Gina's eyes teared up. "I'm beginning to see how He takes care of me every day, on the inside."

"You've been through a rough time of it. Sounds as if you've got two new friends helping."

"Yeah, I'm feeling a lot better about things than I was when we first arrived."

"Good. Is he landlocked?"

"Jesus?"

"No, Olafsson."

It took Gina a moment to follow his line of thinking. "Oh. No, not technically."

"Practically?"

"I don't know. There is a ravine that he says is too deep to easily build a road through."

"Probably would cost him a bundle, too."

"Can I come with you tomorrow?"

A loud thumping and her mother's cries drowned her dad's answer. They rushed to the front room. Dad reached Mother first. She lay in a heap at the bottom of the wooden staircase.

"Margaret!"

She moaned as he gently turned her onto her side. Gina knelt to examine her left ankle, which was swiftly doubling in size. It was bent in an unnatural way. Carefully she removed the ridiculous thing her mother called a shoe. It was a slip-on sandal with a raised heel and probably the cause of her tumble down the steps. She bit back a lecture.

Anne knelt beside her. "How about some dish towels for a splint?"

"Please."

"Margaret!" Dad repeated. "Talk to me, Margaret."

"Reece." Her mother winced and her voice was strained. "You go for days without saying my name and now you're going to wear it out."

"Mom, where do you hurt?"

"Everywhere." She struggled to sit up.

"Good." She saw a knot forming on her forehead. "Dad, can you get her to the couch?"

"Margaret, put your arm around my neck." He hoisted her in his arms and carried her the short distance.

Gina noted her father's face was more ashen than her mom's. She positioned Maggie's leg on a pillow while Anne folded the dish towels. They gently tied them around the leg, making the pillow into a splint. Everyone hovered, expressing dismay over the injury.

"Margaret, what happened?"

"Isn't it obvious?" she whispered.

"How far did you fall?" Gina asked.

"Just the last few steps. I was," she took a painful-sounding breath, "rushing."

"Dad, we've got to get her to the emergency room. I think it's fractured."

Slowly he rose from beside the couch. "I-I'll get my wallet."

"Can somebody tell us how to get there?" Gina raised her voice above the noisy chatter, then noticed her mother's eyes. Only the whites were showing beneath slowly closing lids. "Mom!"

"Margaret!"

"Mom!"

Her eyelids fluttered open, but her eyes were unfocused. Gina wondered if the knot on her head was more serious than it appeared. "Dad, let's *go!*" She had never seen her dad so unsure. He shuffled toward the staircase.

Alec said, "I'll take you all to the hospital. Anne, you bring Grandma Lottie's car so they'll have one there."

It was an agonizingly slow process to get everyone moving in the same direction. Her mother continued to behave in a dazed manner, her father even more so. In the midst of it all, Gina realized how deeply he must care for her. Why was it he didn't show it more plainly?

Good grief. She was beginning to sound like Brady. Illogical and irrational.

~

"Gina, go home," Reece urged. "There's nothing more for you to do here."

"No, I want to wait until they put the cast on."

Lying propped up in the hospital bed, Maggie heard the resolve in her daughter's voice and smiled at her. "You've raised enough ruckus for one day, hon. I'm sure they can manage a cast without your supervision."

Incredulity was evident in Reece's raised brows and in Gina's face lifted toward the ceiling. They stood on either side of the bed. Lauren was at the foot of it.

Maggie squeezed Gina's hand. Promoting optimism was a losing battle. "At any rate, I'm not hanging around for them to redo it! If you don't approve, we'll come back tomorrow. Now go. Have fun at your dinner."

"You're sure?"

"I'm sure. Lauren, take her, please."

Reece ushered them out the door, then restlessly paced the small room, sipping coffee from a paper cup. "Stick a DVM at the end of her name and she thinks she knows everything related to medicine." There was a father's pride in his comment. "Can I get you anything?"

"Just out of here."

It had been a tedious, tedious day. Maggie closed her eyes against the brightly lit room. She wanted to crawl into that black hole she had kept slipping into while the pain pierced relentlessly. But they had given her something for the pain, leaving her to confront...too many things.

Reece and Gina had been almost obnoxious in voicing their contempt for the hospital. True, things were disorderly and incredibly slow, giving the appearance of inefficiency. They had been there for hours. Reece postponed his meeting. She knew he'd rather be working than pacing in a cubicle, had even encouraged him to leave, but he refused. Well, at least it was a cubicle, a room with walls, not just a curtained-off area. The hospital was a fairly new structure.

Then there was that nagging at the back of her mind about what Aunt Lottie had said. Someone called, but he didn't leave a message. She wasn't worried that Reece had paid attention to the comment. She was worried that something was wrong with her friend John, otherwise he would not have called. It had to have been him. What other "he" would call?

"Margaret?"

She didn't open her eyes. "Reece, they said I could sleep. There's a problem only if I don't wake up."

"I know I've said this, but you need to slow down. I can just imagine you flying down the staircase, in a hurry to get nowhere."

There was no need to respond. The subject had been covered. He always wanted to fix things quickly, figure out causes, and offer solutions one, two, and three.

"Mr. Philips?"

Maggie opened her eyes. The doctor appeared. He was mild-mannered, tall, and thin, fifty-something with horn-rimmed glasses and a soft voice. He wore a brilliant white lab coat.

"You're awake, Mrs. Philips? I was looking over your chart and wondered if I could ask you a few questions."

Reece approached the other side of the bed. His tension was palpable, but he didn't say anything. "Ask away, Doctor," she replied. "If you have the time. We're not going anywhere."

"I was curious about your age and broken bones. Are you pre- or postmenopausal?"

"My guess is I'm in the thick of it. Generally speaking, things have gone haywire."

He nodded. "Insomnia, hot flashes, irritability, outrageous laughter one minute, intense crying the next?"

She smiled. "Your wife?"

"Yes. You're not on hormonal replacement therapy?"

"No."

"Well, either that or alternative ways would combat all of the above. My concern today is your bones. Do you take calcium supplements or eat a lot of dairy, salmon, soy, broccoli? Do you exercise regularly?"

"No." She shook her head. "No."

"Have you ever had a bone density scan?"

"No." She heard Reece's sharp intake of breath.

"Doctor," he said, "is there a problem with something?"

"Not so far as I can tell from the X rays." He addressed Maggie again. "I'm just suggesting that you may want to talk to your doctor. You're petite and fair-skinned and, let me guess, you drink quite a bit of coffee and diet soda?"

"Guilty."

"Those things put you in the high-risk category for osteoporosis." He patted her hand. "At the very least, change your diet and walk more." With a smile he strode toward the open door. "Especially down staircases. We'll be with you shortly."

They watched him go, then Reece harrumphed. "Shortly." He removed his glasses and pinched the bridge of his nose. "Speaking of coffee, I'm going to take a walk and get a fresh cup. Do you want anything?"

"No. Thanks."

Maggie closed her eyes again. They burned with tears she refused to shed. How could her body betray her like this? How could she maintain control when it insisted on controlling her? Since Rosie, she had been so very careful not to break rules, not to make mistakes. She worked hard at her job and taking care of her family. How could she do such a stupid thing as fall down the steps and break an ankle? And what was she supposed to do with a future of deteriorating bones and dried-up skin and crazy emotions and—

She took a deep breath and willed the images away long enough to begin a prayer. *Dear God, I feel like I've lost my way. I can't face this alone. I want to believe You're with me. Help me to know what to do about all of it. Diet, hormones. John. Marsha's caterer. Reece.* She paused. *Reece. Dear God, I don't feel anything anymore.*

Her thoughts grew fuzzy and she dozed. A tickle under her nose awoke her. She looked up at her husband. He was sitting on the bed, holding a fragrant, long-stemmed white rose.

"Do I really go for days without saying your name?" He seemed subdued.

She eyed him warily and nodded. When was the last time he had given her a flower?

He studied her face. "I'm sorry. Margaret." He looked away. "Seeing you lying there at the bottom of the stairs, then listening to the doctor's dire predictions...I don't know."

She took the rose from him and smelled it.

"Like I said last night, I do want my Margaret back."

"I'm not sure where she is."

He paused. "Well, I don't think she's here in Valley Oaks with Maggie. Now, will you promise to make an appointment when you get home to talk about this stuff with your doctor? Please?"

A lump formed in her throat. She swallowed. "I think that would be a smart thing to do."

"Oh, I found a gift shop and bought these to take to Marsha's tonight." He gestured over his shoulder.

She eyed a large bouquet of flowers in a clear vase on the table behind him. There were more white roses in it.

"Shall we stop at a market and pick up some contribution to dinner? Appetizers? Dessert?"

No words could get around the lump in her throat now. Which had come first? The thought to give her flowers or to give their hostess flowers? She knew the answer. He was always so much more the conscientious guest than attentive husband. When had she started minding?

The friendly middle-aged nurse who had been in and out all day entered, exclaiming, "Flowers! How romantic!"

Maggie blinked back tears.

"Mrs. Philips, you are so lucky! My husband would never in a million years think of that."

Reece smiled sheepishly. "Actually, I bought them for dinner tonight, for our hostess."

The nurse looked at Maggie with wide eyes and shook her head. "Men are clueless." She pushed on Reece's arm. "Move out of my way, bum. *We* are going to take care of your wife, unlike *you.*"

They bantered back and forth, Reece defending himself while the nurse talked about tarring and feathering.

Maggie wished she could join in, wished she could take Reece's cluelessness lightheartedly and tease him about it. The fact was, he didn't know how to make her feel loved anymore. That was it, wasn't it? That was what Marsha was talking about. She needed to feel loved, and he wasn't fulfilling that need.

Well, whose job was it to clue him in? Hers, probably. Would he talk through it? She owed him, at the least, to try again, this time with specifics that he couldn't refute with "It's just this season of your life; get over it."

The truth was that if they didn't start addressing things on a deeper level, she would soon be beyond caring if he ever understood. She was tired of hurting. Maybe if things simply ended, the pain would go away.

She needed roses and tender words and time with him. She needed him to accept the fact that Margaret was here, buried somewhere in Maggie's past.

Twenty-Eight

Gina didn't know what triggered this all-encompassing sense of well-being. Here she sat in Brady's country kitchen, at the small round oak table with him, Lauren, Aaron, a Scrabble board, Homer at her feet, and this delightful tranquillity almost oozing from her pores.

She suspected it had a lot to do with her new faith. Once she decided to accept as fact that God's ear was tuned to her very thoughts, talking to Him quickly became a habit. With such a powerful audience, it seemed silly to spend every waking moment fretting over her career. Or lack of one.

But, of course, it also had a lot to do with the one who wrote those wonderful books that showed her the reality of Jesus. The creator of tonight's magnificent meal of smoked turkey and twice-baked potatoes and apple crisp. The vocabulary whiz who speculated at the letters she held and suggested words during her turn. The one who smiled at her now across the table and winked. "An 'm' would fit nicely here with—"

Lauren smacked her hand against the tabletop and stood. "That's it!" she cried. "We're playing partners, Brady. Trade places with me. If you're going to keep helping Gina, you have to be her partner. Give me some kind of chance here."

Brady protested his innocence, but did as he was told, sliding his chair close and draping his arm along the back of hers. His shoulder brushing against hers tickled from head to toe.

He was the perfect gentleman. It seemed an old-fashioned term, but she thought it fit him. He was...sensitive to her. Except for that kissing business. He had only kissed her three times. Once on the sidewalk near Aunt Lottie's. Once in the car on the way to dinner, a quick brush of his lips. Once last night.

Last night... The Scrabble letters blurred now as she replayed how after dinner, back at Aunt Lottie's, they had climbed from the car. Brady leaned against it and pulled her to him. She didn't want to awaken from kiss number three. When he released her, she initiated number four.

"Gina," he had whispered, his lips trailing across her face. "I have to ration these."

"Ration?" She looked up at him in the dim light from the porch, the back of her head resting in the crook of his arm. "What on earth for?"

He inhaled a deep breath, then forcefully blew it out. "I get lost just looking in your eyes. That doesn't begin to describe what happens when I kiss you. Do you know what I'm saying?" He straightened then, placing his hands on her shoulders, gently pushing her to arm's length. "It's a little early in our relationship to be struggling with this, but..." His voice trailed off.

Gina swallowed. Maybe he was being sensitive to her in this.

She smiled now as he whispered in her ear about what letters to place on the Scrabble board.

"Brady!" Lauren laughed. "You're partners. You don't have to whisper."

Aaron elbowed her. "I think he likes whispering in her ear." He leaned toward her. "As a matter of fact I think I like whispering in yours."

Lauren giggled uncontrollably as her fiancé nuzzled her ear.

Gina turned to Brady with a smile. "Feel like an intruder?"

"Mmm," he replied, his face somber. He touched a strand of hair that had escaped her ponytail and wrapped it around his finger.

Her smile faded. "What's your ration for today?"

"Just used them all up." Abruptly, he stood. "I'm going to change the music." He headed toward the adjacent living room where the stereo was located.

Lauren had selected the music that flowed through speakers in the kitchen. She pulled away from Aaron. "Brady!" she called. "Don't change that one. It's what we played at the concert."

Aaron grinned, then started humming. When a low, breathy female voice started singing, he missed a beat, but quickly caught up with her. "*Where does your journey lead from here?*" he sang out in a strong baritone. "*O'er mountains not scaled, 'cross oceans still wild?*"

The speaker went silent and Aaron hummed a few bars a cappella. "Da de dum *'I have but one request of you, dear.'* Da da—"

"*Your hand in mine,*" Lauren joined in, "*I'll walk alongside.*" They laughed through a few more da dums. When a sudden blast of orchestral music drowned them, they stood and sang out loudly, "*'Til life's journey is complete, counting each moment with you as eternity held fast.*"

One request? To walk alongside 'til life's journey is complete?

The stereo volume decreased, and Brady came back into the kitchen. Gina caught him glancing her direction, before quickly averting his eyes. He meandered toward the coffeepot. The tips of his ears were red. She couldn't resist. "Brady, *now* do you remember the words?"

Aaron asked, "What do you mean? He knows the words. We all sat around here, listening to his old music, choosing songs for the wedding."

"We almost chose that one." Lauren twisted her head to look back at Brady. "Didn't we?"

His neck was flushed now.

Gina smiled. "At the band concert, he sang the first two lines to me, then said he couldn't remember any more of the words."

Aaron laughed. "As in '*I have but one request of you, dear*'?"

The three of them howled with laughter as Brady stood at the counter, obviously flustered and at a loss for words. He seemed to have a problem knowing what to do with his hands, shoving them into the back pockets of his khakis, then pulling them out and crossing his arms over his chest. At last he sputtered, "I didn't think they were appropriate."

"I should hope not, mister." Gina picked up her coffee mug and walked over to him. "'*What are you doing the rest of your life?*' It sounds like a marriage proposal. May I have some coffee?"

"The first part was appropriate." He still looked rattled. His forehead was creased, and he combed his fingers through his short blond hair. "I mean, you're trying to figure out what to do with your future. The rest of your life."

"Mm-hmm." She was amused at Brady's discomfort. She nudged him aside and reached for the coffee carafe. "Do you want some?"

"The remainder of the song was just too irrational to even mention."

"Absolutely." Gina bit her lip to keep from bursting into laughter again. He sounded so sincere. She picked up her mug and turned. "That's probably why you jumped up so quickly to turn it off. You know how annoyed I get at irrational, illogical sentiments."

"Yeah." He looked toward the refrigerator, then back at her. His tan had deepened. He recrossed his arms. "I don't imagine you'd respond favorably to an irrational proposal."

She shook her head, then sipped coffee.

He cleared his throat. "But what exactly would a rational, logical proposal sound like?"

"Well, first of all the one offering it would have to be a really, really good friend. Then it would probably be a mutual decision. Either one of us might say, 'We function so well together. Maybe we should make it permanent. What do you think?'"

His eyes widened. "That's rational. It's also totally without passion."

"There's passion," she argued. "It's just...subtle."

"Do you take after your dad? You sound like a no-nonsense businessman. Person."

She shrugged a shoulder. "Yeah, well, it works. I don't suppose you could relate to a woman in that way. You'd be too busy sending flowers." *And kissing.*

"Gina." He leaned in, stretched his arms around either side of her, and rested his hands against the countertop behind her. Aaron and Lauren were forgotten. "Has anyone ever sent you flowers?" His discomfort seemed to be lessening.

While hers increased. "Sure."

"I mean, sent you flowers."

She frowned at him, aware of her heartbeat against the coffee mug she clutched between them.

"Dozens and dozens of roses," he clarified.

"Why would someone do that? It's too extravagant for something that will soon be put in the trash."

"He would do it because you have the same effect on him as dozens of flowers. To him you are as beautiful as exquisitely shaped roses, orchids, daisies, and tulips. You brighten every room you enter like a dazzling burst of fragrant, colorful beauty. You influence everything about his life for the better." Brady moved still closer and tilted his head closer to hers. "Too irrational for you?"

"Totally."

"You're all red, Angelina," he whispered.

"You changed the subject. So why did you jump up so quickly to change the music?"

"Now you're changing the subject."

Gina tore her eyes from his turquoise gaze and stared down at the steaming coffee in her mug.

"I changed the music because," he breathed against her hair, "in the park I wanted to sing all the words to you. And that is way too irrational, even for me."

"Yoo-hoo!" It was a loud female voice followed by the solid thump of the front door closing in the other room. "Are you home?"

Brady straightened and crossed the kitchen just as a woman hurried through the doorway.

She threw her arms wide and cried, "Brady!" She rushed to him. Her arms encircled his neck, and she pulled his face toward hers.

The kiss lasted long enough for Gina to exchange a questioning look with Lauren and to see Aaron frown. It lasted long enough for her to observe that the stranger was tall, probably 5'11" or so, with willowy with straight blonde hair. She wore a knee-length sleeveless black dress. It lasted long enough for an air of awkwardness to settle on the gathering. Gina moved back toward the table and stood beside her cousin.

"Kim." Brady unhooked her arms from his neck. "You're back."

She tapped his nose with her finger. "You are observant, dear boy."

Lauren cleared her throat. "Hello, Kim."

She will have blue eyes, Gina predicted.

The stranger turned large blue eyes their direction. Her nose was delicate, the tip turned slightly upward. She smiled. Her teeth were very straight. "You've got company! Aaron, right?" She stepped toward them and shook his hand. "And—?"

Brady offered, "You remember Lauren, his fiancée. And this is...Lauren's cousin." He glanced at Gina. "From California. This is Kim Severson."

He had forgotten her name. Gina shook the woman's hand, not bothering to fill in the blank. Not that she had much of a chance. Kim chattered nonstop, scurrying back to the doorway where she retrieved a paper bag overflowing with sticks of French bread.

"I've brought dinner. Oh, but only for two." She pouted.

"It's nine o'clock," Brady said.

"In Spain the evening is just getting started at nine o'clock."

Between Brady's words tumbling over Kim's, Gina gathered that Kim was a junior college Spanish teacher and had just returned after spending the second semester in Spain with a group of students.

"I got so homesick for you, Brady. I wanted to surprise you. Have you all eaten? We could run back to the store, get some more chicken. They're still open. I was so surprised to see they've extended their hours."

Her strings of sentences wrapped around the four of them like tentacles, holding them all at attention. Somehow Lauren managed to extricate herself, stepping to Brady and giving him a quick hug, thanking him for dinner, firmly stating they were leaving. Aaron followed suit with a handshake. Gina added her thanks and a polite "nice meeting you" as she moved toward the door.

Brady and Kim followed them outside, she holding his arm. Spotlights shone from the garage on the drive. The surrounding woods were dark. They quickly climbed into Aaron's car and left.

In the back seat Gina shook her head, not sure what to make of the last ten minutes. Except for the sound of Lauren's heavy breathing, they rode in silence out to the highway.

"Aaron!" Lauren exclaimed finally, "what is she doing here? I thought that was over!"

"Lauren, I don't know anything. What are you so steamed about?"

"How can he do that to Gina?"

"Do what?"

"Act like he cares about her and then have Kim waltz in behaving as if they're engaged or something."

"He's not responsible for Kim's behavior."

"Well, he could have stopped it. This is so embarrassing."

"For whom?"

"Hey, you two," Gina interrupted. "Don't worry about it. So Brady was involved with Kim. Or is. *Que sera sera.* It's not like we were anything but friends for the time being. It's not like," she paused, swallowed the catch in her throat, "not like it was going anywhere."

"It was rude," Lauren said. "Any sensible, just-friend friend would have seen he was occupied and said good night. Any idiot could have told her he was occupied; he'd call her another day. She walked in as if she lived there. They just dated last fall. I think we saw them at a party last summer."

"Laur," Gina pleaded, "give Cupid a rest. Please. Just take me home."

They rode in silence. Inexplicable emotions churned in Gina. She couldn't think straight. There was literally a physical ache in her chest. *How could he kiss someone else in that same way? What was last night all about? I need a job—*

"Gina," Lauren broke into her thoughts. "It's early. If you don't want to face your folks and Aunt Lottie, come with us to the house. We can watch Aaron paint or something. Okay? Okay, Aaron?"

Her folks?

Aaron's eyes sought hers in the rearview mirror. "Good idea. Come with us. Give yourself some time to get over the, uh, rather abrupt end to the evening. What do you say?"

She didn't want to face her folks. What would she say? *You were right. He is an Olafsson.* But he wasn't, not in that disparaging way. Was he?

"Gina?" Lauren broke into her thoughts. "You won't be in the way."

"Yeah. Okay." It was a lifeline her cousin threw. Good grief, she didn't have a life. She had to get her own place. Job first, then her own place. Put the Wild Creatures Country behind her, put Podunk behind her. Move on. Get a life. Start the rest of her journey...

Twenty-Nine

Maggie repositioned the crutches under her arms in an attempt to find a less tender spot. Her palms hurt, too, from pressing them against the padded rungs. Her ankle throbbed again. The cast was impossibly heavy. Was it time to take more pain medication?

She felt like a klutz, maneuvering her way through the living room toward the dining room. Thank goodness Marsha had moved the dinner to Aunt Lottie's, insisting that Maggie stay put. Now it was after nine. As Maggie shut the door on departing guests, Reece had gone straight to the dining table, attaché case in hand.

A low mechanical hum greeted her at the doorway, flowing on a light breeze. Reece had placed a fan in the window. It pulled in the late night's cooler air. He sat with his back directly to it, laptop computer open before him on the table, piles of papers spread about, weighted down with a coffee mug, a crystal bowl of colorful plastic fruit, and blue racquetballs. The lace tablecloth had been pushed aside.

"Still up?" he asked. The keyboard clicked under his rapidly moving fingers.

She ignored the rhetorical question, pulled out a chair, and carefully lowered herself onto it. She angled the crutches against the nearby wall. They immediately clattered to the floor. She breathed a frustrated sigh.

Reece glanced up. "You've had a traumatic day. Don't you think you should get some rest?"

"I want to talk."

His eyes were on a paper in his hand. "I need to go through these—"

"Reece!" Her tone was sharper than she had intended.

His jaw tensed, but he put down the paper, closed the laptop, and made eye contact with her.

It was now or never. If she backpedaled, she'd lose his attention. It was time to get to the heart of the matter. "Do you love me?"

He barked a laugh. "What kind of a ridiculous question is that?"

"Ridiculous, I guess, but I need an answer."

"Podunk always unnerves you. I wish you weren't spending an entire month here."

"It's a simple question, Reece. I can't remember the last time you told me."

He blinked. "You know my parents weren't demonstrative in that way. I grew up without—"

"You're 56 years old. Let's move beyond our childhoods."

"Like you're doing, spending a month back here wallowing in yours?"

"I'm wallowing in it in order to come to terms with it. And move on."

"I thought you moved on when you came to Northern."

"That was just burying it. I didn't take the time to grieve death and divorce and lost dreams. I didn't take the time to forgive Neil's mother."

"You have to do this now? It's over. It's been over a long time. Some counselor tell you to do this?"

She hesitated. John had helped her conclude this, but he wasn't a counselor. "No."

Reece rubbed his forehead. "I don't understand you. Women and their hormones. Why can't you just let things be? Let them stay buried?"

"Because they're still locked in here." She touched her chest. "And they keep me fearful. They keep me from forgiving and from...dreaming new dreams." She paused. "Your issues keep you from saying you love me."

He looked down at the tabletop and drummed his fingers.

"Unless you just don't anymore."

"Margaret, if I didn't, would I spend a weekend in Podunk with your family?"

"You came for business."

"I do that business for you, for us, for our home, our cars—"

"You do it because you thoroughly enjoy everything about it." How often had he told her that through the years? He was that rare man who found deep contentment in his work.

"You've always been my best friend," he offered.

"But we don't talk on that deepest of levels, about positive or negative things. Do you talk to anyone in that way?" Involuntarily, her breath held and her hand went to her tightening midsection. What if there was someone else for him?

He spread his arms. "I'm a man. I don't know that I even think that way, let alone talk to anyone that way, This is all gray area. I deal in black and white. Black and white says we met, we fit, we married. End of story."

"You used to bring me flowers."

"You want flowers? I can bring you flowers."

"If I have to tell you, it doesn't count."

His eyebrows shot up.

"Reece, do you think I love you?"

He crossed his arms and grunted. "Can't say that I think about it."

"Well, could you think about now?" Her voice rose. "Just for a minute?"

"You're going to wake Lottie."

She grabbed a stack of his papers, sent a racquetball bouncing away, and fanned herself.

"Look," he said, "I guess I just assume you do. You're there when I come home. We have mutual friends. We go to dinner together." He stopped.

"I decorate the house by myself," she continued in his vein of reasoning. "Blanca and I clean it. Ramon and I care for the yard. You go to basketball and whatnot games with your friends. When our friends come over, I cook dinner. You're out of town 16 days a month. At least."

They stared at each other.

Reece broke the silence. "I have work to do." He stood and reached down to pick up her crutches. "And you should rest."

Bracing herself against the table, she rose and accepted the crutches from him. It took a moment to place them under her arms.

"Margaret?"

She looked over at him.

"So do you?" He blinked. "Love me?"

She averted her eyes to the floor and began to inch her clumsy way to the door. At least he had asked. He deserved the truth. "I don't know anymore, Reece."

Gina strolled up the dark sidewalk in front of Aunt Lottie's as Aaron and Lauren drove off. It had been good to spend a few hours with them, letting the shock of that moment at Brady's filter through time and dilute itself. What remained was a touch of sadness, a touch of relief, a touch of clarity, a touch of resolve.

She was grateful for Brady's friendship and how he defined Jesus for her. Evidently she was in worse shape than she realized, vulnerable beyond a healthy state of mind to have fallen for his romantic overtures. How silly she felt! What had she been thinking? Well, she hadn't been thinking—

She saw movement in the shadows of the front porch. "Dad! What are you doing still up?" She climbed the steps.

"Couldn't sleep. You're home early, compared to last night." He sat in the padded, aluminum rocker. It creaked against the wooden floorboards.

In the dim light of a distant street lamp she could make out a tall plastic glass that he lifted. Ice cubes clunked. Iced coffee was a favorite of his, but in the middle of the night? Gina slid onto the swing. "Coffee's going to help you sleep?"

"I thought as long as I was awake, I may as well be awake, if you get my drift. I changed our tickets. Is it all right with you if we leave tomorrow afternoon? We can go straight from Rockville. No need to drive to Chicago."

"Sounds *perfect* to me." The sooner the better.

"Perfect, huh? It must be getting to you, too."

"What is?"

"Podunk."

"Dad, that's so derogatory."

"You sound exactly like your mother, and I admit you're both right. It is derogatory. Excuse me. But you can't tell me this town doesn't unnerve her."

"Oh, it unsettles her, but at the same time she seems to be handling things well. I mean, she finally found the courage to tell me about Rosie and Neil. We had a great time looking up ancestors' history at the courthouse. It gave me such a sense of grounding. I know it affected Mother. And she's laughing a lot with Aunt Marsha. Did she tell you about doing a cheer in a parking lot with her old friends? Can you picture that?"

"Not with a cast on her ankle." He chewed an ice cube.

Gina had never heard her dad sound so negative. "What's with you?"

"Po-Valley Oaks. It's completely unraveling my sense of equilibrium." He paused, then, "Do you think I'm clueless?"

She laughed. "I think I was 16 when I explained that one to you, and you didn't even have to ask."

"I'm serious."

"Okay. On what subject?"

"Flowers. I bought some at the hospital gift shop for your Aunt Marsha, you know, hostess gift thing because we were going there for dinner. I gave your mother a rose from the bouquet. I mean, I know she likes flowers. She has a back-yard full of them. The nurse called me clueless, and I get the impression that your mother would like her own flowers from me, but not if she has to tell me."

"She's a romantic. You know that." Gina felt more than saw his blank expression. "Don't you?"

He didn't answer.

"She cries at sappy commercials. She likes quiet after-noons in art galleries and candlelit dinners and reading by the fireplace and surprise gifts when it's not her birthday."

"Is this a girl thing?"

"Not necessarily. I'm not exactly like that. Mom always liked the guys who opened doors for me and dressed up and brought corsages. All I wanted was one who'd stalk lizards in the backyard with me or dig for worms. I don't care about flowers..." An image of Brady stopped her. He stood a hair's breadth from her, long arms reaching around either side of her to the counter she leaned against. Her breath caught. She fought down the warmth that flooded her.

"You don't care about flowers?" Dad prompted.

"Nooo...but...well, Brady said something about flowers. Something about women having the same effect as flowers, being beautiful and bright. Dazzling. Anyway, I guess they mean something to some people, like Mother."

"After 30 years..." His voice trailed off. "Maybe I am clueless. Why are you in such a hurry to leave town?"

"Brady's a romantic and I'm not, and he has a-another *friend*."

"Did you expect something different?"

"I didn't think enough about it. Guess that makes two clueless souls sitting on this porch in the middle of the night."

They sat quietly for a few moments, then her dad asked, "Would you still recommend the guy's books?"

"Oh, absolutely. They taught me how to see that Jesus was who He said He was. Because of that, I know He won't let me down, not like people do. I think I'm going to find a lot of comfort in that."

"You could use some, honey, after the year you've had."

"I think you could, too, Dad."

"It'll help to get back to work. Do you want to come with me tomorrow to Brady's place?"

She bit back the words that snapped to mind. If her dad would stop hiding in his work, maybe he'd get a clue. Straight words from his daughter like that wouldn't reach his heart though. Friendly as he was, he'd always fit the macho image too well. She smiled now as a new option dawned on her: She could pray about it. "No, I'll stay home and pack. I'll have to see Brady at the rehearsal, wedding, and reception. Three too many times."

"Want me to be tough on him? Teach him not to mess with my Gina?"

"Squish him like a roly-poly bug." She imagined Brady's handsome face, how it glowed with contentment and happiness as they roamed through his woods. "Not really, Dad. He's going to have a hard enough time talking with Maggie

Lindstrom's husband about losing easy access to his beloved property."

"Maggie," he mumbled.

"What?"

"Nothing. I think these two clueless souls had better get some sleep."

Thirty

The flowers began arriving soon after 9:00 A.M. Aunt Lottie, of course, knew the teenage girl who delivered them.

"Erin, it's Sunday! Your mother's shop isn't open today, is it?"

"No. She's just doing a favor for—" The girl giggled. "Well, you're supposed to read the card. Bye." She hurried down the porch steps.

"This is just not like— Oh, Gina! These are for you. Aren't they gorgeous? I can't imagine! On a Sunday..."

Gina had been watching the scene from the top of the staircase. She went down only because of the dear woman who eagerly held out the bouquet. No mystery to her who had sent them. Neither the day of the week nor a closed sign in the florist's window would stop a man who sent flowers because the woman reminded him of— How had he phrased it? "A dazzling burst of fragrant, colorful beauty." A real-life interpretation awaited her, its overpowering scent wafting upward in greeting. Wrapped in yellow tissue were white baby's breath, purple statice, and every color of the rainbow in the form of orchids, daisies, tulips, irises, and carnations.

Aunt Lottie pressed them into her hands. "I'll get a vase. Goodness, I hope I have one large enough. Whom do you suppose they're from?"

Gina could have sworn there was a twinkle in the old woman's eyes. She glanced over at her dad, sitting in the front room.

He quickly hid his face behind the newspaper, not soon enough to hide a grin. "You may want to rethink your opinion of flowers," he murmured.

She didn't want to rethink her opinion, but that didn't seem to be an option. She fingered the envelope. "Angelina" was printed in a masculine hand. Did she have to read what was inside? It would be an apology that would yank more vigorously on her heartstrings than did this gesture. If he hadn't explained his reasoning behind sending flowers, they would have meant little. But she knew their significance. It was affecting her opinion.

With clenched teeth, she opened the card. *I'm sorry for the misunderstanding. Brady.* Her stomach flipped. What was that supposed to mean? What was the misunderstanding? That he forgot to mention he was leading her on? It wasn't as if his friend Kim was a misunderstanding. It was rather obvious who she was.

Mother hobbled in on her crutches from the dining room. "Oh, how beautiful! Brady?"

"Mm-hmm."

"Breakfast is ready, you two." Before turning back around, she lifted a shoulder and wiped awkwardly at her eye.

Gina looked at her dad now standing, watching her mother. He must have also caught sight of the tears. "Psst," she whispered and went over to him. "You may want to rethink your opinion of flowers."

He raised his brows, inspecting her armful. "No roses."

"Hmm."

The first roses arrived at 10:00. A dozen yellow ones, from the other local florist, addressed to "an Angel" and signed with a smiley face. Maggie was resting upstairs, Aunt Lottie was at church, and her dad was out for a walk. They were all back by 11:30 when the red roses arrived. From

Rockville, two dozen sweet-scented velvet blossoms in a heavy crystal vase. More baby's breath and greenery.

She had stayed home from church in order to avoid Brady and here she was reading yet a third card written by him. This one included a Bible quote. *"The mind of man plans his way, but the Lord directs his steps." Your job loss was not in your plans, but surely God ordered your steps to meet Him here. Praying for you as you interview. Brady.*

Gina turned her back to her family and the three bouquets. She crumpled the card in her hand and hurried blindly up the stairs. It was time for a good irrational, illogical cry.

"You could have put in a new road for what you've spent on flowers today." The silver-haired man threw Brady a disarming smile as he approached, removing designer sunglasses and extending his hand. "Reece Philips. You must be Braden Olafsson?"

Brady returned the smile and shook his hand, appreciative of the way the man quickly broke the ice. He wasn't too far from the truth. The cost of the final, most extravagant bouquet—an arrangement of fresh Hawaiian blossoms to be flown in from Chicago this afternoon—would pay for enough rock to cover half his road. "Not to sound like an ingratiating slob, but your daughter's worth it. I was unforgivably rude to her."

"Well, that's between you two, although I must say you caught everyone's attention this morning. Shall we take a walk?"

Like an ice hockey face-off, they had met in the center of Brady's narrow road and parked their vehicles hood to hood. *Let the game begin,* he thought. They walked behind his truck, veering off the gravel onto a field of short, stiff prairie grasses that he regularly mowed. It was a clear afternoon, one of those perfect June moments when the humidity was low, the flies and gnats asleep, the tree frogs' high-pitched humming wove through the gaps between bird songs.

Brady noticed Philips' olive skin tone and dark, expressive brows. Just like Gina's. She had her mother's green eyes, but her height, build, and facial shape resembled more her dad. He suspected she also took after him in that no-nonsense approach to life. Her rational, logical attitude intrigued as well as baffled him.

He knew beyond a shadow of a doubt that he had blown it last night. She would see the situation as an equation. Brady plus Gina did not equal Brady plus Kim. If he had a relationship going with Kim—which it undoubtedly appeared as such—then she wasn't about to develop one with him. Not to mention everything else she had on her plate, such as finding a job, living in California, and recovering from her injury. None of that fit into an equation that included him and Valley Oaks.

Still, he was scrambling to keep the communication lines open. The flowers were his initial reaction, not very creative and not exactly appropriate given her personality. He had called twice. The first time there had been no answer. The second time, Lottie couldn't get her to the phone and made apologies for her, saying she wasn't feeling well. He'd have to go there, talk to her. Somehow convince her that in spite of the fact they had only just met, he was...falling in love? Off the charts for irrational and illogical thinking. Not exactly her style either.

They reached a short wooden stake protruding from the ground. Running along the left side of the road, a row of uniform stakes stretched ahead, about ten yards between each. Fluorescent orange plastic flags were tied to them, flapping in the light breeze.

"Is your attorney coming?" Philips asked.

"Uh, no, sir. I had hoped to have an informal discussion with you about this."

"That's my hope, too. Officially, this is out of my jurisdiction. I only work west of the Mississippi, so I wasn't even in on the decision to purchase this land. But as you know, there's a family wedding." He smiled. "I offered to take a look."

They approached the point where the stakes began lining the other side of the road, to the west. His road no longer ran through his own property. This was where the easement came into play, giving him permission to use this portion.

Philips stopped. "Is this the end of your property then?"

"Yes."

"So you own the land the road is on from the highway up to this point?"

"Right, about 50 feet in width. The road from here curves for about 250 yards through the land your company purchased. Then it swings back onto my property, the other side of this ravine."

"No place for a road, eh? What about that cornfield on the east side?"

"Two problems. The owner's not interested in selling or giving an easement. Second, I'd have to cross the ravine to the south where it grows deeper. The creek at the bottom floods regularly."

"I see."

They continued walking along the curving road, where the stakes lined the right side of it.

"Looks like quite a hideaway." Philips nodded toward the oak canopy in the distance where the stakes were again planted back on the left side. "Good place for writing?"

"Perfect. I'm not looking forward to having neighbors."

"I imagine you regret not protecting this easement."

"Regret's not strong enough a word to describe what I feel. I'm still not clear on how Swanson—"

"The deceased owner?"

"Right. How is it my easement contract with him became null and void when his kids inherited the property?"

"Beats me. Chalk it up to a lawyer you'd rather have on your own side. So what are your options here?" He halted beside the tree-filled ravine, stuck his sunglasses on his head and his hands in the pockets of his khaki slacks.

"Options? My option was to buy this land, but it didn't go on the market. What do you do, read farmers' obituaries and then visit the grieving families?"

"Hey, that's not a bad idea. Wonder if there's some software available so we wouldn't have to read every small-town weekly published in the Midwest?"

Brady gritted his teeth.

"It's business, Mr. Olafsson. Not everybody ends up happy. Your school superintendent is very happy. This housing development will draw families. Your schools need more tax dollars and a higher enrollment or they'll be forced to consolidate, making it an even larger, far-flung district. It's a positive for your community."

"Wide-open spaces and natural habitats are positives. Two other developments are going up in the district, east and south of town."

"True. Tell you what. Why don't you think about what you can do with this." He nodded toward the ravine. "What do you think? Some kind of fill rather than a bridge? Trees will have to come down. Fax me some estimates. Maybe we can offer some sort of compensation. I don't think we owe you anything, but we'd rather make the gesture than go through court."

"You still don't have the Zoning Committee's approval."

Philips ignored the comment and started walking back to his car. He pulled a card from his shirt pocket and handed it to Brady. "My phone and fax numbers are on that. Think about it. I'm sure we can reach some sort of an agreement. We can probably even get a deal by using the same excavator."

Teeth still clenched, Brady felt the beginnings of a headache. "What about selling this slice of land to me? Two hundred fifty yards. Fifty feet off someone's backyard acreage."

"I'll run that by the decision makers. Doubt that they have an alley in mind behind these homes. And with parcels already measured—"

"This isn't even zoned for housing yet."

"We'll be in touch." Philips shook his hand. "It's been a pleasure." He opened his car door, slipped on his sunglasses, and smiled. "Oh, by the way, Olafsson." He paused and the smile faded. "Make my daughter cry again and I'll see to it that your road's permanently blocked."

Brady stared at the receding car. What happened to "That's between you two"? Almost imperceptibly it crept in again, that attitude that all Lindstroms and their relatives were the scourges of the earth. Well, except for Lottie.

Brady didn't often become angry. As he slammed the truck into gear and peeled off the narrow road into a U-turn, gravel shot every direction. A cloud of dust followed him. A stake snapped in two. The crunch gave him a morbid satisfaction. He aimed for two more. They might be on his property, and then again they might not be. Didn't matter. They interfered with his mowing.

The thought crossed his mind that less than two hours ago he had sat piously in church, worshiping.

The afternoon was a blur of phone conversations and swallowing ibuprofen. Two school board members as well as the superintendent called him, urging him to withdraw his lawsuit. Valley Oaks needed this development.

Village board members phoned. All six agreed that as chairman of the Zoning Committee, he shouldn't vote on this decision. It was clearly a conflict of interest. He disagreed.

What had Philips done? Put an ad in the newspaper, offering a reward to anyone who swung a punch at Brady?

Well, he wasn't giving up. This was his property, and he wanted more than 250 yards access added to it. He wanted privacy that the projected 100 neighboring houses would obliterate. He called his lawyer.

By four o'clock the turmoil ended. It felt all wrong, spending Sunday in this way. He should have been apologizing profusely to Gina, holding her hand, coaxing a smile from that Miss America mouth, stroking the hardness from that jaw that looked so like her dad's. He remembered the confusion and hurt in her eyes last night. Would that be gone by now, replaced by cold emerald stone that would shut him out?

Well, he wasn't giving up on this either. Wild as it sounded, he cared deeply for her. She had awakened emotions he thought were dead. Her smile triggered a deafening brightness akin to fireworks in his heart. She fit in his woods as naturally as the shy doe and the raucous bullfrogs and the May apples with their secret blossom. Gratitude washed over him. If his plan to marry Nicole hadn't been derailed, he never would have written the books. He never would have had a chance with Gina.

Dear Lord, please pave the way here! I have to speak with her!

He was struck with his self-centeredness. What did she need? He thought of the fragility of her new faith.

Don't let me be a stumbling block. Keep her eyes on You.

Once more he picked up the telephone, this time to dial Lottie's number.

Thirty-One

"Brady, is that you?" Maggie sat at the kitchen table, left leg propped on another chair, chopping vegetables for a salad.

"Yes—"

"The flowers are absolutely gorgeous! We're all enjoying them. Thank you. I know they meant a lot to Gina." She didn't mention that the reason she knew this was because her daughter cried, and her daughter never cried.

"You're welcome, Mrs. Philips—"

"Maggie. I assume you called for Gina. She's not here. She had to leave right after the fourth bouquet arrived."

"Leave?"

"For L.A. Didn't she tell you?" *Oh, goodness,* she thought, *they haven't talked.* "She and her dad decided they should go back tonight rather than tomorrow. They're going to start the deposition in the afternoon."

"Oh."

She heard immense disappointment in his utterance of that one tiny word. "I'll give you our home number. She'll be there until Thursday. Got a pencil?"

"Do you mind giving me the address, too?"

Maggie smiled. Florists must love Brady Olafsson.

After their goodbyes, she pressed the disconnect button and pondered calling John. He had never called back. It must not have been urgent after all. She stretched up behind her shoulder and hung the phone on the wall. Tonight was for *not* talking.

Why was it the moment Reece left relief flooded her? Marsha would admonish that it was because she didn't want to deal with her disconcerted emotions toward him. No doubt there was some truth to that.

She did love him. She didn't know why she had answered him as she had, with "I don't know." They had spent over 30 years together, more than half a lifetime of ups and downs, tears and laughter, a child, the heartache of no more, earthquakes, and coffee. Of course she loved him. In a practical sense. She just didn't feel it when she was with him. There were unresolved issues, such as his traveling...

He had wavered at the front door before leaving for the airport. They had never parted on such undefined terms before. Speechless, he held her awkwardly, the crutches in the way.

Speechless was an improvement over his endless solutions or changing the subject. "Reece," she whispered, "I need some space. Can you understand that?" He had understood it at one time.

"Two thousand miles enough for you?" He kissed her forehead.

"Dad." Gina hurried down the staircase. "Here's Brady's book. This one's my favorite so far. Mother, I hate leaving you like this. You never left me when I was on crutches."

"Don't be silly. I'll let Aunt Lottie pamper me. You have more important things..."

Maggie continued fixing her salad, wondering if Reece would read the book. It would take a miracle for him to read a novel. Her hands stopped slicing cucumber.

Didn't she believe in miracles now? If God wanted him to read the book, the man would read the book.

She tossed the lettuce and veggies and chicken with some vinegar and oil. Aunt Lottie was gone for the evening with a friend to visit other friends at a nursing home. Amazing how that woman kept going. She didn't want to leave Maggie alone, but Maggie insisted she not change her plans.

Maggie cleared a spot for a pad of paper. Fork in one hand, pen in the other, she took a bite and began to write. It was an exercise that had come to mind while listening to the sermon tape Aunt Lottie had brought home. She wanted to write a list of regrets, of disappointments. Of all those things she had hoped and planned for that didn't come about. All those chance journeys, as Marsha called them. Would they make some sense now? Could she see how that mythical bird, the phoenix, had risen from the heap of ashes? Could she scatter the ashes in the wind, let them go once and for all?

What she knew for certain was that it was necessary and that it would hurt. She would cry, but like that morning she learned to forgive Neil's mother, the tears would heal. Only then would she be able to move forward and address the biggest question mark—her marriage.

The car's headlights swung across the front of their house as Gina's dad drove the car into the attached garage. She noticed a shadowy lump on the flagstone walkway near the front door and knew immediately what it was.

She climbed from the car and walked onto the driveway while her dad flipped on lights and unloaded their luggage. The stars were magnificent. Admittedly dimmer than those above tiny Valley Oaks, but still...she took a deep breath. Ahh...blessed cool California air with just the right amount of dewfall and the promise of no humidity tomorrow.

"What in the world?" Dad had opened the front door from inside the house and apparently just missed stepping on that shadowy lump. "I didn't leave this here."

"Two to one it's from Brady, Dad." She walked over to her fifth floral gift of the day. This one was different. She smelled it long before she reached it. Thick, intoxicating perfume. Gardenia. It was a large potted plant, blossoms bursting throughout it. She liked gardenias.

Dad made a harrumphing noise. "I told him to leave you alone."

"You what!" Gina cried.

"Well, to be precise," he leaned over and plucked the envelope from the plant, "I said if he made you cry again, I'd block his road permanently."

"You didn't."

"It slipped out."

"You told me the meeting went fine, that you even liked him."

"I liked him because he didn't roll over. He's not a quitter. I admire that, even though he's going to cause us problems. But when I realized he was doing the same with you..." He blew out a breath. "A father doesn't stay quiet when his little girl is crying."

"Oh, Dad." She threw her arms around him.

He returned her hug, then handed her the envelope. "You know I keep my word, so if you read that and cry, Olafsson's out of luck."

"I'm done crying for this year." She squinted at the writing in the dim light. *You're from the Midwest when you know that cow pies aren't made of beef. Forgive me for being full of the same. Brady.* She burst out laughing. "He is so corny, Dad. Unbelievable. Listen to this. It's from his endless string of Midwest jokes." She read it to him, chuckling.

"Cute. Good, no tears. Makes my job easier. Shall we leave the plant here?"

"I'll take it to the patio. Mother will like it." She knelt, blinking rapidly. Why did it hurt so?

She walked along the ceramic tiled entryway, past the living room and into the kitchen-family room area, slid open the patio door and walked outside. It was nice to be home. This was the house she had grown up in. There was nothing grand about it, just the right size for the three of them. Just the right size for a couple and their empty nest. The small backyard was her mother's pride and joy. A tall privacy fence bordered its three sides and was covered with different climbing plants. Ivy, honeysuckle, jasmine, clematis. Instead of grass, the yard beyond the covered patio was a flower garden with flagstone paths. The short patio wall was covered with bougainvillea.

She set the gardenia on the round glass-topped table. She'd have to ask her mother where the best place was to keep it. What to feed it. When to water it.

Gina took a deep breath. It was shaky. She tried another. *Dear Lord. I haven't known him long enough to fall in love with him. And besides, there's no future, him there and me in some big city. Why bother? And another besides, who's Kim? Actually, I should thank You for the wake-up call. I don't know why I allowed myself to trust him.*

She found her dad in the kitchen, fiddling with the answering machine.

"Gina, who is this?" He punched a button.

A male voice said, "Hi. My father was taken ill. If you need me I'm at this number." She listened to an unfamiliar area code and a string of numbers.

She shrugged and walked to the refrigerator.

"You don't recognize him?"

"Nope." She heard the tape rewinding.

"Why wouldn't he leave a name?"

They listened to the message again as she rummaged in the pantry closet in search of crackers. Except for a jar of peanut butter, the refrigerator was bare.

"Gina."

"What?"

"Who is this?"

She turned to look at him. His face resembled a deer caught in headlights, eyes wide as if in shock. "Dad, it's obviously a wrong number. I don't leave my name when I call you or close friends. He didn't leave a name because he thought he had called someone who knew him. Mother doesn't identify us on that thing. She only says "Please leave a number," which, in my opinion, leaves it a little wide open—"

"It's not someone who works with her?" Dad raked his fingers through his hair.

"They're all women." She carried a box of crackers to the counter, pulled a knife from the drawer and a plate from the cupboard. "Except the big boss, and from what I've seen of him, I doubt he would condescend to call a lowly employee's home. Besides, they all have Aunt Lottie's number."

Without a word, Dad left the room. She heard him go down the hallway and close his bedroom door.

Gina's throat suddenly went dry, and she could barely swallow the bite of cracker she had just put in her mouth. Aunt Lottie's voice replayed in her mind. Was it just yesterday? They all sat around the dining room table, eating breakfast. "Maggie, someone called while you were in the shower, but he didn't leave a message." *He?*

She grabbed a glass from the cupboard and held it under the faucet. She drank the water, her heart beating faster.

Her mother wouldn't.

Thirty-Two

Gina leaned her head against the plane's window, grateful for the empty seat between her and a businessman, his nose buried in a laptop.

It had been an energy-zapping week. The deposition had felt like the reopening of a wound. There was no anesthetic except for momentary gasps during breaks in the rest room, *Lord, help me!* Every nerve screamed while the Park's attorneys probed deeper and deeper. It went on for two days.

"Dr. Philips, what do you hope to gain from this lawsuit?"

Decent, professional care for the elephants.

"Why did you talk to the press?"

When I was in the hospital—

"Before that. The other time."

I never talked to them before that.

Raised brows.

Other employees had eyes. Visitors had eyes.

"To see...?"

The abuse.

"What you refer to as abuse."

She merely blinked in reply. She sat across the table from them, between her father and her lawyer. Dad gave her hand a quick squeeze. Ben reminded them they had already been through the definitions of abuse and what Gina had seen.

"What was the extent of your physical injuries?"

Ben referred them to the medical report in their possession.

Gina closed her eyes. Fractured collar bone, three ribs, femur, kneecap...dislocated hip.

"Do your injuries limit you in any way now?"

I can't do a decent jitterbug.

Smiles all around.

I used to backpack. I used to take walking for granted. I used to administer painkillers to animals only. I used to not worry about arthritis...

"Are you able to work again as a vet?"

Physically, yes.

She felt it across the table...inaudible sighs.

"Dr. Philips, *will* you work again as a vet?"

She studied her folded hands on the table. They had begun this surgery almost 48 hours ago. For her, this was the crux, this was the last of the cancerous tissue to be cut away, the part she had kept hidden before...until Brady gave her the courage to face it. The money didn't matter. It seemed a cheap shot, but it was the only way to prevent more Delilahs.

Gina made eye contact with the two men and one woman across the table. Intelligent, pasty, indoor faces. Trim haircuts. Matching, big-shouldered navy blue suits. She kept her voice low.

Do you mean will I get my life back again? She managed a small smile. *Will I stand beside an ailing elephant, pat her thick hide, and promise I'll make her feel better? Will I hold hands with a baby orangutan again? Will I touch an awesome lion's mane while he's unconscious during an operation?*

I don't know. And the reason I don't know is because administrators who wore blinders hired an inept keeper, ignored my warnings, and covered up the fact that he not only left his duties, he locked me in with an elephant he knew was out of control. The mere thought of being that close to an enormous animal, my specialty, reduces me to a sniveling idiot. That's why I don't know.

The already pale faces blanched. Her dad's hand tightened on her forearm. Ben sucked in a deep breath. The expressionless female recorder bit her lip.

"Ma'am? Ma'am?" The flight attendant's voice grew louder.

Gina's reverie dissipated, and she accepted a bagged lunch from her, although she didn't want it. She didn't feel hungry. She didn't feel anything except turned inside out.

On a scale of one to ten, the zoo interview in Seattle was a five. Maybe a five and a half. So-so. Maybe it was her imagination, but she felt a positive connection with the administrator. She was honest about her role in the controversy surrounding Wild Creatures Country, about her physical limitations. She didn't bring up the subject of irrational fear. She toured the zoo with a vet. They didn't go inside the elephant enclosure.

Maybe if she could follow around another vet for a while, become accustomed to the elephants, maybe then she could function. She would go forward by going backward, work as a resident again. Did they offer such things to someone with her experience? Oh, what did it matter? The bottom line of her experience was trouble. Nobody would ask for that.

She dozed. In the Minneapolis airport she learned the flight to Chicago was indefinitely delayed. Thunderstorms had disrupted schedules. What else could wreak emotional havoc on her this week?

There was her mother.

She shoved that thought aside. She realized she needed to let go. Too tired to walk it off, she pulled out Brady's book and tried not to think of the author.

But she missed him. Missed the undeniable comfort he had offered, the care. She felt cherished...until she remembered his friend. Kim.

Gina read until at last the flight was called. A short time later she was in Chicago, eagerly checking a monitor to find the gate for the flight to Rockville. She found it, glanced at her watch...no way! The final flight of the night had left 90 minutes ago.

She twirled on her heel, ready to grab the first airline employee within arm's reach. The only body within arm's reach was a tall blond wearing a sopping wet windbreaker and a sheepish grin on his lean, handsome face.

Brady's heart melted at the sight of her. Defeat was written in her stance, in her face, in her rumpled white shirt and jeans and hair. He held himself in check, letting her make the first move. Almost imperceptibly, her jaw tightened.

"Your carriage awaits, Miss Angelina."

"What are you doing here?" She finger-combed chocolate brown hair behind an ear.

"Well, about 6:00 tonight we heard O'Hare was shut down. Learned your flight wouldn't get out of Minneapolis in time to catch the last run to Rockville."

"We?"

"Your mother and I. There was just enough time to drive here before you went off looking for a hotel. I offered to come fetch you."

"That's too much to ask." Her voice was barely above a whisper. Speaking seemed to take great effort.

"Nobody asked. I wanted to do it."

She looked away.

"And I'm here now." He reached over and nudged the carry-on bag's strap from her shoulder. She let him take it. "It's a long walk to the exit."

"Do I have another choice?"

"I can get a wheelchair. Or flag down one of those vehicles—"

"I meant besides riding home with you."

"Sure. Spend the night in a chair. I think there's a 6:30 flight in the morning. Or get a shuttle to some hotel." He clenched his teeth. She was the most stubborn woman he had ever met! "Or swallow your pride and accept my gift."

Her tired eyes flashed. "You have to let me pay for the gas."

"Fine."

She dug into her purse, pulled out a wallet, yanked bills from it, and began shoving them at him.

"Gina, this can wait."

"No, it can't. I didn't even thank you for the flowers. There, that's all I have."

"It's plenty." He pocketed the money. "Let's go."

She didn't follow him.

He walked back to her. Maybe she was in pain from sitting for so long. "Do you want a wheelchair?"

"Thank you," she whispered, "for the flowers."

"You're welcome."

"You didn't owe me anything. It was too extravagant."

He stared at her. Her problem wasn't stubbornness. If pride, then it was from not being loved unconditionally. He suspected her parents loved her. Her father's threat had not been made in jest. But the three of them were the driven, hardworking, results-oriented type. Perhaps unconditional got buried in the routine. Perhaps she really never had received flowers in the way he meant them. "Look, sweetheart, you know how Jesus came, as a free gift to anyone who chooses to receive Him? No strings attached? He came without our asking, without demanding anything in return. He didn't owe it to us. I just want to give you these things because I—"

"No! Don't say it!"

Love you, he finished silently.

She shook her head. "Brady, I'm exhausted."

"All right. Let's just sit down, give you a minute to catch your breath and figure out what you want to do." He firmly grasped her elbow and steered her through a shifting maze of people toward a seating area. They sat down. "Want to talk about your week?"

"No!" She covered her face with her hands and leaned forward, propping her elbows on her knees. "Oh, it was so awful! Everything is gone. I lost my whole life this week. Everything I worked so hard for. Everything I've ever dreamed of. Everything— Oh, I just want to go home." She lowered her hands to her mouth and muffled a derisive laugh. "I don't have a home. Really and truly, I don't. I have a room at my parents' house. Twenty-eight years old and no place to go, no future." She grew silent.

He wanted to carry her in his arms, take her home, and tuck her in...in the guest room? He gripped the back of her chair, knowing full well that at this moment she wouldn't even accept a friendly half hug. "Gina, this won't make sense right now, but sometimes God allows pain like this so He can take us down another path, one that's ultimately better for us. You can count on the fact that there will come a time when you'll be able to see His fingerprints all over this. Some days all you can manage is to just remember that. It'll get you through. I know, trust me."

She sniffed, sat up, and slung her purse over her shoulder. "Trust you?"

He heard the skepticism in her tone and saw emerald stones looking up at him.

"I have to go now." She stood. "I'm so tired. Can we go?"

"Of course." As they walked through O'Hare's busy corridors, he looked down at her bowed head. There would be no more relating tonight. She was asleep on her feet. Not an opportune time to explain Kim or why it was he thought that Gina should ever trust him again.

Thirty-Three

"Mother, sit down. I can get—"

"No, no." Determined to serve her daughter, Maggie hobbled on one crutch to the refrigerator, pulled out the carton of orange juice, and carried it back to the kitchen table. "I'm getting pretty good with just one crutch. I can hop, too. Go without any."

Gina shook her head. "I sure hope the doctor fixes you up with a walking cast this afternoon. You'll break your neck this way." She munched on buckwheat pancakes Maggie had cooked for her.

Her child looked exhausted, even after sleeping late this morning. Maggie sat down across the table from her, eager to pursue the subject of Brady. He had already been by this morning to deliver Gina's luggage that had arrived on the early flight from Chicago. "I don't think I've ever met anyone as thoughtful as Brady. I told him we'd get your bag today. Yesterday he first called about noon, asking when you were coming, then again later when he heard the weather forecast. Then he checked with the airline. I hated the thought of you spending the night alone at the airport or a hotel."

Gina got that "get real, do you know how old I am" look on her face. "I appreciated the ride, so thanks for sending him. He even had a pillow and blanket in his truck. I slept all the way home."

Maggie laughed. "A pillow? He is attentive to detail. Did he send any more flowers?"

"A gardenia plant."

She grinned. "I think you've got yourself a winner."

"Do you know why he sent all those? Why he spent four hours driving in the rain last night?"

"Isn't it obvious? He's nuts about you."

"He's apologizing because on Saturday night his girlfriend walked in."

Maggie felt her shoulders slump. "Really?" *Still,* she thought, *he didn't have to do all of that.* "But—"

"But nothing, Mother. If there was anything, which I doubt, it's over. Drop it, okay?"

"Okay." She studied Gina's pretty face. It looked so hard in this defensive mode. "Will you tell me about the deposition?"

"Didn't you talk to Dad about it?"

"He hasn't called. I left messages— Was he with you for the whole thing?"

"For most of it. He had some meetings on Tuesday." She drank her juice, then met Maggie's eyes. "It was hard..."

She listened to the details, aching for her child and feeling proud of the young woman who refused to back down, who fought for what she believed in.

With scarcely a pause for breath, Gina moved from the deposition into an account of her interview. Maggie watched her struggle with trying to emphasize the positive, but she saw how crushed her spirit was.

"Honey, I'm proud of you."

Gina shrugged.

"For how you handled everything this week. Who knows, maybe you'll get a little money. That would be some compensation and help get you back on your feet, besides influence a lot of people in favor of your elephants. And the interview, after all, was only your first one."

"Mom." She lowered her eyes and pulled something from her pants pocket. "There's something else."

Maggie took the small piece of crumpled paper she offered. An unfamiliar telephone number was written on it. "What's this?"

"Don't you recognize it?"

"No."

Gina paused. "There was a message on the machine at home. A man said, 'Hi. My father was taken ill. If you need me I'm at this number.'"

Maggie thought her heart stopped beating. A distinct wave of guilt and shame flooded through her. She felt as if she would never again have the strength to stand up.

"The message was for you, wasn't it?"

Amazingly, she found her voice. "Yes."

"Mother!"

"He's a friend, Gina..." *Just a friend, because I need—* No, she wouldn't make excuses, wouldn't put any of the blame on Reece in front of his daughter.

"A friend Dad doesn't know about?"

"Yes."

"It's no mystery why Dad hasn't called you." There was anger in Gina's voice, fear in her eyes. "What kind of a *friend* is he?"

"It's not—" *An affair. But it is, though not in the physical sense. It is an emotional affair. Is that adultery?* "It's not in the way that you're imagining."

"How do you know what I'm imagining? What am I supposed to imagine? We come to Podunk, and you're a totally different person. All of a sudden you have an ex-husband, a dead daughter, and a boyfriend!"

"He's not a—"

Gina rushed from the kitchen.

So Reece had heard the message, too. How did it affect him? Did it affect him?

She pushed the question aside. What was this all about again, this coming to Podunk? To find herself. To go through the past. Unearth the hurts, the denials. She had made her list, asking God for grace to forgive and let go, strength to confront where possible. Hopefully in that she would find authenticity, the real Maggie Lindstrom Philips of today.

She adjusted the crutches under her arms, grabbed the car keys and her purse from hooks near the back door, and went outside. Still crinkled in her hand was the unfamiliar phone number.

It took her four attempts to punch in the correct calling card numbers followed by the ones Gina had handed her.

Maggie sat in the car, in the mall's parking lot next to a drive-up telephone. Its cord stretched through the open window. She rested her forehead against the steering wheel, listening to the ringing of a stranger's phone somewhere in Northern California.

"Hello."

"John? It's—"

"Margaret! Hello." There was a smile in his voice.

"How—" Her throat constricted. "How is your father?"

"He had a stroke, but he's getting along fairly well. He's back home now."

"And how are you?"

"Not bad. I've just relocated for a month or so. Dad's timing was impeccable. He waited until my summer term was over. I can write from here almost as well as from home." He paused. "So. How are the baby steps going?"

Her eyes burned with unshed tears. "It...it seems time for one giant adult step." Her voice sounded unnaturally high. "Maybe it's more like a plunge into a...a sea of authenticity."

Silence filled the miles between them. Her tears spilled over, and she heard him take a deep breath. He understood.

At last he spoke. "I hear the water is somewhat cold at first."

She closed her eyes and whispered, "It feels like ice."

"You'll be warm again. And it'll be a clean warm, no more pretense on any front, no regrets."

She wiped at the tears. "I'm sorry."

"No, please, don't be sorry. Never be sorry. That would invalidate our friendship." He took another deep breath. "I've tried to plan for this all along, you know. It's for your best. And I most definitely want what's best for you."

The tears flowed steadily. It was time to say goodbye, but she had no voice and there were no words.

"Margaret, before I start blubbering, we'll just leave the rest unsaid. Thank you for...for everything. All right?"

"Mm-hmm," she mumbled.

"All right. Take care."

"John, wait! Tell me one thing." The words rushed together now, racing ahead of the sobs building in her chest. "Why did you leave that message on my machine?"

He was quiet for a moment. "Part of me hoped you would pick up your messages. I wanted you to know where I could be reached. But, truthfully...I know you're afraid of heights. I thought a little nudge toward the edge of the cliff might encourage you to take that plunge."

It was an act of true love, forcing her to choose between authenticity and duplicity. If she wanted to live honestly, this friendship was outside the boundaries of her marriage. "Thank you," she sobbed.

"Goodbye, Maggie-Margaret." His voice was full of tears.

"Goodbye." She leaned through the window, hung up the phone, and gave in to inconsolable weeping.

The crinkled piece of paper fluttered across the parking lot in the morning breeze.

Thirty-Four

Gina spent the day with Lauren at her house, avoiding her mother and giving vent to her frustrations by wielding a paintbrush. By the time the old dark kitchen walls radiated new life under a third coat of sunshine yellow-and-white trim, the cousins had reviewed Gina's trip, unfinished wedding-related preparations, the upcoming honeymoon cruise to Alaska, and Brady. Brady ad nauseam.

Aaron walked in through the back screen door as they were cleaning up at the sink. "Hi, girls," he called above the oldies music blaring from the radio. Although the kitchen housed only a coffeemaker and refrigerator, he had moved in last week.

Gina turned down the volume and noticed the bouquet of yellow roses he held behind his back as he greeted Lauren with a kiss, leaning forward so as not to brush his suit coat against her paint-spattered T-shirt. Gina tried to blend into the white woodwork and ignore a distinct stab of envy. They looked so contented together, so happy.

Lauren giggled when he handed her the roses with a flourish. "What is this, a peace offering for what you're about to do tonight?"

He laughed. "Yeah, right. A bachelor party in the church basement. Office hours at 8:00 tomorrow morning. That combination could spell trouble." He headed for the hallway, his fiancée on his heels, chattering about her evening plans.

Gina finished washing out the paintbrushes. Above the sink was a window overlooking the small backyard. It was a cute two-story, three-bedroom house, a fixer-upper, but situated on a pleasant Valley Oaks cul-de-sac. They could spend years here and begin a family. She heard them upstairs now, talking in the familiar tones of a couple accustomed to sharing the intimate details of the everyday. When had she last heard her parents' voices comfortable in this way?

The doorbell buzzed. It was a grating sound that Lauren wanted replaced. Wiping her hands on a towel, Gina walked into the front room. The inside door was open. On the other side of the screen door stood Brady.

Without hesitation, Gina turned on her heel, headed back through the kitchen, tossed the towel toward a countertop, and marched out the screen door. It slammed behind her as she strode across the lawn. The yard was fairly private, with a garage to one side, a row of arbor vitae on another, and a ravine at the end. She went to the lone maple tree, leaned against it facing away from the house, and crossed her arms. He had probably come to pick up Aaron. She'd just wait here until he was gone.

The screen door slammed again.

Gina stomped her foot on the ground.

He came around the tree and halted two feet in front of her. "Here in Valley Oaks we usually say hello to someone at the door."

"Even if you have absolutely nothing to say to or hear from the person?"

"It's called being courteous."

"I'd rather be honest."

"Kim means absolutely nothing to me."

She blinked. "That's what I thought." The sarcasm came easily. "That's exactly what it looked like."

He placed his hands on his hips, arms akimbo. His mouth was a grim line. "I just wanted to tell you."

"Message received. Not that it matters. That isn't why I've nothing to say to you." She glared at him. He wore khakis and no hat. A lime green polo shirt made his hair seem blonder, his tan deeper.

"What exactly is the reason, then? You said you want to be honest," he challenged.

She glanced away and released the breath she had been holding. *May as well just spit it out, girl.* "My life is not what you'd call on an even keel these days. It hasn't been for some time, but I have to get on with it, and that's not going to happen in Valley Oaks."

"What's that got to do with us being friends?"

She looked at him. "Being friends with you is like jumping on an emotional trampoline. I don't know why that is, it just is, and I am not up for the exercise."

He opened his mouth as if to say something, then closed it and walked away.

Gina felt a sense of relief. She had been honest. They were back where they had started. That was as it should be—

"Yeah, but," he came back into her line of vision, "would you like to go horseback riding tomorrow? Take a break from painting and shopping? Think about it. Just come out to the farm midmorning." He cocked his head and his expression softened. "Please come. No strings attached." He left.

She looked up at the leafy branches above her head. Oh, she missed him. She definitely missed him. But he was wrong. There were strings attached. Some romantic would probably call them heartstrings.

Running errands around Valley Oaks with Lauren was like politicking for a candidacy. Her cousin greeted everyone in the hardware store, post office, and grocery store. Gina tagged behind her and was introduced to teachers, students, the bank president, countless mothers of students, a cousin, store owners, and every employee on the premises.

Lauren had showered and changed and looked her usual cute self in white overall shorts and a red T-shirt. Not one speck of yellow paint lingered. At first Gina felt downright gauche with her own stringy hair falling out of a ponytail and wearing jeans and an old, baggy white shirt of Aaron's with its sleeves rolled-up. None of it, including her arms and face, had escaped the sunflower splatter, smeared like some child's unpatterned finger painting.

Gradually the homespun tour worked its magic. It was impossible not to be affected by all the smiles turned her way, the laughter, the best wishes directed toward her cousin the bride. It felt like a genuine sense of camaraderie. Knowing her mother's story, she understood that Valley Oaks wasn't a paradise free from conflict, but this general spirit of good will was infectious.

In the grocery store she burst out laughing when a teenage girl apologized for staring at her. The girl said, "I work at The Landing. Didn't I see you there recently, with Brady Olafsson?"

"Oh, yes, that was me." Gina smoothed back her hair.

The girl and her friend exchanged glances. "His books are so awesome!" they exclaimed in unison. "What's he like?"

"Annoying." She smiled. "I mean, he's a real human being. You haven't met him?"

"No."

"Just introduce yourselves when you see him. He loves talking to readers. He's a..." She paused and felt the softness radiate through her. "He's a really, really nice guy." *And he invited me to go horseback riding tomorrow.*

They went to the pharmacy located across from the town square in a small brick building. The year 1904 was carved in a concrete stone above the door. It was cool inside. Cozy scents of candles, soap, and eucalyptus greeted them along with Britte Olafsson, who stood behind a counter.

"How about some lemonade, ladies?" She poured from a carafe.

Lauren's face lit up. "Now she's offering lemonade? This is great. Gina, last week our new pharmacist was giving out homemade cookies."

Britte pointed across the aisle. "Check out this shelf of new pottery."

"Is that Addie's work?"

"Yeah!"

Gina accepted a paper cup of pink lemonade. "Do you work here, Britte?"

"I'm helping out a bit before school starts. Eliana is just getting her feet wet. She's from Chicago and took over the business only about six weeks ago."

"Come on, Gina," Lauren said, "I'll introduce you to her."

At the back of the store was the pharmacist's counter against a backdrop of floor to ceiling shelves perpendicular to it. A woman stretched on her tiptoes to retrieve a large jar of capsules. Thick black hair, tied back with a blue ribbon, hung almost to her waist.

"Eliana," Lauren said. "I want you to meet my cousin, Gina Philips. Gina, this is Eliana Neuman."

"Nice to meet you, Gina." Though her accent was decidedly all-American, the young woman resembled a China doll with a flawless porcelain-like complexion and dark eyes.

They chatted a few moments, saw Isabel on their way out, waved to Anne across the street. Back in the car, Lauren asked her what was wrong. "You're frowning."

"Nothing's wrong." Gina knew that wasn't quite the truth. "I don't know."

"Brady?"

"No, it's this town, Laur. It's getting to me. I mean, you probably knew three-fourths of the people we passed."

"So?"

"It's just a totally opposite world from mine. It's just too *cozy*. Too *homespun*."

"Meaning?"

"I'm not that way. I don't fit in."

"Which doesn't matter unless you're thinking of living here."

Gina didn't reply.

"Meaning the thought has crossed your mind. Meaning this *is* all about Brady."

"Oh, Laur, I can't see him anymore. What would be the point? I'm leaving in a week."

"People don't have to live in the same town to fall in love."

"That's way too complicated. My life is a shambles as it is. I'm too unsettled to trust my feelings, let alone trust him. He was a friend for a few special moments."

"Have a few more with him. Go horseback riding tomorrow. I dare you."

Gina shook her head.

"Double dare you. What else have you got going?"

"Painting your bathroom?"

"Like I said, what else have you got going?"

Back at Aunt Lottie's, Gina headed straight upstairs to shower, glad for the jam-packed schedule. Lauren's bachelorette slumber party would prevent her from brooding tonight. She scrubbed at the paint splotches until her skin reddened and tears mingled with the water streaming down her face.

"Dear Jesus! I'm unraveling here. I don't know how to pray about it. Please help me sort it out. Mother and Dad. Brady. Work." She drained herself of tears and the water heater of its contents. A sense of peace settled inside of her. Why was it that just as her life made sense with God, everything else was falling apart? What had happened to her common sense, her consistently medium demeanor?

Later, as she was combing her wet hair, Maggie knocked on the open bedroom door. "Can we talk a minute?"

She had missed her mom today. This morning's argument had cut deeper than any teenage disagreement. It severed that invisible connection, that inherent cord between mother and daughter. "Sure." She plopped on the bed.

Maggie sat carefully on the vanity bench, stretching out her leg, the ankle wrapped in a new walking cast. Her eyes were puffy, but there was a distinct air of calm about her. "First of all, I am sorry for letting you down. I know I betrayed you and your dad. There is no excuse. I can blame it on crazy hormones, Dad's traveling, me not telling him I was dying inside, or not letting go of the past. But the point is, I found a way out and I took it, thinking only of myself." She exhaled sharply. "I guess I'm not perfect."

Gina felt the sadness draw her lips downward, crease her forehead.

"Secondly, it's over. He was truly just a friend. When you didn't need me at home, we sometimes met after work for an early dinner or just a walk. Occasionally..." She took a deep breath. "I was so deceitful. Occasionally I took the afternoon off and we'd go to the art exhibits. There never was anything physical between us. I wouldn't cross that line." She took a deep breath. "Not yet anyway. So thank you for the phone number. I called him, and we won't talk again. Please forgive me, sweetheart?"

Gina nodded. Her mother slid beside her, and they hugged for a long time. It was somehow comforting to know that the woman was not perfect.

Thirty-Five

As Aunt Lottie headed to bed, Maggie headed out the door to her sister's. It was late, and she knew Marsha was on overload with the wedding just a week away, but there was no one else to turn to. Maggie felt like a fish out of water, flopping around in this strange environment created because of her new consciousness of God.

She had made the correct choice, one she thought would be pleasing to Him. If marriage vows were for keeps, she had to keep up her end of the deal, no matter that she couldn't remember the last time Reece had listened to her with tenderness or spoken a truly heartfelt emotion.

But every breath she took cut like a knife. What was she supposed to do now? How exactly did one depend on God? She needed a voice and arms and eye contact.

When she entered her sister's kitchen, her heart fell. Marsha was beyond frazzled. Her voice hit screech level as her husband and son slid behind Maggie and out the back door.

Marsha burst into tears.

Maggie wrapped her arms around her, surprised that she had more tears to shed herself.

"Oh, Maggie! They can't even pick up after themselves or rinse off a plate!" She grabbed paper napkins from the counter and handed one to her sister. They blew their noses in unison.

"Yeah, but I bet the barn is as clean as a whistle."

Marsha nodded. "You could use the side of the combine for a mirror."

"Well, only if you wanted to look like a green Martian."
Marsha smiled through her tears.

"Marsh, hire a cleaning service for this week."

"I'm an able-bodied woman. There is no reason on earth
to pay someone good money to do what I can do."

"You can't do it this week. You're having all kinds of
people dropping by, out-of-towners on Saturday, 50 for
Sunday brunch. Hire a maid."

"I've never hired—"

"It's not that big of a deal. If you don't, you'll miss the
wedding. You'll either be sick in bed or look as bad as you do
now, and there's no way you'd step out the door looking like
that. Give me your phone book." She plopped onto a chair.

Marsha ran her fingers through her disheveled hair and
opened a drawer. "Danny says I look like a cat with its claw
stuck in an electric socket." She laid the phone book on the
table and sat down.

"He's right." Maggie thumbed through the yellow pages.
"You have a hair appointment, right? And your dress alter-
ations will be done by Tuesday. Do you have some sort of
salon around here that offers the works? You know, nails,
facial, massage?"

"Massage!"

"It's therapeutic. Let's see…looks like plenty of cleaning
service possibilities. I'll call in the morning." She flipped back
to listings under "Beauty," thinking she should take her own
advice. "Marsh, you know we don't have to be perfect. We
can allow ourselves some time off and ask for help. This can
be my aunt gift to Lauren, a calm mother. I think I'll come,
too. I should have thought of this for Liz's wedding.
Remember how sick you were? Here's one."

Marsha leaned over. "Check out the address. No way I'm
getting a massage in that neighborhood."

"Oh. Is that still the seedy part of Rockville?"

She nodded. "Why are you here?"

Maggie lifted a shoulder. She didn't want to unload on her sister. "Here's another one. This looks better."

"Why are you crying?"

"A mingle-mangle of hormones."

"Is Gina all right? She seemed quiet today at the house."

"I heard you were painting. You don't have to add that to your list, you know. She's fine."

"Is it your ankle? Did the doctor say something was more serious?"

"No." She stood. "Why don't you go take a bubble bath? Leave the kitchen for tonight. Leave everything—"

"Maggie, I'll be fine. I'll do just that. After my tirade, the guys will probably surprise me and fold the laundry."

"Good. I'll go then. Maybe I can take a bubble bath, a one-legged bubble bath." She went to the door.

"How's Reece?"

Maggie would have ignored the question and scooted outside, but her body betrayed her. Tears formed again, her throat ached, her shoulders slumped, she couldn't move. "Fine. I don't know."

"Maggie." Her sister's tone implored.

"He knows about John." She sat back down. The story came out then. The answering machine message, Gina's hurt, the farewell phone conversation. She ended with, "So now what, Marsh? Now I don't have anyone—"

"Except God."

"Except God, and I can't see Him. I did the right thing, didn't I?"

"I think so. Reece must be hurting."

"I don't really know if he is or not. It might be an easy way out for him. I'm not sure he feels much of anything."

"Oh, Maggie, just because he doesn't show it doesn't mean the feelings don't exist. Although I know how frustrating he can be."

"It's like I had this dutiful husband. I was the dutiful wife. We functioned well together. But somewhere along the way our emotions disconnected. Then John's friendship took care of that department. Now I've severed that, and I don't give a hoot about functioning well together."

"God will take care of you."

"Don't give me that, Marsha! It's too abstract. How will He take care of me? Will He hold me tonight and tell me He loves me? Will He warm my bed and smile at me in the morning?"

"Yes."

Maggie stared at her.

"He will do all of that." Marsha squeezed her hand. "He will make the pain bearable. He wants to be all that you need, no matter how abstract it sounds. It's supernatural. When you can't take another breath, let Him give it to you."

"I need a person I can touch."

"He knows what you need better than you do. Remember when I said I thought a mailman would be better for me than my farmer?"

Maggie nodded.

"I started to pray for Dan whenever that thought came to mind. Eventually, things changed. I'm not saying this is going to be easy. I don't think there are any shortcuts. And I'm not saying God will make Reece into your dream partner."

"No guarantees for anything, huh?"

"Only that God wants to be number one in your life."

Maggie put her fingers over her mouth and whispered, "It sounds so hard."

Marsha nodded. "Hey, you didn't really mean you want your bed warmed tonight, did you?"

She thought of the evening's 82 degrees and of Aunt Lottie's non-air-conditioned upstairs. Laughter mingled with her tears.

Reece poured the dark amber liquid into a glassful of ice cubes. He gulped a mouthful and grimaced up at the first stars twinkling in a cobalt blue sky.

He never drank, not even during his college days. He never felt the desire. The few times he tried it simply because it was the thing to do, his body reacted violently to one glass of whatever. His stomach churned and his head pounded. He failed to see the fun in it.

Tonight he wanted to get blitzed. Pie-eyed. Sloshed. Inebriated.

Margaret and another man?

His anger was spent. He had tried to mask it with Gina, sitting calmly beside her at the deposition, feeling pride in her responses and yet literally biting his tongue at times, wanting to lash out at the fools across the table. His office staff didn't fare as well. Minuscule problems were met with diatribes. He played racquetball like a madman.

He didn't return Margaret's messages, didn't even pick up the phone when it rang at home.

He sipped his drink.

One time when Gina was little, she had wandered from him in a large department store while they were Christmas shopping for Margaret. He became frantic. Before she was found, he envisioned life without her, and he knew firsthand what a breaking heart felt like.

This was worse.

It wasn't a wrong number.

He took a swig of the bitter drink and gagged.

This was what she had been trying to tell him the night she asked if he loved her. What had he answered? He called her question ridiculous. Blamed his parents for his inadequacy to say those three simple words. The words he thought were just understood in their day-to-day life.

Even the days he wasn't home? Days? Try *weeks*.

She was a beautiful woman, inside and out. She deserved more than what he had been able to give her.

He tried another sip.

He hated Podunk. He always knew it would win out. He had always been afraid of losing her, hadn't he?

His stomach churned and his head pounded.

He tossed the contents of the glass off to the side of the patio. It sprayed over her flowers.

Oh, no!

In the light from the kitchen window, he set the glass on the table, grabbed a napkin, and knelt on the concrete to brush at the petals. Could he wipe away the damage?

A sob erupted. He buried his face in his hand and wept.

Dear God. I'm sorry. I am so sorry!

Thirty-Six

Brady knelt beside the couch, feasting on the soft features of Gina asleep. The impression she gave was something of a cross between what Sleeping Beauty must have appeared to her prince and that of a secure, carefree child who slept soundly through thunderstorms.

Her closed eyelids hid the deserved anger and distrust he had glimpsed earlier. Her mussed chocolate hair shone in the dim lamplight. She lay on her side, one hand under a cheek, pushing her lips slightly askew. An arm, covered in a short-sleeved peacock blue T-shirt, lay atop a patchwork quilt that protected her from the cold air blasting from a window unit air conditioner. Was that a zebra face peeking out from the front of the shirt?

He shouldn't have come. This was sheer torture. Across the room Aaron and two other guys laughed with Lauren, Isabel, and Abbey. It was after midnight, and they were behaving like a bunch of teenagers, minus the beer. It had started with the obligatory bachelor party: dinner and good-natured but unmerciful harassing of Aaron. Following that, they had gone to the farm and played basketball in the old barn. His grandfather had built the wooden-floored, full-size court when he was in high school, and it had been a popular gathering place. After that they did what came naturally: spray painted the corncrib. It was a dilapidated structure, set out at the edge of a cornfield next to a county road stop sign. Its sole purpose for still standing was to display graffiti painted by high schoolers. Different groups regularly painted

over each other's messages, ducking in the shadows whenever a car slowed, hoping the sheriff wouldn't bust them for
breaking curfew. He wondered if the kids would leave this
latest paint job, three-foot letters proclaiming "Aaron loves
Lauren."

Most of the guys headed home after that, skipping this
crashing of the gals' slumber party. He had looked at the
cans of shaving cream rolling around the truck's floor with
the spray paint cans and thought, "Why not?" He knew that
it was the anticipation of seeing this sleeping beauty that
brought him. Just like a teenager.

Could he break through that hard-shell exterior again?
Make her smile that Miss America smile? He had to. It was
simple. He loved her, and he had only a week to win her heart.

Compared to Gina, Nicole had simply been a nice idea.
He cared for her in an adolescent way. She made him feel
good. The natural progression of things was to become
engaged. They had known each other for some time, but he
hadn't known her in the way he knew Gina. Gina filled all
the empty nooks and crannies of his heart. He wanted to fill
her world with laughter, carry her when her leg ached, share
her burdens, be her best friend. Persuade her to move thousands of miles from home.

Was he being totally ludicrous? He still had excess baggage, like Kim. Silly woman. No...hurting woman. What
had he promised her? Nothing.

Not even indirectly?

He didn't think so. They dated. They shared an interest in
teaching. Her bubbly personality had made for hassle-free
times. He had never intended to hint at anything more. Then
she left for Spain for four months. Had she read more into
their e-mail exchanges? What had he said?

Well, she needed to hear "back off." He told her so the
night she had chased Gina off. Not in those words, of course.
Those words he used this afternoon when she stopped by the

house again, interrupting his writing. She didn't seem to understand the subtle phrases. He apologized for what he didn't even know he had to apologize for. He hated it, hurting her feelings.

Women. He wasn't interested in a more serious relationship, thought he never would be...

Until now.

If he kissed her, would she awaken and smile, notice that her frog had turned into a prince?

He'd better start with bridging the gap again.

Gina stirred, shifting over onto her back. Her cheek was rosy, creased where she had lain on it.

Brady closed his eyes. *Dear Lord. Head over heels was not part of this bargain, was it? I only offered You the chip on my shoulder.*

A kiss and sweet words and flowers didn't get her attention. This called for drastic measures. He vigorously shook the can he held, then squirted a globby string of shaving gel along her hairline, careful to avoid the corner of her eye. As it foamed, he gently feathered it into her hair.

She certainly was a sound sleeper.

Gina's eyes widened in disbelief as she gaped at her reflection in the bathroom mirror. Something was wrong with her hair. "Wha—?" she cried. A layer of mint green traced her hairline from one ear to the other and slicked back her hair, covering most of the top of her head. She looked like a woman who'd fled the beautician's chair with a coloring job only partially completed. All she needed was a plastic cape.

She peered more closely and touched the cotton candy-like mess. Dried foam. She sniffed her fingers. Menthol. It was shaving cream!

"Oh!" she shrieked and yanked open the bathroom door.

She strode past the bedroom where Abbey and Isabel still slept and found her cousin in the kitchen pouring coffee.

"Lauren! This is," she pointed to her head, "the dumbest stunt. I cannot believe that at your age you get a kick out of squirting shaving cream on my hair. Like I've nothing better to do than to shampoo and re-shampoo it this morning. It's probably all over your pillow—"

"Brady did it."

Gina stared at her, mouth open.

Lauren took a sip of coffee, then immediately burst into laughter and sprayed it into the sink.

"Brady?" Gina yelped.

Her cousin nodded, caught between laughter and choking, tears running from her eyes.

"But he wasn't here last night."

"He was," she gasped between giggles, "with Aaron and two other guys."

"Where was I?"

Lauren howled and sat down at the table, doubling over. "On the couch, fast asleep."

"No way." She shook her head. "Uh-uh."

Lauren nodded. "Uh-huh. You sure can sleep."

That was true. Ever since the accident, she'd slept like a dead person. It was as if the morphine was still in her system after all these months, or that somehow her body just craved the healing power of sleep and easily succumbed. "I didn't respond at all?" This was scary.

"Nope." She wiped tears from her face.

"What a stupid thing to waste your time and energy on! I can't believe it. It's so...so teenagerish!"

"Exactly. Very teenagerish. It's proof that he likes you. You're really just embarrassed, you know."

"I am not!"

"Well, I would be. I mean, he sat on the couch beside you for a long time—"

"Sat on the couch?! While I was asleep on it?!"

"Then squirted the shaving cream on your face and kind of," she giggled, "spread it around. At least you weren't drooling. You know. Or snoring."

"Lauren!" She was furious. "I have moved way beyond this kind of nonsense."

"That's why you're so embarrassed. Maybe you ought to lighten up a bit. The guy is nuts about you."

Gina turned on her heel and headed straight for the shower.

After the second application of shampoo she still smelled like a man's jaw. Brady's jaw.

She poured out another palmful and lathered vigorously, dismissing the thought that there would be no hot water for anyone else.

Lord, please get me out of this town in one piece. What is it I'm missing here? So what if I'm embarrassed? It's still an idiotic thing for an adult to do. Totally ridiculous behavior.

Boy, that sounded snobbish. Maybe she was a snob after all, like Brady said he thought when they were teenagers. Was she acting like a teenager, stuck up and too good for Podunk?

She shivered in the hot water.

The truth was she turned up her nose at his flowers and his acts of kindness.

Lord, I'm sorry.

She pondered Lauren's words. *Lighten up.* When was the last time she lightened up? Her life had been years of study and work. It was serious work. She had felt lighthearted, truly alive, only when she was with the animals. It was hard work, but she thrived on it, drew strength from ministering to wild beasts. And that had been taken from her. With her life thrown off course, she wallowed in worries and self-pity.

When was *she* going to grow up?

Okay, if God was in control now, steering that car Aunt Lottie had talked about, she could let go of the wheel. Ease up on the self-imposed pressure. Not care if she appeared a loser. Not care if she felt embarrassed.

What she needed was to connect with some animals again. It was her gift, and without using it she felt like an anchorless boat, floating aimlessly across a churning ocean of emotions. She needed to walk through woods again, catch a frog. Maybe ride a horse? There was Brady's invitation for this morning.

A true snob couldn't laugh at herself. She thought of her reflection earlier in the mirror and cringed. She certainly had looked goofy. One hundred percent uncool. Absolutely ridiculous.

The frown lessened.

At least you weren't drooling.

A crooked smile tugged at Gina's mouth. "Thank You, Lord, for small favors."

Thirty-Seven

"Shaving cream?" Maggie laughed into the telephone at Gina's rendition of the slumber party. The young Olafsson must have inherited his sense of humor from his mother.

"I think I owe him, don't you? Anyway, is it all right if I keep the car for a while?"

"Sure. Aunt Lottie and I are tied to the washing machine today. What are your plans?"

"Brady invited me to go horseback riding at the farm. I think I'll take him up on it. I need to hang out with some animals."

"You're probably in withdrawal. Honey." Maggie paused, catching the motherly words poised on the tip of her tongue, words that would only exasperate her daughter.

"Mom, I know I can't ride, but Lauren thinks they've probably got a sidesaddle. His sisters used to be into riding in a big way. We'll see."

Maggie smiled. "At least you'll be near horses."

"Yep. Gotta go. We're plotting how I can get back at Brady, embarrass him to pieces."

She chuckled. "Good luck. See you later."

"Bye."

It was good to hear Gina happy. Her daughter hadn't snapped at her for referring to her injury. There wasn't even a hint in her tone that she was rolling her eyes or lifting her right eyebrow. This was a definite sign of progress in Gina's emotional well-being.

Thank You, Father, she breathed a prayer. *And thanks for my own progress in that direction.*

Aunt Lottie came through the back screen door into the kitchen, huffing slightly. "Maggie, I'm worried about your ankle. Are you sure all this basement-stair climbing and hauling laundry outside to the clothesline doesn't hurt it?"

"Not at all. The walking cast is great. And it's such a perfect day to hang the linens outside."

"It's a gorgeous summer day." She nodded toward the Bible laying open on the kitchen table and sat down. "What are you reading now?"

"Oh, I'm looking up all the references to 'wife,' trying to get a Christian perspective on marriage. I don't understand all this 'be subject to' stuff."

Aunt Lottie chuckled, her blue eyes twinkling beneath her halo of white hair. "I never worried too much about that. Are you in Ephesians?" She pulled her glasses from an apron pocket and slipped them on. "Read this. 'The wife must respect her husband.' Pretty cut and dry, in my opinion. Nothing complicated about respecting another person."

"No, there isn't."

"But it's the easiest thing to lose sight of with the people living in the same house, up close where you can see all their warts."

"The first part of the sentence says husbands should love their wives. It's easy to respect someone who shows obvious love for you."

"But the two don't have anything to do with each other."

"What?"

"It doesn't say respect him *if* he loves you. And it doesn't say love her *if* she respects you."

"Oh." Maggie frowned. "Well, what if the husband doesn't deserve respect? What if he pretty much ignores his wife and doesn't communicate with her?"

"Doesn't say anything about deserving. It's just God's order of things. Reece doesn't beat you, does he?"

"Who said we were talking about Reece?" She smiled. "No, he doesn't."

"He's just gone all the time."

Maggie raised her brows.

"I've got eyes and ears, child. Do you want to know what I think?" Aunt Lottie patted her hand.

"Okay."

"Let him off the hook."

Maggie winced.

"God let you off."

"But He's God."

"And He'll give you the grace and the power to do what you want to do. That's the real trick. Do you want to do it? You think about that while I go check the washer." She stood and shuffled to the basement door. "You've listened long enough to an old woman's ramblings."

"Don't carry anything upstairs. I'll be down in a minute."

They aren't ramblings, Maggie thought. *They are the voice of real, down-to-earth experience.*

She sighed. She really didn't want to let Reece off the hook. He'd think his ignoring her was acceptable, that her loneliness was just in her head and not his fault.

But was his response her responsibility? No.

Her responsibility was responding correctly to God. And according to Aunt Lottie, He wanted her to respect her husband.

That probably meant being honest with him. Tell him she was angry with him, had wanted more from him. Well, she'd done a pretty good job of that his last night in Valley Oaks when she asked him if he loved her. But she hadn't told him about John.

If not for a nagging in the back of her mind to be obedient, she didn't want to do this. Her feelings for Reece had gone...neutral. It wasn't as if she wanted any more from him now, except maybe to tie up loose ends. For the sake of obedience.

Maggie picked up the phone. He hadn't returned her messages to call her this week. He wasn't answering his cell phone, and she didn't want to leave this type of voice mail on his business line. She dialed home, thinking he would be there sometime over the weekend. The machine picked up.

"Reece, I'd rather talk to you than the machine, but...I need to talk. That voice you heard was a friend of mine. Just a friend. Past tense. There were all these emotions in my heart, and I felt like they were disconnected, just empty holes in between them because there wasn't anyone to share them with. You haven't been interested. I...I needed...wanted someone to fill in the gaps." She took a deep breath. "But I know it was...I was disrespectful to you. I'm sorry.

"So," the words rushed out now, "about this quest of mine, this delving into the past. It's helping. I had to let Jesus forgive all those teenage mistakes I made. I had to forgive Neil's mother. I had to forgive the town in general. I don't have that heavy lump of guilt anymore that I really didn't understand I had in the first place, so I guess I had to figure that one out, too. And I don't think I have to be perfect anymore, now that I've stopped pretending with Gina.

"Maybe this is more information than you want. But, Reece, this is the kind of stuff I've needed to say out loud to you, without you making light of it or offering a zillion quick-fix solutions." She paused. She was finished. "Bye."

Maggie hung up the phone and exhaled noisily. Finished, but it felt as if something wasn't. Something was missing. What was it?

She pushed up her sleeves and headed toward the basement staircase. The temperature was low today, not—she stopped mid-stride.

Hot. She wasn't hot. That's what was missing. No internal combustion. And she'd talked to Reece—well, sort of to him—and her body didn't do its usual haywire thermostat number. Interesting. She'd been straight and honest about John, about her feelings, about him not meeting needs, about her working through the past.

Hmmm. Maybe they should just talk one-sided into answering machines, avoid confrontation.

What came next? She'd have to leave Reece's response up to God. And if there was no response? She shrugged as she continued down the stairs. That was fine. There really hadn't been a response in a long time. By this point she wasn't sure she wanted one.

Reece had listened to Margaret as she talked to the answering machine, still too numb from shock to pick up the phone and respond. Hours later, he was just beginning to warm again. Numb was easier.

Many Saturdays he went to the office, but not this time. He replayed the message over and over, letting her voice wash over him, at times soothing the pain, at times feeding it.

Just a friend. A punch in the gut, but not devastating. Not an affair.

Past tense. A ray of hope.

You weren't interested. Guilt, shame, then anger consumed him. What did she want? He listened!

Disrespectful to you. I'm sorry. She was perfect in his mind, always had been. She was a good person. This was *his* fault. He hadn't given her something, hadn't made her feel loved.

I had to let Jesus forgive... He was reading Olafsson's book. This man Jesus was taking on dimensions he'd never thought about. In the fictional account He had the power to remove anyone's guilt and then tell them to try again, His way. If Reece asked forgiveness, like Margaret was saying, would He give it to him? Could he try again?

I need to say this without you making light of it or offering a zillion quick-fix solutions. Female perspective. He didn't get it. If there's a problem, fix it. If it's just emotional, no big deal. Get over it. Right?

No, wrong. She wanted him to...listen.

But he didn't want to over the telephone. He wanted to see her face, sit down across a table and try to understand this time, try not to disappoint her. How could he...?

What had Gina said? That she was a romantic. That she liked surprise gifts. But not, he reminded himself, flowers, because she had told him about those, and if she had to tell him, she didn't want them.

He stared through the patio door at her backyard full of flowers. Such care she put into those things. She put care into everything, him and Gina and their home. He turned and began wandering through the house now, studying clues to the identity of this woman who'd lived with him for the past 30 years.

It was a one-story tract house, built on a slab of concrete in a decent neighborhood, their first. Margaret loved it and had never wanted to buy a larger one. She had upgraded the plumbing and wiring, replastered the entire interior, refinished the exterior stucco. It was probably the prettiest house on the block. The overall feel was light and air with bright splashes of color.

He stopped in the front room, hands stuffed in his shorts. It was just like her. By far the prettiest one in the entire neighborhood. Petite. Blonde. Her smile always a breath of fresh air, her clothing bright splashes of color. She could wear anything, make anything work on her small figure. She had an innate sense of style, always drawing admirable glances from men and women.

He focused on the small things. There were paintings on the wall, art he had never really noticed before. They were just there, part of the wall. He noticed now the floral prints in light wood. He studied the end tables and bookshelf. Empty crystal vases that usually held fresh flowers when she was home. A bowl of potpourri. Candles. A few white figurines. What were those? He picked one up and read the bottom. Lladro. A five-by-seven family portrait. Gina's high school graduation photograph. Another of Gina in her khaki Wild Creature Country's vet outfit, a baby orangutan wrapped around her side.

He wandered down the hall and looked in his daughter's room. Since she had moved back in, she had removed the teenage posters of surfing and wild animals. One bulletin board remained with photos of old friends. He knew the garage held boxes of things from the apartment she had had to give up. He smiled at the four-poster, remembering how at the age of eight she had torn off the canopy's ruffle—the canopy her mother had insisted on—and stuffed it in the dog's house outside. She had replaced it with an army fatigue cape she bought from a neighbor boy.

They both had given Margaret fits through the years.

He walked into their room. More photos of Gina alone and with them were on one wall. An ocean scene on another. He stepped to it. It wasn't California. The colors were too vibrant, the buildings too old-fashioned and too near to the water. Balconies full of overflowing geraniums. Maybe the Mediterranean?

He opened the folding door of Margaret's side of the closet. More vibrant colors. He fingered the dresses. She wore dresses to work, not suits. What was she wearing to the wedding?

He took a deep breath. He didn't know what was missing, which ones she had taken with her.

He stepped to the dresser and opened her jewelry box. It was packed with inexpensive costume baubles, different styles and colors to match every outfit. He had given her the requisite nice pieces. An anniversary ring on their twenty-fifth. No, not twenty-fifth. He hadn't thought of it until Gina suggested it the following year. Then there was the diamond bracelet for her fiftieth birthday. Did she have those with her?

He picked up a perfume bottle, removed the lid, and sniffed. He tried another. He closed his eyes. This one was her. This was the one that nudged memories. He read the label. *Coco.* He hadn't known...

Books and magazines were in the nightstand on her side of the bed. Women's fashion stuff, work-related material. *Pride and Prejudice.* She read classics? A biography on some writer he had never heard of. He knew there were CDs in the stereo. Music he never listened to. Classical. Italian operas.

The perfume bottle was clutched in his hand. He closed his eyes.

Dear Jesus, forgive me for not knowing her. For taking her for granted.

What could he do to give them time together? To give himself another chance to win her heart? He had done it once, hadn't he? It had to be away from the Valley Oaks crowd and it couldn't wait until after the wedding. A sense of urgency enveloped him.

Make it right. Please.

He held the bottle to his face and inhaled deeply.

Thirty-Eight

As Gina turned onto the drive of the Olafsson farm, she spotted Brady. He stood outside the nearest barn, leaning against the white fence, elbows propped on the top rail, one foot braced on the bottom, cell phone pressed against an ear. He wore his green cap, a white T-shirt, blue jeans, work boots, and an unmistakable frown.

She parked behind him and climbed out.

"Yeah," he barked, "that's my final word on the subject." He punched a button on the phone, raised the hand that held it, and stretched back his arm. With all the force of a major league center fielder, he hurled the cell phone across the grassy area almost to the highway.

Gina leaned against the car. It seemed a good time to wait quietly.

Brady gripped the fence rail with both hands, stomped a foot on the ground, and muttered indecipherable words. He yanked off his cap, raked long fingers through his hair, then slapped the hat back on. Finally he turned around, his face dark, unlike anything she'd observed in him before. He stuck his hands in his back pockets. "You came," he stated.

"Bad timing, I think."

"Nah." He took a deep breath, exhaled, then took another.

"Want to talk about it?"

He blew out another breath and shook his head. "Community stuff. Zoning Board and I don't see eye to eye on my new neighbors."

That would be her father's company.

"Come on. I'm almost done mucking out the stable."

She marched double time to keep up with his long strides. "Is it zoned residential yet?"

Again he shook his head. "More than likely it'll pass, though. They don't want my vote. I'm chairman at the moment. Conflict of interest and all that. School board members are pressing the others to vote yes. My privacy is history."

No wonder he was upset. "I'm sorry."

"Not your fault." He continued stomping around the corner of the large barn that housed the combine and other equipment she had climbed on the day of the open house.

"I can go talk to your mom," she suggested. "Give you time to swing a pitch fork with no one in range."

"She's not home." He stopped and waited for her to catch up. When she reached his side, he flung an arm around her shoulders, and they continued walking at a slower pace. "I promise not to take it out on you."

"Even though it involves my dad?"

He smiled down at her. "Nice hair."

She rolled her eyes. *Nice change of subject.* Her hair hung in damp strands, still wet from its multiple washings. "You're in trouble for that one, Olafsson. Big trouble. I'd be afraid to go to sleep if I were you."

They entered the medium-size horse barn. The familiar scent of sawdust from freshly scattered shavings welcomed her. Five stalls lined one wall, three the other. Doors on the far end were open. Bales of hay were piled in a corner to the left of the door they walked through. To the right were shelves and racks chock-full of saddles and tack. She eyed the area, hoping to spot a sidesaddle.

"Brady, do you—" The beating of hooves against a wall broke off her voice. It sounded like—

Brady rushed to the second stall and opened its gate. "Ruby! Hey, Gina, grab a lead rope there, would you? She's cast in the shavings." He stepped inside.

Cast. Gina felt her blood turn to ice as an image seared itself into her brain. Cast meant that the enormous animal would be on its back against the wall, legs flailing, unable to stand up.

"Gina!" Brady shouted. "Hurry up!"

She raced to the stall. Ruby blocked the entrance to the tiny ten-by-twelve enclosure. She must have twisted around in her terror. Long powerful legs thrashed as the panicked horse struggled against the inability to right herself.

"Gina!" Brady yelled above the loud crashing of horse's hooves thumping repeatedly against the wall boards.

She tore her eyes from Ruby. Brady was backed in a far corner, arms over his head. He peeked out from under one and locked eyes with her.

"Gina, get a rope!"

She couldn't respond.

"You can do this, honey."

She shook her head.

"You can! Believe in yourself. You know what to do. We've got to get her hooves down."

"I...I'll get help."

"Nobody's home! Throw me a rope! Ahh—" He stepped sideways, out of the line of one swinging hoof.

Oh, dear God! Dear God!

"Gina! Now!"

I can't! I can't!

Brady's in danger! She whirled around, blind eyes unable to see anything.

"By the first stall! On your left!"

She saw a rope hanging looped around a hook and ran the short distance to grab it. *Brady's in danger!* She raced back. Keeping her distance from Ruby, she caught Brady's eye. "Here!" She flung the coiled rope.

It landed just the other side of the thrashing horse.

"Honey, you're gonna have to do better than that."

Her heart pounded.

"Gina! You know animals! You *can* do this!"

She looked around, spotted another rope and retrieved it. She had to help Brady. *Help Brady.* She had to do this.

Back at the stall she inched closer to the horse twisting on her back. Ruby's front legs rose monstrously before Gina, close enough to loop the rope around—

I can't!

Ruby whinnied, an unnaturally pitched sound.

Gina caught sight of one of her large, brown eyes rimmed white in her intense terror. Her heart broke. "Oh, Ruby," she whispered. "Poor baby."

Her hands shook as she lifted the looped end of the rope. Her first toss missed its mark. As did the second. The third attempt settled the rope loosely around the right foreleg.

Gina took a deep breath and brushed at the hair in her eyes. There was almost enough space to squeeze inside the stall, pull the leg down...

Help, Lord.

She quickly tightened the loop, and with one swift motion slipped around the horse's head and pulled the leg down. In the split second after her hoof touched the floor, Ruby heaved herself up on all fours. After a fleeting glance around, she sneezed, shook the shavings from herself, and gracefully swished her tail. She nickered softly, as if pronouncing everything was under control.

Gina patted her flank and glanced over at Brady. He stared at her, wiping sweat from his brow with a large red handkerchief, his chest heaving. She flashed him a brief, small smile, trying to catch her own breath. Her body began to shake then, and she rested against Ruby for support. Things were not under control.

Brady's eyes never left her face. Slowly he moved toward her.

A corner of Gina's mind sensed she must be in a state of shock, but there were no lucid thoughts, only raw emotion exploding in her head, pounding in her chest. When Brady cupped the back of her head in his hand and wrapped his other arm around her waist, she knew there was only one expression of all the emotion that clamored for release.

Their kisses didn't slow for some time. They had somehow maneuvered their way out of the stall and locked Ruby in, Brady's arm enfolding Gina, his lips scarcely straying from hers in the process.

Now they were seated on the pile of hay just inside the big, open doors, side by side, reclining against the stacked bales. Adrenaline spent, their breathing slowed to normal. Brady studied the face just inches from his. Her emerald eyes studied him in return, her head nestled against his arm. Between them she clutched his other hand in both of hers in a vice-like grip. He felt another quiver roll through her. Like a ripple effect in a pond, it wasn't as intense as the first ones when she leaned against Ruby.

He was shaken himself, less so from the horse's hoof nearly beaning him than from the reality of Gina. At last he found his voice. "You okay?"

"Getting there."

"This sounds woefully inadequate, but thank you for saving my life, Angelina."

Her eyes widened. "Brady," she whispered, "I think you just saved mine."

He smiled. "It was really tough getting Ruby to cooperate like that. We've been practicing all week."

A smile tugged at her mouth.

"Ready to take on an elephant?"

"No problem." Her eyes glistened with unshed tears. "Thank you."

He kissed her forehead, wishing this moment could last at least until...until his hair turned white? "You did it. I knew you could."

"Why did you go in there anyway?"

"Told you, it was the way Ruby and I rehearsed it." The arch in her right eyebrow fascinated him. "How do you do that? Raise just one brow?"

"You didn't answer my question."

"It was stupid to get near her, I admit. Just my natural reaction to immediately scope out the situation. Usually there's a rope nearby to grab. Figured you were right behind me. Why did you come?"

"You yelled—"

"No, I mean today." Time was slipping away. He could already feel the emptiness that would take over when she moved out of his arms. Didn't she belong here beside him?

"I needed the animals. They've always centered me somehow." She shrugged a shoulder. "It's been too long since I connected with one." She flashed him her dazzling smile. "I think I got more than I bargained for. Way more than I bargained for."

Disappointment yanked at his insides. Her visit had nothing to do with him.

"Oh, Brady! I know I can do it again." Her voice rose in excitement. "I've been so absolutely petrified at the thought of simply *standing* next to an elephant—or even a horse!

And now..." Abruptly she dropped his hand and sat up. "The biggest weight has been lifted. I mean, I can literally, *physically* feel it! All of a sudden it's as if there's color in the world and this morning it was still just plain old gray."

He sat up and picked bits of hay from her mussed hair. Sunlight through the doorway caught the dry, top layer, surrounding her in a halo. "I think you've found your answer to that question."

"What question?"

"*Where does your journey lead from here?*"

She blinked at him. "Well, in a way, I guess."

"You've got your work back. All kinds of possibilities in that." *Down roads unseen, midst stars flung wide?*

"Yeah. No specifics yet though."

I have but one request of you, dear. "The specific job offers will come, and you'll be ready. Actually I have one specific request of you."

The startled look on Gina's face was unmistakable. She recognized the song lyrics he paraphrased.

He hurried to complete his thought. "Will you spend the week with me?" He wouldn't say *spend life's journey with me*, not just yet. She might fly out the door.

"Brady, I hardly know you—"

"Get to know me."

She lowered her head.

Hesitation is good, he thought. He pressed ahead. "We can hang out with the animals here. Watch the wild ones at my place. Catch some more frogs. Help Aaron and Lauren move. Watch the sunset from my meadow. Dance at the reception."

She met his eyes. "And then I'll leave." She bit her lip.

"Gina, I don't want to spend the rest of my life regretting not telling you that I'm falling in love with you. I have to find out what that means. Who knows? Maybe it'll mean buying an elephant for you, and I don't even know what color you like."

"Color?"

He grinned. "Give me a week?"

She fiddled with the hay for a long moment, avoiding his eyes. "Remember what I said about an emotional trampoline?"

"I thought maybe you were up for the exercise now. I mean, after all, you did come today."

She glanced at him. Her shoulders heaved as she took a deep breath and looked toward the open door. "Yes, I came. I'm sitting here trying to pretend there's nothing on my mind except the confidence to find a new job." Her voice caught. "I'm trying to be cool and pretend you don't mean a thing to me, all the while my heart is racing like Ruby's was and I'm just as terrified," the words tumbled on top of each other, "because I know the real reason I came today was to be with you." She turned toward him. "And that makes absolutely no sense whatsoever."

"Doesn't fit in your Day-Timer?"

"No way." She scooted closer to him and laid her head against his shoulder, slipping an arm around his neck. "Did I answer your question?"

"A simple yes or no would have been sufficient."

"Yes, I'll give you a week." She reached up and kissed his cheek.

He closed his eyes briefly. *Thank You, Father.* With a finger under her chin, he tilted her face and lowered his mouth to that Miss America smile. He kissed her in a slow, gentle way.

"Hey," she murmured, "what happened to your rations?"

"New system." He brushed his lips across hers. "I plan to steal as many kisses as I can."

"Brady," she chuckled, "you don't have to steal them."

Thirty-Nine

Gina took another paper napkin from the stack on the table and wiped the last of the barbecue sauce from her fingers. She had given up on using a fork and knife after two bites into the delicious ribs. "Mmmm. That was great. I wish I had discovered this restaurant three weeks ago."

Brady reached across the table and touched his thumb at the corner of her mouth. "All clean." He smiled. "I'm glad you enjoyed it. The Rib House has been here since I was a kid. It's a landmark in Valley Oaks. People come from miles around."

She smiled back at him. The place was down-home, just like Brady. No frills, no extensive menu, no breathtaking views unless you counted the four windows that looked out on the highway and silos beyond that. It was a room full of square tables, each with four chairs and paper placemats. But the food was homemade, tasty, and the real thing. The place was packed on Saturday nights, but he had managed to get them in without a reservation. She watched a dish of apple pie à la mode go by and she groaned.

"Want some?" he asked.

"Most definitely." She folded her somewhat sticky fingers together and met Brady's gaze. The way he looked at her was unnerving. His eyes seldom strayed from her, and they danced as if he smiled at some secret. The corners of his mouth often slipped into his easy grin. She hadn't been able to think straight all day.

Of course that was partially due to Ruby. The horse's situation had blasted her fear to smithereens, leaving a clear return to confidence in its wake. It was an ecstatic high, unlike any joy she had ever known. This attraction to Brady only intensified it, creating something akin to an emotional explosion that made her head spin. How could she love a farmer in Podunk, Illinois? She didn't know. She didn't know what it meant or where it would lead. What she did know was that she didn't want to come down from her present mountaintop.

But they had to make plans. "Okay, let's plan the week."

"The frog choir will be in full swing tonight. Let's go back to my place and sit on the porch." He winked. "There's paper and pen at the house so you can write it all down, Miss Organizer."

She rolled her eyes.

A portly, balding, middle-aged man approached the table. "Brady!" His tone made the salutation sound like a command. "Need to talk."

"Hi, Chuck. I'd like you to meet—"

"It'll take just a moment." Ignoring Gina, he leaned toward Brady, supporting one hand on the table, the other on the back of the chair, and spoke in low tones directly into Brady's ear.

She watched, amused at the thought that she had met— or almost met—her first rude Valley Oaks citizen. Brady didn't look amused. He lowered his eyes from hers, listening intently. The tips of his ears reddened and his forehead crinkled. He nodded. His entire face turned crimson.

The man straightened, then nodded curtly in her direction. "Sorry for the interruption." He walked off.

Brady's lips were pressed together. He lifted a hand, signaling to the waitress.

"Who was that man?"

"Village board president. Can we take a rain check on the apple pie? I have black raspberry cobbler at home."

The man's words had obviously distracted him. He was ready to leave. "Sounds perfect."

He counted bills out for the check and stood abruptly. "Ready?"

They made their way through the crowded room. A few people called out a hello to him. Once inside the truck, Gina slid across the bench seat and sat close to him. "Want to talk about it?"

"Nope." He swung his arm up and around her shoulders, pulling her nearer and steering with one hand. His color had returned to the normal tan, though his narrow jaw still appeared clenched.

She'd pry later.

"Let's talk about plans." He kissed the top of her head. "How I'm going to treat you like a princess all week."

She snuggled against his shoulder. Brady and Valley Oaks were getting under her skin, no doubt about it. Her future plans and this week's plans were not on the same continuum. They had absolutely nothing to do with each other, had nothing whatsoever in common. It seemed God had given her something she asked for and something she hadn't asked for. And the two were diametrically opposed. "Brady, maybe I should try it your way for a few days. Just wing it."

He glanced down at her. "What got into you?"

She shrugged. "Tired of being a control freak, I guess."

"Ah, giving God more room to work. I like that." They rode in silence for a few minutes and then he chuckled. "I like that a lot."

Later they sat side by side in the dark on his screened-in porch. He had moved the couch so that they faced directly out onto the pond. Moonlight reflected off of the water and a few stars were visible through the treetops. As he predicted, the bullfrogs' deep-throated song filled the entire outdoors.

Gina mimicked the noise and laughed with Brady until her sides hurt. She agreed with him that they were easily entertained. Tucking her legs up on the seat, she turned to him and stroked the crease in his cheek. His blond hair shone in the soft light. How could she feel so at ease with this man she barely knew? "Will you tell me about that man who made you so angry?"

"It's not important."

"Brady, I only have a few days to get to know you. Is it about your land?"

He nodded. "The board wants me to resign. They say that as chairman of the Zoning Committee I have a conflict of interest and am doing a disservice to Valley Oaks by my stubborn refusal to vote yes on zoning your dad's property as residential."

"It's not my dad's."

"Sorry. You know what I mean."

"I know. So are you doing a disservice to the town?"

"I told God you were a thorn in my side." His grin softened the words.

"A thorn?"

"When we first met. I mean, you were a pain to talk to and, with all the wedding business, I knew we had to spend time together. I wasn't exactly pleased with the idea."

"Hmm. Well, the feeling was mutual, you know."

"It was? I had no idea."

"Liar," she laughed. "Come to think of it, *roses* have thorns. Maybe they're a good thing?"

"They're annoying." He leaned over and kissed the tip of her nose. "But they force you to pay attention."

"I'd say you're diverting attention from the question at hand."

"Right." He took a deep breath. "Yes, I might be getting in the way of Valley Oaks' growth. I know growth is inevitable and necessary for the town to survive. I just don't want all that growth adjacent to this place. There are plenty of other suitable areas for building homes. Two subdivisions are going up east and south of town. What we lack is a plan to preserve the history of the Crowley homestead, not to mention green space."

"From what I can tell, it's all green space between Valley Oaks and Rockville. Miles and miles of farm land. Lots of green corn and soybeans."

"That's not the same. I mean wildlife refuge areas. We have a state park up the river a ways. A zoo 90 miles away in Chicago. Nothing else in a 100-mile radius. These prairies used to be teeming with all kinds of animals. Hey, do you want to see some buffalo? There's a farmer nearby who raises them."

"Buffalo? Really? I'd love to."

"We'll put it on our to-do list." He leaned toward her.

"We're not making a to-do list."

"Oh, that's right." He kissed her gently. "We'll just meander over there some time soon."

Her thoughts floundered for a moment. "Uh, back to the subject at hand. Make this a wildlife preserve. Can you zone it for that?"

"We have the power, but there just isn't much interest. And since I own the land, I can't bring that idea to a vote. That's a definite conflict of interest. But if we did that, we'd have to provide access to it, declare the whole road and then some as part of the preserve."

"Don't move." Gina hurried into the kitchen and fished a dollar bill from her purse, then plopped back down beside him. "Here." She stuffed the money into his shirt pocket and planted a kiss on his cheek. "I'll buy your land. Now go zone it for wildlife and stop complaining."

With an absentminded gaze on his face, he smoothed her hair. "This isn't going to work."

"What's not going to work?"

"This." His whispery voice was lower than usual. "Us. Kissing while the frogs sing."

Her stomach knotted. "Did I miss something here?"

"It's just that..." He caressed her cheek, then withdrew his hand and slid away to the other end of the couch. "You fit too perfectly, Angelina. You fit in my house, in my woods. You fit in my head, in my heart. You fit in my arms. And I want you to spend the night."

Her head swam. Was he serious? She scrambled for a flippant tone. "Well, that ain't gonna happen, mister."

"I take it back. You don't fit perfectly if you can say 'ain't' without gagging."

"It's in the dictionary."

"But it's not acceptable."

"Who says? I'd use it in Scrabble. Shall we play Scrabble?"

Brady jumped to his feet. "It's definitely time for Scrabble. I'll get the board."

Forty

The dishwasher hummed quietly, cleaning the remainder of the Sunday dinner dishes. Windows were shut tight against the early afternoon heat, locking in that blessed invention, air conditioning. Maggie sat with her cast propped on a chair and eyed the others sitting around her sister's oak kitchen table and sighed. No one noticed.

Marsha wore her midlevel frazzled expression and wasn't screeching. Lauren had cut a second serving of her mother's luscious cherry pie and now hunted in the freezer for vanilla ice cream, moaning about eating too much. Gina's eyes resembled a raccoon's.

Maggie's exasperation overflowed into one word, "Lauren!"

Blonde curls whipped around, brown eyes widened as if in shock, her jaw dropped.

Maggie couldn't help but smile at her niece. "The mean aunt is back. Now listen to me. You will *not* be able to fit into that gorgeous wedding dress if you eat that ice cream. Put it back and come over and sit down."

Lauren did as she was told.

"All right, girls," Maggie continued. "It's time to take our emotional temperature here. If we behave like this on Saturday or even at the Friday rehearsal, we will miss the moment entirely. Marsh, you have hair and massage appointments, a cleaning service coming three times this week and twice next week. You're done. You can stop now and enjoy the festivities."

"But there are flowers, the cake, the food—"

"And a florist, baker, and caterer. Didn't you hear the same sermon I heard this morning?"

Marsha wrinkled her brow.

"Jeremiah 29:11 tells us that the Lord has good plans for us."

"That doesn't mean everything will work out."

"I understand that! But it's all part of the chance journeys you told me about. God knows what He's doing. You've prayed over every detail. Whatever happens or doesn't happen is *His* responsibility. Right?"

"R-right."

Maggie turned to her niece and slid the plate away from her. "Lauren, honey, I know you're excited, but you've got to take care of yourself. Why don't you go play a Rachmaninoff piece on the piano?"

She swallowed and waved a fork. "Two more bites?"

"No! There's a bag of celery in the fridge. Marsha, you are forbidden to bake this week." She looked at Gina. "Why aren't *you* eating another piece of pie? You've been eating like a horse, which means you've fallen head over heels for Brady—"

Marsha gasped. "I thought it was a crush!"

"You didn't see the way they looked at each other when he picked her up for their first date. We are not talking crush here. Oh!" She swiveled back to her daughter. "Sweetheart! You're not eating because you and Brady had an argument!"

"No, Mother, we did not have an argument. Leave me out of this lecture. I'm just a bridesmaid, low on the totem pole. Nowhere near the center of attention."

Lauren touched her arm. "Gina, what happened?"

"Nothing."

Maggie recognized the distress in her little girl's crinkled forehead and asked, "How serious are things?"

"Things cannot *be* serious. Brady Olafsson is *not* my kind of guy. Valley Oaks is *not* my kind of town."

Maggie's stomach somersaulted. "That serious, huh?"

"Oh, Mom!" The floodgates opened and her words tumbled out. "You can hang out in the pharmacy and be served *lemonade,* for goodness sake, like—like it's a family reunion! And have you ever met anyone like Aunt Lottie? I mean, she teaches me something new every single day. Then take Anne. She's an absolute blast, and she's basically a stay-at-home mom! She and Alec have their act so together with their kids and each other. I've never seen anyone more contented than Liz. Lauren is so happy, and her house is so cute. And Brady, well, he has a hundred acres of heaven, and he's—" She stopped to take a breath. "Just about perfect."

The women stared at each other. Maggie finally broke the silence. "But there aren't any elephants nearby."

"Exactly!"

Lauren nudged Gina. "What does Brady have to say about things?"

"He brought me home early last night so he wouldn't be tempted to ask me to...stay." She glanced sideways at Maggie and Marsha. "The night."

"Whew!" Lauren whistled. "Nicole never stayed. I doubt she was even invited."

Marsha gasped again. "Lauren! How in the world do you know that?"

"Mom, it's Valley Oaks. Britte told Anne and Anne told me. Brady's always gone strictly by the Book. Capital 'b.' Nicole had a bit of a problem with that. I mean she was a believer, but thought since they were engaged they may as well live together. Brady said no-o way."

Gina frowned. "Get real, Lauren. No guy is like that these days."

"Aaron is."

"You mean...you're waiting?"

Lauren grinned. "Just till Saturday night."

Maggie noticed her sister had turned beet red. "Marsha, isn't it great how open our girls are with us? They're nothing like we were with Mom."

"Sure."

Maggie read uncertainty on her daughter's face. *She's so fragile.* A heaviness of uncertainty nagged, and it wasn't just Gina. Reece hadn't returned her calls. What was his reaction to the last message she left? What did she hope it was? Would he even show up for the wedding? She addressed Gina, but knew she encouraged herself, too. "Gina, keep that Jeremiah verse in mind. God knows what's best, and sometimes, in order to get us to that best place, He has to take us on a detour. Let me tell you about mine."

Monday morning Maggie sat in Aunt Lottie's car parked in the driveway, tapping her fingernails on the steering wheel. Gina was taking forever to leave the house. She had overslept. Then Brady had called, and they talked as if they weren't going to be spending most of the day together.

Maggie wondered about that relationship. What did she really think? Much as the young man impressed her, his being Neil's son was just too bizarre for everyone involved. In spite of the detour talk yesterday about letting God lead them down unplanned paths, Gina would never settle in Valley Oaks. She was too much her father's daughter, all big-city-eyed. Big cities with large zoos.

Maggie glanced at her watch again and considered honking the horn. They were already behind schedule. Convincing her sister that things were under control meant, of course, that Maggie assumed responsibility to oversee the thousand and one details not yet under control. The caterer was a nightmare. The florist—borderline hopeless. Oh, well, it didn't matter. The "mean aunt" could afford to be strung out. The mother of the bride needed some pampering at this point. And besides, the challenge and busyness kept her mind off of her own bizarre relationship with Reece. A week from today she would head back home…

Gina bounded from around the back of the house, waved to her, and continued on past the car. Maggie twisted in the seat. A FedEx truck blocked the driveway.

"Now what?" She climbed from the car.

The driver handed Gina a flat, rectangular package about a yard in length. "It's for you, Mom!"

"It'll have to wait." John wouldn't send her a gift, would he? But it had to be from— "Stick it in the house and let's go!"

"Oh, come on. Take a peek anyway." Gina disappeared through the front screen door.

Maggie sighed and followed. *Oh, Lord. This can't be happening. He never gave me a gift, only his friendship. A gift is too tangible. Too definitive. He knew the goodbye was final…*

Gina glided a knife under the flap of the cardboard and sliced through the packing tape. "Mother, the label says it's from an *art* shop in Chicago."

Maggie sank onto the couch, a fresh wave of guilt sucking air from her lungs.

"You should open it."

She shook her head.

Gina smiled, eyes bright with anticipation, and ripped open the box. She shoved aside packing peanuts, tore apart butcher paper, and caught her breath.

And then Maggie caught hers. An exquisite piece of art glistened in the brown wrappings. Under glass, in a simple black frame, vibrant red and purple irises bloomed against a gold backdrop.

"Mom, it's beautiful!"

"Absolutely gorgeous," she whispered. "I can't accept—"

"This card says it's serigraph on gold leaf—"

"A silk-screened print on *gold?*"

Gina handed her an envelope and whooped. "He sent you *flowers!*"

"What?"

"Don't you get it? *Flowers!* But they're not *truly* flowers, because then they wouldn't count!"

With shaky fingers Maggie pulled out a gift card. Reece? This was from *Reece? I do love you, Margaret. More than ever. Reece.* She shook her head, as if the movement would dislodge some understanding. This was incomprehensible.

Gina propped the painting against a wall. "Way to go, Dad!"

"You knew?"

"He told me something was to be delivered this morning, and he hoped we'd be here. Couldn't you tell I was stalling?"

Maggie bit her tongue. This could have waited. She had waited for years. What was one more afternoon?

Forty-One

Brady whirled Gina around the bright yellow kitchen and hummed what he considered "their" song. *Where does your journey lead from here?* Crazy as it sounded, he did want them to travel the rest of life's journey together.

She pushed him away and answered his unspoken question, "Probably looking for an elephant to take care of. Now move that box and let me get back to work."

"Yes, ma'am." He set a heavy box of dishes atop the counter and headed back outside to help the other guys carry in his cousin's enormous rolltop oak desk.

He and a group of friends were at Aaron and Lauren's house, delivering pickup truckloads of household goods gathered from the couples' apartments and parents' homes. Brady had joined the party at 1:00. Gina had been stand-offish since 1:02, right after she flashed him her Miss America smile.

Not that he blamed her.

"Yo, Olafsson! Heads up!" Cal Huntington climbed the porch steps, desk chair in his arms.

Brady moved aside and held open the screen door.

"You done mooning yet?"

"Huh?"

Cal grinned. "Kind of sweet on that pretty California gal, aren't you, bud?" He carried the chair into the house, then came back outside. Without the brown deputy sheriff's uniform draping his broad shoulders, he appeared larger than usual in jeans and a white T-shirt. "Got your basketball?"

"Never leave home without it."

"Bet you could use a game between that," he tilted his head toward the house, "and your Zoning Committee."

"You know, you should go into law enforcement, Huntington. You'd be good at detective work."

"Ha, ha. How about some one-on-one? Even you and I can't move that desk until the others get back."

They sauntered over to Brady's truck and retrieved the ball. "Think the Johnsons will mind if we use their hoop?" A freestanding hoop faced the paved cul-de-sac.

"Nah," Cal replied. "Neighborhood's quiet this afternoon. Perfect 72 degrees and too hot for the kids."

"Talk to me, Calhoun. What've you heard?"

"Oh, I guess the general consensus is she's sweet on you, too."

Brady punched the ball at him. "Check. I meant about the zoning situation."

"You don't have the votes."

They played, their conversation punctuated by huffing silences, grunts, and the rattling of the backboard when the ball hit it.

"What's your opinion, Officer?"

"It's a shame. All that history out there. Besides the fact that you live in a private park. Got enough developments going up. Town's probably evenly divided. Whatever you guys decide will work out. Course the school board'll be on your case for the next century or so."

"No kidding."

"What'll you do? Move out to California?"

Brady's shot nicked the edge of the backboard. He chased after the ball. Move to California? That was one option he hadn't considered. Wouldn't ever consider. He liked living in Valley Oaks. He liked everything about living in Valley Oaks. Well, everything except for the fact that Gina Philips would be leaving it next week.

Six days left to win her over. And he had probably scared her off Saturday night, letting her know just how serious he was about her. Or confused her by working last evening instead of taking her out for dinner. *Lord, give me some middle ground here. Something between cool and aloof and mooning like a lovesick teenager.*

Maybe he could talk her into staying longer. It wasn't like she had a job to go back to.

⌒

Gina splashed cool water on her face and studied her reflection in Lauren's new bathroom mirror. It had been hot work unloading cartons of kitchenware. A banana clip held back her disheveled hair, but it still needed shampoo. Raccoon eyes...now brimming with tears.

She was tired and her leg ached. She didn't want to join the others for a trip into Rockville for catfish. She really didn't want to intrude any longer. This was a Valley Oaks thing and she was an outsider.

Brady and that big guy, Cal, typified the character of the group. From the kitchen window she had watched these two grown men as they left behind heaps of unfinished work and strolled across the street to play basketball. She had watched them laugh and grimace and pant. She had watched them drink from the hose in the yard and then squirt down their heads and red faces like a couple of kids. That and today's entire scene oozed good-natured wholesomeness. *Homespun.*

She didn't fit.

She leaned over and splashed more cold water on her face. Lauren's comments of yesterday haunted her. "Nicole never spent the night...Aaron and I are waiting..."

Gina buried her face in a new thick towel. It didn't matter. Seattle had called that morning. Aunt Lottie had given the zoo's head of personnel Lauren's number and he had reached her there. He offered her the job.

The wait was over. God had answered her prayer. She was back on track.

Rejoining the group downstairs, she begged off going to dinner. Brady approached just as Isabel was offering her a ride home.

"Gina, you're not going?"

She shook her head, trying to avoid eye contact. "I'm bushed."

He touched her elbow. "Want to have pizza with me in town?"

By now Isabel was talking with someone else. Gina studied the floor.

"Sweetheart, shall I get you some ibuprofen?"

How did he know? Her head felt as if she were on a carousel ride. "I just took some. Thanks."

"Ah, then you'll need some pizza in your stomach to go along with it. Let's go."

She took the arm he offered and leaned against him. The room stopped spinning. "You didn't wink, Brady. You know how I am about getting into your truck."

With a tilt of his head, he came into view and winked in that familiar, oh-so-mellow way of his.

How was she going to tell him?

They sat in a booth with high wooden backs at the restaurant, pizza remains on a platter between them. It was a crowded place with oldies playing just loud enough to mask neighboring conversations. Brady reached across the table and tucked a strand of hair behind her ear. "Feeling better?"

"Colored sugar water always helps."

"Pop," he corrected.

"Soda."

"You say toe-may-toe—"

"I say toe-mah-toe."

He grinned. "I suppose that's the crux of things, eh?"

"Brady—"

"Look, Gina, I'm sorry for confusing you. One night I practically say 'move in with me' and the next we talk a total of two minutes on the telephone. The fact is, I don't know how to express myself."

"Brady—"

"All right, I'll just say it. I'm falling in love with you. No, not falling. I already did that. I love you, Angelina."

"But we've only just met!"

"I know."

"We live thousands of miles apart!"

"I know that, too. Tell me something I don't know. Like what do you think about spending more time in Valley Oaks?"

She tore her eyes away from his turquoise gaze. She hadn't told him yet about Seattle.

"Oops," Brady said, "that might be too much of a leap." He shoved aside the dishes and reached for both of her hands. "Maybe the, uh, interest isn't anywhere near mutual?"

She looked at his slender, workingman fingers wrapped around hers. They felt rough. She had seen them covered in black oil while he worked under the hood of a tractor. She imagined them on a keyboard, tapping out beautiful words that changed her life. Tears sprang to her eyes. "Oh, Brady. I can't trust my feelings right now."

"Too irrational and illogical?"

"Yes, and logically speaking, I don't fit here with you and your friends."

His eyebrows shot up. "Too Midwestern for you? Too beneath your—"

"No! Exactly the opposite. *I'm* beneath *your* standards. You must know that. Until now I didn't know anyone who waited for marriage. Including myself." She watched his face register surprise. Oh, the guy was definitely leaps and bounds out of her league. *Mr. Homespun...* "Please, Brady! Don't keep making me out to be someone I'm not!"

He raised one of her hands to his lips and kissed it. "You're a new woman in Christ."

"But there is baggage."

"We all have baggage of some sort. I love you, Gina."

She closed her eyes for a moment. "The Seattle zoo called. They offered me the job. Starting the first of August. I have to go home next week and move myself up there."

His hands tightened over hers, and he gave her a genuine smile. "Congratulations." He blew out a breath. "And here I thought I had things figured out. I should know whenever that happens, God's going to surprise me. Ready to go? I have mowing to do."

She had given him a way out, and he had grasped hold of it like a drowning man thrown a rope. It was for the best for both of them, but somewhere deep inside herself Gina ached.

Outside they walked silently to his truck. He held the door open for her, shut it, and leaned in through the open window. "You'll join me, won't you?"

"When? For what?

"Now. Mowing."

"Mowing?"

"Sure. You know it's true love in the Midwest when she rides on the tractor with him."

He had done it again, poured a warm, soothing balm on the hurt. She touched his forearm. "Change it to you know they're the very best of friends when she rides on the tractor with him. Then I'll say yes."

Brady's eyes narrowed as he studied her face. "How about if I just stop talking about it?"

"Excellent idea, Mr. Olafsson."

Forty-Two

It wasn't a FedEx truck on Tuesday.

It was a white stretch limousine.

Maggie eyed the chauffeur through the screen door. Hat in hand, he wore the professional demeanor and black uniform with its row of right-angled buttons.

"Mrs. Philips?"

She hesitated. It had nothing to do with the honest-faced stranger who smiled politely. He was gray-haired and thickset, almost bodyguard-like in appearance. No, the hesitation stemmed from the wariness that had settled over her since yesterday's delivery of the painting. That painting...still unceremoniously propped against the wall where Gina had set it. She swallowed. As the mean aunt, she had lost her edge. "Y-yes."

"Hello. My name is Julius. Mr. Philips has asked that I escort you. Your limousine is ready whenever you are. May I suggest that we leave as soon as possible? The agenda is quite full."

"Gina!" she yelled in the cheerleader voice she hadn't used in years, then twirled around.

Gina, Marsha, and Aunt Lottie scurried through the doorway from the dining room. They must have been right behind her when she left the kitchen to answer the doorbell.

"What's going on?" Maggie asked.

Giggles and grins erupted among the three women.

"Mom, just go. Do what the chauffeur says."

"What is going on?!"

Marsha made a shooing motion with her hands. "Go, Maggie. Reece has planned something special for you."

"There's far too much to do here. I don't have time for anything that's not on the agenda."

"Gina's taking over. Everything is covered. We're even going to the masseuse together. While my house is being cleaned, thank you very much."

"I'm really not in the mood for surprises. I was looking forward to a massage myself."

The grins faded.

"Mother, he's trying."

Aunt Lottie spoke up. "Honey, you know I don't like to interfere, but it would seem prudent that you meet the man halfway."

Maggie's heart pounded in her throat.

It was Marsha's turn. "Remember praying about being a loving wife? Here's your chance, Magpie. Go for it."

"But—"

"Take the first step. God will carry you after that."

Dread and anxiety washed through her. She felt as if her bones melted and all thought processes shut down.

Marsha flung an arm around her shoulder and gently kneaded her forehead. "Stop frowning, sis. The man loves you."

Gina handed Maggie her purse. "There, Mom. You're good to go."

Aunt Lottie pressed her way in and gave her a sound hug. "We'll be praying for you."

Marsha hugged her, then Gina. They each grasped an arm and prodded her through the front door. She couldn't summon the strength to protest.

At the limo, Julius opened the back door, revealing a luscious burgundy carpet and matching butter-soft leather seats.

Maggie glanced down at her burnt orange camp shirt and white denim skirt above the royal-blue walking cast and cried out in alarm, "I've got to change my clothes!"

"Mother, there's no time. Besides, you look fine for what you'll be doing." Gina nudged her inside.

Classical music floated on the cool air that greeted her. The other women climbed in behind her, begging to take a peek. They oohed and aahed, declared it gorgeously elegant, discovered the telephone, television, CD player, magazines, orange juice, fruit basket, and croissants. Maggie noticed the white carafe with cup and saucer beside one of the seats. It probably contained coffee. The magazines, the food, and the strands of a Bach concerto all suggested that it probably contained not just any coffee.

The others got out and stood on the curb, waving goodbye as the limo pulled silently away as if on a cushion of air. She unscrewed the carafe lid and sniffed.

Almond-flavored. Her favorite.

When had Reece noticed?

Dear Lord, I'm really not ready for this.

As Valley Oaks faded from view, Maggie asked Julius one question, "Where are we going?"

In the rearview mirror his smile was enigmatic beneath his cap and dark glasses. "I'm sorry, ma'am, but I'm not at liberty to disclose that." He slid the window shut between them.

Once on the interstate, she knew where they were headed. Reece would, of course, bring her to Chicago.

Chicago.

Oh, Lord, I'm really, really not ready for this.

As mile after mile of corn, soybeans, and prairie grass flew by, Maggie fought down incessant, nagging thoughts of what she wasn't accomplishing for her sister and niece. She chewed her lip, drummed her fingers, held imaginary fretful conversations with Reece about his timing. Those all ended with Gina's haunting words, "He's trying." The magazines went unread, the croissants untasted. She fortified herself with the entire carafe of coffee.

She punched the intercom button. "Julius, I need that rest stop coming up."

There was a state highway patrol car in the lot. She could find the officer and tell him she'd been kidnapped. By her husband. *And why would he do that, ma'am? Well, he's trying to win back my heart. How? By taking me to Chicago where...well, I'm just not ready for this; I have too many other things to attend to. Ma'am, did you come willingly? In a way. I'm just trying to be obedient to Christ.* She would have lost the guy by then.

Less than 90 minutes from the time they had left Valley Oaks, the faint outline of skyscrapers appeared in the hazy distance. She closed her eyes and leaned her head back against the cushy seat. It was time to change the prayer. *Dear Father, what do You want from me?*

Maggie imagined Julius would take her to the Art Institute because Reece would remember it was one of her favorite places in the city. He would be waiting. He would stroll beside her, yawning his way through the exhibits. They would wander down Michigan Avenue, choose a restaurant where she wouldn't feel too tacky in a denim skirt and cast. They would sit by a window, watch pedestrians, and not have anything to say to each other. She would thank him for the effort, get back into the limo, and go home.

Except for the limousine's role, the scene had been played.

Too soon they were in the midst of thick traffic on Lake Shore Drive. Lake Michigan sparkled, reflecting summer's deep blue sky. Maggie took a deep breath. *Give him a break. He is trying.*

On Michigan Avenue, the chauffeur turned the opposite direction from the Institute...and pulled into the covered drive of the Hilton.

Tears sprang to Maggie's eyes. Of course. Their honeymoon hotel.

Julius braked and turned in his seat, smiling broadly. He loved the dividing window. "Have a pleasant day, Mrs. Philips."

A doorman opened her door. A young woman wearing a concierge badge greeted her, "Mrs. Philips, welcome to the Hilton." She whisked her right past the check-in counter and into an elevator, chatting the entire way about what was going on in the city this beautiful June day. On the twenty-first floor she led her down the hall, around a few corners to a door where she slipped in a key card and stepped aside. "I'll leave this key with you. Please call my desk if you have any questions. Have a wonderful day."

"But what am I doing?"

"I think you'll find everything you need in your suite. Enjoy."

A magnificent view of Lake Michigan filled the windows lining one entire wall of a large sitting room, but it was the scent of roses that overpowered the room. Bouquets sat on every flat surface. A dozen red here, a dozen orchid-colored ones there, a dozen yellow, a dozen white. She walked through into the bedroom and found two more bouquets of pinks. In the bathroom was a bouquet with a rose of every color.

An array of cosmetics caught her eye. She breathed a drawn out "Oh." Her brand of everything in new, unopened containers filled the vanity counter. Cleansing cream, day and night moisturizers, lipsticks, eye shadow, shampoo, hair spray...perfume. Everything. *What was going on?!*

She hurried back out to the sitting room. There was an envelope propped against one of the vases. Her name was written neatly in calligraphy. She pulled out the card.

You are cordially invited
to a day off.

10:00 – 11:00
Inspect the suite.

11:00 – 1:00
Art Institute—Special Exhibit
and Lunch Inside at
Restaurant on the Park

1:00 – 4:00
Appointments in the Hilton Salon
for Massage, Hair, Manicure, Facial

5:30
Leave for Dinner at
The Signature Room

8:00
"Phantom of the Opera"
at the Opera House

Transportation will be provided by Julius.

Please check the closet
and bureau for necessities.

"Oh!" She hurried past the couch and overstuffed arm chairs. In the bedroom she flung open the closet door. "Oh, my goodness!"

Clothes with tags still attached hung neatly on hangers. A casual pale blue sleeveless dress...perfect for the afternoon. A pale green linen skirt and white knit top...for tomorrow? A black dress. She pulled it out. It was dazzling: short sleeves, ankle length, the bodice covered with iridescent beads. She carefully returned it to its place beside a beautiful, long white silk nightgown. On the floor were shoes that matched the dresses and luggage for packing it all.

She slid open the dresser drawers. Rhinestone earrings and bracelet, an evening bag, underclothes.

Maggie realized she truly did not need a thing...except the desire to receive the lavish gifts from a man she wasn't sure she even cared to see.

Forty-Three

Gina handed Brady a dish towel. "Are you sure you don't mind?"

It was like asking if he minded living in his woods or if he minded writing for a living. His passion for being with her ran as deep. "Do I get to stand beside you while we do the dishes?"

Ignoring his question, she tilted her head downward and slid dinner plates into the sudsy water.

Aunt Lottie shuffled into the kitchen. "You two be sure to leave the light on, just in case Maggie gets home late tonight."

"Aunt Lottie, you said you were going to bed!"

"I am, honey. I just thought the sight of you two snuggling in my kitchen would give me pleasant dreams."

"We're not—!"

Brady threw his arm around her shoulders. "But we could!"

Aunt Lottie beamed. "Good night." She shut the back staircase door behind her. They could hear her giggling all the way up.

Gina elbowed him away. "But we're not because you brought the Scrabble board, right?"

"Right. Speaking of romance, I wonder how the adventure is going with your folks?"

"I can't wait to hear all about it. I cannot believe all the surprises Dad had planned."

"Quite a display of extravagant love. Kind of like Jesus."

Again she focused on the sink full of dishwater.

Brady let it go. From recent conversations he knew she struggled to understand such a love. She was running from it, guilt-ridden from living in worldly ways, not grasping the fact that the kindest, most moral, churchgoing person did not deserve God's love either. He prayed to know how to show her that kind of love.

She changed the subject. "How did things go at your committee meeting?"

He blew out a breath, a sound of disgust. "Biggest bunch of nonprogressive dolts I've ever had the misfortune to work with. There's so much history in and around my property. I cannot believe they'd turn it over so easily to a developer. They may as well dump toxic waste across my road."

"Every one of them is like that?"

"Well, no. Half of them would leave things as is, use the land for green space. Or let me buy it. Without my vote, though, it's a tie. And they all agree I can't vote the tie-breaker."

"It is a conflict of interest, don't you agree?"

"It's not *my* property, only adjacent to it. There are plenty of other acreages for housing."

"Brady." She stared at him, her green eyes serious, and flicked a wet hand at his shoulder.

"What?"

"That chip's back. You're sounding angry and offensive and extremely one-sided here."

"Gina, this is my livelihood we're talking about! There's no way I can work in the middle of a neighborhood."

"Have you ever tried?"

"Haven't had to."

"Well? How can you be so sure then? Besides, there'd still be a ravine between you and them."

"Which is not on my property, which someone will build a deck out into."

"So close your windows."

"I like my windows open. Every season."

"Even when it's -50 wind chill?" She gave him a sly smile. "And snowing?"

"It's the principle of the thing. Valley Oaks doesn't need housing there and it should hang on to its history!"

"Does that mean you're going to offer to fix up the old Crowley place, make it a local attraction? Maybe get it registered with the Historical Society? Open it to the public?"

"No."

She drained the sink. "In other words you just want your privacy."

That certainly sounds selfish, he thought.

"Brady, that sounds unbelievably selfish."

Yes, unbelievably. "Gina." He sighed. He really had no explanation.

"Maybe it is the best thing for the town if it was developed. I mean, if the entire school board thinks it would draw people here and enlarge the tax base for better education—"

"Not everyone thinks that way."

She took the towel from him and folded it. "Why don't you go run around the block? You sound too angry to play Scrabble."

"I'm fine."

She gripped his arms and turned him around, then pushed him through the back door. "You're not fine. Go cool down."

He lurched down the porch steps and looked back at her.

Gina stretched out and touched his face. "You'll never be able to kiss me good night with your jaw clenched like that," she whispered.

It was the best incentive he'd ever had to run around the block. "You'll wait?"

"I'll wait." She sashayed back into the house. "And you thought *I* was a snob."

Brady strode toward the front sidewalk, inhaled the dewy, fragrant night, and glanced up at the stars. His anger dissolved even before he took his first jogging step. He only hoped his jaw would unclench.

Forty-Four

Somewhere between the shearing of her natural curls and slipping into the elegant black dress, Maggie felt an inkling of nervous anticipation. It had been a lovely day and a very special person had ordered it. She recognized this hope to have dinner with him as an answer to prayer.

Her hopes fell when Julius opened the limousine door and she saw the empty interior. At the John Hancock Center she entered the elevator with two other couples. She didn't mind dining alone, actually. She valued her independence, but...this was an evening to be shared. She wanted to thank Reece for his efforts, for his gifts, and most of all, to ask him to his face for forgiveness.

The maître d' surprised her by greeting her by name. "Good evening, Mrs. Philips. Follow me, please."

She wondered how she could again be caught by surprise. It had been happening all day.

The view was breathtaking. An unhindered panorama of skyscrapers shimmered in the evening sunlight. As they neared window tables, she saw him.

Reece stood. The room faded from her vision, but she sensed that heads turned. The silver in his hair glistened in a sunbeam. He was as trim and handsome as ever in his black tuxedo. His wide mouth broke into an easy smile. He wore his glasses, a sign that his eyes were tired. With a start she realized she didn't even know where he had been this past week.

He stepped toward her and took her hands in his, leaned forward, and kissed her cheek. "Thank you for coming," he whispered in her ear.

"Reece, I'm so sorry," she murmured.

His gray eyes bore into hers. "Margaret." He paused. "Maggie, it's all my fault."

She couldn't find her voice as he held the chair out for her.

"Do you want to prop your cast up on this other chair?"

"N-no. It's fine for now."

He sat across from her, scrutinizing her face as if he'd never seen her before. "You're more beautiful than ever. I like your hair that way." He cleared his throat and shifted in his seat. "I've already ordered for you. The special is a salmon I think you'll like. But if you want to look at the menu..." His voice faded. "This feels like our first date."

"All right, I give up. Who are you?"

He smiled. "And what do you mean by that?"

"Reece doesn't kiss me in public. He doesn't call me Maggie. He doesn't *look* at me like that. He doesn't order dinner for me because he hasn't a clue what I like. And he never, ever talks about *feelings*."

His smile broadened into a grin, and his eyes crinkled behind his glasses. "You noticed."

"Rushed off at 8:00 A.M. by a stranger wearing a chauffeur's uniform to an unknown destination? Oh, I noticed all right."

"And? How do you *feel*?"

She picked up her goblet and sipped the mineral water, delaying the honest answer that might hurt him. "I-I'm fighting it. Feeling means I'm vulnerable again. Does that make sense?"

"Perfect sense, Maggie. And it's fair. I don't expect you to trust me just because of a few gifts. We're obviously at square one."

A waiter interrupted momentarily, placing fragrant potato-leek soup before them.

"Reece, we're not exactly at square one. We never ate at a place like this during those square one days."

"I tried to get us a table at that little French hole-in-the-wall. Evidently they're closed."

She laughed. "We thought we were so sophisticated. Gina would call it a dive."

"I thought perhaps we wouldn't talk about Gina tonight. Let's talk about us."

Maggie swallowed a mouthful of hot soup, coughed, and quickly gulped water. "Reece, will you please warn me when you're going to say something like that?"

"I'm going to say something like that."

"Again?!"

"I just realized that I'm only being myself in all this. I'm simply treating you the same way I've been treating clients and business associates for years."

The delectable soup turned to sawdust in her mouth.

"Not to today's extreme. I mean, I never knew anyone else's brand of lipstick or dress size, but I have sent limousines and arranged hotel rooms and surprise schedules. It's just a part of business."

She laced her fingers together in her lap.

"But I've never personally shopped or called a florist or gone to the hotel room and hung up clothing and set out cosmetics."

"You did all that?"

"Yes, I did. Of course I had to call Gina a dozen times to find out where to buy certain items. I've memorized Brady

Olafsson's phone number, of all things." He rolled his eyes in the same way their daughter did.

"We're not talking about her."

"Anyway, it is a despicable way to live. Margaret, I mean Maggie, will you forgive me for ignoring you all these years?"

Tears sprang to her eyes. "I'm never going to get through this soup."

He smiled softly.

"Forgiving takes time, Reece. I'm working on it."

"Fair enough."

"Will you forgive me?"

"As I said, it was my fault. I can't blame you for finding a friend."

"But can you forgive me?"

"I have, Maggie, because I love you."

"And I do love you."

"Thank you. Ah, here's the salad. Honey-mustard dressing on the side, right?" When the waiter left, Reece said, "Speaking of dives, remember our first apartment?"

"That wasn't a dive! It was *cozy*."

They laughed and talked through the remainder of dinner, reminiscing about the happy early days of their marriage when they lived downtown. The city was full of their memories.

"I ordered raspberry cheesecake. Did you save room for some?"

A favorite of hers...of course. "Oh, Reece, this has been an unparalleled day of self-indulgence. I see no reason to stop now. Thank you. I haven't had this much fun in a long time."

"It's not over. There's still the opera."

"You don't like opera."

"But you do. I promise to listen this time when you tell me why."

"Well, for one thing, it's extremely energetic, like you." The waiter slipped a dessert plate before her. A small gold foil-wrapped box with matching bow sat on it. "Reece, this isn't cheesecake." She locked her eyes with his.

"Will you open it? Please."

Something in her hesitated, but she did as he asked. Beneath the paper was a box. Inside that was a black velvet ring box. She lifted the lid. The loveliest of diamonds sparkled up at her. Not too small, not too ostentatious, a solitaire on a band of gold. Simple. Elegant.

"Maggie, will you marry me? Again?"

She saw the crease between his brows, the intense concentration in his eyes. "Reece, it's gorgeous." She bit her lip.

"It's all right. You don't have to answer tonight."

"I didn't the first time either, did I?" She looked down at the original tiny engagement ring still on her left hand.

"Will you just wear it, on your right hand, until you decide?"

"This is difficult, Reece. I have to be honest."

"I want you to be honest, no matter what."

"I don't know yet. Will you...will you keep it, until you know for certain what my answer will be?"

He blinked a couple of times, thoughtful, probably trying to follow her line of reasoning. A smile slowly spread across his face. "You think I'll get to that point?"

"After today? Oh, most definitely."

⁓

Reece slipped his arm along the back of the limo's soft leather seat, behind Margaret. *Maggie.*

During the opera their shoulders had brushed. She had touched his forearm twice, whispered in his ear. But he longed to take her in his arms and kiss her like there was no tomorrow.

She looked up at him as Julius maneuvered the car through the after-theater Chicago traffic. "Reece, I think I'd like to go back to Valley Oaks tonight." Her tone was cautious, as it had been much of the evening.

"My darling," words of endearment rolled easily now, "you don't have to. I have my own room, on another floor. And a cold shower will do me good."

"And Julius?"

"I don't know why he'd need a cold shower."

She poked him in the ribs.

"He has a room, too. But if you're determined to leave, he'll take you. No problem."

"All right," she breathed. "I am tired. If I get back by nine in the morning, that'll be early enough. Thank you, Reece."

"My pleasure." He fingered the ring box in his jacket pocket. She wasn't making this easy. He would win her back though, even if it took the rest of his life.

Forty-Five

Brady was as handsome at the wedding as Lauren had predicted. His blond hair glistened, his tan was deep against the white tuxedo, his eyes reflected more green than blue above the chartreuse shirt that matched Gina's dress.

He caught her gaze, crooked his elbow, and held it out to her.

It wasn't time to walk down the aisle yet, but she slipped her hand through his arm anyway. Close proximity to Brady had become her favorite place. They stood outside the sanctuary with the other attending couples, listening to the final notes from the string quintet before the doors would open and she and Brady would lead the group inside.

She glanced back at Lauren and Uncle Dan. Her cousin's face radiated pure joy.

"Hey," Brady whispered and touched the corner of her eye with his little finger. "Not yet. Let me see that Miss America smile."

She rolled her eyes.

"That's better." He grinned. "Oops, show time."

The doors swung open as a trumpet sounded. Brady squeezed her hand, and they stepped onto the white carpet just as the chamber group joined the brass.

It was the most beautiful wedding Gina had ever been in or witnessed. It was magical. No, more than that. It was supernatural. Lauren and Aaron were clearly being joined in Christ, a dimension of immeasurable depths.

The guilt hit Gina again. She could never deserve a man who would gaze at her as Aaron did at Lauren now. She

326

always knew her cousin was a good person, at times nearly even a Miss Goody Two-Shoes. But she didn't realize until this moment how exceptional that was nor how precious that made her to her husband.

The group turned when the pastor presented the new husband and wife. Brady caught Gina's eye and winked. She tried to smile while biting her lip. This whole scene was becoming way too emotional. The sooner she told Mr. Olafsson goodbye, the better. She *was* the snob he had imagined and worse. An irrational feeling of emptiness hit her like a blow to the stomach.

Oh, Lord, help me get through this day!

Brady stuck beside her in the receiving line outside the church and diligently introduced her to the half of the community she somehow hadn't yet managed to meet. It was a perfect July 1 afternoon with sunshine but low humidity. From the church's front sidewalk she could see the town square. It was a photographic moment, a genuine Podunk moment with white steeple, green grass, most of the town wearing their finest...

"Gina, are you all right?"

She blinked up at his concerned, handsome face. "No, Brady, I'm not all right, and I won't be all right until I get on that plane to California."

He wrapped his arms around her and pulled her close to his chest. Right there in front of everyone, in the middle of Valley—Podunk. It was Podunk. Always had been, always would be.

~

The reception was in full swing. Reece held his hands out toward Maggie. "Dance?"

She eyed the cast that hadn't been there three weeks ago and fought back the niggling resentment toward him for missing the reunion dance.

"Come on, Maggie, I want to dance with you. We'll just inch ourselves around in a circle. Pretend like this band knows how to play slow music." He grasped her hand and led her to the edge of the country club's dance floor.

They danced carefully, the same way they had been interacting since he arrived at Aunt Lottie's on Thursday, a day earlier than planned. Her schedule had been packed full of wedding preparations...and Reece had graciously helped. He even took Aunt Lottie to the hairdresser. But he gave her space, hadn't barged in and taken charge as he used to do. He seemed extraordinarily sensitive to her needs. She was grateful, yet wary still. His behavior didn't undo the years of being nothing like this. It didn't impart automatic trust, and it didn't ignite emotion.

"Mar—Maggie, are you having a good time?"

"I am."

"Gina looks a little out of it."

Maggie spotted their daughter in Brady's arms. He was leading her adeptly around the dance floor. One wouldn't guess that she limped. But she wasn't smiling. "It's Brady. I think she's falling for him."

"Falling—?" Reece stopped them in their tight tracks. "In love?!"

Maggie nodded.

"But she has a new job! Her dream job!"

"Precisely."

"Poor kid."

His sympathy surprised her. "Reece, this is an Olafsson we're talking about. A true-blue Valley Oaks' resident."

"Gina wouldn't fall for a jerk. Besides, I like his books. Not to mention he taught me a thing or two about sending flowers." They resumed dancing, his face thoughtful. "I'll put the pressure on that development. We can force him out. Then he's free to go where she goes."

"Oh, good grief, you're serious."

"It's Gina we're talking about. Of course I'm serious."

"Reece, you always want to *fix* things. We don't need a fix here. She—they just need to work it out and that will take time."

He leaned back and intently studied her. "Is that where *we* are? No quick fixes?"

"Yes."

Slowly he twirled her in a circle, then slipped his hand around her waist. "No problem. I'm in it for the long haul."

Long haul. She felt a hint of comfort in that phrase, but... "Can you prove it?"

"You drive a hard bargain, lady."

She shrugged a shoulder and looked him square in the eye. "Take it or leave it."

He smiled, but his chin tilted and his eyes narrowed slightly. It was his determined business man's expression. "I accept the challenge, Maggie Lindstrom Philips."

"Gina," Brady murmured, his cheek nestled against her hair, "I don't want to leave things in limbo."

She didn't reply. He let it go.

They sat in two outdoor padded lounge chairs that he had carried from his parents' deck to the middle of a grassy field behind the barns. His invitation had been to watch for shooting stars. It was after midnight, after the reception, after the mosquitoes had retired. Gina sat near enough to lean her head on his shoulder, but not too near. The aluminum chair arms protruded between them. He tried not to think about how the two of them could probably fit rather nicely together in one of the chairs.

He plucked tiny bits of dried baby's breath sprinkled about in her hair, most of which was pinned up in a twist. "Can I take these out? They tickle."

"Mm-hmm. These stars are absolutely incredible. Almost as good as a desert sky."

"Did I tell you how absolutely, incredibly beautiful you looked today?"

"Once or twice." She shivered against him.

He slipped off his tuxedo jacket and draped it over her. Reclining again, he put his arm back around her shoulders, ignoring the pain in his ribs where the chair arm poked.

"Thanks. You're warm enough?"

"Been warm enough all day. I cannot figure out why we guys get stuffed inside these long sleeves and jackets and cummerbunds in the middle of summer while you brides-maids run around in short sleeves. Did I tell you how pierc-ingly emerald your eyes were today?" He hadn't been able to take his own from her.

"Brady, stop talking. I can't hear the stars. Listen. They make this magnificent, macroscopically hushed sound."

"Macroscopically?"

"Shh."

They sat quietly for a long time, listening, until he reached his limit. At the wedding and reception, her demeanor had been highly agitated. When he asked her a few times what was wrong, she replied "not now." "Gina, how about now? What was bothering you earlier?"

For a moment she didn't answer. "You."

"You're supposed to say 'nothing.'"

"Another irrational game women like my mother play."

"What'd I do? I didn't tell any jokes, did I? Just that one—"

"Brady, I was coming to terms with our situation. I don't want to leave us in limbo either. The fact is..." She paused. "There is no 'us' to leave in limbo. We've had this...this moment together, but our lives are just too different. The summer fling is over."

He felt like a rodeo cowboy atop a bucking bronco fresh out of the chute. His breath was ripped from him. "Then why are you sitting here with me in the middle of the night with your head on my shoulder, wrapped in my jacket?"

"Well, I'm not gone yet. We can still be friends."

"I don't *snuggle* with friends. You can't deny you don't feel anything but *friendship*."

She straightened. "I deny it, Brady," she whispered.

"That's just your logical self talking. I'll visit you in Seattle, give you time to get to know me better, because I know all I need to know about you, which convinces me that I want to spend the rest of—"

She yanked off his jacket and threw it at him. "Don't you get it, Brady? You don't know me, but I do know you, very well in fact, and I know I don't belong with you! Not in Seattle, not in Podunk!" She swung her feet to the ground and strode away.

Gina had stomped halfway across the dark field before his frozen brain connected with his legs. *Podunk?* What was going on here? He caught up with her near the truck. "Gina!"

"I need a ride. I'd walk, but I think that's an unrealistic expectation considering we're out here in the middle of miles and miles of nothing but corn." She opened the passenger door and climbed in.

He got in his side and had the truck started before he slammed the door shut. "We call them acres, not miles."

It was a quick, silent ride to Lottie's house. The porcupine had returned with a vengeance, and Brady was at a loss as to how to handle her. He pulled into the drive, nearly rammed the front of the truck into the neighbor's hedge, and cut the engine.

She looked toward her window. "I can't get out."

"Gina, please don't leave things like this."

"It's for the best. Actually, maybe we had better say goodbye right now."

"Why do we have to even say goodbye? Give us a long-distance chance at least."

"What did you think, Brady? That I don't have another life to pursue, one that doesn't include 'us'? That somehow my dream to be a vet would just cease to exist?"

"There's something between us. You can't kiss just anyone like—"

"Brady! Of course I can! You are so naïve. This whole town is. It's like a time warp. I don't fit in, not in any way, shape, or form here, and you certainly don't fit in where I'm going!"

At some level deep within himself he filtered through her noise and heard the cry of her soul. She was pushing him away out of guilt, not understanding that in Christ wrongs were forgotten, that in Brady's love she fit in anywhere. Still, he ached. Panic rose, his heartbeat pounded erratically in his throat. Nicole's leaving had simply cauterized his heart, had quickly burned away all feeling. This was a severing that would bleed until he died if he couldn't be with Gina.

"Brady, I didn't mean to lead you on. Your books," her voice caught as she huddled against the door, face averted. "Your friendship...I'll always be grateful for what you've given me. But it just won't work. Please, let me out."

He felt incapable of standing. He started the engine and backed away from the hedge, giving her space to open the door. Neither spoke as she slid from his truck, gathered the long gown in her hands, and hurried toward the house. He winced at the sight of her uneven gait. Like the day he met her, it still did a number on him.

Forty-Six

Maggie took advantage of their last morning in Aunt Lottie's house to awaken Gina with a cup of coffee. Once they returned to California, there wouldn't be moments like this.

"Morning, sweetheart."

Like a little girl, Gina stretched with her eyes still shut. "Mmm, I smell that good coffee."

"It's after eight. I thought you might want to get going."

"I better." She propped pillows behind her and sat up. Maggie handed her the mug and sat on the edge of the bed. "All packed?"

Gina nodded and sipped coffee. Dark circles underlined her eyes, which weren't quite open.

"Aunt Lottie and your dad are cooking up a storm. They invited everyone for breakfast. Commotion will make the goodbyes easier."

"Thought we did that yesterday. What's gotten into Dad, prolonging his stay here?"

"Well..." She sighed. "Well..."

Gina smiled. "He's nuts about you, isn't he?"

"It appears he is."

"Kind of a change, huh?"

"We'll see. We both head back to work tomorrow, go our separate ways again." She shrugged. "Most importantly, he has forgiven me, and I him for not being there in ways I needed. Still, the trust isn't rebuilt overnight."

"Mom, you're 53. When does it get easy?"

She laughed. "Never. But knowing now that Jesus walks alongside makes all the difference. He forgives me, forgave all that baggage from the past, all the ghosts. He loves me no matter what. I am going to make it. How are you doing?"

"Fine." Her stern tone implied she wasn't.

"Your dad called Brady to invite him today. He left a message on his machine."

"We already said goodbye. Saturday night."

"I wondered why he wasn't at the brunch yesterday." Maggie saw the pain on Gina's face. "What are your plans?"

"For what?"

"For seeing each other again."

"Why would we do that? It's time to leave. I have a job."

"I thought—" She bit her lip. "Don't sell yourself short, honey. That man is nuts about you."

"A farmer in Podunk does not fit my agenda."

"Pencil him in. Loving a *non*-farmer and leaving *Podunk* was not on my agenda. Life is full of chance journeys that get us where we need to be." She turned at the sound of footsteps pounding down the hall.

Reece rapped on the open door and walked in, excitement written on his face. "Ben just called from L.A."

Gina asked, "Your attorney works at 6:00 A.M.?"

"He's your attorney and he just received an offer from the Park."

Maggie and Gina exchanged glances.

"For 10 million."

Gina's face crumpled. Maggie took the mug from her and handed it to Reece, then enfolded their daughter in her arms, catching the first sob against her shoulder.

Reece came around so he could face Maggie. "What? Too little?"

She raised her brows, her own eyes filling with tears.

"T-too much," Gina blubbered. "I don't want any. I just want it to be over."

"Honey, it'll be over if you accept this settlement," Reece explained. "And you won't get the *entire* ten after Ben's fees and other costs. At least you don't have to drag things out in court, but you've gotten the attention you wanted for the elephants. What do you say?"

Gina nodded her head.

"Maggie, is that a yes?"

She smiled at him. "That's a yes. Call Ben and finish this mess."

"Done."

"Reece?"

He turned back.

"Thank you."

A gentle smile erased the anxiety from his face, crinkled the crow's feet. At that moment Maggie felt something inside of her melt.

~

Gina slumped in the hard chair, studying the airport's carpet, trying to keep the pain from consuming her. It was as if some internal black hole grew larger by the moment, devouring strength from every part of her, threatening to cut off air to her lungs. It intensified with each passing moment away from Brady. The agony was physical, worse than after Delilah's attack.

The last she had seen of him was late Saturday night, his truck roaring too fast down Aunt Lottie's street.

But that was the last she *wanted* to see of him.

Then why did she miss him so?

She'd be better as soon as she stepped on the plane. Her old life would meld into a new life in Seattle. This little detour, as Mother called it, occupied a mere fraction of life.

It would dissipate in time, making hardly a dent in the large scheme of things.

Except for Jesus.

"Gina." Her dad sat down beside her with a heavy sigh. "I can't stand it any longer. Here." He placed a large manila envelope on her lap.

"Can't...stand..." Each word was separated by a painful breath. "What?"

"Seeing you so miserable."

"I'm...not...mis...miserable."

"Of course you are. You didn't look this bad wrapped in a body cast. That's from Brady."

Her throat closed.

"He came by early this morning, before you were up. I don't know what's in it, but he made me promise not to give this to you until we were on the plane. I'm breaking that promise."

She struggled for a breath. "Why?"

"Because I think you need to hear from him."

"I...don't..."

"Open it, Gina. Maybe it will help you settle the issue. I'll leave you alone." He left.

There wasn't any issue.

Oh, but there was. She loved him, but she could never meet his standards. She didn't deserve him. Why couldn't he see that? She'd never survive in Podunk. Why did he keep prolonging the inevitable?

Well, she was done with prolonging. She'd read his love letter and be done with it.

The envelope was rather large and heavy for a love letter. Of course, he was a writer. It was probably an entire story. With unsteady fingers she tore at the sealed flap and pulled out a handful of papers. On top was a note written on linen paper in Brady's hand. Beneath it was a stack of legal-looking documents.

Dear Gina, no matter where you are, the enclosed is unconditional, like God's love for you. Like mine. Brady.

That was it? What was this? She skimmed the other papers and called out, "Dad! Mom!" She looked up to see them hurrying toward her. "Dad, what is this?"

"It's—" He swallowed and shuffled through the pages. "It's the deed to Brady's property, signed over to you. This says you purchased it for one dollar. Did you give him a dollar for it? This bank statement says the mortgage has been paid off."

"What does it all mean?" she whispered.

"It means you're a millionaire who owns 122.7 acres in Valley Oaks, adjacent to an undeveloped piece of property that you can probably buy for a song once you build your elephant enclosure."

They all three stared at each other.

"He just gave up his privacy. His most precious possession!"

Her mother nodded. "I think it's called love."

She stood. "I have to go to him."

Her parents smiled at her, the two of them blinking back tears as their flight's boarding was announced.

Dad grabbed her first in a bear hug. "Of course. Go right back to the car rental counter. You can probably get the car we just turned in."

"Dad, is this right? It's so irrational!"

"It's right, Gina. Believe me. It beats the rational path of dotting i's and crossing t's."

Mother hugged her, grinning through tears that dampened her cheeks. "We'll have your luggage sent back here when we get home. I love you. Call us!"

Dad handed a carry-on bag to her. "Go!"

She wove her way through the crowd lining up to board, turned back once, and waved to her parents. What in the world was she doing?

The empty highway stretched before her. Gina pressed her foot against the gas pedal. The speedometer climbed to 70, the concrete rhythmically *tha-rumped* beneath the tires eating up the 26 miles. Fields of corn stalks narrowed to a green blur in the corners of her eyes.

He loves me.

She peeked at this truth as if it were a butterfly enfolded in her hands, sure to fly away if scrutinized too openly.

He really loves me.

Of course he had told her, but she hadn't grasped what that meant, didn't even have the capacity to begin to grasp it. Now it had anchored itself into the core of her being and she knew it. Knew that it was unconditional. Knew that she was more important to him than even his property, his privacy, his way of life. Like God's love, nothing would get in the way of its expression, not the past, not the future.

Half prayers formed on her lips. Ecstatic "thank-yous" jumbled over terrified pleas for guidance.

Selling his property meant he could vote on the zoning issue. Development efforts on the adjacent land could be blocked. It meant he was willing to do anything with his place, even leave it and move to Seattle.

He loves me.

Or it simply meant that he wanted to lease the land from her and be allowed to vote.

A car passed her going the opposite direction. Suddenly the green blur of corn turned into a rainbow of flashing lights.

"Oh, nuts!"

She slowed and pulled onto the shoulder. The lights filled the rearview and side mirrors. Her heart raced, beating away precious minutes. She could have been in Valley Oaks by now! She lowered her window just as a large man in a brown sheriff's uniform stepped to it.

"Miss California!" His mouth widened into a grin below dark sunglasses. "Thought that was you zipping by me like it's a freeway out here."

She recognized Brady's basketball-playing friend. "Cal!"

"Kind of racing the wrong direction to catch your plane, aren't you?"

"Oh, Cal! I'm not leaving."

His grin expanded. "Does that mean you're staying?"

"I'm in an awful hurry!" Her breath was coming in short bursts again.

"No kidding."

"I've got to see Brady right away. Can you just mail me the ticket or something?"

"You're headed to Brady's?"

She nodded. "I think he loves me."

"Shoot, the whole town knows that. How about an escort instead of a ticket? We'll swing around here." He gestured with his arm. "You passed the turn for the other route about a mile back. It's a lot quicker than going through town, but it's a narrow blacktop so we can't go 75. You okay? Take a deep breath."

"I'm fine!"

"Okay. I'm sure you'll have no problem keeping up with me." He sauntered away.

Gina raced behind the county patrol car, its lights flashing and siren blaring all the way to Brady's drive. Cal switched things off and waited on the shoulder, throwing her a grin and a thumbs-up sign as she went around him.

She crept down the private road while her heart still raced and fears bombarded. What if Brady really only wanted to pay her rent?

Forty-Seven

Tears still threatened to flow well into the flight, but Maggie sensed their healing power and didn't let them interrupt her monologue directed at Reece. He listened while she poured out her happiness and fears for Gina. He maintained eye contact while she described forgiving Neil's mother and letting go of old resentments. He held her hand while she spoke of lost dreams and finding a new self in Christ. She didn't resist when he cupped her cheek, leaned over, and kissed her temple.

"Maggie, I was always afraid of losing you to Valley Oaks. Thank you for taking care of the ghosts and for not giving up on us in the process."

She felt that melting sensation again. "Thank you for responding."

"What man in his right mind wouldn't? Don't go away." He undid the seat belt, stepped into the aisle, and fiddled inside the overhead compartment. He settled back into the seat, a large manila envelope in his hand. "I figured if a manila envelope was good enough for Olafsson, it was good enough for me."

"I don't want to jump to conclusions, but I think you'd like that guy for a son-in-law."

"I think so, too. Maggie." His voice grew husky and he paused. "I hope that your response is as irrational as Gina's, but if not, that's all right." He handed her the envelope.

She smiled and then giggled. The panic and hesitation she felt last week in Chicago had vanished. With childlike anticipation she opened the flap and pulled out...a

340

small packet containing...tickets...to Venice...Venice, Italy! "Reece!"

He gave her a sheepish smile and lifted another paper from the packet. "Here's the itinerary. It's for the month of September, actually beginning the end of August."

"Reece!"

"I know that's a long time, darling, but I think we owe it to us. We have an awful lot of catching up to do."

"Reece!"

"Look." He pointed to the paper. "We'll see most of Italy, or I should say most of its art anyway—"

"Reece!"

"What?"

The tears flowed freely now and her only response was to nod.

"You'll go?"

She nodded again.

When he pulled her near, she didn't resist. It was time to let him kiss away the hurts. It was time she kissed him with the promise of a new tomorrow.

Gina parked the car beside Brady's truck, relieved that he was at home. Propelled by irrational anxieties, she ran to the front door and rang the bell.

He loves me.

No answer. She pressed the button for an entire minute, then tried the doorknob. Locked. She raced around, across the deck, and into the screened porch. And stopped.

What if Kim were here? Or some other friend she didn't know about? He certainly wasn't expecting her. She was supposed to be on the plane, just now unsealing his little surprise.

He loves me.

"Brady!"

She hurried across the porch, noticed his laptop on the table, a screen saver in motion, and went through the open door into the kitchen. "Brady!"

Where was he? Where was Homer? With a 122.7 acres to roam around, they could be anywhere.

No, not just anywhere. They'd be in Brady's favorite spot.

Gina grabbed a baseball cap from the coat rack and headed outside. It was tick season and warm and muggy and a very long drive to a large zoo, but...but it was heaven on earth because Brady lived here and he loved her.

She jogged her lopsided trot around the pond. At the other side she swerved onto the path they had mowed together. She remembered standing on a bar behind his tractor seat, clinging to his neck, conversation abandoned to the engine's roar. Shoulder-high prairie grasses bordered the trail. Like sentinels they stood, their feather, purple-splashed heads still, no hint of a breeze under the glaring noonday sun.

What if he just wants to visit Seattle, give us a long-distance chance?

Brady named it Gina's Path. Was it hers? Was it the one God had always been leading her toward?

It rose now, leading into the woods, tree trunks barely visible through the wild masses of green. Beneath the cool canopy of leaves, she hurried along the winding trail. Twice, divergent paths halted her. Twice, she cried out, "Which way?!" Twice, she whirled in circles before forcing herself to study the clues. They were there, in the trees, in the ground's slope, in her sense of direction.

The path led back downhill toward the creek. Panting, she slowed and heard the clear notes of a flute. She recognized Brady's halting rendition of "Amazing Grace" on his Irish whistle.

At last the slope leveled out and the path led between two stately walnut trees and scrub bush. It ended where the creek looped into a "c," creating a moss-covered peninsula. Water rippled over rocks, underscoring the flute's song.

He was there. She saw him sitting on the end of a fallen oak that spanned the creek. Homer, lying at his feet, raised his golden head and cocked an ear.

Brady caught sight of her and broke off playing, astonishment in his raised brows. He wore his green cap backward, the sleeves of his white T-shirt rolled up. Slowly he removed the flute from his mouth as Homer yapped and raced to greet her, tail wagging.

Gina stopped a short distance from him, catching her breath, unable to gather her racing thoughts into a lucid sentence. She patted the dog, shushing him.

Brady spoke first. "Miss your plane?"

She nodded. "Just found out I'm a landlord."

"You weren't supposed to know that yet."

"Why not?"

"I wanted you to take time to think about it." His unemotional tone raised an invisible barrier, making him unapproachable. "A long time."

"What is there to think about?"

He shrugged. "How much rent to charge."

"I don't want to charge rent."

"Property taxes aren't cheap here in *Podunk* County. I should at least pay for those."

She blinked.

"Then there are the other implications." He paused. "Your vote."

"Yes, there is that, but who knows what'll happen once the Village board gets hold of it? That no longer matters. I mean, in essence I don't have a home here anymore anyway."

"It's still your home! You don't have to leave! I'll sell it back to you for a dollar after the vote!"

"That wouldn't exactly be proper, would it? And I don't know anyone else who appreciates this land as much as you—"

"Brady Olafsson! You can't go around giving away 122.7 acres! It's too...too extravagant!"

"I can do whatever I please with it. Don't you want it?"

"No!" she cried.

He lowered his eyes and set the flute on the log.

"I only want—" She bit her lip and swallowed the shrill tone. "You," she whispered. "I only want you. I want to spend the rest of my life with you."

Whether it was a shout or Homer's excited barking or merely an inexplicable sense of the majestic oaks clapping audibly, she didn't know, but the woods pealed with a tangible joy. Brady ran to her, caught her in his arms, and laughed as he swung her around.

"Then why, dear girl," he lowered his face and his lips grazed hers, "are we talking about *rent?*"

"I thought maybe you just wanted the vote."

"How could you—? Oh, Gina." He kissed her soundly. "Convinced?"

She smiled. "Almost. Better try again."

"Just a minute. Homer!" He pointed a finger at the dog and spoke sternly. "Quiet. Now," Brady turned to her and slid her cap around backward, "where were we? Ah, yes, convincing you." His second try took a bit longer. "Satisfied?"

Held in his turquoise gaze like this, how could she ever not be? But there was something. "Brady, are you really willing to leave here and move to Seattle?"

"Sweetheart, when you told me goodbye Saturday night, I came home and suddenly I knew it wasn't home anymore. It never would be again without you. And I saw that you were right. I was being selfish about holding on to this place.

Giving it up was the only way I could think of to prove how much I love you. All I need is my laptop, a plane ticket to wherever you are, and a prayer that you'll give us a chance."

"And a dog carrier for Homer."

He grinned.

She kissed his cheek. "I love you, Brady Olafsson. And I'll give us a chance on one condition."

"What's that?"

"That you stop the references to *Podunk*. After all, this is my hometown."

"Hometown?" His grin widened. "Meaning?"

"Meaning I'm giving up the Seattle job. How else can I prove just how much I love you?"

The woods sang with their laughter.

Harvest House Publishers
For the Best in Inspirational Fiction

Sally John
THE OTHER WAY HOME
A Journey by Chance

Linda Chaikin
A DAY TO REMEMBER
Monday's Child
Tuesday's Child
Wednesday's Child
Thursday's Child
Friday's Child

Melody Carlson
WHISPERING PINES
A Place to Come Home To
Everything I Long For
Looking for You All My Life
Someone to Belong To

CONTEMPORARY FICTION
Blood Sisters

Debra White Smith
Second Chances
The Awakening
A Shelter in the Storm
To Rome with Love
For Your Heart Only

Lori Wick
THE YELLOW ROSE TRILOGY
Every Little Thing About You
A Texas Sky
City Girl

CONTEMPORARY FICTION
Sophie's Heart
Beyond the Picket Fence
Pretense
The Princess
Bamboo & Lace

THE ENGLISH GARDEN
The Proposal